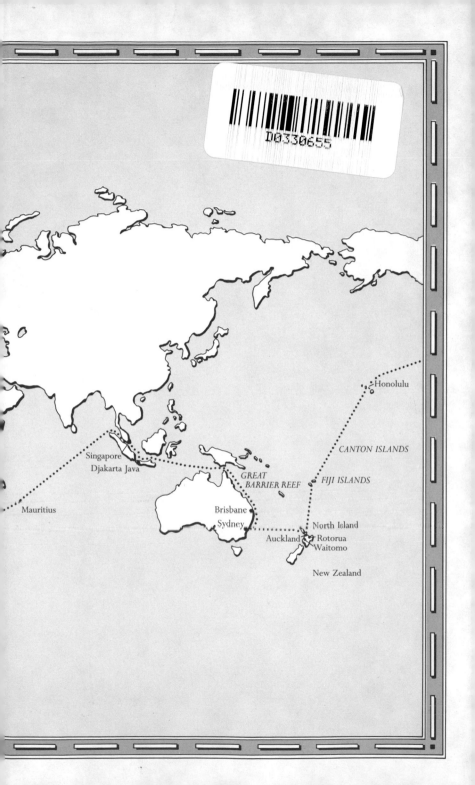

Honolulu

CANTON ISLANDS

Singapore
Djakarta Java

GREAT
BARRIER REEF   FIJI ISLANDS

Mauritius

Brisbane
Sydney
                              North Island
                    Auckland   Rotorua
                                  Waitomo

                              New Zealand

TRAMP ROYALE

ROBERT A. HEINLEIN

⌐ TRAMP ROYALE ⌐

ACE BOOKS, NEW YORK

TRAMP ROYALE

An Ace Book
Published by The Berkley Publishing Group
200 Madison Avenue, New York, New York 10016

Book design by Caron Harris

First Edition: April 1992

Library of Congress Cataloging-in-Publication Data
Heinlein, Robert A. (Robert Anson), 1907–1988
   Tramp royale / Robert A. Heinlein.—1st ed.
      p.   cm.
   I. Title
PS3515.E288T7   1992
813′.54—dc20
ISBN 0-441-82184-7

Printed in the United States of America

10   9   8   7   6   5   4   3   2   1

Preface

TRAMP ROYALE HAS spent almost forty years in the obscurity of the files.

It was written immediately after our return from a trip around the world in 1953 and '54, and sent on the rounds of publishing companies. But, at that time, there was a slump in the publishing business, and no one could see any possibility of publishing it. It was then put in the files and sent to the library at the University of California at Santa Cruz, and forgotten.

In 1989, an editor asked me whether Robert had any unpublished books. I recalled this one. So the library made a copy of the manuscript, and I sent it to that editor.

Now here it is.

It might strike you as odd that an out-of-date travel book should be resurrected and published. But there must be something interesting in it, aside from the dated prices and old hotels which might now be torn down to make room for more modern ones.

Homesickness is ever-present when one travels away from home. It might well have flavored some of this book. I hope that our friends from some of the places mentioned in this book will not take offense at what has been said. Robert wrote his observations of their hotels and cultures without pulling his punches. We both know from later observation that Australian hotels have changed for the better.

On looking back, I find the prices of those days laughable. Where could one get a suite for $22 U.S. these days? I'm sure that Singapore prices are far higher now. And $35 for an alligator bag! If you could find one now, I'm sure it would cost ten times that much.

The title of this book comes from a Kipling poem—"Sestina of the Tramp-Royal"—which you will find on pages 371–72 of this book. The Britannica says of the sestina form: "A most elaborate form of verse . . . The scheme was the invention of the troubadour, Arnault Daniel, who wrote many sestinas . . . The sestina, in its pure medieval form, consists of six stanzas of six lines each of blank verse; hence the name. The final words of the first stanza appear in varied order in all the others, the order laid down by the Provencals being: abcdef, faebdc, cfdabe, ecbfad, deacfb, bdfeca. On these stanzas a tornada, or envoi, of three lines, in which all the key words were repeated in the following order:—b-e, d-c, f-a."

Such rigidity in form is probably not suited to beautiful poetry, and the Kipling verses are not his best, but the poem might have been influential in the writing of this book.

Enjoy this book as a period piece. It does not represent today's world at all. We enjoyed even the horrid parts of the trip in retrospect, but especially the homecoming. Being away from home for an extended period makes one appreciate one's home country.

VIRGINIA HEINLEIN
Atlantic Beach, Florida

TRAMP ROYALE

I

Ten Suitcases

MY WIFE TICKY is an anarchist-individualist. I sometimes suspect that all females are anarchists in their hearts, with no innate respect for law and order . . . but on her it shows more. She is the sort of person who looks the wrong way at tennis matches. When she was in the Navy during the early 'forties she showed up one morning in proper uniform but with her red hair held down by a simple navy-blue band—a hair ribbon. It was neat (Ticky is always neat) and it suited the rest of her outfit esthetically, but it was undeniably a hair ribbon and her division officer had fits.

"If you can show me," Ticky answered with simple dignity, "where it says one word in the Navy Uniform Regulations on the subject of hair ribbons, I'll take it off. Otherwise not."

See what I mean? She doesn't have the right attitude.

I should have known better than to propose a trip around the world to her. Little-did-I-dream that I would spend the next forty thousand miles shaking in my boots for fear that she would wind up in some foreign calaboose while I tried to find the American consul.

The junket came about because we found ourselves last year with a drawerful of old, dirty money and no special use for it. I do not like to keep money around too long; the stuff shrinks like Colorado snow in a chinook—inflation, or they pass a new tax, or an operation, or something. Or

1

someone comes along who can sweet-talk me out of it. It never lasts long.

We had been talking more or less about building another house with it, renting it, and becoming fat and nasty as landlords. But building involves time as well as money; it becomes a demanding vice. The fascinating details of septic tanks and clerestories and insulation move in like Bermuda grass and take over the mind and imagination. For a fiction-writer such as myself this is a road to bankruptcy.

But it was necessary to do something before a distinguished stranger came along and persuaded me to invest in a Wyoming oil lease.

Ticky was out weeding on the terrace when I found the solution. I hurried out to tell her, approaching the matter with the finesse of a sailor on a four-hour pass. "Look," I said, "we're going to make a trip around the world."

I had placed myself to catch her if she fainted, or to join in the dance if her ecstatic response required exercise to work it off. She was able to control her enthusiasm. For about thirty unusually long seconds she continued to fiddle with a johnny-jump-up, then she said bleakly, "Why?"

"Huh? Don't you *want* to go around the world?"

"I like it here."

"Well, so do I. But we can't spend our whole lives in one spot. We grow roots. We vegetate. People will start searching us for sun scorch and scale bugs. Travel is—"

"Speaking of roots, I'm worried about those lilacs. I think I'll have to—"

I approached her gently and took a trowel out of her hand. "Ticky," I said gently, "listen to me. Forget gardening for a moment. We're going around the world. I mean it."

She sighed and let me keep the trowel. "Why? What has Timbuctu got that we haven't got more of right here? Except fleas, maybe?"

"That's not the point. I grant you that Colorado Springs is almost certainly a nicer spot than Timbuctu, but—"

"Then why go there?"

"Why? Because I like to travel. I thought you did, too."

"I do. We went to Sun Valley less than a year ago. It was fun." She thought about it. "If you want to go abroad, let's go to Lake Louise. I've always wanted to go there."

"Huh? Canada is not 'abroad'—it's not a foreign country."

"Ask a Canadian."

"Sure, sure. But it's really just a part of home that happens not to pay taxes to Washington. Pretty clever of them, too, come to think about it. But take Timbuctu, since you mentioned it."

"You take it. Let's go to Lake Louise and watch the glaciers glashe."

"All right, all right! We'll go to Lake Louise. We'll have dinner there tonight. It'll only take about three hours, not counting the hour to drive to the airport. We can discuss the trip around the world and make plans and tomorrow morning we'll come back and start arrangements."

"Mmm . . . no. Your tux is at the cleaner's and I haven't a dinner dress that is fit to wear." She took the trowel back from my limp fingers. "About next Wednesday, maybe. I'll have to buy some clothes and Sweet Chariot ought to be put in the shop for a day, just to be safe."

"What do you want to put the car in the shop for? It runs; if it will get us from here to the airport that's all I ask of it."

"Because we are going to drive to Lake Louise. No airplanes for me."

"What? Now wait a minute, slow up. We are *not* going to drive to Lake Louise. Since when this silly aversion to airplanes?"

"Since all these crashes in the papers. Airplanes are dangerous."

"Look who's talking! Leadfoot Lulu, the gal who thinks she is parked if she's doing less than ninety."

"I have excellent reflexes," Ticky answered with dignity, "but my reflexes are useless if a plane I'm a passenger in runs into a mountain. Which they've been doing."

"Which they do darned seldom. It's—"

"Once is enough. Once is too many."

"It's well known that modern airlines are the safest form of travel. Insurance companies no longer make any distinction between air travel and any other normal hazard. If there is anything as certain as death itself it is that insurance companies don't take risks; they operate on the same simple, straightforward statistical principles as the gambling houses in Las Vegas—the odds are picked so that the house always wins. It's the same with air travel; if these spectacular crashes were frequent enough to shift the odds, the insurance companies would change the rules in a hurry."

"Hmmph!" said Ticky.

"Hmmph yourself. Air crashes rate headlines simply because they *are* unusual. Take the Quintuplets—they got a lot of newspaper publicity, too. But what do you think your chances are of having quintuplets?"

"You aren't Mr. Dionne," Ticky answered darkly.

"That's beside the point. Don't you believe in statistics?"

Ticky pondered it. "Sure, I believe in statistics. But I've noticed that whenever I personally am a statistic I'm always way out at the end of the curve, instead of being comfortably toward the middle. They've got a plane crash all shined up, waiting for me to come along."

"Sheer solipsism. Paranoia. The Ticky-centric Universe."

"How else?" she answered contentedly and went on with her weeding.

I took a deep breath. "Ticky," I said, "listen to me. Put down that trowel and look at me. I'm going to put it in simple, Ticky-sized words and I want baby to try to understand it. I am going around the world. You are going with me because I need to keep you in sight where I can watch you and keep you out of trouble. We are going to fly."

"No."

"Yes. It's either planes or ships, and ships are a stupid waste of time. When you go by plane, you spend your time *being* there instead of killing days and weeks getting there."

"No."

"Yes. I'll bet your grandmother refused to set foot in one of those horseless carriages. But right now we fly, all the way around the world."

"No."

"Yes, we do. And when the time comes we'll take a rocketship tour to the moon, too."

So I firmly gave in. We ordered tickets for a round-the-world tour on one of the President Line steamships. It was a lovely ship, as the four-color folders showed—swimming pool, ballroom, private baths, movies, deck sports, beef tea in your deck chair in mid morning. By the time I got through studying the deck plans and the itinerary I no longer regretted not going by air. We applied for our passports and Ticky started making out lists.

That is, we applied for our passports after we sent in for certified copies of our birth certificates. Do you happen to know where *your* birth certificate is right at the moment? Or did the personnel office ever give it back to you after you applied for that job with Douglas back in 1942? You think it's with the insurance policies? I'll give you even money that the document you have in mind will turn out to be a New Jersey driver's license, expired. Americans, lucky people, even today need birth certificates only on very rare occasions. Hardly a half century ago they needed them not at all and very few had them. If an American wished to travel abroad, he did not need a birth certificate because he did not require a passport. All that he required was a letter of credit from his bank and leisure. It was literally possible for an American to wake up on Monday morning, decide to go to Europe, and be sailing, sailing over the bounding main on Wednesday.

Nowadays he had better allow three months as a minimum for the red tape. Six months is much easier on the nerves.

First the birth certificate: this takes about two weeks provided everything is clear sailing, that is to say that you know exactly what official to write to, his address and the amount of the fee that you must send. If you do not know, then you may be able to save two or three useless exchanges of letters by sending a money order for five dollars to the clerk of the county you believe you were born in. He will either do it himself and send you your change, or will pass it on to the proper official (in populous counties, such as those of New York City) who will most likely take care of it the following Tuesday if the photostat clerk or the vital statistics clerk is not on vacation.

Or he may send back the entire five dollars with a polite note informing you that "the records in question were destroyed by fire when the courthouse burned down in 1919." This is a penalty move and requires you to go back six squares and start again.

In my case the penalty move came in the form of a letter stating that "vital statistics were not kept in this county in the year named." This produced a scramble to achieve what is called a delayed registry of birth. Luckily I come from a family of pack rats; we were able to dig up a family bible entry, my first grade report card (good marks in arithmetic, poor in music, fair in deportment—none of this modern evading the issue), my cradle roll certificate, and a letter addressed to me by name on the occasion of my third birthday. There was also a lock of hair.

The cradle roll certificate had the wrong year on it, so we threw that out, but the other exhibits, in due and leisurely time, produced from the State of Missouri a document which said that my birth had at last been duly registered at the state capital. I breathed relief; at last I was me. I had attended school, been commissioned in the armed services, held two civil service jobs, married, voted, run for office, drawn a pension, and done all manner of things as a citizen and a flesh-and-blood being through more than four decades, all without having had any legal existence whatsoever. Now at last this little 4x6 slip of paper, issued by a clerk who had never seen me, assured me that I was real and therefore could apply for a passport.

I am not opposed to birth certificates. They are a nuisance only if you do not have one. But I am not impressed by them. There must be thousands (more likely, millions) of persons like myself in this country who managed to get born without

benefit of statistics, nor do I find it reasonable to penalize a
new-born infant for an omission on the part of government.
Contrariwise, a birth certificate as a proof of identity—its only
conceivable function—leaves much to be desired, as they are
easily obtained illegally. If I were in the spy business and
needed a U.S. birth certificate, I would—but why should I
make it easy for spies? Especially when they know more about
it than I do? I am sure that no Russian spy in this country ever
lacked for an American birth certificate if he needed one for
his unlawful occasions.

But an honest citizen can be very handicapped by the lack
of one at times. If your birth was never registered, better take
steps, as I did. If it was and you are serenely aware that you
can always send for a copy if you need one, better send for
one now; the courthouse might burn down again. Seven to two
you won't! You will wait until it is indispensable, as I did.

Eventually we got our birth certificates and applied for our
passports, with another short delay for passport photos. Those
passport photos, the sort suitable to hang in a post office under
a "WANTED FOR FRAUD" notice, are not accidental. The
State Department prescribes the lighting and the pose; the
public-enemy result is automatic. I cheated a little by smiling
when I saw it was about to be taken.

Be sure to get at least a dozen and a half copies; foreign
officials have a way of asking for two or more copies unex-
pectedly. I have no idea what they need them for or what they
do with them. Scrapbooks? But failure to produce on demand
can be as troublesome as losing your traveler's cheques. Have
them. Carry them on your person when crossing international
boundaries—a traveler fully fitted out these days to cross
such an imaginary line has bulges all over his person like
Tweedledee and Tweedledum outfitted for battle, and he looks
and feels just as foolish.

In addition to a myriad pieces of stamped paper adding up
to several pounds, he will, if he is wise, have at least two
cartons of American cigarettes within easy reach and which
he is prepared to give away at the drop of a hint. Bribery?
No, "Squeeze"—a bribe is paid to get a man to do something

he should not do; "squeeze" is something he demands of you for doing something you are legally entitled to have done anyhow, such as stamping your passport or passing your personal luggage. Most officials do not expect squeeze; those who do can make you miss trains, or worse.

While I am in a mood of reminiscent irritation let me state flatly that there is no limit to the variety of bureaucratic buffoonery placed in the way of legitimate travelers today and that it is my solemn opinion that none of it is of any use whatever. None of it is efficient enough to stop spies, smuggling, or illegal immigration. But the proof of the uselessness of any particular item of red tape lies in the fact that each procedure required by the laws of Ruritania will be found to be missing from the red tape of Lower Slobbovia, with no equivalent procedure to replace it. Instead, Lower Slobbovia will have a different silly mess of its own. This one impounds your passport, that one requires you to report to the police, this one so help me wants you to file an *income tax return* for a stay of four days, that one requires that you register your Kodak (but lets you take any pictures at all!), this one wants to know where your grandparents were born before it will let you simply change planes inside their sacred precincts. That one requires a cash deposit to guarantee that you will leave, then requires you to submit a freshman term paper to get it back when you do leave. This one—

But I could go on endlessly. Their name is legion and these steeplechase hazards to travel have in common in their endless variety only that they are all obnoxious and they are all useless. Pardon the irritation—I have been keeping my temper and smiling for the past forty thousand miles and my face is tired.

But after all it's their country, not mine, and if I don't like it, why didn't I stay home? True . . . but not the whole story. All of these countries are advertising in the States, ads paid for by the governments, urging you to come to beautiful Boskonia and spend those Yankee dollars; see any copy of *Holiday*. Many of them maintain government tourist bureaus in the States. Why, if they are so confounded anxious to improve their dollar balance with the "invisible export" of tourism, can't they refrain from treating a visitor like a juvenile delinquent being processed into reform school?

In order to apply for your passport it is necessary to appear in person at a court having jurisdiction and bring with you a witness who has known you for two years. You don't see the judge; you simply make out another one of those usual forms covering everything but your blood type, you pay the clerk a fee, and leave. Ticky and I found it no real trouble, since we live only a few miles from such a court and could ask a neighbor to go down with us. But in the open spaces of this country many people live more than a hundred miles from such a court (one empowered to naturalize foreigners). If you want the passport, you'll make the trip—but it is a far piece to drag a neighbor just to say, "Sure, I know him. And here's my driver's license to show who I am." Who feeds the pigs while he's gone?

Since the so-called appearance before a court is simply to fill out a printed form, swear to it, leave some photos and your birth certificate, plus personal identification by some other person who in turn need be identified only by papers, in what way would this weak procedure be further weakened if it were carried out by a local notary public who actually *does* know you?

I would not question the wisdom of the personal-appearance-cum-witness if the procedure were tight enough to discourage foreign agents from attempting to get American passports. An American passport is a valuable document; the black market price on them in some Asiatic ports is reputed to be from two to three thousand dollars and no doubt they bring more when they are then resold behind the Iron Curtain. But the present method for "identifying" an applicant is laughable as a security measure and is uselessly inconvenient to the honest applicant— and to his neighbor's pigs.

In due course Ticky's passport and mine arrived by registered mail from Washington. She examined hers smugly . . . all but the picture. "It says here," she announced, "that the Secretary of State of the United States of America sends greetings and urges everyone to permit Ticky to pass freely. That's pretty nice of him."

I agreed that it was. "But we can't go anywhere with it yet. Now we have to get visas."

"What use," she wanted to know, "is a visa?"

Visas are of no use, none whatsoever. They are the epitome of functionless red tape, as meaningless as stepping on every crack while walking down a sidewalk. Many countries have abolished them entirely for all or almost all visits; other countries cling to them and make the obtaining of one as complicated and as annoying as removing an impacted wisdom tooth—South Africa and Indonesia, to cite two horrid cases. The endless questionnaires serve no purpose, since the desired answers are obvious and the international crook need only resort to cheerful mendacity. The fees are almost always too small to constitute worthwhile revenue in view of the overhead—often there is no fee; it is red tape for the sweet sake of red tape itself.

Saudi Arabia alone has a sensible visa system—eighty dollars for the visa, which is limited to Mohammedans, a head tax on pilgrims to Mecca, for revenue unashamed. My hat is off to Saudi Arabia, the straight bite and no nonsense about it. All the other countries are merely inconveniencing themselves and annoying the tourists they seek.

We started to get visas, then did a sudden about-face; our deposit had been returned by American President Lines. They thanked us for our interest and informed us that their round-the-world tours were booked solid for two years in the future.

I was ready to sit down on the curbstone and bawl. Ticky was not much more cheerful; she had been shopping for evening dresses to wear in the ballroom of the S.S. *President Monroe* and was all over her earlier lack of enthusiasm. She had carelessly and with assumed modesty informed all our friends that we were about to make a world tour. The idea of announcing publicly that it was all a mistake was unendurable.

She suggested that we go to Pueblo under an assumed name and spend three months reading *National Geographics*, then return home from the other direction. I was halfway sold on it.

But Mrs. Feyock took us in hand. Hertha Feyock is a cheerful little person who is the "World" part of the World-Wide Travel Agency in Colorado Springs. She speaks several languages, knows exactly how much to tip a Paris concierge, and has been to many of the places she deals in. "Don't you vorry," she said. "I'll find you a ship. There are some lovely Dutch ships running from South America."

I pointed out that we were in North America.

But she already had her head buried in folders, with a thumb tucked in a loose-leaf book six inches thick consisting entirely of ship schedules. "I'll put together a tour," she said absently.

Which she did. It took a month to do it, a wastebasketful of letters, many toll calls and cables, and recasting of the overall plan as drastic as deciding to go around the world eastward rather than west when it appeared that the tentative schedule could not be made to jibe in Singapore. But she did it. Planning a world tour by various means of transportation (rather than by a single tourist ship) is a project as complicated and unlikely as organizing a political campaign or trying to get six children off to Sunday School, all clean and neat and all on time. It calls for patience, expert knowledge, and optimism.

To attempt it yourself unassisted in the belief—entirely mistaken—that your costs will be less is as foolish as taking out your own appendix. But not as thrifty, for the travel agent collects not from you but from the transportation and hotel companies with no increase in price to you. But if you take masochistic pleasure in doing everything for yourself, go right ahead with either enterprise; the results should be interesting to others.

I can hear that plaint from the lady in the back of the hall: she wouldn't *think* of going to a tourist bureau; she doesn't want to find herself in a crowd of dreadful *tourists;* she wants to go to the *out-of-the-way* places.

"Tourist—(n.)—a person traveling for pleasure."—The Thorndike-Barnhart Desk Dictionary.

You may disclaim the horrid title, lady, but you are a tourist, once you leave your home town for any reason other than removal of domicile or business. That terrible couple over there with the impossible child (and he is a nasty little brat, isn't he?) resents your presence, your table manners, and your personality quite as much as you detest and despise them. You are all tourists together, so why not relax and enjoy it?

Nevertheless the yearning to go to out-of-the-way places where you will not be annoyed by other tourists and where you yourself will annoy only the natives is a legitimate one— in which case Thomas Cook and American Express and Mrs. Feyock and the other travel experts know much more about such places than you are likely to be able to learn unassisted. There are such places and many of them are lovely. Regrettably all of them are woefully short on inside plumbing, comfortable beds, and drycleaning service. Such amenities are directly linked to dollars, pesos, and pounds; they are provided only when there are enough tourists to make it pay.

Sometimes the lack of mass-production comforts is offset by native servants willing to work fourteen hours a day for small change in American money to provide you by hand with the machine comforts you are used to. You may be lucky enough to hear of such a place and go to it before the natives are "spoiled" (i.e., before they realize that they are being exploited). If you hear about such and want that sort of thing, go at once; if you read about it, buy your ticket the day the magazine appears. Otherwise you will arrive at the painful transition period when the place is already bursting with tourists, the prices have gone up, and the plumbing, et cetera, has not yet been installed.

Carry with you your own mosquito netting, soap, penicillin, toilet tissue, and a stomach rugged enough for any sort of cooking; out-of-the-way places have an infuriating habit of being out of the way. The unspoiled paradise, unknown to tourists and unlisted with the travel bureaus, exists in vast numbers throughout the globe. Africa, South America, Mexico, and Canada abound with them; even my home state of Colorado has dozens of them. But don't write to me asking for directions; get hold of Hertha Feyock instead. She will tell you how to get there and where you can hire pack mules for the trip.

Or next time try Mars.

Mrs. Feyock finally put together the following itinerary. (See the map in the end papers, unless they have tucked it in somewhere else.)

Colorado Springs to New Orleans, train or plane

New Orleans to Valparaiso, Chile, by American freighter, via the Gulf of Mexico, the Caribbean Sea, through the Panama Canal to the Pacific, and with numerous coastal stops on the west coast of South America

Valparaiso to Santiago, Chile, by train

Santiago to Buenos Aires, Argentina, by plane

Buenos Aires to Capetown, Union of South Africa, by Dutch cargo liner, with stops up the east coast of South America

Across Africa by local transportation, plane, train, et cetera; rejoin ship at a west African port

Across the Indian Ocean to Singapore, with island and west African stops

Singapore to Australia, via Indonesia (ah, Bali, beautiful Bali—more about that later)

Australia to New Zealand by passenger liner

The itinerary came to a sudden stop at New Zealand. Mrs. Feyock was still trying to book us by ship from New Zealand to our west coast at the time we left. No passenger ship was to be had, but it seemed to be just a matter of patience to book us on a freighter—a long, slow idyllic voyage, calling at mystic islands of the South Seas, all with names ending in vowels and sounding like endearments in an exotic tongue. I could see myself sitting on the fantail of such a ship, strumming on an old beachcomber and idly sipping a planter's punch, while the sun sank in the west and the colorful exotic natives gathered on the shore in their colorful exotic native costumes and bade the ship Aloha with their colorful exotic native songs.

I would feel her screw churning under me and the water, warm as new milk and clear as champagne, chuckling against the plates of the old rust bucket. After supper, served by boys who spoke only Pidgin but knew telepathically what you wanted before you knew yourself, the Captain and I would smoke a pipe on the bridge and swap yarns—then bed, for a night's deep, unworried sleep.

I began to feel like a Somerset Maugham character.

The only nibble we got was from the Matson Lines; all the others were "sorry" for one reason or another. The Matson Lines offered us "dormitory accommodations"—Ticky in a women's dormitory, me in one for men.

Ticky gasped. "What are those Matson Line people? Missionaries?"

We will omit my answer.

"Maybe we should explain to them that we are married. They may have me mixed up with Sadie Thompson." She scowled and then smiled. "Tell 'em 'yes' but that you'll take the bunk in the ladies' dorm and I'll take the one with the men."

"Okay, it's a deal."

"You're entirely too agreeable about it. Anyhow, they wouldn't let us. Missionaries! Well, I'm not going to do it and that's flat. Six weeks cooped up with a bunch of old biddies, watching them get in and out of their corsets and listening to their snores at night, is not my idea of a pleasure cruise. It reminds me of those old slave ships, where the mate would stick his head down into the hold the middle of every watch and tell them all to turn over at once. No!"

We both thought the dormitory plan was obscene and indecent, as well as having a flavor of Botany Bay about it that did not belong with paid passage. But our decision forced us to leave open the matter of passage back to the States. We told ourselves cheerfully that it would be easy to arrange in New Zealand, right on the spot. After all, ships left from New Zealand every day; we would make the rounds of the home offices and pick one that suited us. Our trouble was that we were trying to book passage from ten thousand miles away for a date six months off whereas no ocean freighter has a firm schedule that far ahead.

"Besides," I added, "New Zealand is supposed to be one of the nicest spots on earth. We might decide to stay there quite a while. We might take a room or a flat and hang around while I write a novel, in between admiring glaciers and kiwi birds and geysers and things. I might do a story with a New Zealand background, while I'm there and can check on the correctness of detail. Both of my readers must be pretty tired of the backgrounds I know now. I'm sure I'm sick of them."

"What you need, honey chile, is not a new background; it's a new plot."

I thanked her. Every writer needs honest criticism in his own home. We left it at that and turned our attention to visas and baggage.

The theory with a visa is that you get hold of the consul of the country in question, obtain from him a set of questionnaires, fill them out, mail or take the completed forms with your passport and fee back to the consul, whereupon he looks over the questionnaire, determines from it that you are a safe and proper visitor, then takes a rubber stamp and stamps your passport: "SEEN." That is all that "visa" means, just "seen."

This piece of tap dancing need not take more than a week or ten days if you wish to visit, let us say, Spain and nowhere but Spain. If you wish to visit several countries, it is still possible though tedious to accomplish in a short time provided you live in New York or Washington, D.C., and can take a few days off to walk your passport through from one consulate to another.

In our case we wished permission to visit nineteen sovereign countries, possessions, or colonies. Allowing a none-too-safe ten days for each transaction by mail and multiplying by nineteen gave an answer in excess of six months.

We had started our preparations to travel in mid June; it took until September to get passports and straighten out an itinerary; our first ship sailed in November. We had six weeks left in which to get visas. It began to look like one of those unsolvable mazes used by psychologists to induce frustration paralysis in laboratory animals.

Our State Department puts out a document listing the visa requirements of (almost) all other countries. We discovered that many countries had abolished this kindergarten procedure for the ordinary tourist. Most of these enlightened areas were in western Europe, not on our schedule, but several of them were in South America. The list that remained would still require two to three months if done by mail from Colorado—but the fine print came to our rescue: British consuls could grant visas for other British Commonwealth countries where said countries were not represented by consuls of their own. About two-thirds of our remaining list was British Commonwealth area—good! We would send our passports to the British consul in Denver and clear up most of it in a few days. As for places like French Tahiti, and Dutch New Guinea, and Portuguese East Africa, if we ran out of time before sailing, we would pick them up in person at any of several national capitals—Santiago, or Buenos Aires, or Rio, or even Pretoria. We would not be daunted by red tape, no, sir!

So we sent our passports to the British consul in Denver.

We waited for a week and nothing happened. Finally we decided to drive to Denver and inquire. Perhaps I should have done so in the first place, but I was fighting a deadline on a novel which had to be finished before we left. In my own case, at least, a loss of one calendar day in a writing schedule equals a loss of three writing days.

We arrived about one o'clock and found the consulate closed for lunch but a small sign informed us that it reopened at one-thirty. I spent the time trying to read "Come to Britain" posters through the glass door. At one-thirty-five a nice young lady with an English accent arrived in an apologetic rush, unlocked, and offered us chairs. We asked about our passports.

She dug them out of a file; nothing had been done to them. Nor could she help us; we would have to wait until the consul returned from lunch. Any minute, now? Oh no, he was attending a luncheon—three o'clock, perhaps.

We studied several pamphlets displayed on a rack: *Agriculture in the British Isles, Sports in Britain, Come to the Coronation, Historic Abbeys*. That is, I did so; Ticky spent her time making noises like a kettle about to boil. About three-thirty the consul returned.

He was a tall young man with a beautiful blond beard and he had the perfect, somewhat distant good manners of a top-drawer Britisher. "Awfully sorry to have kept you waiting, my dear chap. What can I do for you?"

We explained again. "Oh, yes, those— I had been wondering what to do with them. I'm afraid there isn't much I can do for you. According to your letter you aren't going to England."

I had come armed with the State Department publication about visas and I showed him the various notes in fine print. "We would like to have you issue visas for the Union of South Africa, Singapore, Australia, and New Zealand."

He blinked at the page and admitted that it did seem to say so. "Too bad, really. Sorry not to accommodate you."

"Then this thing put out by our State Department is wrong? Maybe it would be a good idea to write and tell them so."

"Well, it is not exactly *wrong*. But I once granted an Australian visa and became involved in such a dreadful bother that I decided never to do so again."

Ticky took a deep breath and I could see her muscles tighten. I jabbed her in the ribs, thereby saving temporarily an appearance of international amity. "Perhaps I did not make clear our situation," I went on. "We haven't time to send these passports around to each consulate separately. Couldn't you stretch a point, since you have the authority, and help us out?"

He shrugged. "Awfully sorry."

I stepped on Ticky's foot. "Well, I suppose you can issue the Singapore visa?"

He reluctantly conceded the point and we started filling out the same old forms—age, sex, occupation, place of birth, purpose of visit, means of transportation, race, permanent residence, marital status, ct cetera ad nauseam. I was tempted to emulate a friend of mine who for years has been putting down his occupation as "necrophilist" without once having it questioned.

Presently we handed in our homework with our passports. After about ten minutes the young man with the beard stuck his head out and said cheerfully, "I seem to have ruined one page in Mrs. Heinlein's passport—the wrong rubber stamp. Sorry. I'll just scratch it out, eh?"

I grasped firmly Ticky's upper arm. "Quite all right."

It was about four-thirty when we got out of there, having at last received permission to change ships in Singapore but nothing else. Our British cousin relented a bit as we left. "If it turns out that you simply can't get those other visas any other way, come back another day and I'll see what I can do for you."

I thanked him and got Ticky out of there quickly before she could start quoting Patrick Henry. It was a cold, gloomy drive back in the dusk and Ticky was unusually silent. Once she spoke up. "I'd like to set fire to his beard."

We gave up and loaded the problem on the patient shoulders of my friend and business agent in New York, Lurton Blassingame. His secretary took the passports around by hand to each of the consulates in New York. Even this process cost twenty-seven dollars in long-distance tolls (to obtain questionnaires first) plus (as near as I can guess) about sixty dollars of his secretary's time, plus fees—all totaling around a hundred dollars for a ritual as useless as stamping white horses.

All but Indonesia— The Indonesian consulate in New York refused to have anything to do with our passports. We lived in Colorado Springs; Colorado lies west of the Mississippi; therefore our visas would have to be granted by the Indonesian consul in San Francisco, Q.E.D. and ipse dixit.

I pointed out, by long-distance phone, that while we might be in Colorado, our passports and paperwork were physically present in New York and would be delivered by hand along with the cash; couldn't they *please* stamp a visa on each of them under the circumstances?

"So sorry. No."

I explained with tears in my voice that there was no longer time to have some visas granted in New York and then send the passports to San Francisco. But their spokesman was adamant; rules were rules and had to be enforced.

As we were to learn later the new government in Indonesia is quite unable to enforce rules about murder and pillage, much less rules about public health and sanitation. But when it came to red tape, they had learned fast; they were as Western as a school board. ("Come to Beautiful Bali, Last Home of Romance.")

All during the long campaign for reservations and the subsequent battle of the visas Ticky had been overhauling our wardrobes and we had both been stuck at odd intervals with hypodermic needles—cholera, typhus, typhoid and paratyphoid, tetanus, smallpox, yellow fever. This is one requirement for foreign travel with which I do not quarrel, since it is obviously of benefit not only to the countries visited but to the traveler. For technical reasons of biochemistry the yellow fever shot is very hard to obtain unless you live close to one of the half dozen U.S. Public Health offices which dispenses it. We did not, not by nine hundred miles, but we were able to obtain it as a courtesy from a nearby army post. The U.S. Public Health Service will supply on request a booklet telling what inoculations are required for travel in any part of the world; appended is a list of places dispensing cholera shots, free. They are not available commercially. Any traveler who needs one had better find out how he can get it most easily and plan for it ahead of time; the problem is not one of red tape nor of bureaucratic stupidity but one of inconvenient fact having to do with the present stage of medical art. There is no one to blame.

Ticky did not accept the requirements of inoculation easily. She stated that the navy medical corps had stuck enough needles in her to last her the rest of her life. I agreed and pointed out the alternatives: either she could let me go roam among the señoritas without mama to watch over me, or she could leave the country without inoculations—no one would stop her—and then find herself placed in quarantine for two or three weeks at the first port we reached . . . a process which would be repeated a dozen times around the globe, including San Francisco on return.

She stated positively and explosively that she would not go at all. But in due course she was baring her arms and her thigh and various other parts of her skin in Dr. Mullet's office and wincing as she was jabbed. I don't think the threat of señoritas convinced her. Ticky is as hard to convince as a cat, but, like a cat, she will submit to the inevitable. Just barely.

The first typhoid shot gave me a mild headache; I had no other reactions. Poor Ticky was distressingly ill from each and all of them—even her vaccination "took." I stipulate (though she does not) that it may have been psychosomatic, but the illnesses were real. She lost the better part of two weeks, just when we were busiest.

Because of the book I had to finish writing, almost all the endless running around necessary to get us started had fallen on Ticky. She was especially busy planning and shopping for our wardrobes. I first became aware of this early in the summer when she said thoughtfully, "I suppose we had better get some more luggage at once."

"What for? You take your big suitcase and your hatbox; I'll take my Valapak and the other suitcase. That'll be plenty. I can even let you have some room in my bags."

She shook her head. "We'll use the big suitcase for our skates and I'll pack my skating dresses around them. I was thinking of a wardrobe trunk for each of us."

"Skates—" I said, then took a deep breath and screamed, "Skates! Ice skates? Who are you? Barbara Ann Scott?"

"Don't be silly, dear. This trip is supposed to be fun, isn't it? Won't it be fun to look up the skating clubs everywhere we go? I'm thinking of doing an article for *Skating* magazine about it. Skating My Way Around the World, or Blades under the Southern Cross, or something like that."

I answered with dignity that *Skating* magazine did not pay anything for copy and that I hoped she would never bring up an immoral proposal like that again.

"I'm not asking you to write the article. I'll do it myself."

"It's a bad precedent," I answered sulkily. "Start a thing like that and it could lead anywhere. First thing you know I'd have to take a j-b—if you will excuse the expression—and go back to working for a living. You wouldn't want *that* to happen."

She did not answer. "Or maybe you would?" I went on, not quite so firmly. "Anyhow, it is absopreposterously out of the question. We can't drag thirty pounds of skates and a bushel of skating costumes around the globe just to skate a few times. If you find any rinks open in the southern hemisphere—which I doubt—we will rent skates and try them. I'll go that far with you. You can even take one skating dress. One."

"Rented skates," she said quietly, making the words an obscenity.

"Then don't skate. We live two blocks from one of the best rinks in the world. We are not repeat not spending all this dough just to compare one piece of frozen water with another. Ice is ice in any language."

"No, it's not. In Spanish it's *hielo*. I looked it up."

I withdrew to a previously prepared position. "Look, darling, I had been meaning to talk with you about this. The secret of happy traveling is to travel light. We'll take two bags each, one for each hand. That way we can always move them ourselves if we have to. There is nothing worse than to be stuck out in the middle of a pouring rain with a big stack of baggage and no porters or taxicabs to be had for love or money. And even if you do find a taxi, in a lot of those hot countries the first thing the driver does is size up your luggage. If you've got a lot of it, then you must be rich and fair game; he multiplies the normal charge by the number of your bags."

"So you tell him firmly you won't pay it."

"And sit there in the rain? No, if you have just the baggage you can carry, as we will have, you walk off and look for another taximetro. He follows after you and offers you the right price."

"Robert A., if you think I'm going to show myself to people all over the world in clothes that came out of one bag—and look it—think again. You like to see me nicely dressed. The very first remark you ever made to me was, 'Your slip is showing.' "

"You can be nicely dressed with just two bags. Pan-American puts out a list that shows you just how to do it."

"Written by the same chap who tells how to make tasty meals out of left-over scraps, I'll bet."

"It isn't like dressing here at home. You're not going to be seen by the same people each day, so each outfit is as smart as the first time you wore it."

"So? We are going to be in that Dutch ship for six weeks. Do you want me to wear the same black dinner dress every evening for forty-two days, not forgetting the Captain's Dinner?"

I shifted tactically. "Another thing, if you have a lot of luggage, it takes forever to get through customs."

"Why? It can't take long to mark a chalk mark. I've seen them in New York."

"Honey, do you know what that chalk mark means?"

"Should I know?"

"It means that the customs officer has unpacked everything in it, searched it, and passed it. You have a lot of stuff, tightly packed, and it takes him forever to paw through it."

"Paw through *my* clothes?"

"Of course. That's what he's there for, to search the stuff."

"But that's silly. Where did you get that idea? When Aunt Lou got back from Europe she just handed the man a list of what she had bought outside the country; he took it and made some chalk marks. It took about thirty seconds."

I nodded. "So it did. She had declared a reasonable amount, she had her list made out in advance, and she didn't smell like a smuggler to him. So he passed her. They can't do a skin search on everybody and we are granted such liberal free allowances that most people don't try to smuggle. But if he had been suspicious—well, they are quite capable of taking you to a private room, stripping you down and going through your bags with knife blades and probes. When it comes to dope or jewels they even go after the body cavities—and I do mean *all* of them."

Ticky slapped the table. "That settles it! I'm not going."

"Slow down. Level off and get your flaps down or you'll overshoot the field. That sort of thing happens only when the customs authorities have received a tip from their informers abroad that a particular person is going to attempt to smuggle—and they rarely make a mistake. If a foreign customs officer tried it on us, I'd yell for the American consul so loud that they would hear it in Washington. But they won't. Customs officers aren't fools. What they will do is to search our baggage. Most other countries have much stricter import and tariff regulations than we have—so they search everything that comes in. But nobody is going to lay hands on my redhead, don't you worry."

"And they aren't going to go pawing through my clean underwear either. I won't stand for it."

The discussion continued without reaching a conclusion. Ticky did not insist again that she was not going, but she never gave in to the idea that a strange man should be allowed to handle her clothes. Once she suggested that she could carry along white gloves and tell the inspector to put them on before he touched her things. I was tickled by the picture of Ticky holding them up and saying, "One moment, Señor, before you commence—" But I was scared by it, too. She was quite capable of doing it—and what a proud Latin official would do when he finally understood that the *norteamericana señora* was suggesting that his hands were too dirty to touch her possessions I did not like to think about.

He would not touch Ticky. Latins are much too gallant for that, no matter what the provocation. But I enjoyed no such immunity; *I* would wind up in the calabozo.

What Ticky would do then I did not even dare guess. It would be something like the behavior of a lioness deprived of her young and it would not even have a speaking acquaintance with the amenities of international law.

Maybe we really should stay home.

The question of how much we should take with us got lost in the muddle. I made feeble protests from time to time but the number of evening dresses and sports clothes and accessories grew. Then she started in on me and I got slacks and tropical suits in these new materials that can be washed, so it says on the label, and do not require pressing. This seemed sensible so I shut up. Then a new white evening jacket. Then a stack of sports shirts for shipboard wear. I quit fighting and decided to enjoy the lovely new wardrobe instead.

There were ten pieces of luggage when the day arrived, all packed to bursting. It took two trips to get them to the station.

II

South to the Southern Cross

SANTIAGO, CHILE—*Manuscript found in an Old Pisco Bottle:* "Is anybody listening? Is there anybody there at all? I am stranded on the fourteenth floor of the Hotel Carrera and I seem to be about to fall out of touch with the rest of the world entirely. I can't sleep properly. Almost every twenty-four hours I wake up at least once and have to struggle up two flights or *pisos* to the *piscina* on thee rrroof and sip a pisco sour while I watch the señoritas sunning themselves and swimming in the *piscina*. Then I crawl back down and fall again into the *mañana* coma.

"Orion is upside down and people eat dinner in the middle of the night and a simple request for drinking water requires endless protocol and much waiting. But all forms of alcoholic beverages are readily available everywhere and the chambermaids whisk busily in and out of thee bath while I am bathing, cooing gently at each other like turtle doves (rootly-*boo,* rootly-*boo!*). The hired help work in committees, talking and using their hands and very cheerful, but not necessarily accomplishing anything. The same hired help is evident at all times and everywhere. If Ticky and I close the roof garden at four, the same patient waiter with the Indian ancestry and total lack of English offers us breakfast in the grisly light of noon. They must hang them on hooks.

"Can you hear me? Can you speak English? The guidebook

25

says that almost everybody here can speak it but the guidebook is wrong. I am beginning to feel unreal. I—"

The above is roughly the effect on a couple of gringos of first exposure to the druglike, almost unbearable sweetness of our Latin American neighbors. We visited seven such countries; I state the simple truth when I say that not once did we hear a harsh word, never were we scowled at, no one was ever too tired or too busy to be patient and kind to us. Nor is it fair to attribute this continent-wide courtesy to the Yankee Dollar; most of these encounters had nothing at all to do with money.

It seemed to me to be the finest outward expression of true individualism: each man respected himself; this inner respect, his awareness of himself as a unique person, required him to extend to every other human being everywhere and of any economic station a dignified courtesy which recognized tacitly the unique worth of both his fellow human and himself.

My analysis may be wrong, but the outward fact remains. This account reports what I have seen, with my opinions tossed in to fill up some of the white space. I have never understood how globe-trotting columnists can take a quick look at a country and come up with all the answers to all problems, economic, political, and social. I can't possibly do so because I don't know enough history, geography, psychology, economics, science, anthropology, or whatever, nor can I keep up with the endless spate of new facts. Even my own home town confuses me; every time I think I have reached the "facts" I find another layer underneath, like peeling an onion. How can I do justice to a country, a continent, a globe?

Nevertheless, it does not take a biochemist to detect a rotten egg in an omelet. Some things that are right, others that are wrong, about a country can be seen even from a tour car. When you see a 65-year-old woman staggering along under a load that would cause an American stevedore to fetch a fork truck it does not require a Guggenheim grant to determine that something is crumby about the way that country is run.

I shall set down my opinions whether they constitute complete answers or not.

We left Colorado Springs on 12 November by train, after having shipped half of the ten suitcases by express in order that we might go by air, only to receive a telegram immediately after shipping telling us that S.S. *Gulf Shipper* would be three days late in sailing—a routine mix-up in traveling. So we left in the middle of the night from a bitter cold railroad platform instead of in bright daylight in the gala atmosphere of an airport. But a biggish crowd of our friends came down to see us off anyhow, the Knowleses, the Herzbergers, Eileen Seigh Honnen, the staff of the World-Wide Agency, three assorted young ladies whose names I did not catch, and a Free Press photographer came down to see us off, and Bob Wirt of World-Wide presented Ticky with green orchids and the Nelsons and Mrs. Feyock gave us candy (which we ate to the equator). We had our pictures taken on the steps, then waited through a long anticlimax for the train to pull out late.

We were off! Into the Wild Blue Yonder, enduring the hardships of a Pullman drawing room. Actually, I had forgotten just how dismal a way to travel a train is. Like most Americans I have learned to go everywhere in my own car (needs a tune-up and one new tire, but reliable) or, if really in a hurry, by air. This is not counting a mule descent into the Grand Canyon, or a week's pack trip by horse of which the less said the better. Now a Pullman drawing room is luxury travel and it costs a bit more than air travel. It is noisy, dirty, uncomfortable, monotonous and slow, and sleep is almost out of the question. The engineer employs a spy to make sure that he uncouples the diner just as the razor reaches the point of my chin and the water tastes of old iron.

We changed trains in Fort Worth and soon we were in de land ob cotton. Looked pretty bad, too—not much of a crop this year. The drouth really raised hell with the farmers. We arrived in New Orleans Saturday morning and were delivered to the Maison de Ville at breakfast time, short precisely two nights of sleep.

Unfortunately check-out time was three o'clock and our rooms were not available. We carried the banner through the French Quarter until the afternoon. This is a painful and groggy episode which I remember dimly save for one item, Loni's Vieux Carré Lingerie Shop at 218 Bourbon Street. Loni deals in custom-made frillies for frails of really amazing sorts— panties with clutching hands embroidered on same, others with appropriate mottoes, if you happened to be very broad-minded, things which I dubbed bedroom Bikinis but which Loni assured me were "home G-strings." None of these items were built for heavy wear; all were intended to be removed promptly and (we trust) with care, as they were beautiful and fragile.

One mannequin, the mascot of the shop, was seated, completely dressed and quite naked, in the middle of the shop rear. She is known as "Ophelia."

We were tempted but I limited myself to a pack of playing cards, the only non-wearable item offered. The conventional designs on these cards had been replaced by pictures in gorgeous Kodachrome of young ladies who did not patronize even Loni's liberal establishment. After all, were we not about to barter in the bazaars of the cross-roads of the world?— dickering with and outwitting mysterious Hindus in quaint little stalls in Zanzibar for the mysterious treasures of the Orient, then to wait until we returned to the ship to decipher the mysterious cabalistic mark on the underside saying MADE IN CAMDEN NJ FAIR TRADE PRICE $1.75? After all, Loni plies her trade in the States and promises "Mail Orders Filled Promptly."

We dragged ourselves back to Maison de Ville, taking turns carrying the playing cards, and slept in chairs in the lobby until our predecessors checked out—and were then informed that the ship would sail on Tuesday instead of Sunday. This is known as the Missing Top Step. So we went to bed and slept until dinner time.

There was the usual queue on the sidewalk outside Antoine's; we did not tarry. I have never eaten at Antoine's and do not intend to do so ever; any restaurateur who lets his patrons stand on the sidewalk instead of providing room enough to sit down is welcome to the suckers he gets—but I'll be a sucker sitting down, thanks. We went to Todt's on Bourbon, an excellent French restaurant with a German name. Mme. Todt is a tribute to her own cooking. The place is beautiful, ancient, quiet, leisurely, and the cooking is superb. We began to dig our graves with our teeth, wide and deep, a process likely to continue for 40,000 miles.

We wandered away from Todt's, belching gently and walking carefully. We had no intention of spending the evening in the clip joints of the Vieux Carré, no sirree! We were going to a movie. But careful inspection of a newspaper disclosed that nothing was showing but Hollywood's revenge for television. On the way back to Maison de Ville we decided to indulge in a small spot of social research, as we had heard that the town had been cleaned up. We stopped in one of the joints to find out.

It was true. The girls no longer danced on the tops of the bars, but on runways arranged among the customers, an arrangement more sanitary and more convenient. Nor did they strip completely. No matter how many bows they took, each retained a G-string at least the size of a cigarette package and in place of a brassiere (which might have become dislodged in the enthusiasm of the dance) each wore two little stickers based on the principle of the "Posees" which enjoyed a brief rage a few years back, but differing from that adhesive bra in being smaller, say an inch and a half to an inch and three quarters wide. These little modest stickers were often of a natural rosy hue, but some were silver, some were gold, and some were covered with sequins, giving pleasant variety. Some of the young ladies had tassels appended to these stickers, which accented their movements. One had four tassels, two in front and two fastened to the bulges of her glutei maximi. Such was her athletic skill that she could start or stop any of the tassels independently, swinging them in time with the music. The tassels had been treated with fluorescent dye, producing a giddy and pleasing effect of mobile mathematical patterns.

We left this establishment without having suffered undue financial damage and were just about to turn into our home street when we saw a sign advertising the leopard woman. We went in. The dive was grimy but the show was all that it was billed. I mean to say: where else can you see a naked woman rassle with a full-grown leopard thirty-nine inches from your nose and no bars? This act was all that it was represented to be and it struck me as damned dangerous. Sure, she did her strip by having the leopard claw and/or bite her clothes away, just like Lolita and her Doves and that gal who used to do the same act with a parrot. But the thing that got me was that apparently bad-tempered leopard practically stepping in my half-ounce cuba libre. It made me so nervous I had to sit through the show twice.

The Maison de Ville is a luxury hotel run like a very well run French pension, by a Mrs. Ehrlich, who came down from the Nawth, liked the town, bought this hotel and stayed. It is small, very personal, and very well managed. The new wing was built in 1800, which gives you some idea. The patio is lush, old, and cool, with green moss covering the ancient bricks. There is a wishing well where you may chuck a penny if you have any wishes left unsatisfied, which seems unlikely. A complimentary continental breakfast is served until eleven o'clock in this patio and it opens into the much larger patio of the Three Sisters, where everything is served, from Sazerac cocktails to lobster mayonnaise.

Having seen New Orleans before, we had not intended to spend much time there, but the delay in sailing left us with a couple of days to kill. On Sunday we took a rubberneck trip and found that in New Orleans such a trip is not to be scorned. There are many things there which need to be pointed out and cannot be seen just by poking around—such as the canals that are above the level of the adjacent streets and many old fine antebellum homes which would give a housekeeper nightmares. And there is the cemetery that used to be a race track until one man was refused membership, whereupon he resolved to make it the deadest place in town. He did so—he bought it and it is now a very beautiful cemetery.

Thereafter we wandered down to the waterfront, had coffee at the Morning Call (an obligatory ritual) and found the *Gulf Shipper*. Captain Rowland W. Dillard was aboard and very kindly showed us around. Captain Dillard is usually Chief Mate of the *Shipper*, but had just completed a voyage as C.O. during the vacation of Captain Lee. We soon discovered that he was a retired naval officer, whereupon we admitted that we were Navy files, too, and became *muy simpático* in an atmosphere of "Did you know so-and-so?"

We firmly resolved to see a movie that night, several bills having changed—but found that Hollywood's Chinese suicide was still going on. So we started back to Maison de Ville. At the corner of Toulouse and Bourbon, fifty feet from Maison de Ville, is the Old French Opera House. I pointed out that it was much too early to go to bed; why not sit through one show?

We did. At this point begins the confirmation of the Louisiana Purchase. I now own one New Orleans night club, having bought and paid for it. Through some oversight the deed has not yet been sent to me; however, we have been traveling; it may be awaiting us in the States.

The O.F.O.H. promises continuous entertainment. We sat through one show and were just preparing to leave when the first M.C. sat down beside us, the relief M.C. having taken over. "How do you like our show?" he asked. "Fine," I agreed and presently asked him to have a drink. He accepted.

Three hours later I was still buying drinks for him and for a little blonde stripper named Pam. There is no cover charge but the drinks are very small and the prices are high in inverse proportion. I must say at this point that I enjoyed every minute of it, save that all too often I was busy making change or tipping when I should have been giving careful attention to the artistic and uninhibited dancing going on at a point averaging one meter from my bulging eyes.

These dives on Bourbon Street vary a good bit. I must say for the O.F.O.H. that it smelled clean, it looked clean, the glasses were clean, and the girls were young, pretty, healthy, and looked freshly bathed and not tough. If you are relaxed to the fact that the purpose of the place is to show pretty girls in as much skin as the gendarmes will permit, then the O.F.O.H. is the place for you; it is a nice joint of its sort. The jokes are not too rough and feature neither bathroom humor nor fag humor. Paul, the M.C. who sat with us and helped us complete the Purchase, was half Gypsy, the son of a tightrope artiste and had as his ambition to own and operate a small carnie wild-animal show—toward which he had a fair start, including a boa constrictor that slept with him on cold nights. He was in the market for a mountain lion kitten.

Pam, the little blonde stripper who joined us presently, was suffering from a hangover and love. She and the trap drummer planned to get married, but would have to wait a bit as he was buying a new set of traps. She assured us that she could cook. It seemed that everyone in the show was suffering from a hangover, the preceding night (Saturday) having been very drunk out, including among other things, Pam having had her bar bill cut off by the manager and retaliating by taking off her shoes and throwing them at him. One of the girls had threatened suicide and Paul had had to go into their dressing room and quash it. There was no general agreement as to which girl was threatening suicide but all agreed that someone had.

We were supplying the hair of the dog—at house prices.

I don't know how I got out without paying the French War debt as well, but I did, eventually. Actually, both Paul and Pam were nice kids; Ticky and I liked both of them. Pam was 21 and had been a stripper since she was 13, at which time her mother used to take her to and from work. Ticky asked her if she weren't scared when she started. Oh yes! but now it was just a job, a better paying job than working in an office. The girls make $75 to $90 a week. There is no real future in it, of course, and it is inclined to turn them all into habitual drinkers if not alcoholics. I haven't the slightest idea how many of them end up in bagnios—probably most of them get married. If stripping damages their moral fibre, I was unable to discern it.

We went aboard ship the next day, came ashore for dinner, having been warned by the purser that the crew was being paid off and that there were some beefs which might result in bad language and unpleasantness. We finally went to a movie, *Veils of Bagdad* or some such, featuring Victor Mature in improbable situations. I went to sleep. Ticky woke me and took me back to the ship.

The *Gulf Shipper* was warped away from dock and headed out into the stream by towboats about 1000 Tuesday morning. We spent all day watching the lower or delta reaches of the Mississippi, counting pelicans and one (1) porpoise. (No score is credited for seagulls.) The delta Mississippi is an improbable place. From the deck of a ship one can see right over the tallest trees to the horizon, stretching around through 360 degrees as in the flattest parts of western Kansas. The highest land seems to be roughly 21 inches above water and the black gumbo mud runs down to China. Vegetation is lush, thick and low, something between canebrake and jungle. But there are farms and cattle ranches back in here, paved roads and many oil wells. One wonders what they do at high water.

Almost down to the Gulf the Delta pilot leaves the ship, at Pilot Town, a town built on stilts, and the Bar pilot takes over. The Bar is a neighborhood rather than a channel—the lower portion of the multiple mouth of the Mississippi changes so rapidly that it must be piloted by a man who has taken a look at it just a few hours before. You can almost see him moving his lips as he comes aboard, concentrating on remembering the latest twist of Old Man River. He takes the ship out into the open Gulf as the sun goes down, then with a sigh of relief turns it over to the skipper.

We went to bed.

Next morning we were out of sight of land, on the open blue Gulf, lying in deck chairs and counting flying fish instead of pelicans. The sea was almost glassy with the ship moving gently, rolling almost imperceptibly and lifting a trifle to long, slow, low swells. Nevertheless it was enough to bother one passenger, who started missing meals at once. The rest of us started getting acquainted—Ticky and myself, Vi and Robert from Hawaii and off on a busman's holiday to the tropics, two couples from the same middle west town who kept much to themselves, and Mr. Tupper. Mr. Tupper was known either as "The Cruise Director" or as "The Owner"—it was his third trip in this ship, he had his own sextant and navigated with the mates each day, he had a stateroom right on the bridge, one which had apparently been intended as an emergency cabin for the skipper in wartime. He was not a seafaring man by profession, but a retired insurance executive from Atlanta, Georgia, who had made a hobby of the merchant marine in his old age and had studied navigation in order to enjoy it the more. He was the life of the party, the benign spirit of the ship, with an endless string of anecdotes and "animal stories," always funny, and with a case of Old Parr under his desk in case something—such as sighting a whale, or a boat drill, or such, should make him and his companions "nervous."

He assuaged my nervousness on numerous occasions. GSA should give him his passage free and charge the other passengers extra, should they be lucky enough to sail with him.

We passed the west end of Cuba the next night and were in the Caribbean, which looked just like the Gulf. I looked for the furrows I had worn into the Caribbean as a kid thirty years ago, but they were gone. All is change, there is nothing you can really depend on. The Captain gave a cocktail party which made up for it. He put on a uniform for the first time, too (freighters are *very* informal)—dress whites. Captain Lee is a tall, handsome man in his early forties and looks the way a skipper should look. He has a very heavy hand with a cocktail shaker.

The skipper went to sea as a boy, shipping before the mast, and worked his way up through the hawsepipe through all ratings from ordinary seaman to master mariner. This personal saga of the sea is probably passing today, as a consequence of the founding of the U.S. Merchant Marine Academy. No doubt this transition represents progress, but one thing is sure: the old-style skipper has a knowledge of his ship and the job of every man in it which cannot be learned in a school room.

Captain Lee kept a very taut ship. There was overt evidence in clean paintwork and well-shined brightwork but the most compelling evidence was negative; the ship had no odor. Almost every ship that sails the sea holds a pervasive, inescapable stink compounded of bilgewater and a dozen other ancient, organic whiffs. In a dirty ship it is almost unbearable; in a clean ship it is so slight as to be inoffensive when the weather is calm, the ports open, and the stomach is easy. But one does not expect it to be missing entirely. The *Gulf Shipper* had none that I could detect.

Later on we were conducted through all parts of the ship, engineroom, holds, lower passages, crew's quarters, galley, lockers, iceboxes—and I could see why. The ship was clean. Not just reasonably clean, but clean. The Captain inspected the ship each morning from stem to sternpost. When he inspected during our first day at sea I was asleep, with our door closed. He did not knock but noted down that he had not been able to enter stateroom number three and returned that afternoon to complete his inspection.

He did not simply stick his head in, glance around, and ask us if everything was all right. He came in and tried everything himself—plumbing valves, porthole dogs, medicine cabinet door, wardrobe doors, drawers. There was a steel chest of drawers welded to the bulkhead; Captain Lee found that one drawer stuck, so he squatted down, took hold with both hands and attempted to make it work.

He is a large man and powerful. With a sound of ripping metal the entire steel chest parted from the bulkhead and came away in his hands. He looked at it soberly and remarked, "I'll send one of the engineers up to fix that."

Freighter travel can be very pleasant. If you insist on the combination of swank hotel and organized children's party which characterizes a smart North Atlantic liner you will be bored and miserable in a freighter, for a freighter offers only meals, room, and transportation; the rest is up to you. I am not sneering at luxury liners; real luxury can be a lot of fun. Freighter life is a different sort of fun.

The staterooms are usually larger than any but the most expensive in a liner and they are always outside rooms. Ours in the *Gulf Shipper* had a private toilet and shower, contained two single bunks and a large couch, had three ports, and was roomy enough to set up a card table. Outside the passengers' rooms were wide verandas with deck chairs. There were no deck stewards hovering around; if you wanted your chair moved, you moved it; if you wanted a cup of coffee or tea, you went down to the pantry and got it.

The passengers ate with the officers in the officers' saloon. The service was adequate—one waiter for nine passengers— and the food was the sort known as "good, plain cooking." This can as easily be "bad, plain cooking" but in the *Shipper* it was good. The chef was no *Cordon Bleu* but he had a decent respect for good raw materials and prepared them accordingly. There was usually a choice of three entrées and two desserts; I believe that anyone but a gourmet would have been happy with it. Dutch, German, and Scandinavian freighters have a reputation for setting a better table than do our ships. In some cases this reputation may be justified—but I enjoyed the food in the *Gulf Shipper*.

What you do between meals is up to you. You can sunbathe in a deck chair and count the flying fish, sleep, chat with the other passengers and the officers, read, play cards, study, or even get drunk. Or you can hole up in your room and wish to heaven that you had never left Paducah.

Ticky and I found the three weeks in the *Shipper* one long, gay picnic, its only drawback being that we ran very short on sleep. Both of us had expected to work and study on this leg of the trip; neither of us got anything of the sort done. But I am forced to admit that, aside from a couple of good parties in port, nothing noteworthy happened. We played cribbage, we yarned endlessly, and we had cheerful drinks with cheerful companions. Someone else might have found the trip excruciatingly dull.

Freighter travel is not necessarily cheap. For the North Atlantic crossing freighter fare runs about the same as cabin class in the *Ile de France,* with first-class fare running considerably more and tourist class running considerably less. No direct comparison can be made between passenger ships and freighters on the run from New Orleans and Valparaiso as there are no passenger ships on this run. But it can be compared with air travel. First class one-way by air from New Orleans is now $529, air tourist class is $402, whereas the ocean freighter fare is $410, to which you can add $30 or $40 in tips.

Another way is to compare round-the-world fares:

President Lines tour ships... about $2600
Air First Class............................. $1720
Air Tourist.................................. $1580

Ocean freighter travel—from $500 to about $2000: the catch being that the $500 bargain is almost impossible to get and you probably would not want it if you could get it. A more likely figure is something between $1400 and $2000, or a median cost almost exactly equal to air tourist fare and a top cost in excess of first-class air travel.

Of course air transport simply gets you there, room-and-board on the ground being your problem. A typical trip around the world by freighter or cargo liner might show thirty days in port, during which time you may sleep and eat in the ship. Equal accommodations might cost you $15 per day if you went by air—a very rough guess since cost-of-living and rates-of-exchange vary so widely. Nevertheless, from my own recent personal experience in hotel costs around the world, I estimate the value of freighter accommodations as American-plan hotel accommodations to be certainly not more than $450 for 30 days, i.e., you can buy as many days sightseeing around the world for about the same price whether you go by air or by freighter. If you do not insist on the foreign equivalent of a Hilton hotel, you may be able to do it by air for a few dollars less than by freighter—and *much* cheaper than you could do it by luxury ship.

This may be surprising—I know that it surprised me. Until I made a direct comparison, on paper and through experience, I had always assumed that air travel was comparatively expensive, that in general travel by water was fairly reasonable, and that ocean freighter travel was very inexpensive. While it may have been true once, it is not true now.

The rates for particular trips vary widely. As a rule of thumb you can now expect that first-class travel by air will cost about the same as first-class travel by ship or train and that ocean freighter travel will cost about as much as air tourist travel. But it still depends on where you want to go; New York to London is about $75 cheaper, class for class, on the water, whereas New York to Los Angeles is at least $100 more expensive by water.

It adds up to a matter of taste and convenience. If you like long, lazy days at sea and have time for an extended vacation, ocean travel and freighter travel in particular is a real bargain; if your time is limited and you want a maximum of sightseeing for your dollar, go by air. If you can spare a month, you can go all the way around the world, see as much in as many days of sightseeing as are offered in luxury cruises of three or four months, all for the price of a Chevrolet. (A luxury ocean cruise, counting in tips and extras, will cost as much as a Cadillac.)

But freighter life unquestionably offers the maximum opportunity to rest. When we left Colorado Springs I was in a state of jumpy nerves from overwork. I twitched in the daytime and had insomnia at night. After a few days in the *Gulf Shipper* I was as relaxed as an oyster. It took me five days to work up enough ambition to load my camera.

After some days of sleeping all night, all afternoon, and napping in the morning I did bestir myself enough to poke around the ship a little. The *Shipper* is a typical freighter of the type known as "C-2." Her gross registered tonnage is 10,700 but, loaded, she actually displaces 15,000 long tons of sea water, i.e., that is what she would weigh, loaded with cargo and ready for sea, if you weighed her on your bathroom scales—I am speaking of largish bathroom scales, of course.

The term "tonnage" is used glibly with respect to ships by travel agents, seafaring men, and landlubbers, but the word is as slippery as "democracy" or "love" unless defined each time it is used. The ton referred to is a "metric ton" which the dictionary says is 2204.62 pounds—which is right as far as it goes. But it can also mean space of 100 cubic feet, or a carrying capacity of 40 cubic feet, or 35 cubic feet of sea water which is 2240 pounds in weight. It *never* means 2000 pounds as in a ton of coal delivered to your house.

To add to the confusion any ship has at least four usual "tonnages"—gross registered, net registered, dead weight, and displacement. The first two are measured in cubic feet, the second two are measured in pounds. In speaking of the *Queen Mary,* the *Nieuw Amsterdam,* or any merchant ship, the term "tonnage" that you are likely to hear means "registered gross tonnage" which is a cubic measure of the space enclosed inside her skin. On the other hand "tonnage" of a warship almost always means how much she *weighs,* ready for action. The two scales have the barest nodding acquaintance.

In the case of the *Shipper* her "net" tonnage is less than one third of her "displaced" tonnage, but both are correctly her "tonnage."

(John "loves" Mary; John "loves" bowling—see what I mean?)

Let us call the *Shipper* an 11,000-ton ship—on the same scale under which the *Queen Mary* is called an 80,000-ton ship, by the cubic footage inside their skins. This does not mean that the *Shipper* is small; it means that the *Queen Mary* is fantastically large. A "little" ship like the *Gulf Shipper* can carry as much as two to three ordinary freight trains. She is 460 feet long, 63 feet wide, and draws 32 feet. To push this bulk through the water at 15.5 knots (18 land miles per hour) she uses 6000 horsepower derived from oil-fired boilers and steam-driven turbines—the locomotives used by the Santa Fe's famous *SuperChief* are rated at 900 horsepower; on the other hand the lovely lady *Lexington,* lost in the battle of the Coral Sea, had a rated horsepower of 180,000 and could, by tucking up her skirts a bit, turn up over 200,000 horsepower.

The *Gulf Shipper* carries a crew of forty-seven, seventeen in deck and navigation, seventeen in engineering, thirteen others including the purser, radio operator, chief steward, cooks, waiters, and helpers. Twenty-four of the crew are deck and engineering watchstanders, eight to each of the three watches. The others are either those whose duties never end, such as the Captain, the chief engineer, the purser, or those who work at specified hours, such as cooks and deck maintenance men. The ship's payroll will run around $20,000 a month and the total cost of operating her is about $85,000 a month—which means that she has to run fully loaded most of the time, make fast turn arounds, and avoid excessive overtime in order to show a profit.

American merchant ships are in a poor position to compete with foreign shipping. The ship itself costs more, our safety laws are more stringent than those of many of our competitors, and we pay enormously higher wages. I am not criticizing the wage scale; it is simply what must be paid to persuade Americans to go to sea instead of taking jobs ashore—but it is true that we pay as much to an able seaman as many countries pay the captain of a large vessel.

Because of our high costs many American vessels are being transferred to foreign flags under whose laws they can operate at much lower costs. This flight from the American flag would perhaps be of only sentimental importance were it not usually agreed that a large and healthy merchant marine is an essential part of our national defense. A quick answer is to hit the taxpayers for a shipping subsidy. Another quick answer is "American ingenuity and enterprise." A third quick answer is that merchant shipping is no longer a major factor in war because the next war will be settled from the air in a matter of hours or days.

I am sorry to say that I seem to have mislaid the right answer.

The *Gulf Shipper* arrived off the Atlantic end of the Panama Canal early Saturday morning the 21st, stopped just long enough to pick up the pilot and his handling crew and to drop the purser, then started through the Canal. Passengers could, if they wished, get off with the purser, spend the day shopping and sightseeing, travel across the Isthmus by bus, and join the ship that evening on the Pacific side.

None of us did so. Ticky had never seen the Canal before, but neither had she ever seen Colón and Panama City and the U.S. settlements, Cristóbal and Balboa, adjacent to them. She was torn between the desire to see the first foreign port in our trip and a desire to see the Canal; I persuaded her to see the Canal.

I swear on a stack of wheat cakes that I was not motivated by a desire to keep her away from the bazaars. It is true that the shops of Colón and of Panama City have an effect on all women and some men much like that of a bed of fresh catnip on a cat—and the bargains often are real bargains, for Panama City is a free port. No, like a total eclipse of the sun, the experience of transiting the Panama Canal is one that should not be missed if available. There is nothing else like it in the world . . . and I am not forgetting the Suez Canal.

I still have scars on my arms from sunburn acquired more than a quarter of a century ago when I first went through the big ditch. I knew at the time that I was getting sunburned but I could not bring myself to stop looking and go below. Since then I have seen it many times—and I still can't stop looking.

Any atlas, world almanac, or encyclopedia will provide a winter's supply of sound, chewy facts about the Panama Canal, tonnages, tolls collected, yards of earth moved, and so forth. They are well worth reading but we will not repeat them here. The Canal was started by the French in 1882; you can still see the old French Canal slicing slaunchwise into the channel we cut. Yellow fever and more bad luck than any man ought to have put a stop to the French attempt. We bought the franchise and, with almost indecent haste, recognized a Panamanian revolutionary government which seceded from Colombia in 1903, signed a treaty with the new government and started work again in 1904. Ten years later the first ship went through.

The Canal is fifty miles long and runs northwest to southeast across the twisted isthmus in such a fashion that the trip from the Atlantic to the Pacific (i.e., to the *west*) winds up twenty-seven miles farther to the *east*. This has to be seen on a map to be understood; it is as silly as the fact that Los Angeles is east of Reno. Sea level is a couple of feet higher on the Pacific side than on the Atlantic side but this odd fact is swallowed up by the fact that the major portion of the Canal is eighty-five feet higher than either ocean. Three sets of locks at each end perform the improbable task of lifting and lowering ships of fifty thousand tons or more the height of an eight-story building.

There has been a lot of agitation for a sea-level canal, through Nicaragua or elsewhere. One glance at any one of the locks of the Panama Canal is enough to show why; one pony-sized A-bomb anywhere near one of the locks would put the entire Canal out of use for months or years and leave our navy and merchant marine with a nice, long, chilly trip around the Horn in order to get from one coast to the other. You will correctly assume that the Canal Zone contains anti-aircraft and radar installations—but the bomb need not be delivered by air; it can be in the hold of a ship flying the flag of Ruritania, or even the U.S. flag. There are more than seven thousand ships going through the Canal each year and the only known way to inspect a ship for A-bombs is to unload everything, take a screwdriver and open every crate . . . a process equivalent in itself to closing the Canal to traffic.

I am disclosing no secrets. You may be sure that Mr. Malenkov's assistants have given thoughtful consideration to these matters and that our government has been equally thoughtful. If I knew of an answer I would be in Washington right now.

In the meantime the locks of the Panama Canal remain the most satisfying gadgets I have experienced since the time Santa Claus brought me a toy steam shovel that actually worked. The ship slides slowly and quietly into the first of the Atlantic side or Gatún Locks, towed into place by miniature cog railway engines known as electric mules. The gates close ponderously and magically behind her, untouched by human hands; a guard chain rises to protect the gates. The ship is enclosed in a box; all one can see is the concrete walls.

Water boils up from the bottom of the lock and high, high up she rises! The ship lifts gradually up and up until the sightseers on her decks can again see over the sides of the lock the tailored, tropical surroundings. The gates ahead open, again by magic, and the ship is gently urged into the channel ahead. Three times the ship goes through a water elevator, lifted each time about thirty feet, then she is let free into Gatún Lake.

The lake was made by damming the Chagres River, which supplies the water to work the locks. Here and there, outside the dredged channel, dead trunks of trees still thrust up through the water, melancholy monuments to progress. The extremely broken shore line and the numerous islets, both characteristic of newly-flooded river valleys, form and re-form deep three-dimensional vistas, all in glorious Technicolor. The place seems unreal, as if one had fallen into a Disney musical.

I have heard it said that Gatún Lake is the "dull" part of the Panama Canal. I don't know what to say to such people. They are unquestionably right, since it is all a matter of taste, as the old lady said when she kissed the pig. I once ran across a woman from France who had just finished a tour of the western part of the United States. In her opinion she had seen nothing west of the Mississippi worth looking at—including the Grand Canyon, the Rocky Mountains, Yellowstone, and so forth. As the booking agent said to the man who was flying by flapping his arms: "So you can imitate birds. But what can you do that's *novel?*"

You may not share my enthusiasm for Gatún Lake and, after all, it is just another lake. The whole world is loaded with beautiful scenery; Gatún Lake is one of thousands. But I have been in it at every time of day and in every season and I myself have never grown bored with it. The lights and colors are always changing; the motion of the ship combines with the twisted shore lines to form backdrop after backdrop into mysterious depths. Perhaps it is "dull"—but I am a Missouri country boy with black mud between my toes; I still stare at the Empire State Building whenever I get a chance.

The entire experience of the Panama Canal has always seemed pleasantly unreal to me, as if it all had been constructed by a Hollywood miniature set designer—the blazing sunlight, the quick rain storms, the little electric engines crawling slowly up beautifully curving concrete walls, the locks themselves and the lavish engineering structures around them, the endlessly changing depth on depth of lake and cut and jungle. It was designed more than half a century ago, back when ladies had "limbs" and the shout of "Get a horse!" at an "automobilist" was real wit. Yet it looks like a set for a major production scene in a Hollywood fantasy of the future.

After the lake the ship enters the Cut—"Gaillard Cut" on the maps, "Culebra Cut" in the mouths of most people. This is the part that almost broke the hearts of the builders. This is where hairy engineers in field boots stared through surveying instruments at mountains and decreed that they must be moved. Moved they were—by coal-burning steam shovel and scraper and mule and muscle and sweat. The Model-T Ford was brand new then and the bulldozer was yet to be born. Earthmoving machinery such as any county road department now owns would have seemed miraculous; they made do without.

The banks are very close here and the jungle is almost in your lap. You sit in a deck chair or lean on the rail and let it flow past you, birds and snakes and waterfalls and giant blue butterflies. Once, some years ago, I found myself staring back at an eight-foot alligator, so close that I could see the stains on his teeth. I alert Ticky to watch for them, but we have no luck. One of the pilot crew aboard tells me that there are plenty of them still on the shores of the lake and that it has been necessary to fine people who hunt them for sport, then leave the carcasses to rot in the clean water of the lake.

Back in the jungle here, only shouting distance away in places, is the old Gold Trail, peopled with the ghosts of the Indian slaves who died on the way. Once, twenty years earlier, I rode along a portion of it on a borrowed army horse. It was paved with stone and the jungle had not quite destroyed it, but had arched over it instead, forming a dusky tunnel, a place of enormous butterflies and midget deer and silence. The Isthmus was one of the world's major roadways long before the water bridge was cut through it.

But nowadays the once-heartbreaking journey is soft and easy and no one dies on the way. Traffic lights control the shipping through the Cut, real traffic lights with red for stop and green for go. There are places where the pilot must hold back and give the traffic ahead a chance to clear; the lights tell him, just like those on Wilshire Boulevard. In addition to lights he has been briefed by the control officials ashore as to what ships to expect and where, since the enormous mass of a ship is not stopped by jamming a foot on a brake. The handling of a ship through the Canal is a piece of precision choreography. There are ranges, each a pair of giant targets, at dozens of places along the route; the pilot can sight along one range and know that he is lined up properly for the channel and sight along another at the same time and know to the yard just how far he has progressed along that reach of the channel and how soon he must turn.

The reason for such precision is evident: in some places ships pass so closely that you expect their plates to scrape. Canal pilot is among the most highly skilled jobs in the Zone and is highly paid by civil service standards. But the job is done without swank. Almost all other countries dress their pilots in uniforms like those of naval officers, but the *Gulf Shipper*'s pilot was a young man in a slouch hat and casual sports clothes who carried his responsibilities with the relaxed ease of a truck driver.

We passed through Pedro Miguel and Miraflores Locks in the late afternoon, with the same processes as in Gatún Locks save that we started each time high above the scenery, then sank into claustrophobic depths before being let out into a lower level. At dusk we dropped the pilot and steamed out into the waters of the Pacific, into the Gulf of Panama, with the lights of Panama City on our port hand. We picked our way through islands and submerged rocks and presently Captain Lee set course for Point Charambirá above Buenaventura, Colombia.

A drastic change comes over a ship as soon as it touches dock. The physical change can be easily described but the emotional change is far greater and harder to convey. For some days you have been in a little world, an enclave away from atom bombs and strikes and bills and auto accidents and traffic noises and strange people. Nothing is real but the ship and it is a place of no worries. You leave your stateroom door wide open, leave binoculars or cameras on deck chairs, dress as you please. No one hurries and no one worries. You are home, with only your "family" around you.

Then the gangway touches the dock and all is changed completely, with the suddenness of being dumped out of warm sleep into cold water. Strangers swarm aboard, they are everywhere and they all look like criminals. A percentage of them are indeed petty thieves who will steal the socks off your feet without untying your shoe laces; this is true in any port including those of the United States. You always lock your stateroom door and carry the key with you everywhere. You dog down the ports of your room if you step out even for a moment, no matter how hot it is, as even a moment is enough for the waterfront pilferer; fly screens won't stop him, it takes steel. Nor are you safe simply because your porthole does not face onto a gallery; harbor thieves have been known to operate from the masts of small boats, using a gadget combining the features of lazy tongs and fishing rods.

You return to your stateroom—locked, thank heaven!—and find a villainous-looking stranger trying the door. Unabashed, he claims to have been looking for the purser. Perhaps he was and perhaps he has legitimate business with the purser. Perhaps stealing is only a hobby with him. You don't find out, as the purser is much too busy to talk with you. The Captain, a genial host only an hour before, brushes past you without seeing you, two strangers in tow. You return to your room, bolting the door behind you, and start to change clothes. Then you notice faces at each porthole. They weren't there ten seconds before and the gallery was empty as you came in.

Buenaventura, Colombia, is not worse than other ports; for pure villainy it is not in the same league with the racket-infested docksides of New York City. In fact, the purser tells us that Buenaventura is safer than it used to be, as "the officials are no longer hungry." About six months earlier there was a revolution, or rather a military coup d'état; since then the port officials and the police have been paid regularly. They do not need to steal nor to seek bribes in order to eat.

The notion that a military dictator can produce a better government than an elected regime is obnoxious, but clearly this is an occasion for suspended judgment. Our Latin neighbors move in mysterious ways. Where we would use a recall or simply wait for the next general election, they wake *el presidente* up in the middle of the night, stick a gun in his face and tell him that he is through . . . they hardly ever kill him.

I find it necessary to remind myself firmly that the customs of my own tribe are not the laws of nature.

The stevedores all come aboard carrying empty sacks; when they leave the sacks are not empty. The sacks may contain U.S. cigarettes purchased from crew members and destined for black market ashore, or they may contain anything that is not riveted down. The chief mate tells us that he has found them taking away crumpled pieces of old newspaper—trash—used in stowing cargo and left in the holds. Or they will gather up a few coffee beans left on the floor plates. These people are poor; to them anything is worth salvaging.

It was raining when we reached Buenaventura. During the two days we were there the rain stopped once for about two hours. Buenaventura enjoys, or suffers, three hundred and fifty inches of rain a year or about an inch a day. A freighter skipper hates to rig cargo awnings as it slows up the work greatly and cuts into the slim margin of profit, but in Buenaventura it is done as a matter of course. Much of the cargo loaded there is coffee; to allow it to get wet is financial disaster.

Colombian coffee is precious stuff, much prized for blending. A prime reason why it is almost impossible to get a decent cup of coffee (by American taste) anywhere but the United States is that coffee made elsewhere is likely to be Brazilian coffee, strong and bitter. We use the hearty Brazilian coffee, too, but we blend it with milder coffees of vastly different flavor from the highlands of Costa Rica and from Colombia. The purest water, used with great care in Silex or drip pot, will not produce an "American" cup of coffee if our American blends are not used.

Most of our tonnage for Buenaventura was a couple of dozen big motor buses, carried on deck and in the upper holds. Rain would not hurt them and there was no need to rig tarpaulins until they were out of the way, but rain could and did slow up the work and make stevedores and crew miserable. It was hot, tropical rain. We slept naked on sheets with blowers playing on us full blast, and we soaked the sheets. I used three shirts a day in a hopeless attempt to be neat and the neckties I did not wear nevertheless mildewed on their hooks. Towels never dried, clothing was damp when it was put on, my typewriter rusted to immobility, and I broke out with a superior grade of athlete's foot.

Ticky looked at me with quiet reproach and said, "I thought you told me you *liked* the tropics."

The rain slacked off and the sky almost cleared the middle of the next morning and Ticky and I, Vi and Bob Markham, went ashore. Buenaventura is a very busy port, serving all the west slope of Colombia, but it is a small town, about 14,000. It looks like any number of other small towns through Central America and is rather pretty when the sun is shining. It has a one-sided main street, a hotel, a Catholic church, several cantinas, and a few shops where the rush of trade is slowed down to a tranquil hush. Once you are off the docks and through the customs gate there is little danger of being run down by the traffic, nor are the sidewalks crowded. One swarthy fellow, perfect type casting for the assistant villain in a tropical melodrama, followed us around the whole time we were ashore, but he never attempted to speak to us. Apparently he just wanted to look at the gringos.

We exhausted the sightseeing resources of the town in an hour and had exhausted ourselves in the heat and humidity even at a very slow walk. It was beginning to rain again; we returned to the ship.

I was assured by several members of the ship's company that Buenaventura might be sleepy in the daytime but that it possessed a very rugged night life "up on the hill" with music and liquor and entertainment downstairs and anything at all that one cared to pay for upstairs. I thanked them and let it go at that, saying that I had a date to play cribbage.

The cribbage game never came off because the chief engineer took advantage of our stay in port to give a cocktail party, announced as a meeting of the D.M. Club to induct four new members: the Heinleins and the Markhams. "D.M." stands for "Dry Martini." It also stands for "Dead Man," and is an intentional play on words. The chief engineer made excellent dry martinis; regrettably he served them in water tumblers. I do not have the constitution to play "al seco" or "bottoms up" with martinis of that size and I refused to do so, even though repeatedly urged—nevertheless the drunker I stayed there the longer I got.

I was saved by the dinner bell. We all piled into the dining saloon and started wolfing comestibles. I needed same.

A careful reconstruction of what happened next seems to establish clearly that Ticky fired the first shot. The Captain was sitting across the room from her and failed to answer when she called out something to him. Ticky is not a woman to be ignored with impunity; she wadded up her napkin and let him have it. The first salvo was short and landed in his soup.

For several days we had had bowls of kumquats on the table. The kumquat is a very pretty fruit and makes excellent preserves but they are not much to eat raw. I never saw anyone eat one and I think the waiters simply dusted them off and brought them back, meal after meal.

But they are a nice size for throwing and have excellent ballistics properties in the medium ranges. Very soon the air was filled with kumquats. Each kumquat could be used over and over again (and was) until it got tired and burst, which it did. As the kumquat supply diminished, other things were pressed into emergency service, rolls, more wadded napkins, anything that came to hand. I was very hungry and did not take full part in the festivities, limiting myself to grabbing anything that landed near me or on me and firing it back blindly over my shoulder. There being a solid rank of ship's officers behind me, I stood a good chance of getting the junior third or the mate even if I missed the skipper or the engineer. So I kept on eating.

The officers' waiter, a young Cuban called "Chico," entered into the spirit of the occasion and started running ammunition in from the pantry to the Captain's table, starting with more kumquats and branching out when they ran short. He came in at last with a large platter covered with cold cuts, which was intended for midnight lunch. He offered it proudly to Captain Lee.

The Captain looked at it, grinned, and reached for it—then demonstrated the qualities of leadership, mature judgment, and restraint that had carried him to the top: he firmly refused it and made Chico take it back, much to Chico's disappointment. This act of renunciation turned the tide; a few more desultory salvos and the battle was over.

Bob Markham told me afterwards that the finest moment of the engagement known from then on as "Kumquat May"—a poor pun but it was awfully hot—was an incident that I did not actually see because I was in it. Someone hit me fair in the back of the neck with an entire plateful of tossed green salad, well marinated, and I did not flinch nor cry aloud but kept on eating. Markham seemed to feel that it showed rare aplomb.

I gave him the aw-shucks-fellers-it-warn't-nothing-anybody-else-with-courage-and-a-cool-head-would-have-done-as-well routine. The fact was that I wanted my dessert. It was a plain one-egg cake with icing which I prefer to most fancy desserts; I was durned if I was going to miss finishing my dinner simply because lettuce was dripping from my ears. Once I finished the cake I gathered up everything that I could reach and threw it at the Captain in one saturation barrage. I was not sure that he had thrown the salad at me but I believe in the sound and ancient principle that the commanding officer is responsible for everything that happens in his ship.

I must say that Captain Lee looks well in chutney.

After dinner someone again suggested that we all go ashore and try the entertainment offered up on the hill. Ticky was willing but I vetoed it and was supported by Bob Markham. No doubt a solid phalanx of ship's officers, ably led by the

Paul Bunyan figure of the Captain, would have supported us in any difficulty—but I do not trust remote tropical seaports after dark; I have seen too many of them as a young bachelor. The guardia is never around when you need it and a surprising number of the citizens carry knives. We went to bed instead.

It was clear for almost an hour the next day when we steamed out. Buenaventura is located in a very beautiful estuary which would no doubt be still more beautiful if the clouds would clear away and give a view of the snow-capped Andes only a few miles beyond. I had looked forward to seeing the Andes here, for it was through these mountains that Simón Bolívar the Liberator, a man half devil and half saint, had dragged his consumption-racked body to lead his starved and ragged army on to victory and freedom.

But I had to be content with a view of the harbor and the surrounding jungle. Colombia, although a country of Spanish and Indian tradition and culture, has a major strain of Negro. Accompanying us out into the stream were many dugout canoes paddled by blacks and on the shore we could see grass huts appropriate to Africa but which looked decidedly out of place in South America. Most of the Negroes here are supposed to be descendants of slaves escaped from farther north and who made their way through jungle and along the shore to freedom. It seems plausible, for it looks as if Congo culture had been preserved almost unchanged here through the centuries, only a few miles outside a town having most of the hallmarks of modern Western culture.

The *Gulf Shipper* turned south and soon entered the Humboldt Current, which sweeps north along the coast all the way from Antarctica. The weather turned chilly and we crossed the equator under two blankets—after sweltering in our bare skins only a few miles to the north.

Three days later the *Shipper* stood into the harbor of Callao, Peru, the seaport of Lima, the capital. The metropolitan district of Lima contains more than a million people and is a good place for a gringo to start getting over the notion that South America is an uncivilized back country. True, South America is thinly settled compared with the United States and it still has ahead of it perhaps a century of frontier exploitation whereas our frontier has moved on up into Canada. But Lima is both one of the oldest and in some ways the newest city in the Western world.

As a Western city it dates back to 1530, Pizarro's conquest, ninety years before the Pilgrims landed at Plymouth Rock; its origin as an Indian city is lost in antiquity. Its university is the oldest in the Americas. But in new Lima are mile after mile of homes in the style called "modern" and which perhaps should be called ultra-modern, since nowhere in the United States can there be found modern architecture to compare with these in abundance, in lavish use of color and glass, and imaginative freedom of design. Admirers of Frank Lloyd Wright, of Schindler, and of Neutra, if suddenly plopped down in new Lima, would probably conclude that they had died and gone to heaven.

The ship docked late in the day; it was early evening before we could leave—five of us, Ticky and I, the Markhams, and Mr. Tupper, the honorary "cruise director." Captain Lee had intended to come with us but business with the company agent held him up; he asked us to meet him at the Gran Hotel Bolívar at seven-thirty.

We drove the seven miles from the port to Lima along the beautiful Pan-American Boulevard. The countryside, vegetation, and buildings looked to me much like many places in Southern California, except that the Coca-Cola signs read "bibo" instead of "drink." We could see the Andes from time to time, but not very impressively as they were obscured by the same high haze so common in Southern California. It looked to me as if it might be gathering in for a rain storm and I asked the driver about it. He said that he did not think so, as it had not rained for thirty years.

He was not pulling my leg. All of the water in Lima is brought down from the mountains; there are grown men there who have never seen rain. The incredible change from the never-ending inch of rain per day of Buenaventura to the endless years of no rain at all in Lima only a short stretch of coast to the south is accounted for, so they tell me, by the ocean currents; the cold Humboldt Current laps Peru while the hot Counter-Equatorial Current runs straight into Colombia.

We passed through cuts in hills which had a faintly artificial look to them, being composed mostly of thousands of little boulders, polished smooth to the size of grapefruit. The artificial look was justified; they were Indian burial mounds. Here and there one could see a thigh bone sticking out, or ribs, and sometimes a boulder turned out to be a skull. Indian families had huts here and there among the partly destroyed mounds and babies played among the bones of their ancestors.

The taxi driver let us out in the Plaza de Armas in downtown Lima and charged us twenty sols or one Yankee dollar, seven miles for five people. The present rate of exchange is very favorable to us *norteamericanos* and it does not seem quite fair. We strolled around the plaza for a while, an impressively beautiful place, then sought out the Hotel Bolívar—with a couple of narrow squeaks from traffic. Lima has excellent traffic cops who handle the extremely dense traffic efficiently and with rare dignity—their stylized gestures remind me of a Balinese dance in slow motion. But the signals they use are not the signals our traffic cops use and every Latin American drives with courage. He understands the decidedly different driving customs of his country and he expects pedestrians to understand them also. Getting from curb to curb without any intention of jaywalking can be a hair-raising experience. By the time we reached the Gran Hotel Bolívar I was glad to seek out the bar and have a tonic for my nerves.

Under the favorable exchange martinis cost about nine cents and a pisco sour cost six cents. The pisco sour occupies in west coast South American diet the position that vitamin tablets do in ours. Pisco is a native brandy. No proof is ever shown on the bottle but it is certainly higher in alcoholic content than is whiskey in the States. I estimate that it could stand up to vodka and give away the first two punches. I tried one pisco sour and shifted back to martinis, where I knew the territory.

At the Bolívar we gathered in the purser and the second engineer and a flier from Texas and a big gringo mining operator. When the Captain arrived with a company agent, Vi and Ticky had nine men to split up between them. But the wolves in Lima are gallant, aggressive, and optimistic; Ticky complained to me presently that a stranger present was trying to pick her up. "Every time I look up he lifts his glass to me and motions with his head for me to come over," she said indignantly.

I suggested that if she refrained from looking at him she would not know that he was looking at her. But she continued to simmer. Presently she and Vi left us to find the powder room. When she returned she again had something on her mind. "This place is impossible!"

"Why? It reminds me of the Bellevue-Stratford in Philly. Seems like a pretty nice joint."

"Hmmph! Vi and I just walked through the lobby, minding our own business. At least a dozen men tried to pick us up."

"Well! Congratulations."

"It wasn't funny."

I tried to explain to her that customs varied and that any woman without an escort right at her elbow was assumed to be open to suggestions until proved otherwise. But her attention had flitted elsewhere. "Bob, there was a little Indian girl in the powder room, the maid, the attendant. I didn't have any change and Vi didn't either, so we turned out the bottoms of our purses—"

"Strike oil? Any mousetraps?"

"Don't be funny. I found a nickel and two pennies and gave them to her, feeling apologetic. But she seemed pleased and started talking excitedly and hurried away and came back and showed us what *she* had. It was an American quarter and she had shined it up like silverware. It was rather pathetic. Give me some change, dear. I want to go back and tip her properly."

"All right. But let's figure it out. You tipped her seven cents. That's one sol forty, or the price of a cocktail. Back home, would you tip a washroom attendant seventy-five cents?"

"Why, no, I'd probably tip her a quarter."

"Then did you under-tip? Or over-tip?"

Neither one of us could figure it out. It was our first tangle with a problem which worried us all around the world: whom to tip, when to tip, and how much? How to hold up the American reputation for generosity without adding to the American reputation for being blatant and wasteful suckers? We never did work out a satisfactory formula.

The entire party decided to move on to the "Club 91" for dinner, at which point I attempted to put into operation a previously prepared plan. It had long been established that Captain Lee was the world's worst check-snitcher; it was almost impossible to buy the man a drink because he would make a long arm, grab the check, and push aside anyone who attempted to pay it.

Knowing this, we party of passengers had planned for it and I had been selected to carry it out. I started with a verbal barrage in which I informed Captain Lee that we had taken a vote and decided to stick him with the check. I was very firm about it and he was very hurt, protesting that he did not mind paying his share but he thought it was a hell of a note for the rest of us to decide to clip him—he wouldn't stand for it, no, sir.

While his attention was diverted, I had obtained the check; I handed the waiter our pooled funds.

Captain Lee caught the tail end of the maneuver. With a scream of rage and a fist full of sols he straightened up to his full seven feet and attempted to reverse the matter. I got off with a slight flesh wound, but we kept him from paying the check.

On the way to dinner he kept trying to force money on me. After a while he quit but he seemed pleased about something. Later on Mr. Tupper twitted him about losing, whereupon he said, "Oh yes? Bob, look under your coat collar."

I did so, but there was nothing there. It developed that the Captain had tucked a roll of bills, two hundred sols, under my coat collar while we were crowded into a taxi—but they were gone, had fallen out. We speculated about the expression and feeling of the taxi driver or whoever it might be that found it, then forgot it, with each side feeling that it had won a moral victory.

But the next time I try to snatch a check from Captain Lee I'll wear gloves.

Club 91 is on the top floor of a skyscraper and has a feeling much like the Top o' the Mark, with broad expanses of glass giving a panorama of the wide-flung city, the Andes, and the ocean. It is very posh and has wonderful food, an exotic cuisine in no way resembling Mexican food. Nor is it international-French cooking, it is Peruvian. I don't know what else to say about it; describing dishes and flavors which are truly novel is a waste of words. But when you go to Peru, don't limit yourself to steak; there are delightful surprises in store for you. Leave room for dessert, too. They bring them around on an oversize tea wagon and let you pick by sight instead of from a menu. I don't know whether this is a kindness or not, since by that time you cannot possibly toy with more than one and the others are lost to you forever.

Dinner in South America is not the evening meal; it is a nighttime adventure. Although we went straight back to the ship it was very late when we got aboard and I rolled into my bunk, happy with the thought that the ship was sailing and I could sleep all day tomorrow.

But I learned at seven A.M. that the ship was not sailing, that loading had not been completed, and that the Captain had ordered a taxi and a guide for us. I groaned, took Dexedrine, and decided to enjoy it, reminding myself that I had come a long way and had spent more than fifty cents for the privilege.

Our guide and driver was Señor Rodolfo Gonzales Bueno, a middle-aged Indian of great size and great dignity. Perhaps his ancestry was more Spanish than Indian; if so, the Indians came out ahead. His face reminded me of that carved stone god that stares with timeless majesty out over the water gardens in the grounds of the Pan-American Building in Washington, D.C.

We made a full day of it and I was soon glad that the ship had not sailed even though my head was beginning to ache. We saw Callao first, the harbor, the naval academy, and an enormous market made up of hundreds of little stalls, crowded and colorful. I took the precaution here of leaving Ticky's purse with Mr. Gonzales as I was not anxious to start too quickly the business of dragging plunder around the world.

Then we saw old Lima, university, government buildings, presidential palace, archbishop's palace, cathedral, all impressive and all ornate in a style no longer popular. There were so many of them that I almost felt sympathy for the tourist who came charging up the steps of our own National Capitol at Washington and said to his wife, "Okay, Marge, you take the inside and I'll take the outside and we ought to be through in twenty minutes."

But in the cathedral we saw the mummy of Pizarro the Conqueror himself. There he was, in a glass coffin, a little man who could not have been very impressive alive and who must have looked like a child to the giant Inca gods. Yet he and his "thirteen friends" by treachery and deceit and casual murder brought the mighty Inca Empire to ruin.

Now he lies with sunken eyesockets staring sightlessly up, his shriveled, darkened flesh and untidy hair on display, a sight for any tourist with two-bits to tip the attendant monk to let them stare. "Ozymandias, King of Kings—" Was it worth it, pal? Are you happy now? Or are you groaning in hell for your crimes?

Odd though it seems, although his bloody record is well known and although most of the citizens of Peru are descended from the conquered rather than the conquerors, Pizarro seems to be a popular hero.

I asked to be shown slums. This was not morbid curiosity. All countries have the homes of the rich, whether they be commissars, counts, or capitalists; their homes are all beautiful, they look pretty much alike everywhere, allowing for climate and architectural styling, and you learn very little about a country from seeing them. I always look at them for the enjoyment of seeing beautiful things, but you learn more from the slums, which are not enjoyable to see.

Lima had both shanty town slums and formal, tenement slums. The shanty towns were true international architecture, the grim and pathetic structures built by people who have nothing at all and must shelter themselves with scraps and other people's junk. They were indistinguishable from the shacks of Okies in Imperial Valley twenty years ago, from the barrios of Rio, from the shanties of Singapore's waterfront. The formal tenements were mostly one-story buildings built wall to wall in long rows with narrow alleys. They reminded me of dog kennels and were even more depressing than the much less adequate shanties, for here poverty seemed static and hopeless, a permanent way of life.

Almost next door to these warrens was a palace. It had once been a private home but now belonged to the government and was used by the army. Many of the soldiers' families lived in the nearby tenements; the contrast was sharp and bitter for papá worked in (literal) marble halls, then went home when off duty to a house more suitable for pigs than for women and children.

The palace had been built by a marquis for his "beloved"— a polite Latin expression which concedes the permanence of marriage but admits that love is something else and important in its own way. The social custom of the mistress as a formal institution in Latin America is very disconcerting to *norteamericanos,* reared in a matriarchy. Except for a very few cases, mostly in Hollywood and New York, there is no group or social class in the United States parallel to what is meant by "mistress" in Latin America, and even the exceptions are not truly parallel, for a kept woman does not have the publicly recognized, customary status of a Latin mistress.

When we use the word "mistress"—which is seldom—the reference is often in the past tense and means simply that Mr. and Mrs. Jones had their honeymoon before they held their wedding, a circumstance often factual but usually known publicly only through gossip and conjecture, or known statistically through Dr. Kinsey's tedious tables. Or "mistress" may refer to an informal biological arrangement carefully concealed and usually without any specific financial arrangements for support. Neither of these cases parallels the Latin custom. A Latin American who has a mistress usually has a wife as well and will appear in public with either one of them, but not both.

Each woman has a recognized place in his life and their social spheres ordinarily do not overlap.

But a mistress is not something to hide away in a back street. Her status is limited but much more privileged than is easy for a gringo to comprehend. Some years ago in a South American capital the United States ambassador gave a big party and invited all the local heavyweights and their wives. They came but most of them brought their mistresses.

The ambassador's wife was insulted and the ambassador was outraged and it almost resulted in an open international incident. Yet the mix-up was clearly a failure to understand each other's customs, since no South American would intentionally offend his host and hostess. The word should have been passed around quietly that this party was not intended to be fun; it was simply meant to be attended ritualistically—with *wives*.

The marquis' "beloved" (I don't remember either of their names and it does not matter) was apparently a woman of spirit who did not accept easily the limitations of her status. She was part Indian and from the lower classes; instead of being a well-behaved and modest mistress, respectful to her "betters," she refused to play the game according to the rules they handed her. Whether or not she objected to polygamy in itself is not known, but she certainly objected to the subordinate status accorded her by custom. She went out of her way to flaunt her birth and background under the quivering noses of the Castilian aristocracy of Lima. But her marquis refused to knuckle under to social pressure, but hung on to her, even though she was obviously "impossible" in the minds of all "right thinking" people.

He certainly did well by her. The Peruvian government, although using much of the palace for military purposes, has preserved the grounds and gardens and has maintained many of the chambers as a museum of the splendors of a by-gone day. Among other things, there is a carved marble bathtub on one of the balconies, of Imperial Roman magnificence. No one seems to know now if that was its usual position; the climate of Lima is balmy enough to have permitted her to bathe outdoors if such was her whim, and the tub would be very difficult to move. In any case there is a small swimming pool in the middle of the garden and a small summer house next to it which has a slatted screen like a venetian blind through which the pool can be seen. The old marquis is reputed to have been a bit of a voyeur; this summer house is supposed to have been a vantage point from which he could peep at her while she was swimming. Why in Ned he did not simply pull a chair up to the edge of the pool, or better yet, pull off his duds and join her nobody knows. Maybe he got more fun out of peeking.

There is a marble bust of her in the garden. She was unquestionably a beauty, fit to occupy the palace he placed her in. Now it stands as an inspiration to all women that they, too, can live in a palace if only they will use the depilatories and deodorants advertised in all the best women's magazines.

We then drove through miles of magnificently gardened, ultra-modern-style homes to the country club. We passed several of the embassies, among them the Colombian Embassy where Señor Victor Raúl Haya de la Torre was at that time still a prisoner of asylum, and still was to be so for several months to come. Mr. Haya's story is well known through the newspapers and has been fully covered in his own words in *Life* magazine (3 May 1954); we will omit details, except as they throw light on the striking differences between political life as we know it and the brand practiced south of us. Mr. Haya is the leader of the APRA party of Peru, which is left of center but not communist. He was charged with attempting a coup d'état against the government, but—and this is a South American twist hard for us to follow—the charge was brought against him by a later government, which had itself come to power by overthrowing the very government Haya was charged with attempting to overthrow.

The nuances of Peruvian politics are too complex for me and I doubt if any outsider could gain a real understanding of them without a long, hard apprenticeship. All of the nations south of us are constitutional republics with liberal constitutional safeguards similar or usually equivalent to those found in our own constitution, yet with the shining exceptions of Chile and

Uruguay, their political records seem to us to be an endless list of coup d'état, bloody revolution, unelected provisional presidents, political admirals and generals, states of siege, states of public emergency, exiles and refugees, outlawing of opposition parties, liquidation of opposition leaders, suppression of free speech, free assembly, and free press.

Here is a place to walk softly, to be not hasty in passing judgment; we may not understand all that we see. I found in traveling around the world that a great many people believed the most arrant nonsense about the United States. In particular, a great many people, apparently well educated and sophisticated, were convinced that the people of the United States were in the grip of terror and that free speech and free press no longer existed here. They believed that the United States was fomenting a third world war and would presently start it, with Armageddon consequences for everyone else, and that the government of the United States smashed without mercy anyone who dared to oppose even by oral protest this headlong rush toward disaster.

These people could "prove" their opinions by quoting any number of Americans and American newspapers and magazines. That they were able to quote such American sources proved just the opposite, namely that we *do* continue to enjoy free speech even to express arrant nonsense and unpopular opinion, escaped them completely.

The extremely wide scope of free speech and free press in the United States, much wider than that enjoyed anywhere else in the world including all of the British Commonwealth, is not understood elsewhere.

(More free speech and press than in the British Commonwealth? Surely not! Ah, but we *do* have: our radio is not government owned, we do not place severe restrictions on the importation of printed matter from outside our borders, our libel laws and our limitations on reporting of court procedures are as nothing compared with theirs, our news reporting is the most aggressive in the world.)

The real restrictions against what we can say or print are very nearly limited to only the most blatant of pornography and to classified military secrets. But citizens of other countries neither understand nor believe this; it is too foreign to their own experience. I said to a man in South Africa: "You insist that anyone in the United States who expresses an opinion favorable to Russia or to communism is immediately thrown in jail. How do you reconcile that with the fact that the communist *Daily Worker* is still published in New York?"

He simply called me a liar.

I thought of sending him a copy on my return, but I refrained; such a publication in *his* country was likely to cause him trouble if he was caught with it.

In most cases all around the world these discussions that revealed the extent of misconception about the United States and its institutions started at the same point: why didn't the United States government or the United States people or *somebody* suppress Senator McCarthy and put a stop to the "reign of terror" in our country?

The interest in Senator McCarthy was enormous; the total lack of understanding of what was really going on was even more enormous. Now I am neither a constituent nor an admirer of the Senator, but I found myself repeatedly in the odd position of trying to explain what he was doing, why it was legal in a free country for him to do it, and how it was impossible for a congressional investigation to cause a "reign of terror" in 160,000,000 people.

My task was made more difficult by the fact that many Americans with other attributes of a horse than horse sense were asserting loudly that McCarthy had indeed created a "reign of terror." Are *you* terrified? I am not, yet I have in my background much political activity well to the left of Senator McCarthy's position. The worst that Senator McCarthy can do to me is to ask me a lot of questions and demand answers under oath. I may resent some of the questions but I can answer them without taking refuge in the Fifth Amendment; there is no treason in my record.

To call such investigation a "reign of terror" is to stretch language out of all shape. My notion of a "reign of terror" consists of bandits in the bush who murder and loot in the dark of the night (Indonesia, Malaya, Kenya, elsewhere), jailing the opposition political leaders (Argentina, Spain, etc.), or killing them (anywhere behind the iron-and-bamboo curtain); it does *not* mean questioning people under the safeguards of the most thorough system for the protection of individual rights this world has ever known. It does *not* mean a few dozen traitors and/or custard heads taking refuge behind the Fifth Amendment on the sole grounds that to tell the truth would be to incriminate themselves.

I am not defending McCarthy's thumb-fingered approach nor his sweeping public statements. It has been argued that McCarthy's personality and methods have played into the hands of our enemies and enabled Communism International to make effective propaganda against us. There is some truth in this thesis but, in my opinion, not much. I think that a Senate investigation of communism in the United States would have been fought by propaganda just as angry, just as vicious, had the investigation been chairmanned by Thomas Jefferson with Daniel Webster as his chief counsel. The thing that the communists hate is not McCarthy's unloveable personality but the fact that he is daring to attack communism at all.

The other half is that the thing so many foreigners relish about this investigation is not the issue of communism, not the personality of McCarthy, but the fact that it gives an excuse to take a slap at the Fat Boy . . . Uncle Sam—*Us*. It is easy to hate the rich and the powerful; those who sneer at us for "McCarthyism" are just as ready to sneer at us for our inside plumbing—I have heard both sneers combined in one sentence.

The point of this aside while our party drives through beautiful new Lima is that the political institutions of another country are hard to understand. Outside the United States very few people comprehend the nature of a congressional investigation and it is almost impossible to explain it to them. They have it mixed up with the Inquisition, with Senator McCarthy having all the functions and powers of Torquemada. The idea that a private citizen can answer or refuse to answer a series of questions put to him by a senator, such that the record shows clearly that the citizen being questioned is now or has in the past been actively engaged in treason against the United States—and then get up and walk out a free man—is so foreign to most other people that they simply cannot believe it.

Furthermore, if they did believe it, they would be even more contemptuous of us for being so soft than they now are for "McCarthyism" as they comprehend it, i.e., which they conceive to be a policy of take-him-away-and-lock-him-up-I-don't-like-his-politics. Our extreme leniency, if they understood it, would strike them as preposterous, asinine.

The institution of political refuge as practiced in South America is almost as hard for us to understand. It is as if Adlai Stevenson had found it healthy to hole up in the French Embassy immediately after election day in 1952, for this is approximately what Señor Haya did. He ducked into the Colombian Embassy and stayed there for five years. The Peruvian government never gave up its contention that Haya was a common criminal charged with a capital crime; Colombia, which itself passed through three changes of government by revolution during the five years, never swerved from its determination to give asylum even though the various Colombian governments were not in sympathy with Haya's politics. But, bitter as the issue was, Peru never attempted to remove the refugee by force from the utterly undefended embassy; the principle of asylum was too precious even though Peru declared that Haya was not entitled to it.

Asylum is a necessary part of politics as practiced in South America. When bullets are used as commonly as ballots it is comforting to know that, if you find yourself out of power tomorrow, there are a couple of dozen safe spots right in your own capital where your successor's soldiers cannot arrest you, or possibly shoot you while "attempting to escape." This is as ameliorating an influence as our own Fifth Amendment.

(By the way, I have never heard of one of Senator McCarthy's so-called "victims" choosing to take refuge in the Russian Embassy.)

But why should politics in South America be such a rough and sometimes deadly game? I will spare you a 10,000-word essay on historical background, racial types, traditional institutions, and so forth, and admit that I do not know. But I do know that our northern political attitudes cannot readily be exported to South America. Our Latin neighbors are unanimously agreed on one point: they do *not* want Uncle to tell them how they must behave. Most South Americans are both intensely patriotic and fiercely individualistic. Most of them do not dislike us—we are probably better liked and for less reason in South America than anywhere else in the world. But while they will accept United States capital, products, and engineering, if offered with decent respect for their dignity, they will not accept any "do-gooding" from us in internal politics. They hate Yankee intervention much more than they hate their political opponents.

I suggest that in this they may be right. It took us a long time to achieve political stability; there are those alive today who remember the fratricide of 1861-'65. Political philosophy is still a long way from being a science, revolution is still the refuge and the natural right of the oppressed, and I contend that it is very hard to be sure who are the "baddies" and who are the "goodies" in any overturning of a government south of us . . . at least at the time it takes place. Chile and Uruguay are proof that they are not incapable of achieving stability without our busybody help. In the meantime, a policy of hands-off combined with a warm willingness to help when and how they want help seems to me to be the best we can do.

As we passed the Colombian Embassy we saw two armed soldiers on guard outside. Señor Haya was not in sight, but he was there; his long wait for safe conduct to exile had still four months to run.

The country club at Lima would have been a credit to any city of comparable size in the States and its kitchen would almost certainly have surpassed the comparable ones; we had a wonderful lunch at the ridiculous prices made possible by the exchange. A wedding reception party was gathering as we left; the señoras and señoritas were elegantly dressed and most of them were remarkably attractive, some were very beautiful.

For my taste the señoritas south of here live up to the propaganda about them. True, they do have a slight tendency to be broad-shouldered across the hips, but, as the chief mate of the *Gulf Shipper* pointed out, in these parts two axe-handles across the hips is considered about right. The gringo liking for narrow hips is probably a passing fad if history is any guide. Besides that, girdles are terribly difficult things to manage in hot climates, so I have been told.

All of the women wore hats, just as they do in the British Commonwealth. But the hats of these ladies were brilliantly imaginative and frivolous whereas most British hats for women look like something built by birds in a tree and then abandoned.

Ticky was not wearing a hat and received a few surprised glances, but she carried it off with cold dignity. She had a hat with her on the trip (the one she uses for weddings and funerals at home, her only hat), but she declined to be intimidated into wearing it once she found out about a dispensation which permitted her to enter churches without one.

After lunch we visited the art institute and Jirón de Unión, the shopping center. Lima has gone all out for modern architecture but the modern trends in painting have not made a dent. Nowhere did we find a painting looking like two fried eggs, one addled, or perhaps jackstraws in a high wind. The instructors actually required the students to learn anatomy, perspective, and draftsmanship—very reactionary, of course. I liked it.

Jirón de Unión is the collective term for a narrow shopping street each block of which has its own separate name. This must be confusing to the postman; the tourist does well to ignore the street signs and simply keep an eye out for landmarks. The shops are quite well stocked but not equal to those of cities of the same size in the States, except for silver articles of all sorts, much of it of great grace and imaginative beauty and made remarkably cheap by the ridiculous rate of exchange. Ticky showed remarkable restraint, for it would be easy indeed to go wild and spend oneself broke there. Shortly we had to hurry back to the ship in order not to miss it.

As soon as we left Callao we started running across the furrows and the ship bounced for a couple of days down to Arica, northernmost point in Chile. A roll can be unsettling but a pitch really shakes up the stomach; the *Gulf Shipper* was moving around like a cayuse trying to get rid of a rider. I can now testify that Dramamine actually does stop seasickness, at least for this deponent. I am subject to seasickness and certainly would have been disgracefully and miserably ill without the drug; as it was I missed no meals and ate heartily. But I will never grow fond of excessive motion in a ship. It is annoying to have your soup in your lap, irritating to have to hop madly for balance when caught with trousers half on, not restful to fight the motion of the ship in your sleep.

But *anything* is better than seasickness. I include drilling for gum-line cavities without Novocain.

Arica has no harbor, only an open roadstead; the *Gulf Shipper* anchored and tied to a buoy, thus mooring her against swinging but leaving her still subject to the swells that bounced her around on the way down. Cargo was loaded and discharged by lighters which tied up around the ship like pigs around a sow. Ticky and I watched the first boat load of stevedores come aboard and were struck by their extremely colorful and piratical appearance; we kept expecting them to break into the *habanera*. But it was appearance only; so far as our own experience serves, Chilenos, all of them, are the gentlest and most kindly people in the world.

Sadly, many of them are wretchedly poor. The reason is obvious: it takes heroes to wrest a bare living out of much of Chile. The land back of Arica is as bare as the mountains of the Moon—I mean the ones on our satellite, not the mountain range in Africa. What we call desert in our own southwest is verdant jungle by comparison; there is *nothing* on these hillsides, not a weed, not a blade of grass, not even cactus. Yet the soil is not poor; where they have managed to bring water down from the mountains the ground crops beautifully.

Back of the desert shore the great wall of the Andes was clearly in sight for the first time, majestic and incredible, range on range of snow-covered peaks, awesome at any time, breath catching at sunset. It was decidedly worth while to hurry through dinner and rush up to the flying bridge to watch it, while the bosun birds and guano birds wheeled around the ship and discussed us.

The guano birds used to be a major source of wealth to Chile and to Arica in particular, until artificial nitrates reduced the importance of the trade for fertilizers and for explosives. There are islands at this port that are white with their droppings and any shift of the wind will bring positive, odorous evidence that the birds are still keeping up their end of the business despite new competition. But they are victims of technological unemployment; their end product is no longer indispensable.

Arica, although in Chile, is the great Bolivian tin port. A railroad runs from here to La Paz and Chile has granted Bolivia extraterritorial rights for a dock, a customs shed, and railroad terminus. The dock is not yet in operation but Bolivian tin comes out nevertheless, tin ore being the principal item the *Shipper* loaded there. The precious stuff is handled in small, tight sacks, sealed, marked with serial numbers, weight, and name of owner.

Arica is the site of the only United States sea battle fought on dry land. More than a century ago the U.S.S. *Wateree* was beached here five miles inland by an earthquake tidal wave. When the waters receded the stranded ship was attacked by Indians and the ship's company fought them off from the decks for several days. The boiler of the *Wateree* can still be seen, lying on its side; the rest of the ship has long since been carried away.

Ticky and I went ashore by company boat, by ourselves as the others decided not to risk getting into a small boat from a gangway in the continual heavy swells. It is an easy way to break an ankle if one is not used to it; the knack lies in getting promptly and without any hesitation into the boat just as it rises highest at the gangway, there being then a second when boat and ship are almost stationary relative to each other.

We made it okay, albeit clumsily, and the ride in to the landing was pleasant—a passenger in a liner never has a chance to get close to the water. There were no formalities at customs;

an officer smiled at us and saluted and waved us on through. Arica is a town the same size as Buenaventura (14,000) but it has none of the "tough waterfront" quality of many seaports; you are at once in parks and shaded streets. There are two beautiful parks downtown, impressively large for so small a place, and for a place where irrigation water is so valuable.

The thing that struck us first and with greatest delight was the singing of birds. The parks were loaded with birds singing their hearts out. I have never heard before or since so many birds singing at once. So great was the volume of sweet sounds that we could hear it long after we had left the parks behind.

It does not take long to see all of Arica. There are a few business streets down near the water and a church or two; the homes spill down the rather steep hills back of the business district. It is a clean and pretty town but poor; only a few of the houses would have been considered middle-class homes in the States. As is usual in Chile every householder raised flowers, even if the opportunity was limited to a few pots in the window.

We hired a car and were driven out into an irrigated valley hidden from the sea. Here there were truck farms, citrus trees, figs, cherimoya. The last is a delicious fruit almost unknown in the States, even though there is a Cherimoya Street in Hollywood. It tastes a little like a pineapple, a little like a cantaloupe, but mostly like itself; it is a favorite dessert in Chile and quickly would become a favorite with us, were the trees to be grown on commercial scale here.

The valley was not very extensive and there was no place else to go. The land was green precisely as far as irrigation had progressed and no farther; a foot beyond was the utterly bare and depressing desert. But a new, wide road was being built back into the valley and it was evident that reclamation was to continue. Most of the roadwork was being done painfully by hand and human sweat, but there was a "Plan Marshall" powered scraper. "Plan Marshall" is a term used with approval all up and down the west coast of South America; here, at least, we have been able to help without being kicked in the shins for it and called names.

There was a fine new school in the valley and an older one, although the apparent population seemed to call for no more than one small one. All through Chile we were impressed by an almost feverish pursuit of knowledge. Schools are everywhere, bookstores seem to be more numerous than grocery stores (probably a mistaken impression, that one). Students are everywhere, sitting on park benches, studying, or strolling slowly with noses buried in books, eyes fixed on print.

On the way back we detoured to the top of a small mountain which overlooks the city and the port. The road stopped half way up and the driver, with complete aplomb, turned off onto a railroad track and continued on up. The view from there was magnificent and the odor of guano almost overpowering. We could pick out the *Gulf Shipper* from the others in port. Far below us, it was a toy ship fit for a bathtub.

A flag there marks the spot where a Peruvian general, defeated in battle, suicided by riding his horse off the cliff. The driver and I discussed it and decided that a mule would have had more sense. Looking back, I do not know how we discussed it, for the driver had no English at all and the Spanish I know could be written on a postcard without crowding the stamp; it is suitable only for ordering *dos cervezas* in a cantina. But I recall the conversation clearly even though I don't know how we talked. Somehow, two human beings can always talk with each other if both want to.

We got back to town with a half hour to spare and again looked around the shops and listened to the birds. We came across a boy and a girl, perhaps five and seven, with their noses pushed against the window of a toy shop. By their clothes, it seemed unlikely that they would ever get closer than looking and longing, so Ticky took them inside and told the proprietor to let them each have the item each was staring at. The kids did not take advantage of us; the doll the girl wanted was the one she had loved from through the glass, not the most elaborate and expensive one, and the boy simply had his eye on a large ball, not at all expensive.

They thanked us gravely, coached only a little by the proprietor, and went away looking soberly happy. Ticky and I, having set up our own Marshall Plan, went back to the ship in the warm glow that comes only from playing Santa Claus. One of the real magics in life is the fact that wealth can always be multiplied by dividing by the age of the owner.

(Now if that gent in the back row who just made the snide remark about American tourists who love to flash their money in the faces of people less fortunate will step out in the alley with me, I will try to find out how tightly his teeth are set in his head. With Ticky's help, that is—she has studied judo.)

The next port was Valparaiso, our destination. We were anxious to do something before we left to show our appreciation to the ship's officers for many kindnesses and much hospitality; a party seemed in order. We talked it over with the Markhams and Mr. Tupper and planned one. It had to be held at sea, which meant that some of the watchstanders would be able to make only token attendance and the Captain would not participate in the whole-hearted fashion which was his wont ashore, but there was nothing else for it as Ticky and I would be leaving the ship immediately on docking at Valpo.

Martinis in water tumblers seemed a little rugged for a party held at sea and anyhow Ticky wanted to serve French Seventy-fives. As everyone knows, the French "75" is a small, obsolete weapon, ineffective in modern times. Its namesake is also innocuous, being composed of lemon juice, sugar, cognac, and champagne. The lemon juice supplies vitamin C and thereby helps to prevent scurvy, always a menace at sea, and the sugar gives quick energy. As for the other ingredients, they are so thinned out by the lemonade and cracked ice that they do no more than impart a pleasant flavor. In fact, unless advised, you would never believe that it was anything but a soda fountain drink—at first, you would not.

The exact formulation is a matter of taste. Some like it not too sweet, some like it not too sour, some think that too much ice is bad for the stomach. But it needs plenty of champagne to provide bubbles and cognac to give it body.

Cognac was not available so we had to fall back on pisco, which is a grape brandy, too, although made (I believe) from *very* large grapes. Real French champagne was hardly to be expected but Chile makes excellent champagne-type sparkling wines. I do not know what proof they are. The purser acted as purchasing agent for us before we left Arica. At two hundred pesos to the dollar the total bill was about ten dollars—the bottle alone should have cost more than that, empty.

We stocked up also on assorted nuts and olives and such like munching food and sent out formal invitations, from all the passengers inviting all of the officers to an emergency session of the Horse Latitudes Philosophical Society and D.M. Club. Everybody accepted.

The gals put on formal evening gowns, seldom seen in a freighter, and quite a number of us wore neckties, making it a swank affair. It started out a bit slowly as formal affairs often do, but French Seventy-fives have a characteristic and rather slow effect on the emotions; the first salvo is over, the second salvo is short, and the third salvo is usually dead on, after which everyone is *muy simpático*.

It was an occasion both pleasant and sad. The *Gulf Shipper* had become another home to us, and our shipmates were our family. We danced to the radio and we sang and we told stories but over it all was the knowledge that we would never meet like this again. However, the supply of ammunition held out and it is hard to be anything but merry when one of those salvos hits you dead on. I remember telling the chief mate that I was thinking of selling our house and taking a permanent lease on stateroom number three. He applauded the notion and we had a drink on it.

Around dawn we reluctantly adjourned. I stood the rest of the four-to-eight watch with the mate on watch and then went down to breakfast. Ticky was a little tired but we were both determined to show up for breakfast as a matter of face—after which we went back to stateroom number three and died.

I had no more than fallen asleep when I was snatched out of happy dreams by the most terrifying clamor I have ever heard.

I found myself standing in the middle of the room trying to put on trousers; I had both feet in one leg and it was not working out too well. I became aware that Ticky was shouting at me. "Stop it! Those aren't yours."

I stopped. Sure enough, they weren't. They were Ticky's slacks and were not only much too small for me but had curves tailored in in the wrong places. I passed them over as she said, "What in the world *is* it?" The awful clamor continued.

"General alarm," I grunted. "Man the life boats. *Hurry!*"

We did hurry, for I was reasonably sure the poor old *Shipper* was going down and I had just enough life left in me to wish to save it—or perhaps it was instinctual reflex. We were at our boat stations and quicker than some of the crew. We were fully dressed, aside from buttons and zippers and similar non-essentials, and were wearing our life jackets. The sea was calm and the weather clear; I tried to figure out the nature of the disaster. Perhaps war had broken out suddenly. There was a notice posted near the saloon telling what to do in case of atomic attack but I had not read it since the day we embarked.

Our life boat station was right under the bridge. Captain Lee leaned over the rail and smiled at us with fiendish delight. "Good morning!" he said.

The expression on his face was enough to turn it from a disaster into a boat drill. My mind started functioning again and I understood it all. The Captain, inhibited by his responsibilities as master of a ship at sea, had gone to bed early from the party. He had gotten up early as well, breakfasted in his cabin as was his custom, then had looked around to find a ship deserted and utterly quiet save for those on watch. Being of a sociable nature he had cured that by switching on the general alarm, a sound guaranteed to get Davy Jones out of his locker.

No one can criticize a ship's master for holding boat drills; the book even advises that they be held by surprise and this one certainly qualified as such. But I was convinced at that moment that he had sounded that alarm for the prime purpose of getting me personally out of my sack. Right then I would have beaten him to death with a flyswatter had I had the strength to lift one.

I'm sure Ticky would have held him. I would have needed help; he is considerably bigger than I am.

That man has a low sense of humor.

By evening I was able to grin about it, although feebly. By the time the *Shipper* stood into Valparaiso I had decided to forgive and forget; after all we were *amigos* and brothers. I was fond of him and I knew he was fond of me.

But when he comes to stay with us in Colorado Springs next year he had better watch out for snakes in his bed and not go through doorways too hastily. Maybe I can lure him onto ice skates.

Valparaiso does not have the most spectacular harbor in the world; that honor probably goes to Rio with Sydney and San Francisco fighting it out for second place. But it is one of the most beautiful. The shore line, almost circular, looks like a backdrop painted by a scenic artist with a fine eye for color and composition. We had plenty of time to look at it because the port authorities required us to tie to a buoy in the outer harbor to discharge a few drums of naphtha before we were considered safe to come alongside dock.

The minor heavenly functionaries in charge of such things provide arrangements like this to insure a certain routine every time a ship comes into port: first, the passengers must be required to get up earlier than usual, preferably with a big head acquired at the Captain's Dinner; then they must be examined by the port surgeon and various police and immigration officials just as they are about to sit down to breakfast; next, the actual departure from the ship must be delayed so that they will arrive at customs just as it closes, or so timed as to miss a train, or both.

This is a cosmic plan, not a human plan, for the humans who play parts in it are almost invariably polite, helpful, and anxious to expedite things. Other factors have to be thrown in to foil them of their kindly intentions.

The drums of naphtha almost accomplished the full routine

for us at Valparaiso had not Mr. Thackeray, agent for the Grace Lines and acting for Gulf & South American, owners of the *Shipper,* set himself firmly against the plans. Once the *Shipper* touched dock and put over a gangway he got us through the system with such speed that I am still gasping.

Mr. Thackeray is a handsome, blondish young man who speaks perfect American. I assumed that he had been sent down from the States but he smiled and said no, that he was a Chileno who had never been out of his native country. This was our first contact with the dual fact that Chile is the most Latin of Latin American countries in many ways but the Chilenos do not look Latin according to North American preconception of that term. Tall blondes seem almost as common as they are in Sweden. There are many Chilenos of Irish, German, and English ancestry—but they are *Chilenos,* thoroughly assimilated. Most of them speak nothing but Spanish. Even the English seem to assimilate better in Chile than in most places. In Chile they become Chilenos, even though they tend quite sensibly to hang onto the very real asset of English as a second language.

In the meantime our ten suitcases were piled mountainously on the dock and, as I had dismally predicted, the customs shed was a long way off. Part of my gloomy prophecy was wrong: it was not raining, there was merely a fine mist. But the train we had to catch in order to claim our hotel reservation in Santiago was to leave in only thirty-five minutes.

Perhaps I should add that trains run on time in Chile, better than they do in Colorado.

Mr. Thackeray conjured up porters with two hand trucks. Mr. Thackeray produced a Ford station wagon belonging to the Grace Lines. Mr. Thackeray negotiated the movement of our baggage, which had to be done along the docks inside the customs barrier, then settled us in the station wagon and whisked us outside the barrier into the streets and over to the customs station in comfort.

There were no customs officers at the customs shed. Mr. Thackeray glanced at his watch, looked perturbed and said, "I'm afraid they have gone to tea. It's about that time."

"Do they close down completely? Isn't someone left on duty? It's not very many minutes to our train time."

"I'll see what I can do. Nothing can be done until your baggage shows up anyhow." He went away, leaving me with half a dozen fretful questions about was he sure the porters knew where to come and how far did they have to come and how long would it take and where was the railroad station and when was the break for tea supposed to be over, all unasked.

Ticky and I sat down in the big, bare, gloomy shed and shared a cigarette and thought gloomily about home.

In about ten minutes the porters arrived, slightly wet and very cheerful. I counted the ten suitcases and cheered up a little myself, just to see them. Mr. Thackeray returned, helped me pay the porters and, by request, advised me how much to tip. They seemed very much pleased with the tip—tipping is not as common in Chile as in Peru or as it is at home—and began spreading our baggage around the inspection tables. "*Las llaves, Señor?*" one of them asked.

"Give him your keys," Mr. Thackeray advised. "It will save time. I think I'm going to be able to get one of the customs officers to come in." He went away again.

The porters promptly got into trouble with a Valapak and I promptly had trouble with Ticky. It was not their fault; a scarf was packed immediately under a zipper in the Valapak. The thin silk caught in the zipper and jammed it; they tried to force it free and it got worse. Ticky sprang to the defense of her cherished chattels and tried to push them aside. With courteous gallantry they assured her that they would take care of it and did not give way. They spoke in Spanish but the meaning was inescapable.

Three of them continued to sweat and strain while Ticky skittered around them, trying to push her way in, wringing her hands, demanding that they back away and let her do it, and shouting for a pair of pliers in a language known among her hearers only to me and I did not have any.

Shortly there was a ripping sound and Ticky burst into tears. She then started expressing an emotional opinion of the country and its people. I took her firmly by the elbow and led her to the bench. "Sit down," I said fiercely, "and shut up. Remember what I told you eight thousand times on the way down. No matter what happens at customs, you must smile, smile, and smile some more."

She sniffled and said brokenly, "I think it's an *outrage* that I have to sit here and watch while those men *ruin* my things."

"It was just a scarf. Forget it."

"I am *not* going to let anyone paw through my underwear!" She sniffled again. "I want to go *home*."

"Too late. We can't even get back aboard ship. Somebody else has our cabin."

"I am not—"

"You are going to sit still and shut up."

She shut up but she had all storm warnings still flying. Mr. Thackeray returned with a customs officer. But now it was my turn to get off on the wrong foot.

The *aduanero* had left his tea a good twenty minutes early to help the gringos catch their train. I think he must have regretted it at once when he saw that the *norteamericano* did not have ordinary good manners. I could see that he was not exactly jovial and attributed it to his being interrupted at meals; I tried to be ingratiating, but I did not put it over.

Mr. Thackeray touched my arm. "*Take your hat off!*" he whispered insistently. "He is growing quite annoyed."

I snatched it off and blushed. "Please tell him I'm sorry."

I had forgotten an elementary fact, a common element in many other cultures but unknown in the United States. This tired little official was not expecting me to take off my hat to *him*. He would never expect such a thing, unless we did so mutually as two equals meeting. But we were not meeting as equals; he embodied at that time and place the *sovereignty of his country* and he damn well expected me to show respect for it. It was symbolically equivalent to standing up for "The Star-Spangled Banner."

In the United States the President himself is almost the only official accorded such respect *for such a reason;* even governors don't get much of it. We show respect to individuals when and as it suits us, according to the respect that individual has earned in our eyes. We show respect to high office in government, business, church, professions, or the military on the assumption that the holder of high office, be he bishop or brigadier, has probably earned respect or he would not have gained rank. But the notion that the most minor public servant embodies the visible presence of the sovereign state is an idea that has passed us by. An American, if he thinks about it at all, is likely to carry it one step farther and recall that *he* is the state, he himself—not that cop over there.

Of course the cop is a sovereign citizen, too, but *as a cop* he is not sovereign but a servant of sovereigns . . . and the same for all other public officials, servants not masters.

But our attitude is far from being universal. The phrase "On the King's Business—" conveys a very different notion. In Germany a few years back (and for all I know today) there was an offense which freely translated read: "Disrespect to an Official of the State"—by which was meant that you could be fined for arguing with a street car conductor! There are many places in the world where all public functionaries—policemen, school teachers, postmasters, train conductors, assessors—receive formal, hat-in-hand respect quite different from ordinary courtesy. To fail to offer it is to court inconvenience or even more serious trouble. In some hot-tempered places such as Indonesia a mistake in such protocol can be dangerous to life and limb.

But not in Chile. The *aduanero* was mollified at once when I uncovered. He quit frowning and stalling with the declarations and went through our bags with great speed and very little disruption of the packing, so fast that I was pushed to keep up with closing and locking them. Mr. Thackeray said, "That's all let's go wc'll catch that train yet!"

"Where's the station?"

"Just across the way." He hurried out, followed by me, Ticky, porters, and suitcases. He shoved money through a ticket window, seemed to snatch two tickets out of the air, and rejoined us without slowing down. "This way!"

There was no time to check bags; Mr. Thackeray arranged with the assistant conductor to stow them in the vestibule of a car, then urged us on board. The train pulled out as we sat down.

With the departure of Mr. Thackeray we at last found ourselves truly in a foreign country and a long way from home. Up until that time the *Gulf Shipper* had kept home with us, no matter if the stars changed and Orion stood on his head. Mr. Thackeray's sophistication, skill, and linguistic ability had sheltered us through the complexities of transition, but now we were alone. For the first time we felt twinges of homesickness.

We soon discovered that we were cut off in another way: there was no one at all around us who could speak English. I wanted to find out when the train reached Santiago. I was not dead sure that the train ended there; perhaps in our mute ignorance we could be carried on past it. Or even if Santiago was the last stop, it might have several stations, like Philadelphia; we might wind up many miles from our hotel.

I tried each member of the train crew as he passed down the aisle—no luck. I tried English on everyone near us—still no luck. I glanced around farther to see if anyone had looked up at the sound of English—not a soul. I felt around in my pockets and confirmed what I had suspected; all three of the Spanish phrase books we had with us were packed in our luggage. I recalled sourly the guidebook which stated that most metropolitan Chilenos spoke English and that all hotel people, all taxi drivers, and all persons connected with railroads and airlines spoke it fluently—I wondered if the hack who wrote that guidebook had ever been out of Dubuque and decided that he had probably smoked up his lies in the public library.

I was not blaming the Chilenos. The fault was mine for not having learned the beautiful and easy Spanish tongue; I myself would be little help to a Chileno lost in Colorado Springs. It was simply unfortunate that both Ticky and myself had elected French in school, rather than Spanish.

I considered tackling them in French, then got cold feet. My French is only a bit better than my Spanish; I am not a linguist.

At last I again tackled the exceedingly English-looking

young man seated in front of us. (He looked as if he *must* know English.) With the aid of a card and a pencil and a monumental effort by which I recalled that the Spanish word for "hour" was the same as the Latin I established that we were indeed on the train for Santiago, that it arrived at 8 P.M., that the distance was about 150 kilometres, and that we should get off at the last stop in order to reach Hotel Carrera. I had interrupted his reading but he was all patience and friendliness.

It was the only time I was ever troubled by a language barrier. I never will be worth a hoot at any other language; I am eye-minded and even the English language can go too fast for me. But patience and friendliness are everywhere, and the use of writing (to tie down both the question and the answer and allow it to be studied), plus the use of the universal numerals, plus a cognate or two, are enough for any situation. Besides, the chap that wrote the guidebook was not too far wrong; there is usually someone within earshot who is happy to help.

("What sort of people," the frightened boy asked, "are there in this great city?"

(The gatekeeper considered it. "What sort of people were there in your home village?"

(The boy's eyes filled with tears and his voice choked. "They were the most wonderful, the kindest people in all the world!"

("Go on in, son," the gatekeeper said gently. "You will find them much the same inside.")

After I had settled my old-maid worries we relaxed and enjoyed the ride. The train was very fast and the scenery varied from pleasant to magnificent. Santiago sits at the foot of the Andes at 1800 feet; the railroad winds up the valley of Río Mapocho to reach it, through farms and foothills and mountains. We were in the southern rainfall belt and the hills and fields were green. The countryside looks like that near Santa Barbara, California, and numerous eucalyptus trees added to the impression.

Presently the train's news butcher came around with tea.

We had been advised to be wary of the local water but tea seemed a safe bet, and we were both hungry and thirsty, it being far past dinner hour in the *Shipper*. The train attendant hung little trays for each of us on the backs of the seats in front of us, then sold us, at charity prices, tea and sandwiches and strange little cakes. One sort seemed to be expanded nitrocellulose with sugar added but it was probably principally white of eggs.

Then I bought magazines from him. We looked at the pictures and tried to puzzle out the text and told ourselves that we were "improving our Spanish." Perhaps we were, since any change would have been an improvement. I remember one cartoon strip which showed Perón of Argentina cussing out Uncle Sam for the benefit of an audience, then, in the next frame, falling into Uncle Sam's arms with shouts of "*Amigo!*" But most of it was not that easy.

When we reached Santiago, the young man in front of us, the train butcher, the assistant conductor, and several passengers all told us that it was time to get off. "Taxi" and "Hotel Carrera" were all the words we needed. During the ride to the hotel we could not see much of the city as it was after dark, but it was evident that it was a big, bustling, modern city. The Carrera itself is a hotel equal to any anywhere in its standards of luxury, modernness, and convenience. It differs from similar hotels at home in that the service is better and the prices are less than half what we would have to pay at home. The doorman spoke fluent English with an Irish brogue, the night manager, Señora Falco, spoke English with an Oxford accent, and we had no more troubles. Not having had time to get other advice I asked the head porter himself how much to tip him and his assistants; his suggestions were most moderate.

Our room was quite large and beautifully furnished. The night maid bustled in and turned down the beds. When she had gone I heard Ticky's voice from the bathroom. "Bob! C'mere!"

I came. She was pointing at the fourth fixture in the bath. "Look at that!"

"Well," I said, "surely you have heard of them. You didn't think it was a drinking fountain for a dog, did you?"

"I've heard of them," she said thoughtfully, "but I guess I didn't really believe in them. I don't think I would dare use one. Look." She fiddled with a valve.

"Don't splash the ceiling!" I said hastily.

"That's what I mean," she said, shutting it off. "I'd be afraid of being blown through the roof."

III

First Steps

WE MANAGED TO do quite a lot of sightseeing in Santiago and outside it but I don't see quite how we did it; the routine does not provide for it. It starts to get out of step with our habits at dinner time. The first night we were there we washed up quickly and got down to the dining room about half past eight, starving, as the sample of tea aboard the train had not substituted for the hearty dinner at five P.M. we had grown used to in the *Gulf Shipper*.

The dining room looked like an undertaker's parlor ready for a funeral—banks of flowers, hushed quiet, sad-faced Indian waiters, maitre d'hotel immaculate and dignified in white tie and tails . . . no diners, no cheerful sounds of food and drink.

But I was assured that we could have dinner although it was evident that our arrival was unexpected. "Perhaps M'dame would like a cocktail before dinner?" M'dame would, and so would M'sieur; it restored the tissues, soothed travel-weary nerves, and helped to kill the time while the chef was coping with the emergency. Presently food, wonderful, lavish, beautifully cooked food, was spread before us. I had a mixed grill which contained eight or nine things I did not recognize but wanted to know better and Ticky had a steak that had died happy. There were soups and salads and a variety of breadstuffs, too, and other things I can't remember, and delicate light wine and the inevitable bottled water served in tiny glasses. They were used to gringos and there was no trouble in getting *agua sin gas*. Afterwards we had to make a Solomon's choice among desserts.

I was tempted by pineapple slices drowned in champagne but finally settled for "happy cherimoya"—*cherimoya alegre*, thin slices of the fruit in orange juice and powdered sugar. We were both happy, the cherimoya and I.

By the time we were sipping coffee the room was filling up. By the time we left, somewhat after ten o'clock, dinner hour was in full blast. We had come to the right place; we were simply too early.

This late dinner hour throws the whole day out of gear for a *norteamericano*. We were not used to going to bed on a full stomach; with dinner over about eleven at night that meant lights-out not earlier than one in the morning, and still later if we chose to do a little dancing. We did not do that very often as my Coolidge-Era foxtrot does not fit a rumba beat too well.

But even without night life the late dinner hour means getting up late. Breakfast plus formal guard mount last until about ten-thirty. We were not required to watch formal guard mount, of course, but there it was, right under our window in the Plaza de la Constitución in front of the presidential palace, complete with army band in dress uniform, small boy to pretend to lead the band along with the director, and small dog whose international duty it is to help out with parades everywhere.

After guard mount there is time to sightsee before lunch but it is also the best time to go up to the swimming pool on the roof. This hazard can be avoided by staying in a hotel which does not own a *piscina,* at least not one on the roof—but who wants to avoid the temptation? The view from the open-air restaurant & swimming pool seventeen stories up in the Carrera is the best in Santiago, whether you look out at the city and the mountains, or inward at the señoritas swimming and sunning themselves. For thirty-five cents you may use the beautiful pool yourself, or you can sit and drink Coca-Cola or what you will and ponder on the fact that you are nearer to heaven than you are ever likely to be again.

You can sit right there all morning and have lunch there, if you choose, and it is a good choice. Santiago sits in a big level bowl with mountains all around it and the main range of the high Andes crowding close to it on the west. The lights and the cloud formations on the snow-covered peaks are always changing and the city below is a Christmas window display of toy automobiles and ant-sized people. You can see from here that many, many roofs in Santiago have roof gardens; anywhere a Chileno can poke a flower and coax it to grow he will do so.

Whether you lunch there or make the effort to go two blocks down the street to the world-famous French cuisine of the Crillon, after lunch is time for siesta, not for sightseeing. The shutters ring down in the small shops, the doors lock in the big shops, and even the traffic policemen go home. Why bother to direct traffic when no sensible person is on the streets.

So we return now to the Carrera, start to write a letter or a few postcards—then find ourselves overcome by the spirit of siesta. How can one stay awake in the drowsy afternoon when a million and a half people are sleeping?

When at last we come to, awakened by the post-siesta increase in traffic noise, the city is wide awake again. But now it is time for tea, a meal not to be skipped in a country which allows nine hours between lunch and dinner. Tea may be had on the mezzanine with live music, or on the roof with sunset over the Andes. After tea the shops are still open until seven P.M. or later, and the interval from tea to dinner is also the favorite time to go to the movies. It is also a wonderful time to stroll along Alameda Bernardo O'Higgins, a boulevard of smart shops and mansions. (Do not be misled by the County Cork name: O'Higgins was the George Washington of Chile.) Or one can wander through the park by the river, a few blocks from the hotel. Any of these activities, done not too strenuously, will give one an appetite for the late dinner and keep one away from the hazards of a two-hour cocktail hour.

After dinner it is much too late for sightseeing; it is a choice of night life, letterwriting, or reading, then to bed.

You see? A day broken up by four meals and a siesta leaves very little time for anything else. The Chilenos themselves put in an eight-hour work day, from nine to one and from three to seven, but a tourist, already geared down by the holiday spirit, finds this broken up day lapping over on itself.

Nevertheless we saw a great deal. One day we drove down to the beach through a different valley from the one we had come up by train and ended up at beach resorts about twenty-five miles south of Valparaiso. Most of the route was rolling hills and farms, then one drops rather suddenly to splendid beaches and lovely summer homes. The flower gardens around the homes are startling in their banked profusion and unreal, Kodachrome color. Even in Southern California or Florida we do not attempt to grow flowers in the bursting quantities which a Chileno householder seems to take for granted. Driving back we passed many huts of extremely poor peasants; in every case the tenant had splurged some part of his precious irrigation water to put a flower garden around his humble home.

On the trip back we passed a number of vassos, which helped to satisfy Ticky's desire to see colorful natives in colorful native costumes; the blanket and hat of the vasso are indeed colorful. (U.S.—cowboy & ranch; Chile, vasso & fundo; Mexico, vaquero & rancho; Argentina, gaucho & hacienda.)

We visited a dairy fundo as we neared Santiago and were shown around by Señor Quirigo, the *gerente* or manager—in Argentina he would be a majordomo. It differed mainly from one of ours of equal size in that hand milking was used rather than power milking; sanitary precautions were up to standard and pasteurization was used. The home of the Quirigo family and that of the owner were in the style we call "California Spanish" with white walls and red tile roofs.

I had only feeble French in common with Señor and Señora Quirigo, but Ticky used botanical Latin. To become a ranch manager in much of South America a college degree in agriculture is usually necessary, which includes of course a firm scientific grounding in botany; Ticky and Señor Quirigo would agree on the Latin name for some tree, shrub, or flower among the profusion in the garden of the fundo, then would exchange the common English and Spanish names to their mutual great satisfaction. I stumbled along behind, agreeing that yes it was a pretty tree, *lindísimo* in fact.

Our driver had simply driven into the fundo and stated that he had some *norteamericanos* who would like to see a fundo; the Quirigos entertained us as if they had been waiting for the privilege.

The shops in Santiago are, if anything, poorer in most respects than those in Lima. The country is undergoing a disastrous inflation and has never recovered from the blow of the collapse of its nitrate industry. As yet they have very little manufacturing of their own and anything that must be imported is tremendously expensive in their currency. This shows up in a rather startling fashion with respect to paper. We use paper and paper products of all sorts in lavish, wasteful fashion; I doubt if there is a single paper napkin in all of Chile. Kleenex cannot be purchased. Wrapping paper is scarce; a clerk appreciates your willingness to accept a purchase unwrapped. He will wrap it if you wish but he uses precisely the minimum of paper necessary.

Linen napkins are freely available; Chilenos are not afraid of the labor of laundering. But a cheap paper napkin is another matter.

It is distressing to see a decent, industrious people in such straits. This is not a country kicked around by revolution after revolution, with each new boss looting the treasury; they have a tradition of stable, democratic, free government as strong as ours. It is simply that they are faced with real physical economic problems. But I am convinced that they will overcome them; they work hard and they are honest.

We attended an outdoor, free symphonic concert in the grounds of the Palace of Fine Arts in Santiago. By accident, we happened to be coming out of the palace (a fine gallery, with an amazing number of European old masters hanging) just as the seats were being set up. By spikking the macerated, lacerated

Español that I had acquired—a Pidgin of no tenses, numbers, genders, or other non-essentials—we found out what was about to happen and got seats early . . . which was a good thing as all of Santiago and cousin José from the country showed up.

The program presented one number by a Chileno composer, one by George Gershwin, and several by traditional European composers, with none of the atonal modern stuff, which pleased me as I am as black a reactionary in music as I am in art. It was pleasant to see Gershwin classed without apology as "symphonic" even though the notion may strike some of our own highbrow critics as terribly bourgeois.

In the midst of the concert a little boy about five, very well dressed, came pushing through our row, stepping on feet and hurrying. He really was in a hurry; there was a tree a few inches from my right knee and he wanted frantically to use that tree. He used it, sighed with relief, buttoned up his fly and went back to his parents in less of a hurry. Ticky and I did our best to keep our faces straight and pretend that we had not seen anything; we were both aware that South Americans are much more casual and frank about such necessities; anyone with eyes could not help but be aware.

No one around us in this polite and well-dressed crowd paid any attention, except a señora on Ticky's left. This unfortunate lady, having spoken with us, was aware that we were *norteamericanos;* it became at once evident that she was sufficiently cosmopolitan to see the incident through the eyes of a North American, and she was distressingly, terribly embarrassed.

Anything at all that we could have said would only have made things worse. There was nothing to do but let her suffer. But I can see that a compounding of such harmless incidents will in time and a rather short time cause the fierce pride of all South Americans to drive them into ending this carefree custom lest they be laughed at by the gringos—as sure as the missionaries put Mother Hubbards on the pretty Polynesians.

The French, on the other hand, don't care whether we laugh or not.

There are two *cerros* in downtown Santiago, each of which is a park; a *cerro* is somewhat more than a hill, somewhat less than a mountain. Cerro Santa Lucía is the smaller but in some ways the more charming. It was once the headquarters of the Spanish conquerors but is now nominally given over to a museum of Chilean history. I say "nominally" because its real functions are to provide in the daytime a lovely study hall for the many students in Santiago and to provide in the gloaming a perfect place for lovers to court.

It is a series of terraced gardens and winding paths and garden seats. Admission is a cent and a half, our money, which makes one wonder how they can support a gatekeeper even if they let him keep all the admissions. In daylight hours it is crowded with hundreds of students, highschool and university, all studying, none loafing. Quite as many are strolling as are sitting down, but the studying never stops.

As soon as it starts to get dark the park fills up with couples. The chaperone is a thing of the past in Chile; señoritas are not tagged around by duennas keeping a close eye on the property. There is a cop in the park but he is not there to bother them; he is there to see to it that they are not bothered. But *honi soit qui mal y pense;* one is justified in assuming that Cerro Santa Lucía, where romance is accepted as one of the good gifts of God, is in truth a bit more proper than any lookout point or drive-in theater in the states.

In South America, praise be, you can kiss your wife on a crowded downtown sidewalk without causing anyone to stare. You can even kiss another man on both cheeks for that matter, although personally I have never cared for whiskers.

Cerro San Cristóbal is much more nearly a mountain and is ascended via a funicular railway. The vendor sold us first-class seats (at six cents) instead of second-class (at three cents) before we opened our mouths—being a gringo must show, though I don't know just how. All the natives rode second class, the only difference being that the cushions on the seats were thin in second class. I looked for, and did not find, the safety device for funiculars where a catch drops into place immediately if the tension on the cable fails. I did not mention this until we were down again as I had assured Ticky that all funiculars were so equipped everywhere. Probably Saint Cristobal protects this one; nobody has ever been hurt.

Or it might be the Virgin, as the *cerro* is the site of a great statue of María Inmaculada, seventy-five feet high and weighing about 400 tons; it must have been quite a job to get it up there and put together. The mountain as a whole is too large to irrigate but the top is gardened and a little church nestles under Her skirts. The view is what you would expect—we've been over that ground.

Further down the *cerro* are the National Zoological Gardens. I am a sucker for zoos. We visited the one in Lima, which consisted solely of South American birds and animals; the zoo in Santiago was a global one but seemed to lack the one thing that made the zoo at Lima outstanding: Andean condors. The condor is not only of noble size; he seems also to like to spread his wings for display, an effect like a Stratocruiser coming in for a landing.

We climbed a great deal of Cerro San Cristóbal several times, trying to find more condors. I am not sure they don't have them; they may have been inside somewhere. But time at a zoo is never wasted; we saw lots of other things including that repulsive oversize South American rat about the gross of a fat shoat. We were the only spectators, it being siesta time; the zoo staff were stretched out here and there, snoozing and sometimes looking up at the *locos norteamericanos* walking around in the hot sun.

We walked back to the hotel, as the taxi drivers were taking siesta, too. The Chileno is a very sensible fellow.

Regrettably the day arrived to leave Chile. It was necessary to be out at the airport nearly an hour early in order to go through outgoing customs and police check, both of them useless ceremonies. In the last-minute scurry Ticky remembered that we had not left a thank-you gift for the night maid; since she was not around I called the desk to get her name. "Señora Hoan-Ace," I was told.

"Spell it, please."

"Hoan-Ace—J, O, N, E, S."

"Oh—"

We flew in Pan American's *El Inter-Americano,* a luxurious, pressurized DC6B. The hostess had a luxurious and pressurized look about her, too. Airline hostesses have probably done more to popularize air travel than all other factors put together, but where in the world do they find them? They all have beauty, intelligence, friendly charm, and the hard, practical ability to cope with impossible situations more to be expected of barroom bouncers.

We were lucky in that it was a beautiful, clear day which permitted the pilot to detour and drop down to let us have a look at the Christ of the Andes which stands on the border between Chile and Argentina and celebrates eternal peace and friendship between the two nations. We had a quick view and then it was gone; from the air at more than three hundred miles an hour is not the way to see a statue. But the Christ of the Andes is not easily seen any other way; high up in the Cordillera, it is probably as hard to reach as any statue in the world.

Our real luck was the view of the mountains permitted by the good weather. The Andes are magnificent from a distance but terrifying from above—and from the sides, as we flew between peaks more than 22,000 feet high. The endless snow fields, the sharp, raw cliffs and crests, are frightening; I felt relief when we were at last out of the mountains and over the endless plains of the Argentine, even though I had relished it immensely and would not have missed it.

I had wondered from time to time just why the Andes are so much more impressive than other mountains. Ticky and I have our home on the foothills of a mountain more than 14,000 feet high. We are very fond of it and it really is a big mountain, but it is not in the same class with the Andes. A little arithmetic shows why and proves why the Andes may reasonably be considered the highest mountains in the world, despite the Himalayas—thus: heights of mountains are measured *above sea level.* This is crucial to an alpinist half dead from anoxia on the crags of Mount Everest but it has nothing to do with how tall a mountain looks; its majesty depends on how high it thrusts up above the plateau at its base.

By this rule:

Pikes Peak—14,000 minus 6000 gives 8000 feet apparent height.

Mount Everest—29,000 minus 15,000 gives 14,000 feet.

The Andes—22,000 minus only 2000 gives 20,000 feet, which leaves the Andes the winnuh and new champion by more than a mile in height which you can raise your eyes and see.

There are other criteria. Mauna Loa in Hawaii is 32,000 feet high from summit to base, but 18,000 feet of it is concealed by the Pacific Ocean; you can't see it. Nor can you see barometric pressure or "sea level" height. A barometer states that my home is 6015 high; unfortunately only the last fifteen feet of that shows from our garden; the Chrysler Building, a full mile "shorter" than my home by the sea-level scale, is nevertheless a bit more impressive.

The same common-sense criterion that makes a great skyscraper more impressive than a one-story house states that the Andes are the tallest mountains in the world.

The transition from the Cordillera to the prairies and the plains in Argentina is much like the same transition in the United States, except that the great open spaces are even more so than our own, even though we were flying over the most populous part of the back country. There were hundreds of miles of open range and farm with only an occasional village and very few roads. It was impressive in scope but monotonous.

I stared at it and tried to get my thoughts straight about Chile. What was the spirit of Chile? What characterized it? The guidebooks emphasized the Chilean wines, and the fish both for catching and for eating, and the outdoor sports of all sorts, from skiing to surfing. All those things were true but they did not seem to me to spell Chile; take them away and the spirit of the country would remain.

No, not fish, not wines, not sports—but flowers, and serious pursuit of knowledge and an overwhelming kindliness. These were Chile.

IV
==

The Land of "Papá"

ONCE UPON A time a big, sleek, fat Argentine dog met a little, skinny, wretched Chilean dog at the border between their two countries. They exchanged sniffs and discovered that each was headed for the other's native land. "But *why?*" the Chileno mutt wanted to know. "You don't know what you are getting into. I love my native land but I've just got to make a change; I haven't had a square meal in months. But Argentina is already your home and you are well fed, fat, healthy, obviously in the pink—so why don't you stay where you are well off?"

The Argentine dog glanced over his shoulder, then whispered behind his paw: "I want to *bark.*"

I heard the above anecdote in Brazil. It is a fair thumbnail sketch of the difference between the two countries. When Ticky was laying out our itinerary she planned only four days for us in Argentina on the assumption that four days was the longest she could possibly keep her mouth shut. I felt that she was overly optimistic; Ticky makes a vice of telling the truth. I simply hoped that Perón's police would be either too gallant or too cautious to throw a señora from the States into jail.

As it turned out we stayed much more than four days, as our ship, as is customary with ships, was much delayed in sailing. Then much to our surprise we found that we liked Argentina very much. Wait a moment, I do not wish to be mistaken for a crypto-fascist or whatever the communists these days are calling an authoritarian who is not a communist authoritarian. I do not like police states. Like the fat Argentine dog, no matter how good it is some ways I still like to bark. But we did like the country called Argentina and we liked the citizens thereof very much.

However I am going to say some fairly gentle things even about the present government of Argentina. I ask that it be kept in mind that I am simply trying to report what I saw and heard and that there can be qualitative differences between dictatorships, say between Argentina under Perón and Germany under Hitler. The observations made imply no approval of suppression of free assembly, of press, of free speech, of opposition parties, nor of the jailing of opposition leaders. As this is being written, Argentina has just held another election. Perón won it as usual and, also as usual, the opposition party, brought out and dusted off for the campaign, was promptly suppressed once the election was over. This is not our notion of free democratic choice.

But we received a very strong impression that President Perón enjoys a very wide popular support and probably could win an honest election by a good majority. True, he is not taking any chances. There have been several elections since he seized power and he has won all of them, but they have been much of the quality of an election in a social club which is dominated by a clique which controls both the nominating committee and the membership committee; the opposition might as well stay in bed—or over in Montevideo where a lot of them have taken up permanent residence in exile.

Nevertheless I think there are about as many Argentinos who like "Papá" Perón as there are of us who like Ike. As one of them told me, "Practically all of us like *him,* or at least most of the things he has done, but practically everybody hated *her.*" I was not able to judge the latter half of his statement; Eva Perón had already gone to her reward when we were there and very few people mentioned her name. Not that one could forget her, for her name and her face were everywhere, but she was no longer an issue. But it did seem as if Perón were the prisoner of a myth he had helped to create. I do not see how he could marry again should he wish to do so. He set up his deceased wife as a *de facto* saint; it would be awkward, to say the least, were he now to marry an "ordinary" woman.

I asked my informant why Evita was disliked when Juan was liked. "I'll give you a couple of examples. When Eva was a young actress she was beaten out for a part in a play by another and better known actress. She swore that she would get back at her. She did—when she became the President's wife she not only used her influence to keep the other woman from ever being cast for any part, she also drove the other actress right out of the country. That's the sort of senselessly vindictive woman she was and a lot of people knew it. Or take this case— A while back the girls that clerk in the department stores needed a raise, so the heads of their union went around to see Eva about it. She ran everything of that sort.

"She said she would think it over. Things went on for several months while she 'thought it over.' Then suddenly a raise was announced for women clerks, effective at once—but with the pay scale retroactive to the first of the year. A big bonus for the girls? Oh no! The accumulated difference was to be paid over into the Eva Perón Foundation; the clerks are pleased with the raise and they know who got it for them— Evita—and Evita has her hands on several more millions of pesos."

"Then she would spend it on herself?"

"Well, no— Yes and no. She *couldn't* spend very much of it on herself, no matter how many fur coats she bought. There was too much of it. But there never has been any accounting made of the money that goes through the Foundation, either where it comes from or where it goes. Evita used to give audiences in one room in the Foundation; people would file in and tell their stories. If the stories appealed to her, she would reach in a drawer that was stuffed with money and hand over fistfuls of the stuff—no system, no records.

"Mind you," he added, "I'm not saying the Eva Perón Foundation didn't do any good. It did a great deal of good and it still does. Hospitals, orphanages, all sorts of things."

I do not know how true the above stories are, but they seem to be typical of popular opinions. One of the odd things about Argentina, as a police state, was that the ordinary citizen seemed quite unafraid to talk about politics and to express criticism of the government. There is no possible doubt that the *Peronistas* have curtailed civil liberties and suppressed opposition, yet most of the citizens seemed to feel that they were free and well governed.

I do not understand this, nevertheless I will express a few horseback opinions—I can't be much farther off than are most professional pundits. I suspect that the typical South American is such a free soul that he simply will not stand for outright thought policing; if he can't speak his mind, he will rebel. Consequently a South American dictator can't get away with the sort of stuff that the commissars pull; the South American boss must seek real popular support to stay in power. Certainly Perón has sought, and gotten it, from the "shirtless ones." He seems to have much middle-class support as well.

Besides that, Argentina does not have our firm tradition of civil liberty and democratic process; the citizen is more likely to judge results than methods—the "Mussolini-made-the-trains-run-on-time" school of political science. All through Buenos Aires we saw big signs: PERÓN CUMPLE—which freely translated means that Perón keeps his word, Perón finished this or that public work just as he promised he would. This sort of thing makes an impression even in the States. The city I was reared in was dominated by the Pendergast machine; I can testify that my neighbors were more interested in the quality of the paving in their own block (which was good) than they were in the graft in the city hall concerning that pavement (which was scandalous).

In many ways Perón looks good compared with his predecessors. We heard contemptuous remarks about the President he chucked out, to the effect that he spent all his time enjoying the night life of Buenos Aires and never did any work. No one can accuse Perón of being lazy. His working day starts about six A.M. and almost anyone who wants a personal audience with him can get it if they will get up in time to see him at that hour.

His love for children seems to be sincere and it certainly adds to his popularity. He recently gave his country home to the children of Argentina, stating that a bachelor had no need of it. Everywhere in Buenos Aires one runs across this quotation: *"En la Nueva Argentina los únicos privilegiados son los niños."*—President Juan Perón. ("In the new Argentina the only privileged ones are the children.") This boast is not entirely true by a great deal but he seems to be sincere in making it and it fits beautifully the temperament of the people; children are highly valued there.

In addition to the above he is a skilled spellbinder. We heard him speak once; his style was as effective as Hitler's. The content was a semantic blank; he was boasting that Argentina was a great nation because it had ideals and heart and such like vague abstractions. But at one point he stopped suddenly, changed his manner abruptly and snapped, "Tell those policemen to quit bothering the citizens and to go away!"

The crowd ate it up.

It might have been a spur of the moment inspiration of a talented public speaker, or it might have been a carefully prepared plant. Either way it was smart politics.

Now let's drop the subject of politics. It took us three hours to fly across South America and three more hours from touching down until we reached our hotel, what with entrance formalities and an interminable ride from the airport downtown. Airplanes have done half the job of making travel simple and fast; the other half remains to be done.

As we registered at the Plaza Hotel, we were politely told to surrender our passports; the police wanted them. Ticky firmly said, "No!"

The desk clerk was embarrassed, patient, and equally firm. I finally agreed that we would but insisted on receipts by the serial numbers of the passports, which the clerk gravely provided, as well as police cards for each of us. I have not the slightest idea what Perón's police wanted our passports for, but they kept them for several days, then returned them.

The Plaza Hotel is not as new as the Carrera but it is equally luxurious. Our room, a semi-suite twice the size of most hotel rooms, could be split into living room and bedroom by big drapes. The furnishings and decorations reminded me of the Mauve Decade but the beds were modern. The most startling item was the bath towels which were much too much of a muchness. They were enormous Turkish bath sheets, five feet by six feet, large enough to wear as a toga. I would wear myself out trying to get dry with one; I needed a flunky to hold the other end. A chunk cut off one end would have been much more practical. But after the modest scraps of water-resistant rag issued as towels in some United States motor courts I was not disposed to complain.

The next day was Sunday. The shops were closed and the streets deserted; we strolled and tried to get the feel of the city. Buenos Aires is a really big city, big as Los Angeles or Chicago and much handsomer than either. It is so large indeed that it is too large for its back country, from a standpoint of healthy economic balance. If New York City were proportionately large, New York would have *forty million* people.

But it is not surprising that most Argentinos want to live in the capital, if possible; it is a charming, beautiful metropolis, not an overgrown village in search of a soul like some of our own that I won't mention for fear of being lynched. It has more than two hundred parks and plazas, some of them of great size, all of them of great beauty, abounding in flowers and trees and statuary. I happen to be very fond of statuary and I have searched the United States from border to border and coast to coast, looking at statues wherever I could find them. It is a very poor crop. Why the richest people in the world who will willingly dig down in their pockets for anything from flood relief for Siam to a 21″ TV screen won't pitch in together and buy statues I do not know—but there it is. Any city in South America is loaded with statues, some of them run-of-the-mill equestrian, some of them excellent, quite a few superb.

Buenos Aires being a big city has many statues, possibly more than its proportionate share. Most of them were academic in concept but in a large park near the President's city residence we saw something that looked vaguely like a ship, or equally like a giant prospector's hammer balanced on its head. It was heroic in size and conception and the shape was pleasing but I could not figure out what it was intended to be; I asked the guide who was with us at the time.

He smiled gently. "Uruguay gave that to us as a mark of friendship between our two countries, so we set it up here. But we never have been able to find out what it is."

On Monday it seemed time to get down to serious sightseeing. In any country for most travelers, such as ourselves, it is an always frustrating choice whether to see things haphazardly, enjoying oneself and trying to soak up the flavor of the country, or to set about it with grim determination to get the maximum use out of limited time and money. The first method is by far the best—provided you are wealthy in time and money and can afford to spend several months in each country and a lifetime in traveling. The second method is almost Hobson's choice for most of us, but it is hard work.

Ticky and I usually tried to do a little of both, which meant that we necessarily missed a lot of things. ("What? You were in Ruritania and you didn't see the *labyrinth*? My dear, you wasted your whole trip!") The world is a giant smorgasbord; you can sample a bit here and there with pleasure, but if you try to gulp down everything, you will simply become ill. It may be more important to visit with a cat and her kittens in an open-air book market than to try to see all the labyrinths in all the Ruritanias.

Ticky and I went down to the head porter's desk at the Plaza and asked if there was a taxi driver around who spoke English. We knew that Buenos Aires had a subway system that would get us anywhere faster and cheaper than would a taxi, but sightseeing from a subway is something like kissing over a telephone. The porter found us such a driver, a licensed guide named Herman Freudenberger, who was to become our closest friend in Argentina. He was a handsome, well setup young man and was a college graduate in ranch management, but he had given up agriculture to become a tourist guide. As he explained it, an assistant to the manager of a large agricultural estate has nothing to look forward to but the death of the manager; he wanted to get married and the guide business was quicker.

Herman spoke Spanish, Portuguese, English, German, and French; it was a rare tourist who could stump him. He had something else of equal importance: he loved his country, was proud of it, and knew its history. His parents were German Jewish; Herman was as Argentino as San Martín the Liberator.

He did not have his hand out. If we added a gift for special service he accepted it courteously, but if we paid the exact fare by mileage or time he was equally gracious, being at all times a Latin American gentleman and our host in his country, rather than a hired employe.

Herman took us first for a quick tour of the major points of the city. Let's take it for granted that we saw such things as Casa Rosada, the statue of San Martín, the monument to Columbus, embassies, ministries, Plaza Congreso, the Obelisk commemorating four centuries of Buenos Aires, the national art gallery; of course we saw such things and so will you when you go there. But you can learn more about such from five minutes of looking at pictures in the *National Geographic* than you can from ten thousand words of description. Describing a public building is as futile as describing a beautiful woman; the proper medium is a picture.

All of the above took more than one trip on more than one day; Buenos Aires is big. But we saw other things. Herman drove us down to the estuary to let us see the Dutch ship we were to sail in the following week. The waterfront in Buenos Aires is prettier than most, although docks and warehouses of a big and busy port cannot compete with other sights in beauty. But while we were there he gestured toward a big municipal steam-electric plant. "There is where we burned coffee during the War."

"*Coffee?*" I answered, thinking with horror of the present dollar-a-pound prices.

"Yes. We had coffee we couldn't sell or give away and we were short on coal. It gave the whole area quite an aroma."

I was too stunned to comment. It struck me as the most tragic waste of raw material since the time of the Aztec practice of sacrificing virgins.

Later he showed us Avenida Nueve de Julio, the widest street in the world. If you translate the name as "Fourth of July" instead of "Ninth of July," you end up with the proper local meaning: Independence Day Boulevard. It was certainly wide, making even Canal Street in New Orleans look like an alley—about eight taxicabs to a side, not counting broad, gardened parkways.

"How did it get so big?"

"Oh, President Perón decided that we needed a major boulevard through the heart of the city so he told them to tear down all the buildings in one row of blocks and merge the adjoining streets. Look at this."

We drove down a chute and found ourselves in an underground parking and service garage. "This is the biggest underground parking space in the world. This is where the Buenos Aires businessmen leave their cars during the day."

I was not prepared to dispute it; the caverns seemed to run endlessly on back until lost in the gloom. It accounted in part for what seemed to be a total absence of parking lots in downtown Buenos Aires and very few places to park at the curb. This four-hundred-year-old city was not laid out for automobiles. "But suppose they do park here," I objected, "that would still leave most of them a mile or more from their offices."

"Eh? Why, their chauffeurs drive them to their offices, then leave the cars here, then pick them up later."

"But how about those who don't have chauffeurs?"

"Excuse me? Oh . . . here in Argentina any man who can afford to own a private automobile can certainly afford to hire a driver."

I learned that the car he drove was not his own but was an investment on the part of a wealthy man for whom he drove it on shares. We were finding and were still to learn that the Detroit automobile is the most universally coveted piece of wealth in the world. In Argentina and in many other countries import of American cars is strictly controlled and a license to do so is hard to obtain; often it is a cherished piece of political patronage. Under these conditions a car from the U.S.A. is fantastically expensive, not just a mark-up for ocean freightage and tariff, but with the F.O.B. Detroit price tripled, quadrupled, even quintupled.

But even at such monstrous prices they are greatly desired; we were assured that, despite the cost, they were more automobile for the money than were the much cheaper European cars. A Ford or a Chevrolet will be driven "three times around the clock," more than three hundred thousand miles, and will stand up under it; a European car, except the Rolls Royce, will fall to pieces under much less abuse.

I am neither an automotive expert nor a field agent for the Detroit Chamber of Commerce; I report what I heard from drivers on four continents, many of whom were not especially friendly to the United States—in fact in many cases they seemed to blame us for the fact that their own governments had made it so hard to import American cars. The answer to this is tied up with the knotty question of dollar exchange and controlled currencies, but there is a potential market abroad for millions of American automobiles which we are not at present able to use.

Herman took us out to the cattle market, which looked much like the stockyards in Kansas City or Chicago and was comparable in size and in modern methods, Argentina being butcher to the whole world. The cattle were mostly big, beautiful Herefords, large square steaks with ears at one end and tail at the other. Being from cattle country ourselves, they were interesting but not novel. What did interest us were the gauchos and their horses.

Cattlemen are cattlemen, no matter what language they speak. While the gauchos looked odd in their dress to us their costume is as practical as the typical gear of our own cowboys. They wear baggy pants (*bombachas*) in place of Levi's and chaps, a different syle of sun hat, and different styling in their boots; these differences are no more significant than the differences in uniform and insignia between American Marines and French

Legionnaires. Poncho and *bombachas* make a gaucho look fat; our western dress makes a man look leaner than he is— no matter, they are both colorful and dressed for the work they do.

But their horses are not like our dainty, little cow ponies. The gaucho makes little or no use of the lasso; he has instead the *boleadoras,* three strands of braided rawhide bent together at one end of each and with a metal weight fastened to each of the other ends. He can swing this over his head, let it sail through the air, and bring down an animal by tangling it around the beast's legs from a greater distance than is possible with a lariat.

But the gaucho does not use even this tool very often against cattle, but saves it for ostrich or simply for hunting for sport. They believe in treating cattle gently—no sense in subjecting a cow brute to a spill and a nervous shock when you are trying to fatten it for market. Their horses are bred short, wide in the chest, and heavily muscled; they are trained to manage cattle by breasting against them, nudging them the way they want them to go.

Later we discovered that the cattlemen of Australia do not use any sort of rope. If an Australian cowboy finds it necessary to throw a steer for any purpose—which is not often—he will ride up to it, reach down and twist its tail and trip it. Australians do not use the lariat either. Nor did we see any roping equipment being carried by the cattle hands in South Africa. I begin to wonder whether or not the proud art of the American rodeo might not simply be an obsolete stunt, about as useful as rapier fencing. Maybe we shake a lot of hamburger off our brutes unnecessarily just to show how clever we are with a rope.

I risked my pretty business suit and tried the gaucho saddle. The horse turned out to be neck-reined, but he did not speak English and the gaucho uses both quirt (*rebenque*) and heavy spurs so I did not stay up long. The gaucho saddle is nothing like a western "rocking chair" stock saddle; instead of sitting down in it you sit up on top of it and it is built like a feather bed, with layer after layer of blanket, sheepskin padding, and leather. There is so much between the rider and the cayuse that it is hard to feel the beast. I like to be more intimately in touch with a horse if he and I are expected to form a close committee, not separated from him by an inner-spring mattress.

The saddle had stirrups, big metal disks with boot-size holes in them, but I could not see that they did much good; they seemed simply to let the gaucho know where his feet were. They are derived from a much simpler stirrup, a rawhide thong tied around a small stick. The gaucho of the early days placed his toes over the stick with the thong between his big toe and the second toe; it served as a stirrup but it did not look as if you could put much weight on it in a pinch.

Herman pointed out this old-style stirrup on a statue titled *El Gaucho* which stood in a little park in front of the main entrance of the stockyard. It was a beautiful piece of work, comparable in artistic quality and style of execution to "The Scout" or "The End of the Trail." The sculptured horse looked like the same wide-shouldered, chunky little animal that had just patiently let me try him, but the gaucho portrayed was of an earlier century with a strong, hard-bitten Indian face unmodified by European blood.

Herman pointed out his boot, which came all the way up his calf but did not cover his toes at all. "When a horse died the gaucho would make two circular cuts in the hind leg above and below the hock, then he would strip off the hide as an unbroken cylinder the way you would peel off a stocking. Then he would put it on his own leg, with his heel at the hock joint and let it dry and shrink in place; this made him a new pair of boots."

Ticky examined the statue. "But how would he take it off?"

"He didn't, not until he cut it off to replace it with a new one. Those old-timers lived very much the way the animals themselves did. They slept on the ground in all sorts of weather, they never washed, they never took off their boots. They were a tough breed."

Ticky looked at the portrayed boot with the splayed toes sticking out, wrinkled her nose and turned away—Ticky used to bathe fourteen times a week until her doctor made her cut it down to once a day. I myself was wondering just what sort of athlete's foot would be incubated inside a rawhide boot that was never removed, but decided that the tough hombre sitting up there would never have noticed anything short of gangrene.

That afternoon Herman took us to see a very special sort of school, Escuela Pedro de Mendoza. It is the home and studio of Maestro Benito Quinquela Martín, possibly the greatest living Argentino painter; it is also an art museum, a grammar school, and an art school. Señor Quinquela was a very poor boy in the waterfront neighborhood, a wharf rat. From his paintings, now sought by all galleries everywhere, he has become wealthy, but he lives and works in the poor neighborhood where he grew up. The *escuela* is a beautiful modern six-story building by the water; the Maestro owns it, pays the expenses, pays the salaries of the staff of teachers. The poor children of the neighborhood attend free.

A child who attends is not especially likely to become an artist; it is in most respects simply a well-run grammar school. But a pupil there who happens to display artistic talent has every opportunity to study art under a renowned master. Señor Quinquela named the school for the artist who gave him his chance, Maestro Pedro de Mendoza.

One of the pleasant things about the place is that the museum is loaded with works of other living Argentino artists, purchased by the Maestro. Besides that, he has named each classroom for some earlier artist of the Argentine. We did not get to meet Señor Quinquela (although he is readily at home to casual visitors and tourists) because he was away, but his benign personality was everywhere. His favorite subject is still his own poor waterfront neighborhood and so high is the regard in which he is held by his neighbors that all around us we could see that shopkeepers and warehouse owners and householders had painted their properties in bright colors—because the Maestro likes to paint bright colors in his pictures!

Each classroom has a mural done by the Maestro—a feature that may be more impressive if I add that his pictures bring twenty to thirty thousand dollars in the open market. Each grade is decorated appropriately for the age level, starting with Bugs-Bunny-Mickey-Mouse things in the kindergarten. For these small children each door in the part of the school they use is done in a different color, so that a child too young to obey, "Go to room nineteen," can be told, "Go see Señorita Gómez in the room with the red door."

We left the place feeling happy.

I took advantage of where we were to ask to see slums. Buenos Aires turned out to have the cleanest slums we ever saw. They were still slums, substandard dwellings for the very poor, but they were swept and washed and painfully neat, with never an uncovered garbage can, nor a trash heap, nor a bad odor. President Perón decided that all citizens must be clean, so he made each local policeman responsible for the cleanliness of his beat, with his responsibility extending even to compulsory inspections of housewives' kitchens. A housewife can be fined for failing to wash dishes, failing to scrub floors, failing to keep her yard, or passageway, or stoop clean and neat. The results are homes which are clean and healthful and cheerful, though still poor.

I could not help wondering what would happen in tenement neighborhoods in our country if the local cop tried to inspect the kitchens. What would they do to him? Take his club away from him most likely and beat him to death with it—and good riddance, too.

There are other things more important than cleanliness.

In Buenos Aires as in all Latin American cities I have been in there is a nerve-racking din of automobile horns. I had heard that the system was that the first driver to sound his horn had the right of way, which naturally would result in endless horn-blowing and probably endless accidents.

Only it did not result in endless accidents. I asked Herman about it and was told that I did not quite understand the system; it was not a race to see who could toot his horn first. Each driver, as he approached an intersection, gave a short blast on his horn at about the same distance from the corner, around forty feet. Thus the signal of the driver nearest the corner would be heard first and cars coming at right angles to him would give way.

The system seemed to me to be chancy in the extreme but it worked, although the racket was distressing. However, Buenos Aires was quiet as a chess match at night, whereas Santiago was so noisy at night that we could not have gotten to sleep early even if the schedule had permitted it; I asked Herman about the contrast.

"Oh. See this." He flipped a switch on the dashboard. "Now the horn is disconnected and the horn ring flashes the highway lights. President Perón decided that people ought to be able to sleep at night. So at sundown we all flip this switch, drive with the dim lights in the city, and use the bright lights to signal at each corner just as we use the horn in the daytime. It's a fine if you sound your horn at night."

Herman collected parking tickets just as many American drivers do; his business almost required it. At the moment he was not paying them as there was a Christmas amnesty coming up and he expected that the slate would be wiped clean. The notion seems exotic to us; later we were to run into a much stranger use of amnesty in Brazil. In accounts of automobile accidents in Brazilian newspapers the same sentence frequently ends such news items: "Both drivers fled from the scene."

With us, leaving the scene of an automobile accident is just short of carving up your wife with an axe. Not so in Brazil. The courts are years behind in their work; if a driver is arrested on a charge of causing an accident he may wait in jail almost endlessly before he can be tried; therefore he runs away and tries to avoid arrest.

The wonderful part about it is that if he manages to keep his freedom for twenty-four hours amnesty works; he will never be arrested. I am not sure of the law or lack of it in this custom; it may be just a well-understood convention based on the common knowledge that the courts could not possibly in all eternity handle all the cases if the cops arrested everyone who deserved it. In any case, the drivers do run and hide.

Amnesty in misdemeanors and lesser crimes does not seem so out of place in cultures in which amnesties for revolutionists, political prisoners, and exiles are common and almost a necessity. The spirit of forgive and forget makes some of the fiercer aspects of Latin ways more tolerable.

We heard of one other custom much more wildly exotic. I was not able to check on it as it referred to Paraguay, a country we were not able to visit. But here it is: it is alleged that Paraguay has no law against murder, killing being considered a private matter; either the deceased is a no-good and everyone is glad he is dead, or the friends and relatives of the departed can be depended on to avenge the matter themselves.

My first impression was one of horror, but the idea has a certain wild logic about it that grows on one. Almost anyone can make up a list of people he would like to lure into Paraguay— they never would be missed.

We did not spend all our time driving around with Herman although it would have been cheaper for me. The Plaza Hotel is at one end (the more expensive end) of Calle Florida, one of the finest shopping streets in the world. During the business day it is blocked off from traffic and shoppers can wander back and forth as they please.

Ticky is the sort of girl whose eyes bug out and whose face gets flushed at the sight of bargains in a shop window— somewhat the expression that Marilyn Monroe produces in a man; it may be a related mechanism. The greatest hazard in Calle Florida is the alligators, empty ones made up into women's handbags; they are snapping and yapping at a man's financial standing every step of the way down the street. They will savage you in a tender portion, your wallet, at the drop of a hint.

It is no good to tell me that a handbag is "cheap" at thirty-five dollars simply because the same handbag would be priced at a hundred and fifty dollars in New York; if I were in the States I would not be buying a handbag for any century and a half—nor for thirty-five dollars either if I could avoid it; my cornbelt ancestors would spin in their modest graves.

Ticky was moderate; she bought only three alligator bags.

Of course each bag had to have shoes to match. Besides that they were actually giving away (almost) bags of other sorts. Then there were sweaters and blouses and gloves and other things. I kept reminding her that we had been sixty kilos over the weight limit in flying the Andes and that we were going to have to pay excess air baggage several times more; I don't think she heard me.

Once I had anesthetized myself to the inevitable it was really pleasant to see her have so much fun. For most women, to be in Calle Florida is something like dying and going to heaven. So far as I have seen or ever heard nowhere else in the world are there so many smart shops catering to women jampacked into so small a neighborhood. Add to that the fact that a favorable rate of exchange makes any purchase a bargain (in feminine logic) and that many things really are wonderful bargains by any standard.

I offer this hard-earned advice to others who may follow: give her a flat amount and take her traveler's cheques away from her. Tell her solemnly that when the amount is gone the fun is over. Then stay in your hotel room, quietly quaffing San Martíns and thinking serious thoughts; if you go along you will be tempted to let her have more money.

I went along, of course.

Ticky encountered for the first time the custom of dickering. She was no good at it, as she believed instinctively that it is immoral to attempt to get anything below the asking price, equivalent to taking bread out of the mouths of the shopkeeper's hungry little ones. But she finally got it through her head that, except in the large department stores that advertise "firm prices," each sales transaction in Latin America is a social event, more valued for the ritual than for the regrettable economic aspect. But she never did acquire any skill at it. Fortunately most sales people are not disposed to swindle a señora, even if she is from Estados Unidos and therefore conclusively presumed to be rich.

She encountered, too, the lovely custom of making the purchaser a little gift after the transaction is over, and was delighted with it. So am I, for that matter; it is probably an uneconomic practice that results in higher-than-necessary prices, or profits lower than proper, or both, but it does not cost much and adds grace and warmth to life.

In the course of an afternoon's shopping it was necessary to stop for tea. By "tea" I do not mean a cup of lukewarm tannic acid solution with skimmed milk added; afternoon tea in Buenos Aires is somewhat simpler than a Thanksgiving dinner, but not much. The place to go is a *confitería*—which should not be translated as "confectionary shop." (Knowing little or no Spanish I often tried to struggle along through translating by cognates, as indicated above; this can lead to trouble. In a cocktail lounge in our hotel I saw a sign which seemed to me plainly to read: NO PROPAGATION PERMITTED IN THIS ROOM—which seemed to me a reasonable restriction, even in a broad-minded hotel. I learned later that it read: NO TIPPING. And it did not even mean that.)

A *confitería* is a combination soda fountain, cocktail bar, tea shop, and restaurant, usually with live music and other elegances. The best are as swank as the Stork Club; our favorite had the end of the room caged off and filled with dozens of song birds which sang along with the strolling musicians. Around four-thirty or five in the afternoon entire families gather in them, Papa has his highball, Mama has tea, the kids have sandwiches and cakes and malted milks and ice cream sodas or anything they wish. We have no institution for the entire family which compares in wide choice of hospitality, but it is high time we imitated it. We won't of course; the bluenoses would have fits—corrupting the young, and so on.

Ticky and I always picked ice cream sodas, French pastries, and fancy little sandwiches. I had always thought the soda fountain was "Made in U.S.A." and perhaps it was, but our neighbors can teach us some tricks, in particular the "Everlasting Soda" as we called it. The first time I ordered a soda I was fetched the usual large glass, but, while it was packed with ice cream, whipped cream, and crushed strawberries, it contained no bubbly water nor very much room for same. Instead the waiter put a quart seltzer bottle with squirt top down by it.

I was charged a very modest price for one ice cream soda, but it took me more than an hour to finish off the combination. I did not use all of the fizz bottle, of course, but whenever the glass ran a little low or a bit flat I gave it a transfusion. When it was over and we were looking regretfully at the quantities of sandwiches and pastries we had not been able to eat (even though we had made marked inroads), the waiter came along, noted that we had not eaten everything—and reduced our bill accordingly.

It cost us forty cents each.

Most of one morning was killed by a newspaper interview and a radio broadcast. I usually try to duck such chores, as my voice over the air sounds like a rusty saw and, as for news stories, I am leery of any copy that I do not proof myself. I was more anxious than I would be at home to avoid both of them as a foreigner's remarks are likely to be held against his nation, whereas if he waggles his jaw at home his boners reflect on no one but himself. I don't have a diplomat's special training in how to walk a tight rope and I certainly did not want to be an international incident, even a minor one.

I pointed out to the radio chap that I did not speak Spanish. No matter at all, he informed me; it was the government Servicio Internacional, the Argentine equivalent of The Voice of America, beamed in shortwave in six languages. This made me more edgy than ever, so I protested that I had a very full schedule (which was a lie, unless you counted in *confiterías*); I did not have time to come to the studio.

Oh, they wouldn't think of asking me—a crew would come to the hotel with recording equipment. I gave up and scheduled both for the next morning. The reporter arrived first and could not speak English, which almost gave me an out, except that the red-headed Irish maid was in the room; she pinch hit and made an excellent interpreter. Presently Herman showed up and we were able to let the maid get back to her work.

Instead of translating one question Herman started to argue with the reporter. Presently he turned to me and protested, "He insists that I ask you how much money you make a year."

"Tell him I won't answer that one."

"I *told* him that that was a question no North American would answer, but he insists on its being put."

I thought about it. "Tell him I really don't know, that my business agent handles such things. Tell him that I am just a writer with no head for business."

"Okay."

The men from the broadcasting station showed up and started stringing wires around; the reporter closed his notebook and left. An outline had been prepared and most of the items were innocuous enough, things I could discuss without offending anyone. But it was strongly suggested, orally, that I really should finish up by saying something really nice about "Papá."

I did not want to say anything about President Perón, pro or con; a tourist who sticks his nose into politics is asking for trouble, for himself and for his country.

They did not twist my arm but it was very hard to refuse. I tried to think fast without much success—then suddenly remembered the sign we had seen all over town, the one about the kids; it was as non-political as apple pie, as non-controversial as being in favor of good roads and good weather, but it was a direct quotation from President Perón.

So we finished the broadcast with that, quoting it in both English and Spanish: "In the new Argentina the only privileged ones are the children." I said that was an ideal that appealed to all nations, and wiped my brow as the little red light went out.

In the evening paper I saw that I had stated that no atomic blast could destroy the Earth, which was fair enough; I believed it, it was consonant with our own national stand in the matter, and more or less what I had actually said. I saw also that Ticky and I planned to return home via the North Pole, which was a lovely notion, though not true, but it hurt nothing. Further down I discovered that I made so much money that I could not keep track of it but was satisfied as long as I always had money enough for beautiful cars, enough to take care of my mansion in Colorado, and enough always to travel where and how I pleased.

Well, I suppose I asked for it. Stated as ambitions rather than as accomplished facts it was not too far off the mark.

My present car is getting a bit old and the house needs some repairs. It would be nice to have too much money.

I asked Herman about it the next day. "Oh, you wouldn't answer so he filled in what he needed." He frowned. "Things are different here. They should have sent a reporter who could speak English and who understood North Americans. Here one of the first questions a reporter always asks a man is, 'How much money do you make?' and the man being interviewed always gives a flat answer: 'I make such-and-such thousand pesos a year.' It is a polite question and a perfectly proper answer."

"Not in the States."

"I know. Although some of your Texans don't seem to mind."

"Well . . . Texans are a special case. They have their own rules, more like yours."

"Yes, but not quite. Just recently there was one in that hotel you are in. He wore one of those big hats and high-heeled boots and he was boasting about how he could paper his hotel room with thousand-dollar bills if he felt like it."

"Hmm . . . one or two too many San Martíns?"

"He may have been drinking but I don't think so. It was in the daytime and he called down to the desk and told them to send up thirty thousand pesos in change; he was buying some things for his wife. Then he got angry when they didn't do it."

I had no comment. Herman went on, "I've noticed that my guests from the States often mention proudly that they were poor boys. You said something like that yourself."

"Yes."

"I've learned that it is something that a North American is proud of. Here, if a man has become wealthy from poverty he tries to keep it quiet. An Argentino likes to boast, if he can, 'My father and my grandfather left me so much money that I can have everything I want and never have to work.' "

At a later time I ran into a confirmation of this major difference in attitudes. I was at a social event with an Argentine minister of state who had once served his country in New

York City. He was speaking to someone else but turned to me to have me confirm something he said, in that I was the only "Yankee" present. "I was telling so-and-so that my salary in the States was three thousand dollars a month and that that was a very good salary there. That's true, isn't it?"

I assured him that thirty-six thousand dollars a year, tax free, was a very good salary anywhere. He seemed very pleased.

To our regret the morning arrived when we went down to pay our bill. When we got back to our room it was dominated by an enormous bouquet of flowers; the card attached read: "Bon voyage, from your friend and guide in B.A.—Herman."

Herman took us down to the ship, got us smoothly through outgoing customs, loaded us aboard with advice as to tipping the dock porters, then took us back uptown. We had lunch with him rather solemnly and he took us back to the ship. Shortly the M.S. *Ruys* warped away from the dock and out, side bedecked with streamers and band music playing. I found my eyes filling with tears, something I had surely not expected to have happen at leaving "Papá" Perón's too-well-policed paradise. I looked at Ticky and found that she was having the same trouble. She looked at me and said, "We *will* come back, won't we? You weren't just kidding Herman?"

"You bet we will!"

V

The Good Little Country

THE MOTOR SHIP *Ruys* intimidated us at first. It was big and shiny and beautifully furnished and filled with well-dressed people all of whom seemed to know each other and who laughed among themselves and stared right through us. The officers wore gold braid and crisp white uniforms and answered questions politely in correct formal English but were obviously too busy for us to bother them with our trivial affairs. We found ourselves homesick for the good old raucous, comfortable *Gulf Shipper*.

But the beds were comfortable and our stateroom had a polished, spacious perfection. Our bathroom had both a shower and a full-sized bathtub and was roomier than many ashore. There were two wash basins and many mirrors and a large divan and two wardrobes and enough stowage space to put all the ten suitcases out of sight, as well as lots of drawers and shelf space.

Our cabin steward, Kwai Yau, had arranged Herman's mammoth gladiolus in a vase in front of triple mirrors on the dressing table, making the room cheerful as well as luxurious. Kwai Yau could give Jeeves pointers on how to take care of people, but we were yet to become acquainted with his virtues. We showered and changed and decided to face the outside world.

The *Ruys* is the flagship of the Dutch Royal Interocean Lines. "Royal" is a decoration awarded by the Queen in honor

115

of the many ships of the line—more than half—lost in war service. The *Ruys* herself had a long and honorable war record but came through intact. She and her sisters now ply between South America and the Far East, via the Cape of Good Hope and Singapore. She is neither a passenger ship nor a freighter, but a cargo liner, which means that while she carries a great deal of cargo, more than the *Gulf Shipper,* she carries also hundreds of passengers of all three classes.

Such a ship carries only a hundred-odd first class passengers but it offers them greater luxury than do the fashionable giants of the North Atlantic run. In a cargo liner all first class rooms are outside rooms and they are usually bigger than those in a passenger liner. There is plenty of deck space for games and walking and sunning, the swimming pool is never too crowded, there is always room to sit down in the bar, one never has to rush to find a seat at the movies—whereas many so-called luxury ships are crowded as cattle cars.

Second class in a cargo liner is comfortable but not fancy. The less said about third class the better; the best you can hope for is that it be clean. In the *Ruys* it was clean; I have seen some that were filthy.

To our surprised relief the operating language of the *Ruys* was English. The officers were Dutch, the crew was Chinese. Dutch was spoken only by the officers in private; the passengers never heard it. The Chinese petty officers all spoke English and it was this which caused the Dutch officers to manage the ship in English, it being the only language in common with the crew. Most of the other Chinese spoke some English or Pidgin (Kwai Yau spoke excellent English, in which we were fortunate; some of the passengers could communicate with their room stewards only through the petty officers).

Nine tenths of the first class passengers spoke English; there were only a few who had only Spanish. Our days of struggling to make ourselves understood were practically over. There were more South Africans aboard than there were South Americans, and there were only a handful of others, such as Ticky and myself—a few from the Far East, from Australia, from Mauritius, and one other couple with United States citizenship but who lived in South America and kept rather much to themselves. We were the only residents of the States aboard.

It seemed rather lonely for a day or two. We crept out of our stateroom that first day, got lost—the *Ruys* is big enough for that, until you establish landmarks—finally found the bar and ascertained that our signatures would be honored on chits. The bar seemed gloomy as a monastery at first, impressive with carved wood and dark beams and brass. But the drinks contained authentic joy juice. When the dinner chimes sounded we were better able to face it.

The dining saloon was two decks high, with an open, railed well above it and a leaded sky light. It is entered by sweeping, curved stairways which call for music by Strauss and is a place with crisp linen and shining, superfluous silver. The Chief Steward asked our names in a hushed voice and ushered us in slow march to a table; the head steward and the assistant head steward seated us. About then I caught sight of Kwai Yau standing in the background; he caught my eye and grinned. I felt better.

We introduced ourselves and found that our four table mates were all from Buenos Aires—Señor and Señora Rubenstein, two unrelated señoritas. All but Señor Rubenstein spoke English; he spoke Spanish and French and we could struggle along a bit with him in a sorry mixture of both. The fact that we had just been visiting in their home town loosened things up a bit and we got rather chummy.

But we never did get the hang of South American table manners and remained intimidated by them as long as we sat at that table. I have no apology for our own national table manners; in my prejudiced opinion most of us conduct our self-stoking sensibly, neatly, and unobtrusively. I don't see why a soft-boiled egg *must* be eaten from the shell.

But have you ever seen a well-bred South American tackle a piece of fruit? It is an exhibition of surgical virtuosity which would take me a long time to learn, if ever. One of them will tackle an apple, an orange, or a banana with a fruit knife and a tiny fork, peel the fruit and demolish it without ever touching human skin to any part of it. Consider what this means with a banana, for example; under the rules you can't even help yourself with your thumb to get the peel started. "Untouched by human hands."

They cope with a melon in much the same aseptic way, instead of steadying it with the left hand the way we do and spooning it out.

Ticky and I admired these stunts but were scared off by them. We did not eat much fruit that stretch of the trip.

Montevideo lies less than a hundred and fifty miles down Río de la Plata from Buenos Aires; we were there in the morning. The estuary is about thirty miles wide at Buenos Aires; at Montevideo it is more than a hundred miles wide and is practically open ocean although technically still a river. It was here that the British chased the *Graf Spee* almost up onto the beach and fought a naval battle well inside the legal borders of Uruguay, for which they paid an indemnity and an apology with their tongues in their cheeks; the *Graf* was not a prize to let slip on a technicality.

The usual boarders swarmed into the ship before we were up. We arranged a tourist trip before we went to breakfast, as the schedule of the ship permitted but two days in Uruguay and there was no time for leisurely poking around. Señor Roitman, guide, interpreter, and host-by-temperament, agreed to have a car waiting for us and two others after breakfast.

The other two were an English lady (I use the word intentionally) and a shaggy young gentleman from the Canadian diplomatic service who had that careful carelessness in his appearance which characterizes the "top drawer." We found both of them extremely "veddy, veddy" at first. But I knew from other experience that the English are not actually unfriendly; they are merely shy, embarrassed, rather afraid of strangers. Ticky and I firmly ignored the chill they handed us and went on being friendly, informal, and talkative; it worked, as it almost always does. Almost all Englishmen are nice people individually, once you get past their guard, and they are quite willing to decide that you are a nice person, too—for a Yank, that is.

Montevideo is a large city, as big as Saint Louis. The first impression of it is its cleanliness. Underlying this surface impression is a standard of real sanitation as high as any in the world and higher than that of many of our own cities—Philadelphia, for example. You need not fear the water nor the food in Montevideo; they are clean.

The second impression is one in reverse: no policemen. This negative condition probably would not have impressed us had we come directly from home, since we don't see many police-men at home and the few that are seen are usually controlling traffic. But in most of Latin America a cop or a soldier (they are much the same thing there) is always staring down the back of your neck. They won't bother a gringo tourist ordinarily but they are always there, as ubiquitous, conspicuous, and depressing as a chaperone on a hay ride.

There probably are some policemen in Uruguay but I do not recall seeing a single one even though I looked for them. I don't think you could stir out a policeman in Montevideo even by parking in front of a fire plug.

I asked Señor Roitman about this and he got straight to the (Latin American) point. "Our President doesn't need any bodyguards." We were seated at the time in a sidewalk café; he glanced across the plaza and added, "In the afternoon when he finishes his day's work he comes out over there and walks across the plaza alone. He runs across you and you know each other, so you sit down right here with everybody else and you have *café exprés* together. Nobody takes any notice; it wouldn't be polite."

The President of Uruguay is not the boss and he most cer-tainly is not a dictator ruling by decree; the system resembles the Swiss system in that he is chairman of an executive council. I do not recall the name of the incumbent, as his name was not plastered all around in public places as in Argentina.

The third impression was the usual one in South America of parks and plazas and monuments and outdoor statuary. I had assumed up until then that the superior beauty of South American cities was a result of age. But Montevideo is a mere youngster, founded in 1726, more than a hundred years after the founding of New York. Where are New York's statues and monuments? Not that thing over the pond at Radio City, surely? And don't mention Grant's Tomb; I've *seen* Grant's Tomb. They shouldn't do it to a dead man.

My passion for statuary almost got me into difficulty. We were driving through one of the many parks and passed their monument to the Covered Wagon; I insisted on stopping for a good look. It was a fine academic bronze, a life-size group consisting of covered wagon, pioneers on horseback, triple span of oxen, relief oxen following behind, all executed in detailed realism which nevertheless achieved satisfying composition from any approach. It was an opus suited to crown the career of a great master and it made much "modern" sculpture look like the kindergarten blobs so many of them are.

I was interested in it from three points of view: as a work of art, in the strong parallel to our own pioneer history portrayed by the group, and in the mechanical and engineering problems which in a thing of that size are as difficult as the artistic problems. I stepped up onto the base of the group to take a closer look at one of the figures.

A park attendant sprang up out of nowhere and informed me emphatically that it was *prohibido* to molest the statues. I tried to explain most humbly that I had not meant any harm and that I had not touched anything but my frail Spanish broke down completely and Mr. Roitman had to intervene. He made himself personally responsible for my good behavior and I left sheepishly, under parole.

I suppose the park attendant could be classed as a policeman but he was armed with a rake instead of a gun.

We drove for many miles through the old city and through the new city which spreads downstream along Playa de Carrasco. Much of old town was rococo in style, even baroque, but in Carrasco we found miles of the light-hearted, imaginative modern architecture which we had first noticed in Lima, then had encountered repeatedly in Chile and Argentina—and were to encounter again in Brazil. I again asked to see slums, sticking to my theory that a worm's-eye view of a culture is the only one with a true perspective.

Mr. Roitman did his best to oblige. Presently I said to him, "When do we get to where the poor people live?"

He stopped the car. "This is it."

I looked around and said, "No, no, I mean the *really* poor people," then explained what we had seen elsewhere.

"But these *are* the poor people. These are the poorest people in Montevideo."

I looked around me again and was tempted to call him a liar. These were not tenements nor the hovels of the poverty-stricken; these were small and simple single-family houses, each with its flower garden, quite evidently the homes of self-respecting lower-middle class. I already knew that Mr. Roitman was proudly patriotic and I suspected that his national pride had caused him not to show me the seamy side of his city. My own home town of Colorado Springs has little poverty and its slums are not slums at all in the sense in which the word applies to New York, Chicago, Rio, or Sydney, but I knew and was graveled by the knowledge that the worst of Colorado Springs was depressingly worse than this by many stages.

Unsatisfied, I checked on him later. Señor Roitman was right; these were their "poor." Uruguay has no poor. It is a welfare state that works, without, so far as we could see, the dreary drawbacks of other welfare states. How they have managed this I do not know, for I have seen other welfare states which appeared to have much the same sort of legislation and the results I did not like at all—repressive laws, endless bureaucracy, chain gang regulations. Uruguay is not that sort of a place, yet it has cradle-to-grave social security, free education through college, free medicine for the lower incomes, and retirement at fifty without loss of comforts for anyone who wants to retire that young.

Maybe there is a catch in it; if so, we did not find it. Our investigation was as quick and superficial as a congressional junket to Europe; nevertheless I am for the present convinced that they have somehow managed to work a miracle. Someday I plan to go back and dig in deeply; if there is a secret to be learned, we must learn it. Just now I feel strong sympathy for the farmer who said on seeing the giraffe, "There ain't no sech animal!"

Uruguay has the Latin fondness for designating famous events simply by their dates. (Was it Mark Twain who said that a French politician could make an impassioned and effective patriotic speech simply by rattling off a list of dates?) In driving around I noticed the following street names: 14 July, 18 July, 25 May, 26 March, 4 July, 31 December, and 24 September. This is a random sampling, not a complete tally; they may have the calendar (and their streets) as loaded up as we are with Mother's Day and Chew-More-Gum Week.

Note that they complimented us with a street named for the Fourth of July, our only holiday that fits into the date system. This sort of gracious gesture is to be found throughout South America; one is always coming across Woodrow Wilson Boulevard, Roosevelt Highway, George Washington Plaza— nor is it a matter of toadying to Tío, for they have not neglected the national figures of other nations besides ours. I wonder to what extent, if at all, we return these courtesies? I have never run across at home Bolívar Boulevard or San Martín Road. Perhaps I did not look in the right places.

While all of our neighbors to the south follow this gentle custom Uruguay really goes whole hog. Here are a few samples: Avenida Simón Bolívar, Rambla República de Argentina, R.R. de Perú, Rambla Presidente Wilson, Calle George Washington, Parque Franklin Delano Roosevelt (the biggest one in the city), Rambla Presidente Bernardo O'Higgins, more ramblas named for Mexico, Chile, France, and Great Britain (a *rambla* is a fancy boulevard, one with trees and flowers and a view), Avenida Italia, Avenida General San Martín, and even Calle Missouri and Calle Mississippi. After that comes heroes, heroes, and more heroes; they rarely waste a street by naming it something like Chestnut, Pine, or Fifth.

A man can get into their street guide without being a general, a politician, or a Uruguayan celebrity. Emile Zola and Herbert Spencer both made it; you can too. So did Darwin, Cervantes, Clemenceau, Magellan, and somebody named Samuel Blixen. Go climb a mountain or write an epic poem; eventually the city council of Montevideo will award you a few miles of paved immortality.

I think that the only word for this custom is "gracious."

The following morning we drove out to the cattle market, which differs from that in Buenos Aires in that it is some miles outside the city and affords thereby more opportunity to see gauchos at work. It still is not real cattle country, which is farther to the north in the great plains; the countryside around Montevideo is more like Iowa farms, except that some of the vegetation is subtropical. It never frosts in Uruguay, but there are not many really hot days and there is enough rain, around thirty inches a year over all.

I could not see much difference between the gauchos of Uruguay and the ones of Argentina, but their horses here seemed to be finer boned with more Arabian strain and so far as I could see they were not taught to breast the cattle. Representatives of the major North American meat packers are stationed permanently at this cattle market and buy a large portion of the supply, this being their major export to us. We "took maté" with them and the gauchos in the gauchos' clubhouse at the market—"*tomar* maté" is the idiom, literally "to take the pot" but it means to drink *yerba* herb tea through a silver pipe from a gourd pot called a "maté." Socially it means still more; it is the Uruguayan symbol of hospitality.

Custom requires that all in the same circle of friendliness drink from the same pot and the same silver pipe. The English lady with us was offered it first, then Ticky, and then myself, after which it made the rest of the rounds. There is a belief that germs cannot live on the hot silver pipe, that it is self sterilizing. I hope that the belief is true, for the rite is as unavoidable as kissing the bride.

Maté is not unpleasant, being much like green tea, but it is an acquired taste. Uruguayans and Argentinos set much store by it and believe that it is food, drink, and vitamins all wrapped in the same package. There is a story of a besieged garrison that lived for weeks on maté alone. The story is almost certainly true but I would find it a thin diet.

Returning from the cattle market we drove to the top of the Cerro. This is the mountain from which the city got its name: Montevideo—"I see a mountain." There is an old fort there which once dominated the harbor; now it is an historical museum and Uruguay, very sensibly for a country of three million people, simply has given up competing in the military arms race. Mr. Roitman pointed out an island to us in the harbor spread before us and referred to it as the "political prison."

I jumped on the remark. "I thought this was a land of freedom? No political prisoners?"

"Oh," he said, "that is what it used to be, more than a century ago, when the Spaniards ran things. It is empty now, just a landmark."

I thought of the anti-Peronista refugees in Uruguay and looked out across the water at Argentina, invisible but close over the horizon. "Aren't you a little afraid that 'Papá' may come over someday and change all that?"

He smiled grimly. " 'Papá' would like to—but he knows we have an 'Uncle.' "

Later on that day Ticky and I were walking alone down Avenida 18 de Julio, the major shopping street. We were much surprised to hear a cheerful voice say, "Hello! You're Mr. and Mrs. Heinlein."

Facing us was a handsome young chap with a wide smile on his face. He was not one of our fellow passengers, I was fairly sure, and we knew no one in Uruguay—but his face was familiar. I shook hands while saying, "I *know* we've met you, but I can't for the life of me remember where or when."

"Don't you remember? The little dog?"

On the day before, Ticky and I had been seated in a sidewalk café in Plaza Independencia. Near us was a party of people and with them was a little butterfly spaniel bitch. Ticky offered the spaniel peanuts and a potato chip or two. The international amity established with the dog soon extended to the dog's people and we chatted between tables with them. They were a family party, father, mother, and grown son; the two men could speak English.

The encounter was most casual, hardly more than mutual agreement that Primavera was a fine doggie, yes indeed! We did exchange names with them but the chat lasted no more than five minutes; there was no intention nor expectation of following up the brief encounter. We had simply patted their dog.

I had hardly noticed the son. His mother was a woman of extraordinary beauty; my choice in such circumstances is not a choice but a reflex. I had looked at the men in the party just enough to be polite—I *hope* I was polite.

But when the young man who stopped us on the street said, "Don't you remember? The little dog?" the wheels clicked and the numbers popped up. I said, "Oh! Of course!"

Maurice Nayberg took us home with him and we stayed all afternoon, being treated in the fashion expressed by the Latin saying: "This house is yours." The hospitality of the Naybergs was the more appreciated in that it was utterly unexpected; they were under no slightest obligation to be kind to us.

We had been treated with similar open-handed friendliness by the Quirogas in Chile, again under circumstances "over and above the call of duty." Was this warmth characteristic of South America as a whole? I don't know; one certainly should not attempt to fair a curve on the evidence of two data. To do so is not scientific evaluating but mere wishful thinking. Yet a thousand other lesser data all pointed in the same direction. My horseback opinion, admittedly gathered too quickly, is and remains that the vast majority of South Americans have their hands extended in welcome to all gringos who have the gumption to see it.

A more soul-searching matter is the question as to whether our own beloved country is equally open-handed? It is difficult to give a fair opinion; I am inside it, a part of it, and it is hard for a fish to see water. Would strangers and foreigners without any sort of contact or introduction be equally likely to encounter such treatment in New York? Or in Colorado Springs?

I have pondered this and tried to be fair, turning over in my mind cases in point. We as a people are lavishly hospitable to those who come with any faint sort of introduction, granted—but do we make welcome the stranger who has none of any sort?

Yes, I think we do, provided the stranger and foreigner himself is open to it—a proviso which applies just as firmly to South America. Possibly we are a shade more shy about it but not much, not enough to matter. Certainly we are more provincial, less cosmopolitan, than they are, for the same reasons that New Yorkers are so much more provincial than are people in the rest of our country.

But the willingness and friendliness is present everywhere among us. Any foreigner who finds America "cold" had better look for the coldness in his own heart.

Is this ready hospitality, then, a characteristic of all peoples everywhere? Need the frightened boy only go through the gates of the Great City to find inside the same "kind hearts and gentle people" that he left behind him in his own village? I was ready once to assert that it was so, but I was wrong. While the trait may be potential in all humans, it is a cultural trait and some cultures do not have it. Just to nail this down see Ruth Benedict's frightening description of Dobu culture in her *Patterns of Culture*. If a Dobu offered a drink to a stranger it would be only for the purpose of poisoning him. Yet the Dobus are genetically precisely the same sort of humans as are those of certain other warm and friendly cultures around them.

But I did not change my mind through reading scientific anthropology; I had it changed for me, through visiting a country later where we were not treated with ordinary civility, much less open-handed hospitality. The experience cured me of the romantic nonsense that people everywhere are just like the folks back home. Some are not.

The delightful visit with the Naybergs ended our stay in Uruguay as the ship sailed later that day. We left bearing presents and numerous cards of introduction to persons in half a dozen other countries, for Maurice himself was in the Uruguayan diplomatic service and his father was in the import-export business; the family was well acquainted abroad. Maurice walked us down to our ship.

Perhaps, having penetrated a Uruguayan home, I should describe it; actually there is no need to do so. It was a large city flat of an upper class family and would have looked equally at home in any large city in the world. I will mention Clarita instead. She was a little pigeon hen who had had the misfortune to break her wing; Mrs. Robert Nayberg found her and nursed her back to health, then set her free. But Clarita declined to leave. Oh, she joined the other pigeons that flutter around the many monuments of the city but she roosted on the Nayberg balcony at night and spent a good deal of each day inside the Nayberg flat, visiting and making occasional messes on the floor; it was her home by her own choice.

Which showed amazing good sense for a bird brain and showed still more about the sort of people the Naybergs are.

No description should be entirely flattering; there should be some criticism at the very least, for contrast and to lend conviction to favorable statements. But it is very hard to find anything to criticize in Uruguay.

This will have to suffice: sometimes it is not possible to find a taxi down where the ships dock, in which case the visitor must walk almost half a mile to the nearest tram. Obviously this could be improved. Of course the weather will not be cold for walking and it is unlikely to be unpleasantly hot.

But it *might* be raining.

VI

Wakening Giant

BRAZIL IS LARGER than the United States by more than 300,000 square miles, by an area equal to Texas plus the State of New York. It is the largest country outside the Iron Curtain.

This chapter should be served with a side dish of superlatives, to which you could help yourself when you pleased without risking surfeit. Almost everything about Brazil is biggest, largest, longest, or greatest. In addition, after four hundred years of progress moderate to slow, the joint is jumpin' in all directions. Steel mills, factories, hydroelectric plants, oil refineries, office buildings, superhighways, airports, railways, all are going forward everywhere despite the oppressive tropical heat which prevails in so much of the country most of the time.

Although bigger than we are in area Brazil has only about a third the population we have, around 54,000,000. Nobody knows how many people the country can support. Although discovered in 1500 the country is to a considerable extent still unexplored; some of those 54,000,000 are naked Indians who have never seen a white man. The only thing we can be sure of about Brazil is that we haven't seen anything yet; it is entirely conceivable that the Brazilians may be the New Romans of the next century, just as the British were of the nineteenth century, and as we seem to find ourselves elected in this century (if the Russians do not take from us that uncomfortable honor, of course). Brazil has enormous resources of thorium ore, the world's second largest betatron, and an extremely active nuclear research program; she does not lack any potentiality for greatness and dominance.

Brazil has been successively an unknown territory awarded by the Pope to Portugal, a colony, a kingdom, an empire, and a republic. She has suffered and still suffers from political growing pains but has been fairly stable politically for some years now; it may well be that her future will be relatively free of the internal upsets that interfere with economic and social progress. Brazil was late in getting rid of human slavery (1889) yet this is a country where no color bar can be seen and black and white mix socially without tension—or so it looks to an outsider.

Because M.S. *Ruys* spent only three days at dock in Brazil Ticky and I had only opportunity to nibble at one corner of the Colossus of the South, just enough to sample it for flavor. We liked the flavor and want to go back for a full meal someday, but, as always, we were forced to hurry on if we were to get all the way around the planet. (The man who first said, "It's a small world," certainly must never have tried it; the durn thing is *much* bigger than I had ever believed.)

The ship called first at Santos, major port of the State of São Paulo, the booming Texas of Brazil. Brazilian police came aboard and required all passengers to surrender their passports for police cards before permitting them to go ashore. Ticky did not like this at all and I did not like it too well, nor do I see that it was necessary or useful since other countries get along all right without it. Nevertheless it seemed harmless since the passports were not removed from the ship but stayed in the custody of the cop on watch at the gangway. In any case if we were to go ashore compliance was inevitable; we turned in our passports.

Santos is not a tourist town and the docks are not laid out to accommodate tourist ships. There was an endless, uncomfortable, and somewhat hazardous walk along the piers, dodging cranes and trucks and railroad cars and rope slings loaded with cargo before we reached one of the guarded exits, where again our permission to go ashore had to be checked. This merely put us on the right side of the fence; there were no taxis nor any prospect of same, nor any public transportation near by. This is not a complaint, because so far as I know Santos does not advertise for visitors. In Rio, a city which does so advertise, ships tie up at the foot of their "Fifth Avenue," Avenida Rio Branco. Fair enough, both ways.

But the inconvenience does not add to the charm of Santos. After several blocks we came at last to a street with tram rails and presently were able to hop a street car. The trolleys in Santos are Toonerville affairs, dinky, open to the weather at the sides, old, and very crowded. They are a treat to ride, unless you are the sort of person who can't bear to share a taxi and would not think of using the subway; they put me in mind of the San Francisco cable cars and have much the same out-of-date charm. We lurched through narrow streets and swung wildly around corners while the conductor climbed over feet and reached over heads for fares. People swung aboard from either side and jumped off and clung to the sides and ends, all without caring whether the car was moving or stopped. I gathered the impression that the car came to a full stop only for cripples, babies, and sissy *norteamericanos*.

I do not see how the conductor managed to collect all the fares; it would be easier to fold a newspaper in a high wind. Perhaps an honor system helped him—the South Americans we met seemed painfully honest in small matters. Or perhaps he was satisfied to collect a good percentage of the fares.

All the transportation systems we encountered in Brazil were extremely crowded. This is not a criticism; I simply note a fact that is historically an unavoidable growing pain of boom times anywhere. We have not licked this problem and I do not think it can be licked. A booming, prosperous area is always one where people pour in faster than services can be built to accommodate them, which means crowds, choked subways and highways, long waits in restaurants, poor service, high prices—and an overall feeling of excitement, hope, and nervous tension.

The quiet, leisurely places of cheap servants, low prices, and *dolce far niente* are stagnant and poor; this is a law of nature and it calls for the lobster-shelled conscience of a Bourbon not to be affected by the poverty underneath.

Brazil is both of these things at once. The older pattern of extreme wealth and peasant poverty with no middle class still exists side by side with boom times, peasants streaming into the cities to find industrial jobs, and a growing middle class. The *barrios bajos* of Rio may not be the world's worst slums but they surely win dishonorable mention. They are almost vertical shanty towns, built of trash on hillsides too steep to be useful for commercial buildings; they have not even water, not even a neighborhood faucet, and of course no other services. Here many of the penniless poor from the country wind up, a reservoir of labor, and of disease, vice, and crime . . . and riot and rebellion. The government and the better-off Brazilians are striving to cure these sores, but the problem is mammoth.

But we were still back in Santos. Santos is an old city and looks it; it is necessary to get far into the outskirts to find the twentieth century. The plazas, the venerable trees in them, and the age-encrusted buildings around them look like a set for a South-of-the-Border musical comedy. The traffic and crowds of the industrial boom swarm through the old streets, a noisy affront to their sleepy, eighteenth century charm.

We took a bus from Santos to São Paulo, a bus which was as out of place in the plaza of Santos as a spaceship in a corn field, it being at least three per cent more shiny, modern, and gadgeted than the best of Greyhound and Trailways in the States. Once outside the city streets we entered a superhighway toll road straight out of *Fortune* magazine. It is of the same sort and quality as the Pennsylvania Turnpike, but here the engineers had no railway tunnels already built to help them through the tough places, of which there are plenty.

The road ran first through miles of banana plantation; the bus ate up this stretch at about ninety, vibrationless on perfect pavement. Then the road reared up and jumped at the Serra do Mar mountains; the bus eased back to seventy and zoomed up and over them, a three-thousand-foot climb in a few minutes, piercing mountains, leaping chasms. There were no hairpin turns, no bad grades, no stretches to make the timid nervous; only on looking back was one aware of the concrete spiderwebs on which we had crossed the gorges.

But one did look back. The spanking climb right up the face of the mountains produced swiftly changing, garishly dramatic vistas, unreal and improbable. The hot, water-soaked air was not perfectly transparent; we could see the ocean but not the horizon. Instead the tropical haze produced endless stereo depth on depth, a misty Land of Oz in colors too bright and miniature modeling too perfect to be convincing.

The bus plunged on into the mountains, the skyline pulled in and things came back to their proper sizes. There were signs of intense industrial activity all along the hundred or so kilometres from Santos to São Paulo, tire factories, artificial lakes for water and power, high-tension transmission line towers marching over hill and horizon. The great double road was gardened throughout its length but beyond the dedicated expanse there were many big signboards of the sort that disfigure our own roads but are not very common elsewhere in South America. I could not read them but pictures are pictures and trade names persist; I amused myself by trying to pick out the influence of the Yankee Dollar. The majority of the foreign firms appeared to be ours, with England pushing us hard in second place, and Germany a fairly strong third. The incorporations were Brazilian but the trademarks and names usually made the parent foreign corporation obvious. "Esso" was everywhere, along with "Delco" and "International Harvester" monograms and General Motors and many other heavy-industry firms from the north.

And Coca-Cola, of course—we rich barbarians have been accused of having added nothing to world culture. This is a most unfair canard; we have contributed Coca-Cola, jukeboxes, and comic books, all worldwide in scope.

I am only half joking. When the water is not safe to drink, as so often is the case abroad, and your stomach rebels at the idea of more strong coffee, strong tea, or alcohol, Coca-Cola really does offer a pause that refreshes—and you can buy it almost everywhere. As for jukeboxes, the quality of the music is up to the man who inserts the coin; the machine itself is a worthwhile accomplishment. Comic books I won't defend.

I myself am very weary of being told by scornful Europeans that we have no culture. In the first place it simply is not true, even in the snooty sense in which the sneer is usually put, as in painting, music, and literature we are lustily productive. But in the widest sense we have made the greatest cultural contribution of any society to date, by demonstrating that 160,000,000 people can live together in peace *and* freedom. Nothing else in all history even approaches this cultural accomplishment, and sneers at *our* "culture" are both laughable and outrageously presumptuous when emanating from a continent that habitually wallows in its own blood. I'll take Coca-Cola, thank you; it may be vulgar, no doubt it is simply impossibly American, it may lack the bouquet of a Continental wine—but it is not flavored with ancient fratricidal insanities.

During the trip to São Paulo I sat next to a local citizen. We chatted throughout the ride, he in Portuguese and I in English. I found Portuguese even harder to chew than Spanish, but we got along all right as his acting was more than competent. When we pulled into the outskirts of São Paulo he pointed out places associated with the emperors of Brazil and, at last, helped us off the bus and directed us to the hotel where we had been advised to have lunch. My Spanish had been no trouble to him at all; he simply thought I was speaking English the whole time.

(Only three words are necessary to travel all over South America: "*gracias*" and "*por favor*." They cover all situations.)

The parks and plazas and monuments to Emperor Dom Pedro II in São Paulo are old; practically everything else is brand new. This is the Dallas of the boom country. It has almost as many people as has Rio de Janeiro—as of 1953, that is; by today it may have more than Rio. It is bursting its britches and new construction is going on all the time and everywhere, even during Christmas holidays. It is not safe to lean against a building there; workmen may come along and yank it down, letting you fall into the excavation. But there will be a new building in its place almost at once.

We enjoyed a gourmet's lunch on the top floor of a skyscraper hotel. View windows looked out in all directions and I looked out through them. It did not look like Latin America; it looked like Chicago. São Paulo being on a plateau of almost 3000 feet elevation its climate is not as oppressively hot as is Santos; the people are exceedingly energetic. So far as we noticed there was no slow down during the traditional siesta time; they seem to have given up the afternoon nap, which seems deplorable. Progress can be overdone.

The traffic was fast and hazardous. All Latin Americans drive with courage but Brazilian drivers seem to have even more careless abandon than the others. But their conventions are much like those elsewhere in the continent and we were now somewhat used to them; there were no casualties—which was just as well; in Brazil, if a driver runs you down, he usually sues *you;* the pedestrian is not assumed to have the right of way.

We shopped along a street of smart women's shops having the unlikely name of Rua Barão de Itapetininga. I complained that I had seen the inside of every retail shop for ten thousand miles and that we might as well have settled for Denver, but it did me no good. Ticky answered that she had been dragged into every bookstore over the same route and, besides, everybody knew that the quickest way to size up how a country was getting along was to take a look at what was offered for sale there—quantity, quality, variety, and prices.

I muttered that looking was all right but if she kept up her pace she was going to ruin the economic structure of each country we visited, but she did not hear me; she was already plunging into a blouse shop, her nose quivering like a bird dog catching a scent. The shops certainly did have pretty things and the handmade blouses were among the prettiest. Ticky insisted they were "bargains" and I suppose they were. I never will understand about such things; to my mind a bargain is something I need at a price I can afford.

Somehow the *senhoras* were less intimidating than the grim, firm-bosomed females that jostle one in our own department stores. Where do those women go when the stores close?

You rarely see them (thank heaven!) anywhere else. My own intense dislike of shopping is based on a fear of being trapped on an upper floor by a mob of them; I think I suffer from a subconscious conviction that they are carnivorous.

But the *senhoras* and *senhoritas* are soft-voiced and gentle even at a stocking counter.

We had to buy some shoes. That was understandable; South American shoes do even more for the female foot than does a hot water bottle. The designs are indecently sexy. Ticky found, and bought, a pair of black high-heeled slippers the tops of which were nothing but nylon diamond-mesh. They turned bare feet into naked feet, an effect similar to that achieved by dressing a woman in opera-length black hose and a G-string.

I pointed out that if she wore them she might be arrested; she could not be nakeder if she wore nothing but the shoes because no one would look at anything but her feet—and gasp. "That is exactly the effect I want," she said smugly, "a simple, modest dress and my feet looking out in those and leering. I'll take them." She did not even ask how much they cost.

Satiated at last with shopping, we loafed for a while in a dreamy, old garden filled with fountains and birds, which is surrounded by the swarming São Paulo retail district and is near the bus station. There was time still to hire a car and a guide, but the garden was so pleasant that we decided to take for granted that São Paulo had public buildings, a race track, and points of historical interest. We knew that it had; the pamphlet we had with us told us so, but we gave them the rest of the day off and stuck with the birds and the fountains.

At last we walked slowly and reluctantly back to the bus station. The interurban station there is an extremely busy place with a bus pulling out every few seconds and a dozen loading at once; it had a population density as thick as you can get without stacking people in two layers. All seats are reserved and tickets must be bought ahead of time.

The bus for Santos has some other name, I never did find out what. I was trying unsuccessfully to buy tickets and succeeding only in holding up a queue of others equally anxious when a man came to my rescue. He had the face of a jovial hawk and about twenty words of English, which was eighteen more than I had of Portuguese. With his help I got the tickets, then he firmly kept us from getting on the wrong bus.

He stayed with us then, to keep us straight, and flipped his lapel to show some sort of shield; I understood from the gesture that he was a plainclothesman. But he was not satisfied that we understood his status. He pulled down his lower eyelid to show that he was an "eye," then pantomimed in detail the operations of a pickpocket, plus other gestures adding up to a charade that he was assigned there to protect the crowd from pickpockets.

It was clear to us and I suppose it was equally clear to any pickpocket present. But he was a most successful goodwill ambassador for his country. He kept us from getting on several more buses, put us on one at last and spoke to the driver about us, then waved us out of sight.

The run by sea from Santos to Rio de Janeiro is only overnight. The *Ruys* stood into Rio Harbor before breakfast; Ticky and I got up early and watched it from the bridge by invitation of the Captain. The regulations of every ship state that passengers are not permitted on the bridge; I have yet to be in a ship in which the master felt it necessary to enforce the rule. This was the first time Captain Verwijs had invited us and it was a treasured privilege, for Rio has the most glorious harbor in the world.

Oh, I'll admit that it is not a scientific statement; I have not seen all the harbors in the world. But in the course of some years at sea as a youngster, plus other trips since, I have seen a lot of them and I have compared notes with others who have seen the important ones I have missed. I am not counting uninhabited fjords in Norway nor anything like that; I speak of seaports. I stick by the statement and strongly doubt if anyone can be found who has seen Rio who will vote for any other harbor.

Sydney Harbor has its backers for the honor, but, while Sydney's harbor is beautiful, it is not in the same league. The approach to Seattle through Puget Sound is lovely but the Seattle roadstead is not much to see. Golden Gate has one fine view; Rio has a hundred. As for New York Harbor, the approach up Bedloe Channel is essentially ugly, despite the famous skyline and the beloved Statue of Liberty.

Rio, lovely Rio, is the one harbor without fault or blemish, a sight for travelers which cannot disappoint, a case where the glorious reality exceeds the build-up.

Provided the weather is good, of course, since the inside of one rain storm looks much like the inside of any other. We were lucky indeed to draw a golden day. I hope you are equally lucky but don't expect it; Rio has heavy rainfall right through the year.

I do not understand the geology of Rio. The bay looks like a flooded river valley among mountains, but no major stream runs into it; the principal drainage of the back country parallels the coast line behind a row of mountains and discharges a couple of hundred miles away. The land must be slowly sinking into the sea here to produce this wonderfully complicated shore line, but what accounts for the curious conoidal mountains? Are they the cores of volcanoes laid bare by eons of erosion?

If I could tuck in a souvenir picture folder at this point I would not attempt the silly task of describing Rio. On second thought I won't attempt it anyhow but will risk only brief comments. Can half a ton of blueprints and a dozen thick books of specifications convey the breath-taking beauty of a jet bomber in flight?

There are hills, mountains, inlets, points, bays, and beaches in such profusion that it cannot all be seen from any one point, even from the top of Corcovado. There is a great city spilled like gems into this three-dimensional primitive beauty. There is lush tropical jungle, rain forest, covering all but the city itself, the bay, and the hunching summits of rock.

The much-pictured Sugarloaf is only one of a dozen sugarloaf mountains here. The compass-scribed sweep of world-famous Copacabana has a dozen rivals, each unfairly overshadowed in fame by the misfortune of being too close to the one with the famous name.

I had known as everyone knows that Copacabana was backed solidly by tall buildings in a dazzling modern style designed for enjoyment of tropical climate, but I had not known that this free and generous architecture framed all the beaches and spread throughout the city. Rio looks as if it were fifty years into the future. By comparison all of our own cities look as antiquated as a rolltop desk.

The *Ruys* spent only one day in Rio, which left no time for leisurely poking around; we were forced to hire a car and a guide if we were to see as much as possible. We were not too lucky in the guide; he spoke French, Spanish, and Portuguese but only a half dozen words of English. He could point things out to us and tell us what they were but we missed the sophisticated and idiomatic discussions with which Herman enlivened Buenos Aires.

Our first impression was of overpowering, suffocating heat. If the car stopped for only a moment to let traffic change, we found ourselves panting, almost ready to pass out. We were there in their summer (late December). The records show that July averages eight degrees cooler with less than half as much rain, so July is the time of year that we plan to go back and do Rio properly. That means that we will never see Carnival in Rio, since Mardi Gras must fall either in February or the first week in March, which are even hotter than late December.

I hate to give up forever the prospect of Carnival in Rio, but I can't be gay in a steam bath. They say that Mardi Gras in Montevideo is just as much fun and the weather is ten degrees cooler. Or perhaps the trick is to roister in the streets all night and sleep all day in an air-cooled hotel room. Hmm—

Presently our guide got us out of downtown and we began to perk up. Rio is even better equipped with parks and gardens than is Buenos Aires, and tropical rain forest growing conditions make it inadvisable to poke a walking cane into the dirt—it might sprout. After a long and confusing tour of parks and plazas and public buildings we started out along the beaches, where it was so cool that it was just pleasantly warm. The beaches of Rio are so long and so wide (most of them) and so numerous that they aren't very crowded, not so much so as Laguna Beach and nothing like the solid mass of pop bottles, chewing gum, and sweaty bodies that hides the sand at Coney Island. But Australians would find the surf a little on the nice-old-lady side since the enclosed bay keeps the rollers from having room to work up much muscle.

But the sand and sea are just a sidewalk away from the hotels. The wiggly-patterned sidewalks, so conspicuous in postcards, are not limited to the Copacabana; the other beaches have them, too, and so does downtown Rio. We saw them in Santos as well. This pleasant, useless custom gives dull stretches of concrete a holiday air; I would like to meet the light-hearted gent who started it.

I noticed just one Bikini suit and only a few bare-midriff models. South Americans are a bit conservative about displaying female hide.

After the beaches we started up the Corcovado. This mountain is twice as high as Sugarloaf and is the site of the Cristo Redentor statue. We had time for one viewpoint or the other, but not both. I wanted to ride the famous cableway to the top of Sugarloaf, but Ticky gets a bit dizzy on step ladders and grew downright mutinous at the prospect of being locked in a cage and then being swung spiderlike high in the air on a string.

So we compromised her way and I did not regret the choice. The drive is spectacular and exciting. The road is very narrow, barely two cars wide, filled with hairpins and blind corners, and engineered like logging track. It leads through lovely suburban home districts, parks, and virgin tropical forest, past waterfalls and canyons that got me to thinking of Coleridge and *Kubla Khan*. I thought about them still more when we stopped at a restaurant half way up and discovered that the restaurant grounds included a labyrinth grotto that wandered almost endlessly around the mountain—an enchanted place of silence and cool moss and dim, religious light.

The climb was very steep and our ears began to pop. Ticky dug out chewing gum and gave me a piece to relieve the discomfort. We had with us the English lady with whom we had first teamed in Montevideo. She was unattached, a widow, and was good company once she was convinced that we did not sleep in our boots; we had formed the habit of inviting her to go ashore with us. Ticky now offered her a stick of gum.

She accepted it gingerly. "What do I do with it?"

"Just chew it. It will help your ears to adjust to the altitude," Ticky assured her.

"What happens if I swallow it?"

We assured her that every American child had swallowed a piece or two without any ill effects. "Chewing gum is a custom we learned from the South and Central American Indians. It's quite harmless."

I think she tried it rather than risk offending us—she was in all respects a lady. But I am not sure she liked it.

Cars cannot go quite to the top of Corcovado; there are a hundred-odd steps up to the foot of the Christ statue. We climbed them very slowly, as the heat and humidity were bad even on the mountaintop. But the view was worth a much harder climb; we had the great bay spread around us, the great city in our laps. But I balk at describing it. I can think of three city vistas in North America which deserve to be classed with it: San Francisco Bay from the Top o' the Mark, New York from the 86th floor of the Empire State Building, and Los Angeles County from Mount Wilson. The view of New York is equal in interest; none of the three is equal in beauty.

With that I will leave it. Go see it for yourself. Put it at the head of your "someday" list.

The Christ statue is impressive and huge, but as statuary it is a stylized scarecrow, not in the same class with the Christ of the Andes, which is worthy of Michelangelo. It is so posed and simplified as to appear as a cross from the city, rather than as a human shape; to that end it is very effective.

The trip down was even wilder than the trip up. Despite the long drive there was still an hour or so before we were required to be back aboard ship so we had the driver drop us on Avenida Rio Branco, the main shopping street, at the foot of which the *Ruys* was tied. Downtown Rio is not too much to my taste. Basically it is no worse than other big cities and in some respects is better, in neatness and general appearance. Rio Branco, for example, although a skyscraper canyon of a street, is edged with trees right downtown. But city crowds are bad enough at any time; in oppressive heat I find it easy to hate all humanity.

For once Ticky felt too dragged down to shop; her bounce had melted down in the heat. We looked in a few shop windows and I noticed that Rio named streets the way other South American cities did—the 1st of March intersected the 7th of September at a corner of 15th of November Square, also there was a President Woodrow Wilson Avenue, a Buenos Aires Street, and a Uruguay Street all in that one neighborhood. We saw citizens patiently lining up in queues two and three blocks long for the privilege of a seat to get out of the city at the end of a difficult day. Rio is wonderful but they should throw a dome over the whole city and air-condition it in toto—this should not be too hard for people with the energy to build this wonderland in spite of the climate.

We found the flower market, big as a general farmer's market in most cities, and saw orchids too numerous to guess the number. But we did not find a green orchid which was what we wanted. After that we looked in on one of the many fine jewelers, "H. Stern" it was. Rio is the place for amethysts, aquamarines, and topazes; they are magnificent and so cheap that samples are given away to visitors. I risked letting Ticky go in because she does not really care for most jewelry. She has simple tastes and even diamonds leave her cold; all she wants is emeralds, nice big squarecut ones—and Colombia is the place for emeralds, not Brazil.

The ship was an easy walk down the street, provided we took it slowly and avoided sunstroke. But the weather shifted gears and we made it to the ship just in time to be soaked to the skin in the last two hundred yards.

VII

The Farthest Place

THERE WAS A feeling of excitement in the *Ruys* after we left Rio, caused by the possibility that we might receive radio orders to turn aside and make an unscheduled call, a stop at the most remote port in the world.

The world is conceded to be a small place these days, with airlines straddling the oceans, with boats and trains and buses linking No Plumbing, Kentucky, to No Hope, New Zealand. No place is more than a week away from the nearest airline ticket office, plus a possible day by bus or train, or at the most three days for some South Pacific islands.

Is there any really remote place left? Behind the Iron Curtain? A political barrier, not a physical one. The North Pole? The North Pole needs traffic lights these days to keep the Russian patrol planes from bumping into our own. Antarctica? Yes, but Admiral Byrd's continent is uninhabited; I had in mind places where people live. There are a number of places very hard to reach which are unfit for human habitation; that is why there is no transportation to them. What is the most remote *settlement* in the world?

There is an Indian village in the Grand Canyon that is almost never visited by outsiders. But you can make it in two days from New York, by airline, by hired car, and by hired mule. There are pygmy villages deep in the Congo, but safari companies will outfit you and provide professional guides. One way or another almost any inhabited spot can be reached by recognized commercial means. But there is one place left on earth which has long been settled and has a recognized, established government which cannot be reached by any regular means whatever, but only through lucky chance.

It is Tristan da Cunha, a British colony in the South Atlantic, almost precisely midway between Antarctica, South America, and Africa. It is 1500 miles from the nearest land, St. Helena, a spot itself so remote that it was picked as a safe prison for Napoleon Bonaparte after he crushed out of Elba.

There is *no* way to buy a ticket to Tristan. No South Sea island is so hard to reach, so hard to leave, so far from other inhabited land. It is the most remote settled spot on this planet. The *Ruys* was being considered for a special stop there because the government meteorologist and radio operator stationed there had been waiting seven months since the end of his three-year tour of duty for opportunity to get himself, his wife, and baby back to the mainland—any mainland.

It meant adding nine hundred miles and about three days to the voyage from Rio to Cape Town, but there was opportunity to pick up fifty tons of frozen lobster tails there for Cape Town; most of the great cost of detouring a big ship could be charged against pay cargo. But the real question was whether the stop could be made at all. Tristan has no harbor of any sort. Sheer cliffs face the sea on all sides; at their feet are narrow beaches. A ship must anchor off shore and send in small boats. But dense fogs, fierce winds, and mountainous seas are common diet there and whole gales, with winds of seventy-five miles an hour or more, blow up without warning from the subarctic regions below it.

For several days after we left Rio the common subject in the ship was the latest radio weather report from Tristan da Cunha. Would the Captain risk it? Or would we turn aside and go on to Cape Town? No company agent could order him to attempt it; he must decide for himself whether the bet was worth taking— not so much risk to the ship, for a ship as big as the *Ruys* would not be risked for all the lobster tails in the South Atlantic, nor to help a family (safe where they were) to get home. The risk was something on the order of $10,000 in ship's operating costs, a fairly big gamble to take on very treacherous weather against the chance of a modest profit.

We discovered presently from radio reports that the islanders were even more excited at the prospect than we were. No ship the size of the *Ruys* had ever called there in all the history of the island. Any ship at all was a great event, but this was the greatest thing in the memory of the oldest inhabitant. The colony was preparing to welcome us in every way that they could.

About two days before we were to arrive Captain Verwijs decided to take the bet—subject to the possibility of pulling out at the last minute and accepting his losses if the weather turned sour.

We all got up early on landfall morning. The Captain must have been living right and saying his prayers; the sky was clear and brilliant, the ocean was blue and calm, Chamber of Commerce weather. Tristan was a great, flat cone in the distance, a textbook volcano. The two other volcanic rocks in the group, Nightingale and Inaccessible, both uninhabited, were on the horizon. We anchored a mile off shore opposite the one settlement—Edinburgh, known simply as "The Settlement"—in water so calm that the ship did not roll at the hook and so clear that we could see schools of fish twenty, thirty, fifty feet down.

The Chinese crew, all who were not on duty, promptly dropped lines out of every porthole on the lower decks. The Chinese ran their own mess and were paid their rations by the company in cash; they fished at every opportunity. But this was something extraordinary; a hook hardly had time to get wet. Shortly passengers joined in the sport—if it can be called sport to get a large bucketful of fish in a few minutes.

The entire able-bodied adult male population of Tristan swarmed aboard. There are only two hundred and seventy-six men, women, and children in the colony; about eighty of these are men old enough and young enough to handle pulling boats in the surf. The oldsters, the youngsters, and the women had to be content with a view of the wonder ship from afar.

They had a rummage-sale appearance in their dress; store-boughten clothes are scarce and precious on the island. Most of them wore home-knitted long heavy white woolen stockings and home-made leather moccasins. A few had shoes for such special occasions. Save for their footgear they looked like anyone else.

But their manner was different. The difference is hard to describe without sounding snottily supercilious since "child-like" is the word that comes most easily to mind. But they are not childlike, not morons, not savages, but they are people who have been out of touch with the rest of the human race, save for rare visits from passing ships, for generations.

Their isolation would have been only a little more nearly perfect had their ancestors moved to Mars. Whatever the nineteenth and twentieth centuries have done to us has not been done to them. Wars, psychoanalysis, mass production, traffic, atomics, Marxism, airplanes, female emancipation, Hollywood, Kaiserism, suffragettes, paved roads and automobiles, market crash and depression, Sex Appeal and "It" girls, ENIAC— these things *never happened*.

We are closer to Benjamin Franklin than we are to these people. Although the good doctor was born two and a half centuries ago and knew none of the things listed above, he was up to his ears at all times in the same continuing struggle we are now in, whereas these islanders seceded from it. They have come very close to resigning from the human race, both culturally and biologically; they have been a separate breed and a separate culture for more than a century.

It was very hard for us to talk with them. We shared the same language, English, and their accent and idiom was not as difficult for American ears as, for example, Yorkshire; what we lacked was common experience. A detective in São Paulo could tell us, without language, that he was watching for pickpockets; we both knew what pickpockets were. We shared with the detective a common culture, Western and urban; lack of language was a mere nuisance to be circumvented.

But with these islanders, although our language included theirs (their vocabulary is, for obvious reasons, quite limited), there was very little that could be said with it. We could ask direct questions about simple things—boats, sheep, weather, potatoes, fish. They would answer, readily enough, in simple declaratives—and there the conversation would bog down. Discussion was out of the question.

Chief Repetto, the headman of the island, had arranged for boats to take us ashore. The Captain had not granted permission for this and, while we awaited his pleasure, the breakfast call was sounded. As the islanders had not eaten either, some of the passengers took them in to breakfast as guests; Ticky and I took the headman to our table.

It was a painful meal, at least for us. We tried to bridge the strangeness with social chit-chat, but it was impossible. When I found myself asking for the third time how many people there were on the island, I gave up. But I do not think that Chief Repetto was shy and I think he enjoyed himself—I hope he did. The islanders seldom have meat to eat; the breakfast menu of the *Ruys* was rather lavish, including ham, bacon, several sorts of sausage, and a variety of cold cuts. The Chief started at the top of the page and ate stolidly down to the bottom, neglecting nothing.

To the disappointment of all of us word came from the Captain after breakfast refusing permission for passengers to go ashore. I felt a sharp pain in the pocketbook: the loneliest island looked like a sure-thing slick-magazine article provided I could get ashore and take a few pictures. But the Captain expressed his regrets and explained that his decision was forced by the necessity of being ready to up-anchor and run, with no delay, in case of a shift in the weather . . . to which we had no logical counter argument.

So we spent the time trying to talk with the islanders and bought stamps from them (it was the first day of their first issue) and watched the loading of cases of lobster tails and gazed at the village through binoculars and fished. The lobsters were loaded from a little steamer whose masthead barely came up to the level of our forward welldeck. This vessel itself was used to ferry the catch to Cape Town when no larger ship was available, but it was easy to see why the meteorologist and his family had waited; she was larger than a soup tureen but not much—utterly unsuited for a woman and baby. I misdoubt the lobsters got seasick.

Eight-power glasses brought the village up to within a city block. The houses looked all much alike, one-story buildings of big, shaped lava blocks with thatched roofs. The thatch is New Zealand flax, which grows on the island. The dwellings were local-material equivalents of sod houses or of log cabins, one step ahead of a cave. But I did see the glint of glass in some windows.

The Administrator from the British Colonial Office, the Honorable Mr. J. P. L. Scott, was aboard; when he was through with his official duties I cornered him and quizzed him. He is the government, "The Law West of Pecos," "—the cook and the captain, bold, and the mate of the *Nancy* brig, and a bosuntight and a midshipmite and the crew of the captain's gig." He is the postmaster, the chairman of the council, the recorder, the tax collector, the port captain, the magistrate, and anything else which requires the attention of Her Majesty. His job as magistrate is not onerous; there is no crime.

The islands were discovered in 1506 by Tristão da Cunha. For three centuries they were visited only occasionally, but in 1811 one Joseph Lambert, an American citizen, claimed them as his personal empire (and sealing station); he published his claim and designed a flag. Offhand his claims seem as valid as any other in history and less presumptuous than most. This left-handed American occupation came to an end in 1816, when the British established a garrison there to keep the islands from being used as a base from which to rescue Napoleon. Only one of Lambert's colony was left at the time; Lambert himself had drowned in a sealing accident.

The British pulled out the garrison the next year, but Corporal William Glass got permission for himself, his wife and two children, and two sailors to stay on; this started the present colony. Over the years a few others joined them, including some women from St. Helena, but the colony grew mainly by natural increase; even today there are only seven family names on Tristan. Mrs. Glass did her part by having fourteen more children, a fact less surprising in view of the very limited recreational facilities.

The soil is poor and, while rainfall is adequate, the bad weather and high winds are no help; potatoes have always been the only crop they could rely on. Even that sometimes failed, or was devastated by rats or caterpillars; many times they have been close to starvation. The British government regarded the islands as unfit for occupancy and more than once tried to get them to accept relocation. But they won't go; they like it there despite the material hardships. Perhaps in view of the mess the rest of us are in and the prospects facing us their attitude is not really cracked.

Fish, potatoes, and birds' eggs collected on Nightingale are their only important foods; sheep and oxen are considered too valuable to slaughter. Of recent years attempts have been made to grow fruit trees but nothing much has come of it as yet. The biggest change has come since the War, through the establishment of the lobster-packing plant. The "lobsters" are our west coast lobster, or spiny crayfish; not the true lobster of Maine. You are probably now buying their lobsters, packed as "Union of South Africa" for the company is a Cape Town company. This company employs all of the men part time and for the first time in its history cash money is coming into Tristan, making it possible for them to buy things made in the outside world. Possibly this is the thin wedge that will eventually place Tristan on the map, join it by regular service to the outside world. Possibly—though it has not as yet; lobsters can be sure of a berth; a traveler cannot.

The Cape Town company has hired an agronomist and a doctor for the islanders. The agronomist has a real job cut out for him to find ways to grow something other than potatoes, but doctor would appear to have a sinecure. There is almost no disease, except colds picked up from passing ships, and it is customary to die of old age in the eighties or nineties. They don't need a dentist—perhaps there is fluorine in the water; I could not find out.

Although the company has been bringing some cash wages into the island for the past four years they are still painfully short on clothes and beg for cast-offs from passing ships. The Administrator is trying to break them of this habit; nevertheless many of us in the *Ruys* contributed. I had some shirts I did not like anyway and Ticky somewhat tearfully parted with her honeymoon suit—years out of style and useless on this trip, but which she had kept and fetched along for sentimental reasons (and partly to prove that she was still as slender as ever; Ticky is a fine piece of aerodynamic design). She dug out some shoes for them, too, having just stocked up in South America. I could not spare any, nor would mine fit anyone else; my feet aren't mates.

We stood out of there late in the afternoon and set course for Cape Town. Some of the Chinese had purchased two baby penguins from the islanders; in the course of the voyage it was needful to teach them how to walk. A baby penguin is not hatched knowing how, any more than a human baby knows how instinctively. The process is much alike for both types of babies—hold out your arms and say, "Come to Papa!"

Whereupon the baby penguin tries his earnest baby best to oblige, flapping his tiny stub wings and hopping manfully in a two-footed hop like a choir boy in a sack race. I laughed until I had pleurisy—and wanted to cry, too; the infant was so willing about it and so serious.

Penguins are very nice people and they don't mean to be funny. A baby penguin is funnier than an adult by inverse square ratio. They feel nice, too; their hairlike feathers feel like soft, warm fur. At that age they are not yet oily and have not acquired the full fishy fragrance that makes the adults something to stay upwind from.

Albatrosses, about six of them, joined us at Tristan and followed us for two thousand miles. So far as I could see not one of them ever flapped a wing the whole distance. They sail without effort, at twenty or thirty knots, rising much higher than the masthead, dipping down to the water for a fish or some tasty garbage, rising again to any height, all without apparent exertion of any sort—just willpower, personality, and clean living.

The albatross is deceptively large. I mistook the first one I saw for a gull, having nothing to judge it by—I suppose the best way to see how big one is would be to hang it around the neck of an ancient mariner. They have been measured up to twelve feet in wingspread, more span than the condor, largest of the flying birds. A little cross-eyed triangulation enabled me to estimate that those following us ranged eight to ten feet in spread, once I got it through my head that they were big and then waited for a chance to see one between me and part of the rigging. On another occasion one made a crash landing in the swimming pool of the *Ruys* and could not get out. He crowded the pool all by himself and almost beat the boatswain to a pulp before he could be evicted.

Ticky worried greatly over how the albatrosses would get back home, since no ship would be going that way. (We had concluded that their miraculous powers of levitation were based on the thermals raised by the ship itself.) I pointed out that albatrosses had managed all right for thousands of years before men got around to sailing the oceans. But she refused to be reassured: those poor birds were *lost,* and somebody ought to do something about it.

The meteorologist's baby daughter enjoyed the trip back; she was a cute little carrottop and a favorite with everyone. But her mother had a very bad time of it. After nearly four years' unworldly peace and quiet of Tristan she found the *Ruys* (which is really a very quiet place itself) almost unbearably noisy and exciting. The change was too sudden and the poor woman had to spend most of her time in her room.

The rest of us were driving her to distraction.

VIII

The Country With a Problem

Lived a Woman Wonderful . . .
. . . Neither Simple, Kind, nor True—
South Africa: Kipling

OF ALL THE countries we were in the Union of South Africa was the most difficult to evaluate.

It is a wonderful country, a glorious country. We liked everything about it—except the race problem. Which is like liking the Pacific Ocean except for the water in it.

South Africa is a paradise where you expect to wake up some morning with your throat cut. By comparison, our own racial problems are trivial and ninety per cent solved. Before some colored compatriot of mine, smarting under the wrongs of generations, jumps down my throat, let me add that I *know* that the ten per cent remains to be done, should be done, must be done, but let me point out that the ambition of every literate black man in South Africa is to emigrate to Birmingham, Alabama, or some place else in our Deep South, where he can be among his own kind and still enjoy freedom.

He stands no chance at all of realizing this modest ambition. Carefully contrived laws and rigid customs make it next to impossible for a black man to save enough money to escape. His gross earnings as a farmhand are about twenty-five cents a day; as a contract laborer in industry, in the mines or factories,

151

wages run from twenty-five cents to around sixty cents a day— about what a Pullman porter gets as a single tip.

Apartheid, translated literally as (racial) apartness, is the most pervasive single fact about South Africa. But it is much more than Jim-Crowism, or simple segregation; as legislated by Dr. Malan's Nationalist Party it means that a native must either live in a reservation or indenture himself to a white man; if he shows up in town without a work card he is liable to prosecution.

It means no voice in government, almost no chance for education, no hope for the future. If the native reserves, which are vast in area, were decent land, the system might be defended, but they are not. Only about seven per cent of South Africa is good arable land; the white man has it and the native has been assigned rocky, hilly, dry and almost unusable acreage that the Afrikander does not want. Almost the only way a black farmer can get decent land is by hiring out to a white farmer; then the white man lets him till a little piece of it for himself.

If a native youth refuses to go along with the cheap-labor racket, his position is hopeless; he can never buy oxen, he can never pay for a wife. So he signs up.

It is a legal system to enslave an entire race, without placing on the bosses the personal responsibility for the slaves entailed by chattel slavery. The South African native is neither a free man nor a chattel and he has the privileges of neither.

The Nationalist Party is not a majority party, but it stays in power through an entirely legal rotten-borough system similar to that which obtains in the California State Senate whereby a farmer's vote counts for more than that of a city dweller. In general the Nationalist Party is Afrikander while the Unionist Party is English just as most of the farmers are of Dutch descent and most of the city folks are of English descent. But it is most unlikely that more than a handful of the opposition party could be found which did not favor some form of racial discrimination. Looked at coldly, their reasons for this stand can be understood, for, no matter what might be or what should be, the vast majority of the natives are still illiterate savages. The South African white man who does not believe in Dr.

Malan's brand of *apartheid* nevertheless believes that if the native were given his full rights as a human being overnight, the white men would be swallowed up.

There are other approaches, of course. Up in the Belgian Congo a black man can work hard and become an *evolvé,* a man with a certificate which makes him a statutory white, entitled to the same wages, entitled to live in white neighborhoods, entitled to place his children in white schools, even entitled to marry a white woman if he can manage it. All of these things are utterly prohibited in South Africa.

I am not arguing in favor of the *evolvé* system, as I never saw it in action. I give it as an illustration of the fact that there are middle ways between the extreme of *apartheid* and the other extreme—an extreme which the Nationalist always cites to prove that *apartheid* is necessary and unavoidable . . . when in fact it is neither one; it is an inhuman racket for the exclusive benefit of the white man.

On the other hand, do not be misled by the crocodile tears of Mr. Nehru; the very worst exploiters of the black man are the Hindus. The only real public disorder modern South Africa has known was when the natives turned on the Hindus and tried to chuck them back into the Indian Ocean. If South Africa were opened wide to the hordes of India the black man would not stand a prayer. As it is, world opinion and the more liberal elements among the South African whites may eventually force an improvement in his lot—though it looks hopeless today.

"Americans don't know how to deal with natives"—(or "coolies," "niggers," "Chinese," "boys"). So the British have blandly told us and so also have the other breeds who have held colonial empires. But the fact is that we are the only dominant people on earth who *do* know how to deal with the human beings designated by the above disparaging terms. *Proof:* when we inherited the Filipino from Spain, we promised him forty years of education and help, then full and unconditional freedom; we made good our promise. Whereupon, when we needed him, he fought for us and with us, and is now our staunch ally and friend.

Compare this record with Indonesia, with Burma, with India, with Kenya, with Indo-China, with South Africa itself. The Hollander can hardly get a visa to the country he once proudly called "Holland in the East," the Englishman in Kenya sleeps with his rifle in his bed, South Africa is as yet free of "incidents" on any large scale but every South African knows that the natives are waking and listening and stirring, aware of Mau Mau to the north. It spoils the white man's sleep; it makes him careful to lock every door, every room, every cupboard; it makes him install flood lights around his beautiful Johannesburg home. It makes him very cautious on the streets of his own city at night.

He knows he is sitting on a powder keg, but he does not like to talk about it. He prefers to talk about how you must "handle the natives," how you "mustn't spoil them."

These "pukka sahib" laddies who know so much about "how to treat natives" fail to see the native as an individual. In the *Ruys* the South African passengers thought it was funny, ridiculous, a bit bad for our face really, for Ticky and I to bother to know the names of the Chinese crew members with whom we came in daily contact. Many of them (I inquired) did not even know the names of their own room stewards—said names being posted on little cards outside each stateroom door. As for the barmen or deck boys, they would whistle and shout, "Hey! Charlie!"

This attitude applied even more strongly to the Dutch officers. The Dutch once had the worldwide reputation of being the perfect colonials . . . until the Indonesians chucked them out. An engineering officer in the *Ruys* told me that he did not know the name of a single Chinese among his own engineroom watchstanders; he simply knew which one was "Number One" through whom he bossed the others, nor did he know "Number One" by name. I inquired further and found that most of the Dutch officers did not know the names of their own room servants, although in some cases they had been waited on by the same Chinese for several voyages.

We sat successively with three Dutch officers in the course of the trip. As is usual aboard ship the same waiters would serve a table meal after meal, day after day. Yet the Dutch officers who sat with us seemed to find it amusingly odd, somehow undignified, and a rather startling exhibition of memory that Ticky and I always knew the names of the waiters.

They failed to notice that we got better and quicker service than they did, even better than the Captain got.

Of course, we weren't doing anything odd for Americans; I am not pinning a rose on myself. The usual run of American, if he eats twice in the same restaurant and draws the same waitress, will find out her name and call her by it thereafter. He may find out her name the first time, even if he expects never to eat there again, simply because he dislikes shouting, "Hey, you!" If he is served regularly by the same waitress or waiter he is certain to know the name.

This common American habit is not in itself democratic; it is just horse sense. I have emphasized it because, while it is a minor matter to us, simply good manners and convenience, it is a major, important, even crucial difference between us and most other Western white nations. Hell's bells, even a dog is easier to handle if you call him by name! Why can't these lunkheads see that?

The most important possession of any man is his own name. Without a name he has no face. The white man in the East has always emphasized the importance of keeping face himself, but he seems to have given little thought to the deadly danger of not giving face to natives.

In most other ways the South African white (or "European" as he always calls himself) is a remarkably pleasant fellow— jovial, sociable, warm, not at all distant with strangers, being much more like us than they are like the English in this respect. They tend to be somewhat anti-American in general, but not toward individual Americans. This anti-American attitude seems to derive first from a belief that we are stirring up a third world war (they have swallowed the Moscow line on that point), on a dislike for us as business competitors, and a generalized nationalism—South Africans are among the most nationalistic people in the world. They seem to dislike the

English even more than they dislike us and speak of the day when they will divorce themselves from England completely—not "if," but "when."

This xenophobia takes the curious form with the Afrikander South African of tending to be a little surly with those who speak English instead of Afrikaans. The country is officially bilingual but a civil servant will be a lot more civil if addressed in Afrikaans—but he will be just as difficult about it with an English-speaking fellow citizen as with a foreigner.

This clinging to a national language spoken by no one else anywhere (Afrikaans is *not* Dutch, just as Pennsylvania Dutch is not German; it is a highly bastardized dialect derived from Dutch), this insistence on Afrikaans, is perhaps the most cross-grained symptom of their neurotic nationalism. Afrikaans is a language unnecessary and useless. It is spoken by less than two million people practically all of whom speak English as well—and English is spoken by more than a half billion people on this planet. It has no tradition worthy of the name, it has little literature; to use it for science or technology requires borrowing all the technical words from some other language. It requires almost everything in South Africa to be printed twice; it requires wasted years of study to acquire a second daily language, when the time could be spent learning Spanish or German. It has no use at all save to shut out the rest of the world.

Which is exactly what many South Africans, most particularly the Afrikanders, want to do.

Many of them want to make South Africa self-sufficient in all respects; the policies of the present government are aimed at making the country independent both in food and in manufactured goods. They still would like to sell, but they don't want to buy anything if they can possibly help it, and aside from the regrettable necessities of trade they wish the rest of the world would go away and forget to come back. Clinging to a language which no one else can talk makes it easier for them to maintain this attitude. Psychiatrists have a name for this symptom when exhibited by individuals.

But since they still need dollar exchange they advertise heavily in our country to attract American tourists, then their real feelings toward outsiders show up in making it exceedingly difficult for a tourist to be admitted. We ran into this same curious ambivalence in two other small, nationalistic and suspicious countries: Indonesia and New Zealand—plead for tourists, then treat them like convicts being processed.

Despite everything, it is an extremely pleasant country to visit—if your skin is the approved color. Cape Town is English in the very nicest sense, Durban is much like Florida, Johannesburg is like a boom city in Texas. The Johannesburgers show an American enthusiasm for the new, the big, the different, and the expensive; they speak of how much things cost and of the big operations they are in with the unashamed candor of a Texan or a Hollywood movie producer—they are so un-English that it is a bit of a shock to run across a cricket field there.

But most of all, the beauty of South Africa makes one gasp.

The *Ruys* was a very sociable ship, particularly with the South Africans aboard. There was a party of some sort almost every night; the ladies dressed for dinner and most of the men did, too, either in evening clothes or summer whites. On New Year's Eve there was, of course, an especially big party.

I was away from the ballroom floor for a few minutes to replace a dress shirt that I had melted down. When I returned, a tall, handsome man was kissing my wife. Gathered in his left arm was a plump blonde, apparently a reserve.

When Ticky was able to talk she said, "Dear, I want you to meet Sam."

Sam stuck out a hand—a third one, I think—and shouted, "Hi, Bob! Have a drink! It's my birthday." He was red-faced and his shirt had melted down, too, but he did not seem to care. There were three silver ice buckets each with a magnum on a table by him; I congratulated him, sat down, and started sopping up champagne. Sam sat down with us for a moment, then got up hastily. "I missed one! Be right back—" He dashed across the room, grabbed another female, and bussed her.

He ran down the whole female, first-class passenger list, plus the stewardess—who was not the usual old biddy, but should have been on an airline. I poured more of his champagne and hoped that there was no trench mouth aboard.

This was how we happened to drive across South Africa.

Sam invited us to do so with him about ten minutes later. The next morning it appeared that he had not forgotten it and really meant it. For the remainder of the trip to Cape Town we were bombarded with advice from other South Africans not to do so; according to them the Karoo Desert through which we would drive was unbeautiful, uninteresting, and unbearable in the summer; we would be hot, dirty, miserable, and bored—take an old hand's advice, son, and take the Blue Train, or fly.

At last I got a little huffy about it and told one of them that we would go with Sam if we had to walk, dragging our sled behind us; he had *invited* us, damn it, and that was more than anyone else had done! It shut up the talk but did not change their minds.

They were wrong. We enjoyed every mile of it.

We arrived in Table Bay early in the morning, as usual, and with the customary morning-after malaise from the Captain's Dinner of the last night. Even so, I found it possible to second Sir Francis Drake's logbook entry of 1580: "This cape is a most stately thing, and the fairest cape we saw in the whole circumference of the earth." The Cape of Good Hope is as lovely as its name.

Table Mountain, sitting over Cape Town and Table Bay, is a separate sight, some miles to the north of the Cape. The Table is a pleasing sight, but it is an ordinary mesa or butte, made exceptional by being the only one of its sort in the neighborhood, instead of being scattered around in quantity, New Mexico style. It forms a splendid background for an unusually lovely city.

My own first glimpse of South African life was of stevedores on the dock. They were resting and playing a finger matching game—a game which I had played the same way in school as a boy, which is pictured in murals in ancient Pompeii, which is played also by the Australian aborigines, and by Hawaiians half a world away from Cape Town. This may have some great anthropological significance; for myself I was simply delighted with the odd fact.

We were processed with exasperating slowness. It was long past lunch time before we were through customs. The customs examination was not outstandingly lengthy itself and we had Sam with us to smooth the way; the only mild hitch came over cigarettes. We had taken ashore the number which the regulations appeared to permit free of duty, but somehow we were wrong. I never did understand just how we were wrong, but it may have been that a single customs return for husband and wife was allowed one exemption, not two. In any case I was told to pay duty on half the cigarettes we were taking in for our personal use and I did so; the duty amounted to a hundred per cent.

In the mean time Ticky was poking me in the ribs and urging mutiny. Her ultra-free soul had already been tried that morning by some exceptionally silly immigration questions. "Don't pay it!" she whispered, loud enough to be heard back on the ship. "Tell him to go to the Devil! If they don't like it, we'll go back aboard and not spend a damn cent in their confounded country. We aren't even asking to take enough in to last us through— it's an outrage!"

The cost was not much but with Ticky it is always the principle of the thing—mere expense never fazes her. I hurriedly promised to skin her alive and sell her pelt and hustled her out of there. Sam and I closed in on her from both sides and marched her away while the customs officers pretended not to hear and looked smugly pleased. We found a taxi and headed up town.

The plan was to pick up Sam's car, load all baggage in it, then see Cape Town. Departure into the desert would be made at sunrise the next morning. We would sleep aboard ship, as there were no hotel rooms to be had in Cape Town, it being the tail end of the holidays. In fact there were no train or plane reservations to be had for the same reason; had we not stuck with Sam's offer we would never have been able to cross Africa while the ship went the long way around the coast.

Sam lived in Johannesburg and had left his car in the company garage of the Cape Town firm he represented in the north. We drove out to the plant and Sam left us with one of the company officers while he got his car. This gentleman was affable but I at once ran into something which seems to me to characterize the odd attitude of South Africans toward Americans. This man, whom I shall call "Mr. Smith"—he was not an Afrikander—said to me, "New York is filled with gangsters, eh?"

I silently cursed Hollywood for the distorted impression of the U.S. given to the world by the movies and answered as quietly as I could, "Why, no, I wouldn't say so. Most of that sort of trouble died out with the repeal of Prohibition."

Mr. Smith looked startled and said, "You misunderstood me. I meant the businessmen in New York."

It seemed to be an unanswerable remark. Sam arrived with his car at that point and saved me from having to cope with it. But I asked him about it once we were out of earshot. "What did he mean?"

"Oh, that—" Sam frowned and answered, "Nothing, really. It's just an expression. It means a man who is a good bargainer, aggressive. Almost a compliment."

"It did not sound like one."

"Well . . . some people aren't very tactful."

I shut up as Sam obviously did not like the subject. But I do not think the term was complimentary; I think it was a smear name used so habitually by them about us that "Mr. Smith" forgot himself. From this and other remarks I reached the conclusion that the notion that Americans are all gangsters in business matters is something that "everybody knows" in South Africa.

I am not an economist and I certainly shall not attempt to psychoanalyze an entire nation. But one does notice attitudes and there is always the itch to try to understand why. I confess that with respect to South Africa I could never figure out why . . . why the United States was regarded with a mixed aggressive-defensiveness.

The reasons why we aren't liked in many nations are fairly obvious and have been discussed too often to warrant rehashing here, but none of the usual reasons seem to apply in South Africa. The Union of South Africa is not even faintly communist, so that cannot be the source. "Dollar Imperialism" does not seem to be the trouble; while we have a little money invested there, you will not find American trade names spread around and American businessmen are conspicuous by their absence. We certainly have not displaced South Africa from world leadership, nor has South Africa experienced the sour taste of gratitude, either during or after the War—her role was more like our own, on a smaller scale.

It is true that we are the main bulwark (perhaps the only one) between them and conquest by Moscow, but they certainly do not seem to be aware of it, so they can hardly dislike us for that.

One remark we did hear repeatedly; someone would say that he would like to buy this or that, made in America, or would like to travel in America, but "—we can't get the dollars, you know." This remark was always delivered accusingly, as if it were the fault of the United States and of this American, myself, in particular.

We tried to point out that American goods were very nearly forbidden entrance to the Union by embargolike restrictions placed by South Africa itself; we got nowhere. As for dollars for travel in the States I pointed out that there was an open-market quotation for South African pounds on the New York market; their money was acceptable.

This last was greeted with a shake of the head. "Oh, no! Currency restrictions, you know. We can't get the dollars."

The currency restrictions are entirely those imposed by South Africa, not by us—but it is true that South Africans are not permitted to take outside enough money for much travel. (When was the last time you met a South African tourist in the States?) This is an odd status for the nationals of the world's biggest gold producer. South Africa mines over half a billion dollars in raw gold each year, almost half of the free world's supply and enormously more than we produce. Yet her gold reserves are small, her national debt is very large (proportionately about the same as ours), and her currency is "soft" and is kept near par by drastic exchange regulations.

The conventional answer is that they are helping England, an answer I don't understand as there is no love lost between Dr. Malan's government and England. The conventional solution offered by South Africans is that it is up to the United States to do something about about it, to wit, devalue the dollar.

I was first tackled on this subject as soon as I boarded the *Ruys;* a Johannesburg businessman and financier asked me how soon I thought the United States intended to raise the price of gold? I answered in some surprise that I did not know it was in the wind.

He seemed startled at my answer and made it clear that he thought it was a certainty; the question was when? Later I heard him discussing my answer with another Johannesburger; my answer seemed to worry both of them.

This subject came up again some weeks later with an entirely different group of South Africans. Ticky and I were invited to have a drink with this group; the moment we were seated we were tackled bluntly and aggressively: "Why doesn't your country buy our gold production at sixty dollars an ounce?"

The tone was truculent; I could see that I was already accused, tried and convicted. But Ticky took over. "Why *should* we?"

"Eh? It's obvious. You can't expect us to buy your goods if you won't buy our gold."

"We *do* buy your gold . . . all of it you offer to sell, at thirty-five dollars an ounce."

"But you ought to pay more. You ought to pay sixty dollars an ounce."

We had heard this a wearisome number of times; Ticky rapidly reached her flash point. "Why should we? You wouldn't buy our goods if we did so; you've rigged your laws to shut us out. What sense is there in digging gold out of Johannesburg, us paying you sixty dollars an ounce—and then sticking it back in the ground in Fort Knox? What's sensible about that? If you don't like the gold price of the dollar, why don't you keep your gold and go on the gold standard yourselves? Then you could set the value of your pound at anything you wanted to and it would be hard money, at least as hard as the dollar. You could buy anything you wanted with it anywhere. That's all it takes; just quit complaining about the price of the dollar and go on the gold standard yourself!"

There was a shocked reply amounting to, "Oh, no, we couldn't do anything like *that!*"—as if Ticky had said something in terribly bad taste. No counter argument was offered and the group broke up with considerable chilliness on both sides.

I know that Ticky is not much of a theoretical economist and neither am I, but it does seem to me that there was more hard sense to her side of the argument than to theirs. I am not going to go into a discussion of the merits, demerits, and effects of devaluation, inflation, etc.—but I can't see anything in their argument but greed. It seems to me, too, to be a greed that is utterly reckless of the consequences on others; I may be wrong but I suspect that sudden devaluation of the dollar at a time when all other currencies are keyed to it might set off the biggest crash in history.

But this curious delusion that we are deliberately and wrongfully withholding their lollipop, from sheer meanness when we know better, may be the key to the oddly ambivalent attitude that we ran into all through South Africa. They have cast Uncle Sam simultaneously in the roles of Santa Claus and of the Devil.

After we left the factory of Sam's firm he dropped us downtown; we set out to do some sightseeing. Time being limited I hired a taxi—a licensed guide and tour car seemed unnecessary since it was an English-speaking city. Taxis park in the middle of the street in Cape Town; I located one and asked the driver for a rate by the hour.

There was no rate by the hour, only by the mile . . . so I told him what we wanted to do and asked approximately how much it would cost by the hour. His answer indicated that we would probably cover twenty to thirty miles in city driving in an hour, which seemed reasonable, so I hired him, telling him to drive us around the city and point out the sights to us.

Thereafter we got just one piece of "information" out of him; I asked him how many people there were in Cape Town. He said that he did not know exactly but it was somewhere between eight and nine million. I did not argue but contemplated the beauty of it. Cape Town is actually a little over half a million and looks smaller, as much of the city is spread out down the Cape peninsula in formerly independent communities. The downtown part in front of Table Mountain has a lazy, sleepy quality more suited to a much smaller community and the suburbs are garden villages—the whole city is lovely.

Our driver immediately thereafter lost all command of the English language. Instead of driving us inside the main city he hunched over his wheel and tooled his car out into open country as quickly as possible; once on the open road he stepped his speed up to about sixty or better and held it there. Protests had no effect.

Having dinner in mind, I had set a time limit of two hours; he delivered us back into town and to the gangway of the *Ruys* exactly on time—having accomplished the maximum mileage possible without fatal accident. I paid the exact amount without a tip. But I was unable to be really angry at the trick he had played on us; by pouring on the gas and running up the mileage he had managed to take us all around Table Mountain and far down the Cape on a tour which we had reluctantly decided to forgo through lack of time. As it was we saw almost everything usually covered in a leisurely full-day tour.

But the scenery certainly whizzed past.

What we could see of it looked good. There are beautiful homes and gardens in the hills back of Table Mountain, fine bays and beaches and impressive formations, in particular the Twelve Apostles on the Marine Drive down toward Hout Bay on the Atlantic side; these are a dozen rugged mountain bastions facing the sea which might be apostles or anything else but are worth seeing. As we swung across the peninsula to return we had our first view of the Indian Ocean.

On our way back to the ship we passed a Dutch windmill, a relic of early colonial days. Many of the houses in Cape

Town show Dutch gables, a particularly ungraceful architectural conceit which is loved uncritically by the local gentry for its historical associations. Cape Town was originally settled by the Dutch as fortress and revictualing station for their ships sailing to the Indies; it was not intended to be a colony at first. It changed hands several times but the principal settlers were Dutch burghers and their slaves. As a result of the Napoleonic Wars the English moved in and hung on; freeing of the slaves, the famous Voortrek north, the creation of new states, the Boer War, and today an independent nation muttering about seceding from the Commonwealth all followed the advent of the British almost as historic necessities. It would be a deceptive over-simplification to say that the Afrikanders hated the British for freeing the slaves and are still sullenly determined, a hundred and twenty years later, to hang onto slavery—but this abstraction has an element of truth in it.

We arranged with the night steward in the *Ruys* to be called at four A.M.—a horrid hour—and asked could we *please* have coffee, or at least tea. A few minutes after we were called there came a knock at our stateroom door and there was, not the night duty man, but the incomparable Kwai Yau, bearing a big tray. He had decided that we should not start off without a proper breakfast and had gotten up even earlier than we had to prepare it for us. If Kwai Yau were not about forty-five, with a home and family in Hong Kong, I would like to adopt him.

So we started out feeling merely a bit short on sleep instead of feeling three days drowned. It was not necessary to go through customs (which was not open then anyhow) since our baggage was all ashore; we merely had to present our gate passes and breeze on through. The early morning was chilly even though it was midsummer, January; Ticky had worn a coat. I had seen without noticing that she looked a bit lumpy in it.

Once outside the guarded gate she began shedding cigarettes. She had tucked packs of them all over her person; the number totaled exactly the number we had been required to pay duty on the day before. I looked on helplessly, then turned to

Sam. "We seem to have a smuggler. Want to turn around and turn her over to the guard?"

Sam grinned and answered, "No time this morning. Some other time."

"I am *not* a smuggler!" Ticky insisted. "This is just the legal amount that I was entitled to, only you let 'em gyp us."

"Look, darling, the law is what the local authorities say it is, not what you decide it is."

"I wasn't going to let them clip us!"

"Why in the name of habeas corpus would you risk jail for a few shillings? You wouldn't like the food. If I ever get you safely back aboard the *Ruys* I'm going to put a collar on you and chain you to your bunk!"

She stuck out her lower lip and said nothing, so the discussion ended. Deep in my heart I felt the same way about it she did, but it is not good to encourage lawlessness in Ticky; she is too ready to slug policemen at any time. The spirit of anarchy on which our country was founded shows gene reinforcement in her . . . if it is a genetic factor, as I strongly suspect it is.

We passed the statue of Jan van Riebeeck, founder of Cape Town, and headed across the sand flats that connect the peninsula with the mainland. Along here are slums, shanties called *pondokkies* lived in by "Capies" or Cape Town mixed-bloods. Cape Town itself seems to have no slums, for the reason that the natives and the "coloureds" live outside. This is a standard South African pattern; near every white city is a dreadful place called a "location" assigned to non-Europeans, where they may live out of sight of their legal betters.

After the flats we came to some lush farm land, then only twenty miles or so farther on we started up Du Toit's Kloof (or cliff), a steep climb up and over the mountains. Sam had a new Pontiac and was a skilled driver; we sailed up and up, through clouds and around sharp bends surrounded by fine rugged scenery. For the next fifty miles we seemed to be in Colorado.

Then we burst out of the last pass and into the desert— and had I been dumped there without warning I would have identified it as Route 66 through New Mexico and Arizona.

The only evident difference was that we drove on the left side of the road. Beside the road was a railroad that should have been the Santa Fe; around us was arid open range and distant buttes. We stopped at Laingsburg, one hundred and seventy miles from Cape Town, for a second breakfast. It was still only nine A.M. but it was already quite hot. Laingsburg looked like any of a hundred small highway towns in our southwest, with Bantus substituted for Indians.

The restaurant was no better and no worse than we would have found in the New Mexico counterpart; lamb chops and eggs and toast and coffee were substantial and well-enough cooked. Ticky reported that the ladies' room in the garage was spotless, as was that of the men—I mention these two points, cooking and rest rooms, because both were satisfactory-to-excellent all through South Africa, whereas they certainly were not in countries we had yet to visit.

The car had been parked in such shade as could be found but was boiling hot to enter nevertheless. Once on the road we were quickly comfortable. I shall mention no more about the heat nor the appearance of the desert; driving through the Great Karoo is precisely like driving from border to border across New Mexico and Arizona, minus the Painted Desert and the Indians. Some people cannot stand the dry desert heat in either desert. I like it.

The differences lay in *fauna*—the desert *flora* looked familiar, even to yucca under another name. I suppose the varieties were different and many of the species, but from a car window these were not noticeable to me—I can tell an oak from an elm, but just barely.

But African *fauna* are unquestionably African. Even the cattle are different, most of them being Afrikander cattle, a breed almost as rangy as a longhorn but without quite so much spread to their horns. Each of the cattle had two companions— tick birds.

There are two entirely different birds in South Africa known as tick birds. One is a little brown fellow about the size of a robin which you will see mostly in the bush, crawling over deer and searching for ticks, as busy as a pup in a flower bed.

The tick bird of the rhinoceros may be a third sort; I'm not sure. But the most prominent feathered friend called a tick bird is what we would call a snowy egret. Yes, I mean the bird which, if you are caught with its plumes in the United States, the Man puts you in jail and welds the lock solid. They may be a slightly different variety but the difference would matter only to another egret. (I may be weak on botany but I once won a prize for identifying birds . . . another bird guide.)

The pastures in South Africa are cluttered with white egrets.

They have the silliest way of behaving of any bird I ever saw (except possibly the Magnificent Bird of Paradise of Australia; we'll get to him later). The egrets stand guard over the cattle, two to each beast, one on each side and facing forward at attention, solemn as sideboys and perfectly motionless. They look as if they had each been assigned to that post by the sergeant of the guard and did not dare stir until relieved.

They are an unbelievable sight when first seen and they are still impressive after one gets used to them—which one does, for there appear to be exactly twice as many tick birds as cattle in South Africa and there are an awful lot of cattle. These tick birds introduced us to a springbok whom I will always cherish.

The springbok is a type of gazelle which is the national symbol of South Africa. Almost everything there is "Springbok"—the national airlines, a chain of theaters, the trademark of the government tourist corporation, their national teams in sports, almost anything you might expect except their Boy Scouts who are "Voortrekkers" instead. Springboks used to be exceedingly numerous; now they are common but not in the great herds they used to exist in. I heard a story about this which sounds incredible but which is told soberly: the springboks are alleged to have committed a lemming-type of mass suicide . . . poured out of the bush in countless numbers, pressed on to the Indian Ocean, waded in, drank sea water, and died.

If this is true, it is at least as hard to explain as any of Dr. Rhine's ESP researches. In any case, springbok are now not so numerous.

Our first springbok came to our attention through watching tick birds. I had kept my eye on them because I could not figure out what they did for a living. Their passion for standing sentry by cattle did not seem to fill the craw; we never saw one stop to eat, not once—yet birds have a very high metabolic rate and *must* eat, early and often.

We had crossed the Orange River into the Orange Free State late that first day and were in green, fenced pastureland rather than open, arid range; cattle were more numerous and so were the egrets. Suddenly Ticky said, "Look!"

A springbok had jumped the fence and was mingling with the cattle, off the road to the right. Sam slowed to a crawl and identified it for us. But this creature had not crashed the party to enjoy the superior salad inside the paddock, oh, no! He was a practical jokester and he was there for the sole purpose of chasing the birds. He would advance in a series of graceful leaps, duck his head and butt an egret; the bird would squawk indignantly and fly away.

He did this again and again. The cattle went right on grazing and the other tick birds each stood fast, staunch as the boy on the burning deck, right up to the horrid but inevitable instant when it was fly or be knocked silly. The springbok cleaned the silly creatures out of that pasture, then jumped the fence again and trotted away, perhaps in search of more tick birds.

We asked Sam if they always behaved that way. He said that it was the first time he had ever seen it in all the years he had been traveling commercially along the highways of the country. We concluded that this our favorite springbok was a deviant, as exceptional and as touched with genius among his sort as was Mark Twain or Thorne Smith among us.

The Southern end of the Karoo is very dry and is sheep country. A little farther north the range improves and is cattle country. With the cattle come the tick birds and, as the country gets greener, more wading birds, storks, cranes, secretary birds, and others. There were ostriches, too, but I believe that all we saw of these were domesticated. Much of the land is ruined for farming by termites; their hills are often so thickly clustered as to turn otherwise level ground into badlands. The hills come in three types, tall church spires up to a dozen feet high, little mounds the size of a bushel basket or larger, and big mounds which are almost small hills or *koppies*. The dried mud, after having been chewed by the white ants, is a concrete too hard to break with a plow and apparently not soluble in rain. If the Martians ever have to decide who really owns Africa they will probably award it to the termites on adverse possession.

We stopped for tea at Colesberg in Cape Province just short of the Orange River. This town did not have a U.S. southwest appearance but was much like a county seat in Iowa or northern Missouri. From there on through the Orange Free State and across the Vaal River into Transvaal the country was green and lush, like the best of our farm land in the middle of our country. Having traveled more than six hundred and fifty miles we stayed that night at Bloemfontein, capital of the Free State and site of the famous Harvard Observatory. As usual, Sam seemed to know all the girls there; we had stopped several times on the way up to greet his female acquaintances, once right out in the middle of the desert when he spotted a familiar female face back of the wheel of a car coming toward us at a relative speed of a hundred thirty miles per hour. I was gathering the impression that Sam managed to stay a bachelor only by being constantly on the move.

The hotel was delightful and modern in equipment, but old enough to have fine, big rooms and ample baths. In South Africa they do not think a request for a private bath an eccentricity and are prepared to satisfy it. By request, a Bantu knocked on our door at five-thirty with tea for an eye-opener; this is an English custom we would do well to imitate on mornings requiring early starts. It is more effective than a cold shower and much easier to take.

Unfortunately my eyes were not open when the knock came. I forced myself out of a warm bed, grabbed blindly at my robe, and in so doing snatched my glasses off the night table. They hit the floor with a pretty tinkle of broken glass.

I am the sort of person who needs to put on his glasses in order to find his glasses. Being so dependent I am not careless enough to travel with only one pair, but a second pair had been broken the day before during our wild ride around Table Mountain; I was rapidly reaching the point where I would need a little boy to lead me around.

I turned to Ticky, still snug in bed, and said, "Now see what you've done!"

She raised her head and blinked at me. "You spoiled the loveliest dream—I was home. What country is this? And what have I done?"

"Africa. I've just broken my other glasses."

"Poor baby! Poor stupid baby . . . how did it get to be Africa?"

"I don't know. If you had gotten up and answered the door like an ever-loving wife, I wouldn't have busted them."

The polite knock came again. "You're the one with one slipper on and a robe partly on," she pointed out. "You can bring me tea in bed and after breakfast we'll see what can be done about your glasses."

Some women are heartless. I brought her tea in bed, then took a look out into the corridor. Sam's shoes, freshly polished, were outside his door and so was his tea; the night man had been unable to wake him. I kept at it until I woke him, along with everyone else in the corridor, then went back and gulped my tea and felt sorry for myself.

I told Sam about it at breakfast. "Do you suppose we can find a dispensing optician? Our schedule is so confounded tight that I'll have to get them fixed on the fly; the *Ruys* sails for Singapore the very afternoon we reach Durban."

He frowned thoughtfully. "We would have to waste more than two hours here until one opens, when we ought to be chopping a hundred miles off the road to Johannesburg— it's still more than three hundred miles. Just how bad off are you?"

"Not too bad for the moment. I still have an old pair left, with an obsolete prescription I can get by with. But I hate to think of all those weeks to Singapore with the wrong specs. Look, let's find an optician in Johannesburg and I'll have him airmail them to Durban."

"Today is Saturday. I think they'll all close at noon."

"Lordy! Any chance we'll make it by noon?"

"I doubt it. Possible . . . if we all lean forward all the way."

"Then let's lam out of here and get rolling!"

"Finish your coffee and quit worrying about it."

I sighed. "You've got twenty-twenty eyesight. You don't know."

"I said not to worry. I'll get my girl friend to take care of it."

"Huh? Which girl friend? Be more specific."

"The one in Johannesburg."

"Only one in Johannesburg? I thought it was a big city."

"Don't be rude, dear," Ticky advised me. "Sam is trying to help you." She turned to Sam. "He's a beast at this hour, Sam, but useful once the sun is higher."

"I wasn't being rude," I objected. "I just thought Sam made them queue up and show a priority. I admire him. I wish I were like him."

Thereafter the conversation rapidly went to pieces as Ticky tried to make logical her assertion that she thought Sam was wonderful but would break both my arms if I tried to emulate him. We let it rest that Sam would ask his girl friend, serial number one, class Joburg, to have the glasses repaired in time for us to pick them up on our return to the city en route to Durban. I felt very happy over the whole thing; my megrims rarely last past breakfast. I have a sweet disposition and children love me.

During that morning we gradually got into more densely populated country. It was still farm country, but with more cropping and fewer range animals. Wild life almost disappeared except for an occasional meerkat (or "mierkat" or "meercat," take your pick). This little mongooselike critter loves to streak across the road just ahead of cars. Too many of them don't quite make it; we saw their pitiful little bodies oftener than we saw the grey blur that marked where one had just been.

As we got closer to Johannesburg we saw an occasional mine tailing among the farms. The Witwatersrand gold field is the richest gold strike in history—possibly the Incas had something better; if so, it has been lost. It is an underground reef of gold at least sixty miles long and is regularly showing new and unsuspected wealth. Some of the mines are down more than half a mile below sea level, nearly two miles straight down from the 6000-foot plateau on which the Golden City rests. At those awful depths you can put your ear to a rock pillar and hear the stone creak with the incomprehensible weight resting on them.

We arrived in the city proper about one o'clock, too late to find an optician open, but I was no longer worried. We looked up Sam's girl friend, Ida, who was a tall, supple, blonde creature and a professional model, and Ida's sister Laura, who was tall, supple, and brunette and should have been a model but was not, through some oversight. Sam's plan worked out save that it was Laura who took my problem in hand and agreed to see to it that my two pairs of spectacles were repaired. After that they took us out to see the city.

Johannesburg is a seething million people today, where only seventy years ago were only fields of mealies. The town is booming more than ever and buildings are shooting up as in São Paulo. It looks like a mixture of Pasadena and Hollywood, with beautiful gardens, fine parks, and one of the world's most nearly ideal climates, its elevation keeping it from being too hot and its location only a few miles below the Tropic of Capricorn insuring that it is never cold. Its wealthy whites, of which there are many, run to private swimming pools, garden parties, and swank country clubs.

More than half, about six hundred thousand, of the population is non-European, Bantus and a smattering of East Indians. The Hindus are the retail merchants; an "Indian store" is anything from a country general store to a fashionable downtown department store. (We saw a sign in one: "Dogs and bare-footed people are not allowed on the escalator.") The gold industry employs about 300,000 of the blacks, most of whom are contract laborers whose families, if any, have been left back on a reserve and who themselves live in barracks near the mines. Most of the others live in the native locations outside of town. These locations are sometimes shanty towns and are sometimes rows of mass-built little one-room boxes, grim and kennellike.

Some of the native population simply drift on the town, without visible occupation or residence. Their presence there is illegal under the *apartheid* laws and the police and the courts are constantly catching them and imposing sentences which have the effect of forcing them to hire out to the farmers, but they are as elusive as smoke and there are always more to replace those caught. These are natives of what anthropologists speak of despairingly as "fringe" culture, no longer of their ancient culture, not yet part of the new. These drifters have the whites constantly worried. It is not safe to park an automobile in downtown Johannesburg in broad daylight with all doors and windows locked, unless a constant watch is kept on it. The drifters working in pairs, one with a polish rag as camouflage and the other with a tire iron or other jimmying tool, will break into it and loot it, right under the eyes of a crowd of people on the adjacent sidewalk.

At night the streets of Johannesburg are not safe.

We were surprised to see black policemen there. However they are intended only to restrain their own race, they are not armed, and have conditional authority to arrest a white man only under extreme circumstances to prevent immediate violence and then only until a white policeman can be summoned. I never heard of one doing it, even so.

Despite the black cloud of potential racial trouble brooding over it Johannesburg deserves its name of the Golden City. It is young, beautiful, lusty and cheerful. From the many high points in the city you can see that it is surrounded by hills of brown mine tailings, which grow even faster than the constant efforts to plant and garden them. Its white homes are luxuriously beautiful and its downtown district is as modern as any and made exotic by Bantus of both sexes and many tribes in savage splendor only a little modified by white customs— the women cover up a little more but it is not unusual to see a "blanket" man who refuses to wear trousers of any sort and covers up his nakedness with a large blanket. The natives are free to come into the retail area to buy during daylight; curfew must find them out of town, or in the quarters of their white employers.

We were to leave that evening early for the big game country and had to pick up a railroad ticket. I had attempted to make a round trip reservation for us from Johannesburg to Nelspruit and return while we were in Cape Town; a telegram received in Johannesburg confirmed the trip out but not the return trip and advised me to pick up the ticket at once.

I discovered that buying a railroad ticket in South Africa is considerably more complicated than getting married in Nevada. But my good angel, Sam, got me through it.

First we went to the city railroad station, an enormous place suited to the busiest railroad junction in the country and a city of a million. However, over the weekend it closes like everything else, even though the trains still run. All the ticket windows were closed but I had been told to go to the "Emergency Booking Office"—in South Africa, buying a train ticket on a weekend is classed as an emergency.

We managed to find it hidden away far from the main hall. There was a clerk there, doing nothing, and he had a record of my reservation but was disinclined to issue it; instead he lectured me on doing things properly. I tried to explain the circumstances that had forced me into the course of action I had followed, but Sam stepped on my foot and addressed him in Afrikaans. With great deliberation and reluctance he issued, not the ticket, but a document which authorized me to go to another part of the station, knock on a door, and ask another clerk to sell me a one-way ticket; he refused to sell me a return, on the grounds that I should have gotten there sooner. Two processes took the best part of an hour—the railroads are government-owned, of course, and have no competition other than from other government-owned bus and air systems.

We then rejoined Ticky and Sam's friends. Sam warned me that we must be down at the train at least thirty minutes before train time—forty would be safer. I wondered why, since we had tickets and a sleeper reservation; I did not understand the explanation but we took his advice, which was excellent. Instead of being able to go directly to our car it was necessary first to push through a crowd gathered around a bulletin board on which was posted the train's diagram of reservations; from this we found out where we were supposed to be. Then it was necessary to look up the conductor of the train on the platform, check in with him and have some more mysterious paperwork done, a lengthy process since a couple of hundred other people also wished to see him for the same purpose. We got aboard just barely in time.

I had time while waiting in queues to ponder the purchase of two tickets in Chile for a train ride of the same order of mileage—much shorter in time because Chileno trains run very much faster than South African trains (the crack Blue Train, the limited from Cape Town to Johannesburg, averages a dizzying thirty-seven miles an hour). In both cases we had been dependent on the kindliness of a local citizen to catch the trains at all, but under Chileno rules Mr. Thackeray had purchased our tickets in about seven seconds and had had us actually aboard in another fifteen seconds whereas Sam, sophisticated in the red tape and knowing the inner-sanctum language, had been forced to waste two hours of his time in two trips to get us on a train for which we already had made reservations before his efforts commenced.

As I recall, the Chileno railroads are government-owned, too—at least they operate without competition. On the whole, their equipment is poorer than that of the South African railroads. I am forced to the conclusion that the difference lies in the people, in some fashion.

At the steps of the train Sam kissed Ticky good-by and I kissed good-by both Sam's (Joburg) girl friend and her sister Laura, which made me one up on Sam for the first and last time. In a country that had polygamy those two sisters would make a wonderful package deal.

We sat down in our compartment as the train pulled out and proceeded to munch sandwiches that Sam had purchased for us in lieu of the dinner that we had not had time to get. The train had a quaint 1890 elegance about it, carved woodwork and pictures on the walls. The roadbed had been left over from 1890, too, although I've encountered some on the Main Line of the Pennsylvania which was equally bad.

The compartment was of a sort known as a "coupé," a wide seat for two running thwartships which could be opened out into two narrow single beds, one above the other. After a while a "coloured" came around and rented us bed clothes (they don't come with the ticket) and made up the bunks, which left no room for baggage or feet, so we went to the dining car, which was nice in the same out-of-date style; there we had tea and killed time.

Coupés are located over the truck, the middle of the car containing compartments big enough for the largish Afrikander families. The location heterodynes with the roadbed to produce an exciting but not restful ride. Nevertheless we dozed until the attendant showed up with morning tea. I brushed off a blanket of coal cinders and looked out. At last we were in the African big game country.

The countryside along the tracks looked remarkably like Illinois.

Ah, the romance of the safari! Stalwart native porters, their ebony bodies glistening with sweat, lift up their burdens, balance them on their heads and set off single file through the bushveld. The professional white hunter, bearded and taciturn, scouts ahead, ready to bring down meat for the simple evening meal. Suddenly the number-one boy, his eyes popping, trots back to your spot in the safari. "Bwana!" he cries. "Come quick! Simba!" You rush silently forward, followed by your gun bearer. The beast—

You can do it this way, if you want to. The tourist companies will probably conjure up the ghost of Allan Quatermain, for a price. There are porters to be had in Africa and professional white hunters as well; you can have a safari of any sort you want, even one with artificial refrigeration.

But if your object is simply to get into big game country, the more usual way is to pick up the phone book and look up "Southern Cross Safaris" or some other of the safari companies. They will send around a car for you, of the largish sort used by airports which have a baggage rack on top; a uniformed driver will drive you out to the bush and keep you and the other tourists out of trouble with the dangerous animals. This is known as a safari.

Another way is to hire a taxi and go out on your own. This is what Ticky and I did.

There is nothing wrong with hunting lions in a taxi. I'm reasonably certain that Allan Quatermain would have preferred it to his six-span teams of "salted" oxen; it is faster, cheaper, and much more comfortable. At the railroad station at Nelspruit we hired a taxi, driven by a mother of three, an Afrikander farm wife. I can neither spell nor pronounce her name but it was something like "Morgan."

She took us to a hotel for breakfast, went home to feed the baby, then came back and picked us up and we went out after lions, in a "Henry J." American cars are preferred for the bush, as the roads are not really roads but tracks, and the superior ruggedness of any American car, even a little Henry J., is much appreciated. Nelspruit is the nearest town to Kruger Park, which is the place to go if you simply want to see animals and not kill them. Kruger Park is 8000 square miles of everything, from lions to elephants; it runs from the Crocodile River north to the "great grey-green greasy Limpopo River all set about with fever trees" where Kipling's Elephant's Child got its nose stretched for its 'satiable curtiosity.

It was a pet project of Oom Paul Kruger, who feared that the strange and wonderful wild life of Africa might be killed off entirely by hunters not content with a trophy or two, but who would often kill two or three hundred beasts in a day. The whole world can praise him for his foresight; here is a place where a hunter could kill a thousand head in a day if his shoulder could stand the shocks. Kruger Park has in quantity every major animal for which Africa is famous except the rhinoceros—and rhinos are preserved in another park farther south.

An hour's drive over good paved roads brings you to the gate of the park. Inside there is no pavement, nothing has been done to tidy up the bush (we would call it "jungle") save to cut tracks and to build widely separated rest camps with kraals to keep the lions out at night. The route to the park is through Swazi farm country, between fields of mealies and grass huts. Piccanins are beside the road here and there; as our car approached they always started dancing, a sort of a Charleston combined with shoving the arms in and out as if rowing strenuously. We stared.

"Why do they do that?" I asked.

"Oh," said Mrs. Morgan, "it's a welcome. They don't see many people out here, you know, and when one does show up they dance for him to show they are glad to see him."

We entered the park, paying a few shillings for the privilege, and started searching, driving slowly and always staying in the car as required by the rules. Almost at once we saw our first game, a buck kudu, which is a big fellow of the antelope type, with stripes, a goatee, and fantastic twisted horns. After that bucks of various sorts (and does and babies) came thick and fast; frequently we had to stop the car to let a herd of thirty or forty impala yearling bachelors wander across. The impala, pretty little things about the size of our eastern deer and very slender and graceful, were most numerous, but we saw a dozen other sorts, among them the cross-word puzzle gnu, better known in Africa as wildebeest, which looks as if it had not been able to make up its mind whether to be a horse or a cow, got discouraged and decided to be a mule. It is remarkably untidy in appearance.

There were delightful little duikers, too, antelope the size of a fox terrier, so fragile in appearance that you want to pick them up and take care of them.

I was searching the grass on each side for lion; bucks are all very well but I had come half around the world to see lions, wild lions in the bush. I had been warned that it was the wrong time of year and that I could stay three weeks and probably not see one, but I was hopeful, even though braced for disappointment.

The way to look for lions is this: look at every one of the smaller, rounded termite hills that you pass. If it raises its eyes and looks back at you, don't get out of the car; it's a lion. So far I had seen hundreds of termite hills the right size and color but none that stared back. Ticky was watching ahead; I heard her shout.

"Lion?" I asked hopefully.

"No—*look*!"

Crossing the road was a warthog mama, followed in single file by four of the ugliest and cockiest piglets ever, each with its tail straight up in the air. Mother was a Miss Africa among warthogs, with fine curving tusks and a wonderfully misshapen figure. We watched them until they disappeared in the tall grass and nothing could be seen but mama's proud tail like a little flag.

Ticky spotted the first baboon, too, a big bull sitting up on a bare limb about ten feet off the ground—a lookout. Each baboon family posts a guard, against leopard primarily as the lion prefers venison.

Leopards are tricky things, rated by the great professional hunter Mr. J. A. Hunter as the most dangerous animals, worse than lion, elephant, or African buffalo. They will enter a car to attack a man, which the lion is most reluctant to do; every time we passed under a branch Mrs. Morgan made us roll up all windows, sweltering hot though it was in the thick bush.

Ticky spotted three more baboon lookouts, all in similar positions on bare, medium-high branches, while I continued my termite-hill check. A baboon can outdistance a leopard in the trees, given a fair start, even though the leopard climbs like a house cat. I had just looked up to admire one of Ticky's bull apes, then looked back at another termite hill.

This one looked back at me.

"Stop the car!" I gasped. "*Lion!*"

Sure enough, it was—a beautiful, black-maned male, about forty yards from the car. It lay still but never took its eyes off us. When I could stop trembling I got out the field glasses, and gave them to Ticky—after taking the first look myself.

Forty yards split by a magnification of eight is five yards through the binoculars. It brought him so close we could see the yellow stains on his teeth when he yawned. I am prepared to swear on a stack of Baedekers that a lion in the open is *much* bigger than one behind bars. I don't think it was entirely my excitement, either; I think they probably grow bigger out where they lead a normal healthy life—for a lion, not for impala—with fresh meat and enough exercise. I can't prove this but I think it is true.

Ticky handed the glasses over to Mrs. Morgan, then said, "Hey! There's his mate."

And it was. In plain sight, not ten feet from the male, was a lioness, also lying in the grass and watching us. We had been so intent on our first lion that we had not looked. "Maybe there are more around," Ticky said nervously.

"You look—I gotta get a picture of this one—these one—both of them." I did so and she did so, reporting that none of the termite hills on her side were staring at her. Lions do stare with the unnervous steadiness of one who is utterly self confident. I took the picture . . . and it turned out badly; not only was the distance too great for the only lens I had but apparently I was shaking like a bride, even though my own recollection is that I was cool, calm, and dignified. I now find it necessary to tell my friends when I show it: "It really *is* a lion—it just *looks* like a brown ant hill."

I realized at the time that the grass was preventing me from getting the picture I wanted so I did something that I certainly should not have done, something quite properly forbidden by the government of South Africa: I shouted at the beast.

The results were pretty good. The male raised up and started lashing his tail slowly and forcefully, while measuring with his eye the distance between us. But I did not get my second picture; Mrs. Morgan let in the clutch and we scrammed out of there. She did not scold me for it at the time, but she put all speed onto the car possible. Later she told me about lions, balked at getting inside a car, which had clawed all the tires to shreds, including the spare if exposed. I had no suitable comment.

When we were a short piece down the road and it was evident that *Felis Rex* was not following she slowed down again. Then I pulled one of the longest double-takes on record: "Hey! That *really was* a lion!"

"Of course," Ticky said coolly. "That's what you came for, wasn't it? Who did you think it was? Bert Lahr?"

Then she stuck a match in her mouth and tried to strike a cigarette. "There was a lion," I said slowly. "There were two of them. They were *lions*."

Shortly I was puffing a cigarette nonchalantly myself and feeling very good about it, as if I had just won a Pulitzer Prize. They said we couldn't find lions! Francis Macomber Quatermain can find lions any day—just step off the train and flag a taxi. When we rounded the next curve and saw a car stopped and people outside it I leaned out and said, "Don't look now but there are two lions just back down the road a block or so."

A man looked up from an open bonnet. "Thank you," came a clipped British voice, "but at the moment my engine is over-heated. Tell them to wait; we'll be along shortly, I hope."

We drove on.

No more termite hills stared back at us that morning, though we stared at plenty. But one more alarm took place: I had grown used to the routine of rolling up windows for every overhanging tree and was not especially surprised when Mrs. Morgan started rolling them up once without taking time to stop the car. I looked around, saw that there were no such trees. "What's the matter? Leopard on the ground?"

"Mamba!"

I was too ignorant at the time to be impressed. A green something slithered rapidly down out of a bush beside us and slid across the road with amazing speed—a snake more than six feet long and as thick as my wrist. Even in my ignorance it looked mean. Mrs. Morgan got us well out of the neighborhood as fast as the little car would go.

The mamba is the subject of many grisly stories in the bushveld country, most of them depressingly well authenticated. Its bite is much more poisonous than that of our rattlesnake; seven minutes from being bitten to death in agony seems to be about the average. If struck, you may possibly save yourself by taking a bush knife and whacking off, without any delay at all, the bitten hand or arm or foot. Worse still, this snake is not the peaceloving gentleman the rattler is; it seems to like to kill and it is terribly fast; a mamba has been known to chase and catch a man on horseback, strike from the ground—and kill him.

The Afrikanders seemed very casual to us about the big carnivores; they are not casual about mambas.

We had lunch at a rest camp called Skukuza—tea and sandwiches served by a barefoot black giant who called me "Mahster"—a custom I was never able to get used to. Inside the kraal at Skukuza we saw two large dead trees which nevertheless appeared to be loaded with fruit. A closer look showed that the "fruit" were birds' nests, nests of the weaver bird which constructs a nest not unlike that of the Baltimore oriole. But, unlike the oriole, these birds are destructively sociable; once they pick on a tree, it is doomed; they turn it into an avian slum, building so close together that the tree dies. There is probably some deep moral lesson in this but my philosopher's license has expired.

During lunch it started to drizzle, which depressed me until Mrs. Morgan pointed out that rain would bring the game out; on a hot dry clear day the animals tended to hide in some shady cool place and wait for sundown. Sure enough, we saw more game than ever, mostly varieties of antelope, including eight of the rather scarce water buck, more kudus, roan antelope, wildebeest, eland, the lovely little duiker, and enough impala to cause traffic jams. We were rather bored with impala by now, pretty as they are, but we searched each herd carefully for zebra, as zebra have a habit of hiding themselves among impala in order to evade the lions—no luck, no zebra.

But there were plenty of baboons and swarming families of monkeys and all sorts of strange birds, including one called a bush turkey although he is not one. He is as big as a turkey but has a bill like a toucan, which makes him look as if he had put on a false face for Hallowe'en.

We came to a small natural clearing in which there was a herd which I at first mistook for gnus. Then I realized that these were bigger, thicker through the body, heavier in the horn, and most emphatically did not look like a frivolous cartoon of some other animal . . . most especially the bull of the herd did not look like a joke. He looked like Satan himself headed for a coven.

"Buffalo," Mrs. Morgan said softly.

I picked up my camera and rather shakily started to take pictures. We had not expected to find buffalo. Having found them I was not sure that I was glad we had. The African buffalo is mean, treacherous, stupid, and unpredictable. A high-velocity, steel-jacketed bullet will bounce off the boss of horn that protects his idiot brain. In size and muscle he gives much the impression of a medium tank.

I took several pictures while the herd gazed and the bull of the herd stared at us. Finally he started ambling toward us, then broke into a trot. Mrs. Morgan let in the clutch and we got away from there as fast as possible. Apparently the bull decided that his duty was done in chasing us away from his family; he did not follow us down the track. I do not know whether or not a Henry J. can outdistance an African buffalo on a straight-away or not, and I don't ever want to find out.

About twenty minutes and two hundred impala later we spotted two cars ahead of us, stopped under some trees. A car at rest is always a signal to approach cautiously and stop to see what they have stopped to look at; we did so. I craned my neck. "What are they look—*umph*!"

I found myself so close to a male lion that I could look down on the top of his head.

About ten feet beyond him was another male in the same pose, couchant. There should have been a flight of public library steps between them. There they lay, as steady as stone statues, and stared back at the dozen or so humans staring at them. They were both big, magnificent, black-maned beasts. I won't attempt to estimate their dimensions; I feel sure that the fact that they were uncaged distorted my judgment. But they were not small.

Nor can I explain why three out of three males that we saw were black-maned, since black manes are supposed to be scarce.

I should have been able to take a perfect close-up, save for one thing: the light was too poor for color film . . . late afternoon, under trees, and a fine drizzle. It would have required a flash bulb, and I certainly would not have fired off a flash in a lion's face even if I had had one—I don't claim to be bright but I am not suicidally stupid. Sure, sure, it says right here in the book that lions will not molest people in automobiles, but the lion might regard a flash bulb as a violation of protocol. Anyhow, lions have been known to take umbrage at the automobile itself and claw all four tires to ribbons. With lion no farther away than a parking meter I felt not at all anxious to call attention to myself.

So we stared and they stared. I don't know how long we stayed. The lions seemed perfectly willing to sit through a second show. After a long time Mrs. Morgan suggested that we had better be moving on if we were to get to the hippo pool before dark.

Either somebody moved the hippo pool or there was something wrong with the map we were using; we never did find it. Hippopotami are the only animals you are assured of seeing when you visit Kruger Park, because they always stay home in one curve of the Sabie River. Our guide had been there many times before; nevertheless we could not find it and lost so much time looking for it that we barely made it out the gate before sundown closing time.

I didn't care—we had seen four lions.

The booking clerk at the railroad station in Johannesburg had refused to give us a return booking from Nelspruit to Johannesburg and had given me a lecture instead. I had attempted to book our return as soon as we arrived in Nelspruit but had been told by the station agent there that it was too late to book except directly with the train conductor; he advised me to come down a bit early and see the conductor.

I was baffled. How it could always be the wrong time to make a train reservation, when we disembarked in Cape Town, when we arrived in Johannesburg, and when we arrived in Nelspruit, I did not understand and still do not. But there it was—jam yesterday, jam tomorrow, never jam today. So we hurried through an excellent dinner at the Hotel Paragon in Nelspruit—the Paragon deserved its name—and Mrs. Morgan took us down to the train in good time. When the conductor stepped off the train we planned to buttonhole him.

So did fifty other people. We didn't even get close to him.

Not that it mattered, he was letting no one on. We did hear him tell one woman with a baby that she could stand up all night in the vestibule but that was the best he offered. It was a holiday crowd, returning from the seaside; even the seats in the dining car were occupied. The next train was twenty-four hours later and we had no assurance that we would be able to get on even that train—the station master either could not or would not issue reservations for it.

The railroads in South Africa are atrocious, not because of equipment but because of management—sort of a Long Island Railway on a grand scale. True, the equipment could be better in many ways, but the real defect seems to be a total absence of any notion of traffic management. The bureaucrats who run it seem to have borrowed a slogan from an earlier, ruggeder day in American industry: "The public be damned!"

This weekend was the end of a school holiday; any traffic engineer owning a slipstick, having access to the records of previous years, and possessed of enough savvy to figure his own retirement pay could have predicted the service needed that weekend after finishing the morning paper and still have had time to take a long coffee break. But oh no! they had to run it like a game of musical chairs, with children left standing when the music stopped as an expected part of the game.

I have already noted that it was Sam's hospitality and Sam's Pontiac that got us out of Cape Town; all trains were booked solid three days ahead—with no intention of adding more equipment. The same conditions prevailed all over the country. Compounding the annoyance was the barely veiled insolence of Afrikander civil servants, an attitude of who the hell are you to even expect to ride our railroads.

I would have no right to complain if it were not that South Africa maintains tourist bureaus in our own country which publicize, among other things, how wonderful their railroads are.

Sure, sure, I'm just a sorehead tourist who could not manage to get on the train he wanted—but note this: South Africa has plenty of coal and exports it. But Cape Town imports foreign coal, it being cheaper to do so than to bring it down from the north. Inasmuch as the country has a markedly unfavorable balance of trade and the government has a firm policy of preventing the importation of anything at all where it can possibly be avoided, this one fact seems to me to underline the inadequacy and inefficiency of their railroads.

The same Transport Commission which runs the railroads also runs the bus lines and the air lines. Competition is intentionally eliminated.

Never mind—I admit that their railroads, or any railroads, are better than the means Allan Quatermain used. Mrs. Morgan drove us back to the hotel; during the ride I arranged with her for her to drive us to Johannesburg the following day. We checked back in at the hotel and went into the bar lounge. We were soaked through from a drizzling rain while standing on the station platform, exhausted from a long day in the bushveld, disappointed at not being able to board the train, and we each needed about two ounces of universal solvent in a tall glass to place a warm glow over our homesickness.

The bar was closed.

It was the first time we had run into the British Commonwealth customs of "hours." I have been assured by others that "hours" are carefully arranged throughout the Queen's domain to keep a weary man from taking a drink when he needs it most. Actually, closing hours are not much trouble to travelers; they are exempt from most of the restrictions. I don't know how we got caught at Nelspruit as I don't know the rules.

Presently the manager-owner, a very nice chap, found us, condoled with us at not getting the train, and was hospitable— so much so that I never did get up the courage to say, "Hey, Mac, how about a drink?" After a while we went to our room. The beds were good, there was plenty of hot water; the Paragon really is a good hotel.

Mrs. Morgan picked us up in the morning and we set out for Johannesburg. This meant that we paid for another five hundred miles of taxi service, or a total of three days. One day by taxi to see lions seemed reasonable; that was what we were there for and we had already invested much time and money in the preparation. Two more days (one for her to drive us to Johannesburg, a second to return empty at our expense) seemed a little steep, especially as we held train tickets which had not been honored and which we could not cash. But it was either that or be stuck in the interior of Africa with a strong likelihood of missing our ship for Singapore.

Actually Mrs. Morgan charged about half what the same service would have cost us in Colorado, even though her little Henry J. represented an investment equal to a Cadillac and petrol cost more (and gave poorer mileage) than does gasoline in the States.

I have been told by South Africans that the Afrikander farmer is the laziest man on earth, given to sitting on his stoep, smoking his pipe, and watching his black farmhands make him rich. If so, Mrs. Morgan and her husband must have been exceptions. They owned and lived on a farm, which they worked through a black foreman. As is usual, his compensation was permission to crop part of the land for himself. They owned a general store for the natives, which was managed by a "coloured." Mrs. Morgan ran the Nelspruit Taxi Service and was its principal driver, although she had three children at home including a young baby whom she had to stop by to feed occasionally—she had, of course, a Bantu housekeeper-cook. And Papa had a full-time job as a boiler inspector on the railroad.

She told us quite simply that they wanted to make a lot of money. I'm sure they will.

Inside of ten minutes after leaving Nelspruit we were glad that the train had gone off without us. It was a glorious day and glorious countryside. The Transvaal is some of the lushest rolling farm land on this globe and I can understand how the Voortrekkers felt that they had reached the promised land when they reached it after crossing the grand but pitiless Karoo. All they asked of life was fertile land, cattle, and plenty of slaves to do the work—the simple things in life.

Nelspruit is not much above sea level. We climbed through the low veld, the middle veld, and the high veld in the course of the day, gaining more than a mile in altitude but so gradually as to be not noticeable. It was rolling, open prairie, lightly sprinkled with trees, like the best of our middle west farm country. The wide, almost flat-topped flamboyant tree, a trademark of South Africa, was usually in sight somewhere, reminding us that this was not the middle west, but a page out of the *National Geographic*.

There was also a little bird which did not look like home. It was known locally as the widow-of-paradise bird and looked much like a redwinged blackbird save that it had two long, black, floppy tail feathers, perhaps three times the length of its little body. These gave it quite unfavorable aerodynamic characteristics and it proceeded in series of frantic attempts to gain altitude to overcome the drag, then pulled down again, so that it traced a sine curve through the air. Nevertheless it seemed quite happy and no doubt thought that was the only way there was to fly.

In late afternoon we drove through Pretoria without stopping and turned south toward Johannesburg. Pretoria is a clean and beautiful small city of gardens and fine public buildings and is one of the three capitals of the Union, the seat of government—the supreme court is in Bloemfontein and the legislature is in Cape Town. In the outskirts to the south is the Voortrekker Monument and for this we did stop, it being a world-famous Afrikander shrine.

The monument is a large, square, ugly building of great dignity. It sits on a hilltop surrounded by a sculptured circle of covered wagons. The interior is empty save for an altar on a lower level which is struck by sunlight through a hole in the roof only at noon on December 16th, their national holiday. There are bas reliefs running around the inside which portray the struggles of crossing the desert, fighting natives, coping with broken wagons, etc. Ticky and I were struck by the strong resemblance in equipment and costume between these pictured pioneers and those of our own old west. Only in that the "hostiles" were shown as flat-nosed rather than hook-nosed could a difference readily be seen. The men wore spade beards, the women wore Mother Hubbards, the prairie schooners looked like ours. It made us think of the pictures and statuary of the Mormon Trek as seen in Salt Lake City—not really surprising since the Mormons trekked in 1847 and the Cape Dutch in 1838 and following. I could not forget, however, that the two sets of pioneers trekked for very different reasons: the Mormons were attempting to escape religious persecution whereas the Voortrekkers moved on (in part at least) because the British had freed their slaves.

Of course it does not look that way to the Afrikanders and no doubt this book will be added to the long list of books banned by law in South Africa. Mrs. Morgan evidenced the first emotion I had seen her show; she looked around at scenes of Boers fighting Bantus and said very solemnly and softly, "They did it for us."

The Voortrekkers seem to have won. The edict from London emancipating the slaves is still law but Dr. Malan's government has succeeded in substituting a serfdom for the entire black race which leaves the black man no more free than he was more than a century ago without putting the Voortrekkers' descendants to the inconvenience and expense of being personally responsible for the welfare of chattel slaves. (And on the other side of the world we are still persecuting the polygamous dissident Mormons of the Arizona Strip.)

There was a sign outside giving visiting hours and limiting "non-Europeans" to one afternoon a week. I wonder if any of them visit it.

Before I am accused of a double standard let me say that I am aware that our own treatment of the American Indians was in many instances a scandal and a crime, but we have made many amends. There is now no legal distinction between the red man and the white, save that the Indian may, if he wishes, avail himself of certain legal privileges denied to the whites. But he is not required to.

American Indian blood is a matter of pride with us today, e.g., Will Rogers. And we have had an Indian Vice President. I will concede that the Afrikanders treat the Bantus "no worse" than we have treated the American aborigines the day Dr. Malan has a black deputy prime minister. Oh, that will be a day!

Before somebody points out that the barefoot Bantu savage is not capable of full modern citizenship *as he is* let me concede the point—and let me add that he never will raise himself up to the status of Dr. Ralph Bunche or of Dr. George Washington Carver as things are now; the Nationalist Party is firmly determined not to let him.

And in answer to that raucous voice in the back—the man with the sheet over his arm—let me say that my sister is already married. Anyway, it's her business, not mine. The meeting is adjourned.

South Africa has wonderful roads even if the railroads are a practical joke. We were in Johannesburg well before dark. It is a modern city even to its traffic jams, which would do credit to New York; it was well past dark before we reached our hotel. We took a quick tub and grabbed another taxi to a lovely home in the suburbs, owned by people we had met in the *Ruys*. We had cocktails by a swimming pool in a beautiful walled garden, dinner by candle light which was served by white-gloved black servants. I noticed that our hostess called her butler "Sixpence" and asked her what his real name was?

"Why, 'Sixpence,' " she told me.

"I mean his Bantu name."

She shrugged. "So far as I know, that is the only name he has." Then she changed the subject.

I learned later that "Sixpence" is the usual nickname of any Bantu male house servant. I had again shown a gauche ignorance of local custom. But in the United States even the goldfish have names.

In that household wardrobes and cupboards are kept locked, inner doors as well as outer are locked at night, the grounds are surrounded by a high wall and can be floodlighted. There is a story, possibly apocryphal, about a South African lady in Durban who was disturbed at the rumors of an impending native uprising. She called in her houseboy and said, "Sixpence, you wouldn't cut my throat—would you?"

He opened his eyes wide in horror. "Oh, no, Missy! I cut throat of lady missy next door—*her* boy cut your throat."

You hear this story in South Africa but the laugh is a little forced.

The next day we flew to Durban to join the *Ruys*. The ship was a DC-6B, a plane which appears to be the work horse of the world at present, just as its smaller and older sister, the DC-3, was for so long—not but what there are plenty of DC-3s still flying all over the world. Like the Model-T Ford, it is necessary to bury a DC-3 at a crossroads with a holly stake through its heart to make it quit flying.

As we took off from Johannesburg we saw that it was surrounded by manmade mountains of sulphur-colored mine tailings. That was the last of the scenery, as we saw nothing but the top sides of clouds from there to the coast. As a means of sightseeing airplanes are better than subways, but not much. So I looked at the hostess instead. As always, she was well worth looking at. I like to look at pretty girls and Ticky indulges me in this hobby, one which is, after all, inexpensive, harmless, and does not damage the goods. I hope to live to be a nasty old man, with that as my last pleasure in life.

The most nearly perfectly beautiful airline hostess we saw on this trip was a Polynesian girl, but this Springbok hostess was well up in the money. Presently she came over and talked with us. We learned that she was engaged to a doctor who had just left for postgraduate work in San Francisco. She had been unable to go with him because the terms of his fellowship required him not to marry for two years, and now she was worrying that he might forget her for some American girl. We assured her solemnly that if he did, he had rocks in his head—an obvious truth. But it did not console her. She told us that she would have been happy to go with him without being married, but she had not been able to arrange a visa that would let her work.

Sometimes I think the rules are rigged to require at least one fly in every bowl of soup. This planet is not too well run.

After the balmy veld and cool Johannesburg, landing in Durban was like being plunged in a steam bath. By the time we had landed and taken a long, hot, sticky ride to the docks we were tired and irritable. We then had to go through outgoing customs, a practice infuriating through its sheer uselessness, but one which I learned to take with a fixed smile and mendacious good nature.

Not so Ticky! We had to fill out long forms to get ourselves, our camera, and our binoculars aboard ship, which made the third time that we had gone through the rigamarole for South Africa alone. South Africa specializes in empty rituals to slow down the traveler, most of them having the flavor of children's games—"Penalty Square: Go Back Four Spaces"—that sort of thing. For example, Mr. Tupper, our jovial companion of the *Gulf Shipper,* got caught by their requirement of a cash deposit to insure that he would leave the country (we were excused because we had a ticket to Singapore). He put up the deposit in dollars, attempted to collect it when he left and was told that it was returnable only in South African pounds. He pointed out that he had deposited dollars but it did him no good to argue; they had planned it that way.

While I was filling out forms and trying to convince the customs officer that I could not show him the serial number of my camera because it was on the inside where it could not be seen without ruining a partly-exposed roll of film, Ticky was standing behind me making ominous teakettle sounds. As they began to boil over into recognizable epithets I finished hurriedly, paid some minor clearance fee, and rushed her out of there. As soon as I got her back aboard the *Ruys* and inside our stateroom with the door closed I started giving her what-for, explaining in short, bitter words that we were strangers in a strange land and that we had to conform to the local rules whether we liked them or not. Then I attempted to exact from her a firm promise never again, under any circumstances, to be anything other than cheerful and co-operative when going through customs, no matter how much it hurt.

Ticky stuck out her lower lip and looked determined and I found out why the word "obey" had become obsolete in the marriage service—I didn't make a dent. (I must read Robert Louis Stevenson's *Travels with a Donkey* someday. Is it possible that he was describing his honeymoon?)

Reconsidering it coldly and much later I am not sure that I was right and she was wrong. Men are much too law-abiding and will put up with nonsense that women know instinctively is wrong. Males receive a sterner discipline in childhood, then when they reach the age when they might break free of it they are usually subjected to a term of military service which leaves them forever after pliable in the face of queues, red tape, nonsense forms, and protocol for the sake of protocol—they disapprove but they conform.

Not so the female race! They evade or ignore rules and regulations wherever possible without the slightest feeling of guilt, and their husbands are often involuntary and unhappy accessories before and after the fact. Possibly this is a good thing, albeit uncomfortable for the male. Somebody has to strike a blow for freedom before we drown in a sea of red tape.

Speaking of donkeys, we almost bought one. The usual equivalent of a farm truck for a Bantu farmer is a long, narrow flatbed wagon drawn by four or six donkeys. Sam had told Ticky that these cunning little beasts cost only two-and-six, or thirty-five cents U.S., which seemed incredible. I asked Mrs. Morgan about this and found that Sam was almost correct, as she had just recently bought two donkeys for ten shillings for her farm foreman, the price per head thus coming to seventy cents or the price of a pound of butter in Colorado Springs.

Ticky immediately decided to take one back to the States as a pet.

I tried to argue her out of it, though I should have known better. Mere words have never affected the diamond-like quality of her will.

At last I dug into my pocket and handed her two half-crowns. "Here, buy yourself a donkey. You arrange deck passage for it, you get it through quarantine at Singapore—six months. Get it through again at Sydney and Auckland—another six months each, I believe. Same for San Francisco. Write me a letter occasionally and tell me how you are making out."

She took the money and I heard no more about it. But much later aboard ship, when I needed change for something, she told me firmly not to touch the two coins on her dressing table because they were the money for the donkey. I concede the logic of it.

The ship stayed over an extra day in Durban which gave us time to go into Zululand. I wanted to go a bit farther into the game preserve at Hluhluwe (pronounced "shloo-shloo" as if you were rinsing your teeth) in order to see white rhinoceri, but it was just a few miles too far away; one flat tire and we might miss the ship. So we settled for Zulus and the shade of Umpslopagaas.

Mr. Brown, guide for Thomas Cook, Ltd., drove us north to Eshowe, capital of Zululand. I do not know what I expected to find; Zulu history was no part of my formal education and my impressions of the Zulu Empire had been derived largely from Sir Rider Haggard's wonderful but fanciful romances. However, Sir Rider was no mere spinner of fairy tales; his descriptions of the valiant Zulu impis, or regiments, of their military system and tactics, of their stern character, must be taken as factual; he had seen them at the height of their power just before their defeat by the British in the Zulu War in 1879.

What we did see was a rolling, sun-drenched land planted mostly in sugar cane but interspersed here and there with smaller fields of mealies (Indian corn), the staple of the natives. The hills were dotted with beehive grass huts. Here and there were women working in the fields. Along the roads were naked piccanins, older lads dress in breech-clout equivalents of animal tails, barefoot matrons with the high hairdress of married women, adolescent girls with their hair short, and a very occasional rich native on a bicycle. Men were scarce.

The impression was one of overpowering, bucolic peace. It was hard to remember that these sleepy farmers had produced some of the bloodiest fighting ever seen before they were subjugated. Around the time of Napoleon, King Tshaka (or "Chaka"—their clicks are not equivalent to our gutturals) introduced the stabbing assegai, and a military enveloping tactic much like that used by Alexander the Great; he and his successors consolidated all of this part of Africa into an empire. Every Zulu man was a warrior.

The warriors now are pulling rikshas in Durban (still in full war panoply) or are houseboys to the whites. They must work, to pay their head taxes and to buy wives. But waste not too many tears on the lost glories of the Zulu warrior. The Zulu was a conqueror, enslaving and killing—then had the bad luck to meet someone with the same idea but with better weapons. Without defending British colonialism one may at least note that Victoria's troops did not indulge in senseless orgies of blood after a victory. It was Tshaka's habit to kill off all above the age of adolescence when he conquered a tribe. He is reputed to have killed seven thousand of his own subjects when his mother died.

Eshowe, where the Zulus laid siege to the British, is a peaceful modern village now, where the Queen's commissioner supervises the administration of law, tribal and the white law over it, through the paramount and lesser chiefs. My impressions of it are neat brick buildings, a movie theater, a soda fountain and news stand, and an excellent lunch at a clean, modern hotel. Allan Quatermain would never have recognized it.

After lunch we left the highway and drove far out into the fields to visit Ntuli, a native sculptor who enjoys a measure of world fame. His home was the usual group of beehive huts surrounded by farm land. He was not there but his daughter set out his wares and we bought a bust of a Zulu woman. His style is realistic and accurate, with neither the exaggerations of traditional African art nor of the blobs called "modern" in our culture. He shapes what he sees and his eye is good.

We paid seven-and-six, $1.05, for this bust; at these prices Ntuli has become rich, for Zululand. As we left we met him coming home; he was riding a bicycle while wearing a Harris tweed jacket, trousers, shoes, white shirt, and necktie. The weather was such as to make any clothing, any exertion, an invitation to sunstroke, but he kept the jacket on, a perfect classroom example of the symbolism which Thorstein Veblen says is the fundamental motivation of our own society. His outfit was a *reductio ad absurdum* of our own symbolisms in dress but was laughable only if we are willing to laugh first at ourselves—and concede every argument of nudists.

Speaking of nudity, most pictures in travel magazines give the impression that Zulus still dress largely in beads and feathers with the skin mostly uncovered and with the mammary glands living their own lives, wild and free. This is both true and untrue. Those same travel magazines give the impression that the residents of the American far west (of which I am one) dress only in high-heeled boots, Stetsons, and Levi's. I do not own high-heeled boots, although I live in cattle country. But my next door neighbor hardly ever wears anything else. Much the same thing obtains in Zululand; the traditional tribal dress, or lack of it, is extremely common on the reservation. But the Zulus one encounters on the road or in town look much like poor country Negroes of our own deep south, being dressed usually in shabby equivalents of white man's clothes. Our guide told us that the natives were required to cover up when they came into town and that the ones we saw on the road were mostly going to or returning from town.

This explanation satisfied me until later in the day. We had returned the hundred miles from Zululand and were driving through an expensive residential suburb of Durban, which is a wealthy modern city. Suddenly I saw on the sidewalk near us a white child about four years old who was being hotly pursued by a young Zulu woman. An open front door made it evident that the child had made a break for freedom and was being chased down by its nursemaid. The only oddity about the scene was that the young woman was naked except for something wrapped around her waist.

I called Mr. Brown's attention to it. "How about *that*?"

He frowned. "Well, it is not exactly against the law; it is just considered bad form."

That evening Ticky and I attended a performance of a company of the Folies Bergère; it had its customary nude tableaux, as naked as any country scene in Zululand. There may be some thread of logic running through our tribal taboos concerning skin covering but I am unable to figure it out.

The following morning we had a few hours free in the city itself; we spent it, without success, in tramping or riding from one steamship booking office to another, trying to tie down passage from Singapore to Australia. All we achieved was sore feet and a detailed view of downtown Durban. The city spreads along the waterfront the way Chicago sprawls along the Lake; it is as modern as Chicago and much prettier. There are East Indians, Europeans, and Zulus in about the same numbers, each living in their own areas but mixing in the business district. Except for some in the Transvaal this was our first encounter with the East Indians. They are merchants and businessmen of great skill, equal to or exceeding the Chinese. They save every penny, save for a prevalent weakness for powerful, flashy American automobiles, and many of them are extremely wealthy, although they were originally imported as coolie labor in the cane fields.

The blacks hate them. The grave race riots of recent years in Durban were between Zulus and East Indians; the British were not directly involved. They have a reputation for cheating the Zulus at every turn. I cannot vouch for this either way, but it does seem evident that if unlimited immigration from India were permitted (which is what India wants) the Zulu, already crowded onto insufficient land by his present masters, would soon have nothing at all left. The Zulu is already extremely poor. The population density on his reservation land is already half again as high as it is elsewhere in the Union. He makes a slim living as a servant to the whites or working for the large corporate sugar cane plantations that surround his land; it may take him years to pay for his first wife. Marriage is expensive on their scale—eight oxen for a healthy fourteen-year-old maiden, up to twelve oxen for a princess. (Prices are almost twice that high in Swaziland, I never learned why.) After sweating for years to pay the *lobola* for his loved one (don't let the purchase custom fool you; these are love matches usually), he may still have to live away from home most of the time to gain cash for taxes and necessities while his wife sweats in the fields to keep food in the bellies of the piccanins.

Underneath the Zulu is still a warrior; if he finds, or believes, that the East Indians are making his present almost intolerable lot still harder there will be more bloodshed.

We sailed from South Africa later that day with very mixed feelings. I think relief predominated. South Africa is a country wonderful, beautiful, and rich—and terrifyingly mismanaged. There is no indication of any possibility that it will gradually evolve into a better and more humane civilization; the dominant minority is grimly determined not to give an inch. The whip is still their answer to the mutterings and rumblings from underneath. Mau Mau has not yet reached South Africa, but it is only a few miles to the north and there are known to be secret societies spreading among the Bantus, brotherhoods determined to avenge their wrongs and waiting for the Day.

When that day comes the houseboy from next door will be waiting to cut throats. In the meantime I can't see a blessed thing that we can do to prevent it.

IX

We Learn About Oriental Service

THE DEPRESSION ENGENDERED by South Africa we shook off almost at once; the voyage across the Indian Ocean to Singapore was almost idyllically pleasant. The weather was warm without being hot, the sea was calm, the motion of the ship almost imperceptible. We had acquired status and seniority now; we were invited to the Captain's table. The day we first boarded the *Ruys,* when we had been intimidated by her size and luxury, frightened by the brisk, well-dressed passengers who looked right through us, seemed remote and unlikely. We were old-timers who had been in the ship as long as anyone and longer than any but a couple from Buenos Aires. We were almost plank-owners and we enjoyed the status.

The crowd of first-class passengers was down to about half and still further reduced by East Indians who kept to themselves and by French-speaking Mauritians who kept almost as much to themselves. But there was a dance, or movies, or "horse races," or bingo, or some social event every night; there was a cocktail party before dinner each evening; there was swimming, sports, loafing, and long siestas in the daytime. It was hard to remember that somewhere over the wide blue horizon men were dying wretchedly in jungles, the veto was being exercised in the U.N., and the planet as a whole was moving steadily toward what threatened to be the final Armageddon. Under our keel slid the prehistoric continent of

Gondwanaland and I lost the cribbage championship of the Indian Ocean—John Lloyd cut the jack when it was my first count and I was certain to go out. There ought to be a law!

John was a young Englishman fresh out of Oxford, who had joined the ship in Africa. Young, handsome, urbane, and invariably good-natured, he was an asset in any social group. When Ticky told him that his cumberbund should be Dubonnet in shade, rather than claret, he agreed, stripped it off and threw it overboard, and resumed dancing, all with smiling aplomb. (Ticky was left speechless.) We learned that he, like his father before him, had been a member of the "Gonfal Loungers" at Oxford, a club devoted to sitting on the steps in front of one of the buildings there and "observing ye good things God hath made."

"Women, you mean?" I asked.

"Oh, yes, but not necessarily. Just 'ye good things God hath made.' "

"Sounds like P. G. Wodehouse's Drones Club."

"Not exactly. Though I will say that some of the members of the Drones Club would be welcome in the Loungers."

In order to qualify for the Loungers after nomination it was necessary to get oneself arrested on Boat Race Night and be held overnight in jail. This, as John explained, was not easy to do—the second part, that is, about being held in jail overnight, because the University's proctors waited at the police station each Boat Race Night in order to take charge of any young gentlemen who had celebrated too boisterously; it was necessary to change one's appearance, accent, vocabulary, and manner so convincingly that a proctor with years of experience would not recognize the culprit as a University student and invoke the ancient immunities.

Another major asset was Bert and Molly, two Australians who sat with us at the Captain's table. Bert had been serving the United Nations all over the world for the past five years, as a forester in the Food & Agriculture staff. His last job had been to survey the potentialities of the Amazon Valley, and now they were returning home to buy a plantation in Queensland. Bert and Molly were as perfectly Australian as

John was British—in accent, vocabulary, and attitudes. Bert maintained that all Australians grew to look like kangaroos; he illustrated it, with gestures, on himself and his wife. "They get long, pointed noses, ears that stick out, big soft brown eyes, and pear-shaped behinds. Watch for it, you'll see."

(When we got to Australia we could not help but remember this—and it did seem as if he were right. The power of suggestion, no doubt.)

There were Earl and Marianne, of Princeton, Buenos Aires, and Caracas. Earl was an investment banker by profession and a student of yoga by preference; he could assume the full lotus seat, then stand on his head—this, mind you, on the deck of a rolling ship. If you think this is easy, try just the first part: sit down on the floor and wrap yourself into the lotus seat, with the soles of both feet turned upwards in your lap. If you can untie yourself thereafter and walk away unassisted, you are about ready for your beginner's license.

There was the Captain himself, who managed always to be a warm and convivial host while continuing to be a very taut shipmaster. The *Ruys* was clean from stem to stern and perfectly run, but the Captain was always ready to dance all night and his table was usually about thirty minutes late for dinner because, ten minutes after the gong had sounded, the Captain would smile sheepishly and say, "I sink we haff time for annozzer one." So we would.

There were minor frictions, of course, such as South Africans demanding to know why we did not pay more for their gold, people who read us lectures on how the world would be perfectly safe if the United States would just refrain from trying to start a new war, and people who found everything about the United States just too dreadfully quaint and repulsive. Ticky and I tried to avoid such useless arguments but sometimes we were cornered. One South African demanded to know of me why Americans insisted on making such funny sounds instead of speaking English?

He himself was speaking a county dialect I could not identify but which I could hardly understand, but I pretended a politeness I did not feel and tried to explain that American was an independent variation of English, with its own spelling, pronunciation, and rules. This struck him as silly. So I asked him what English accent he wanted us to imitate?—Yorkshire, Oxonian, Cockney, Devon, or what? This ended the discussion without convincing either one of us.

The United Kingdom shows a much wider variation in speech in one tight little island than we do in our continent-wide spread. To have our American speech patronized sets my teeth on edge.

Ticky tangled to the point of brass rags with one English-woman in the ship. This female had insisted on inquiring into one aspect of our economy: "You don't really mean to tell me that you have to *pay* for medicines and hospital care? How dreadful! Why don't you have socialized medicine?"

Ticky glared at her. "We can't afford it! We've had to pay for *British* socialized medicine!"

I've tried to impress on Ticky the necessity of keeping her temper when needled, but I am afraid that she will never qualify for a job with the State Department.

But I have a sneaking suspicion that her uncivil hyperbole contains a legitimate criticism of most of our foreign aid program. Have we really been getting our money's worth in most cases?

We made only a dawn-to-dusk stop at Mauritius. Mauritius is a place I must have missed when I studied geography as a kid but it turns out to be a large and populous island. It exports sugar cane and imports everything else. The language is French, the flag is British, and the population is overwhelmingly East Indian. This is another one of those odd chunks of real estate that England took over during the Napoleonic Wars and never turned loose, like Tristan da Cunha, and, for that matter, South Africa itself. The dominant French population are largely royalists; they appear to believe sincerely that a restoration of the Bourbon crown would fix up all of the ills of France. I don't share the belief myself but I have no objection, as I doubt if it could make things worse. Port Louis is well equipped and beautiful but very busy; the *Ruys* had to anchor and we went in by launch. The shopkeepers, taxi drivers, money changers, and such are mostly Moslem Indians; the field laborers are Hindu; they look alike and have no use for each other.

I changed South African pounds for Mauritian rupees and we hired a taxi. A rupee appeared to be about nineteen cents but the three-way conversion was so complicated that I could not have solved it without a sliderule—if I was cheated, I never knew it. Certainly we were not overcharged in the long run, as a day's drive for four of us, lunch, beer, baksheesh, and the launch came to less than eight dollars each.

Port Louis is a picturesque and cleanly little town of narrow streets and cobblestones. We left it and headed around the island, which is basically one large, long-since-extinct volcano. It used to be covered with tropical rain forest; now all but about a fifth has been cleared and planted. As to climate one need only say that the inhabitants go to Durban, if possible, during the worst months to escape the heat—while the Durbanites are going to Transvaal or Cape Town for the same reason.

We stopped to see the botanical gardens, which are beautiful, old, and very lush. Ticky trotted happily around, pointing to things and spouting Latin, and I identified a mango. There were giant tortoises in a pen there, which looked much like the famous Galápagos tortoises and seemed almost as big. About then mosquitoes started harrying us and I insisted that we move on; Mauritius has malaria.

All day long we kept running into religious processions; it was the festival of "Cavadee" for the Tamil Hindu coolies. Who Cavadee was, or what; what he did, or it signified— these I never found out and my interest in trying to discern the sense behind it was considerably cooled by the fact that the central figure in each procession was a "holy man" with skewers stuck through his cheeks, in one side and out the other. To find nonsense posing in the name of religion it is not necessary to go outside my home town, but most of it seems harmless at worst. Mutilation seems to me another matter. I have no patience with any so-called religion that practices it, and would not bother to study its claims save through morbid curiosity.

We crass Westerners are often urged to study the exquisite spiritual beauties of Hindu religion and philosophy and I will readily admit that some of their religious poetry reads pretty well. But I contend that the disgusting behavior of many of their alleged "holy men" relieves us of any intellectual obligation to take the stuff seriously. No amount of sanctimonious rationalization can make such behavior anything but pathological.

These parades wound around through the streets and into the open country, where the Tamils gathered under trees and piled flowers in front of holy pictures. Their prayers, speeches, and hymns were strange to us but the air was more that of a Sunday School picnic than of Sunday School itself—little children scurried around underfoot, only slightly restrained by their solemn, sari-clad mothers. I noticed caste marks on foreheads and asked our driver what each meant. But he was Mohammedan and not only did not know but was contemptuous of such things.

Our driver took us to a pleasant hotel high up in the hills where we got an excellent lunch . . . only to find out after lunch that the hotel had refused him even back room or back door service because he was not "European." It was infuriating but there was nothing we could do. We urged him to stop at once somewhere where he could eat, but he shrugged and said that he would wait.

But his son, grandson, or nephew will probably someday own the hotel. The sahib's sun is setting in those parts.

We drove around the rim of the extinct crater, an awesome sight of textbook perfection—then dropped back down into Port Louis. The ship sailed late that afternoon. It had been worth a day but Mauritius is not a place I want to see again.

We crossed the equator without ceremony and turned into the Straits of Malacca, dropping back down toward Singapore. After days without raising a ship we were suddenly in heavy traffic and amidst numerous small islands, as well as having Sumatra on our starboard hand. I was surprised at the large numbers of lights visible on the Sumatran coast at night and had it impressed on me in a fashion that the *World Almanac* figures do not: these islands are very densely populated. We think of them as jungle and they are—but all of them are much more heavily populated than the States . . . New Jersey, not Wyoming, is the reasonable comparison. I think perhaps the strongest impression that we brought back from the Far East was the tremendous problem of population pressure. This is going to give us headaches, big ones, long after the communists are forgotten—and I have no idea what to do about it. It may be that there is no solution other than the ancient, tragic checks of famine, pestilence, and war.

It is all very well to answer glibly with "birth control." Actually it is no answer but simply a piece of verbal magic, like, "The Lord will provide." But the Lord *won't* provide and birth control *won't* work on this wholesale scale, for obvious reasons of education and economics and for much deeper reasons of human psychology and body chemistry which we do not fully understand. I once saw a sucker ad for a method of exterminating cockroaches; the device was two blocks of wood: place the cockroach between them and squeeze.

Birth control is about that effective—excellent on a retail scale; worthless at the wholesale level.

But don't blame any religious opposition to birth control. In the long run, religious opposition to or humanistic support for birth control are both as irrelevant and as ineffectual as prayers for rain; the numbers on this planet keep increasing just the same—fifty-five thousand more people at today's breakfast table than there were yesterday morning, twenty million more this year than last year, in each decade an increase greater than *the entire population of the United States.*

Occasionally one sees stories which "solve" this problem by emigration to other planets. I wish it would work but it won't. Oh, we will colonize the other planets someday; that is as certain as tomorrow's sunrise. But it will have no effect at all on the problem of population pressure on our own beautiful and tragic globe. To stay even, not gain an inch, we would have to persuade or coerce nearly sixty thousand people to take to the sky every day of every year. Bypass the psychological problem, assume that it is solved—by force, if you like. The physical problem remains: we can build spaceships but we can't build that many. There isn't enough steel, aluminum, uranium, or anything else on this whole planet to permit us to build enough space ferries to move the daily increment and keep on doing it, day after day, year after year.

The real problem of the Far East is not that so many of them are communists, but simply that there are so many of them.

The above is somewhat out of its proper order, for we have not yet seen Singapore, where I first learned the meaning of the word "teeming"—nor Djakarta, especially Djakarta. We arrived in Singapore early in the morning, my own first impression of it being a shout from Ticky: "Hey! Look!"

Passing by our porthole only a few feet away was the ribbed sail of a Chinese junk. It brought the Far East into my lap. While I knew that those funny sails and odd ships were as contemporary as atomic piles, subconsciously I had had them classed with pigtails and the old Dowager Empress as something out of an earlier era. So we hurried into clothes and topside to watch the junks.

Arrival in port was accompanied by the usual hoorah, some of it necessary, some of it questionable. As usual, Captain's Dinner and arrival in port almost overlapped, with about three hours sleep only between. As usual the port doctor wanted to see us while we were at breakfast, the immigration officer required our presence while we were packing, and the steward's bill contained a major error which had to be corrected. There was the staff to tip, chief steward, head steward, table stewards, room steward (we were sad at leaving the incomparable Kwai Yau), lounge deck boys, night man, etc. Mail, messages, cables, addresses to be exchanged—it was past ten o'clock before we were checked in at the Raffles Hotel.

There was a cubic foot of mail waiting for us there, much of it business mail, and I sat down to sort through it to determine what was important while Ticky settled us in. In about five minutes I looked up and said peevishly, "Have you unpacked?"

"No."

"Then don't. I'm going to see if they can move us to a quiet room." The room we were in, actually a bedroom, sitting room, and bath suite, was excellent, but it was on the ground floor and right at the corner of the building and ten feet outside was a traffic light. Every time the light changed the traffic would pour in one window and out the other. Traffic in Singapore is thick, enthusiastic, and noisy. Singapore is just above the equator and the climate is a steady hot and humid, like being soaked in warm oatmeal. Little men with sledges were playing *Hammer Ring* inside my head and I was beginning to realize that I should have gone to bed early after the Captain's Dinner even though I had wanted to say good-by and drink a cup of kindness yet with everyone in the ship. My morale is never improved by the irritations of quitting a ship, moving baggage, and getting through customs, and it had not been helped by an incident at the gate. When the customs officer had asked us if we had had anything to declare, Ticky had looked him in the eye and said, "Two pounds of heroin."

His eyes bugged out, then he decided to treat it as a joke, laughed hollowly, said, "Yes yes, no doubt," and refrained from searching us. But I did not draw a breath until we were outside and in a taxi.

Then I took a deep breath to load me for what I had to say. "Look, you red-headed juvenile delinquent, don't you know you can get us into trouble with pranks like that?"

"Nonsense! I didn't have any heroin."

"Sure, sure—and you got away with it. But suppose he had been one of that large number who despise Americans? He could have decided to teach you a lesson in respect for Her Majesty's officers, you know."

Ticky said something rude and irrelevant about Her Majesty's officers. Having little respect for vested authority at home she seems to believe instinctively that the very notion of authority abroad is presumptuous and probably unconstitutional; the spirit of the Boston Tea Party is always just below the surface.

But it was not a joke to me. I was seriously worried that she might grow restive at the wrong moment and get herself or both of us into trouble that the American consul would be hard put to straighten out. She was behaving like the fictional heroine who insists on doing something foolish and dangerous which then gives the hero a chance to be heroic. But I was no hero; I was just a middle-aged man in glasses who had no influence in foreign ports and no Lone Ranger tricks up his sleeve.

"Look, baby," I answered wearily, "we've been all over this before. Don't you realize that he had the authority and the right to keep us there for three or four more hours while he subjected us and our baggage to a probe search? How would you like to be stripped to the skin?"

"I'd like to see anybody try it!" She leaned forward and got herself unstuck from the cushions of the taxi. "Though this would certainly be the weather for it."

All in all, my nerves twanged like a harp by the time we reached the hotel; the traffic noises and the damp heat of our room were simply the insupportable last straws. I sought out the manager, an imperturbable East Indian, and told him my troubles.

He showed me several rooms, all of which were for one reason or another no better than the one we were in. Then he somewhat reluctantly showed me one which suited. I took it and hurried back.

"Any luck?" Ticky asked.

"Yes. Grab your purse; we're going out on the town. They'll move our baggage while we are gone."

"But what about our new room? Can't I look at it?"

"Never mind now. It's upstairs and clear across the hotel, a couple of blocks away. It's okay, you'll see it when you get back. Come on now, let's see the town."

She came somewhat reluctantly but soon forgot about the change in room once we were in a taxi and on our way. Singapore, one of the "Seven Sinful Ports," is probably the most fascinating city we saw all the way around the world . . . even though we did not see much of the seamy underside which forms the basis for romantic fiction. No opium dens, no beautiful Eurasians held captive in international brothels, no sinister agents of Dr. Fu Manchu, or (much more probably) of Chou En Lai. All three of the above, plus a knife in the ribs in some dark alley, are (I feel sure) available in Singapore, but they do not come to the attention of middle-class couples traveling in each other's company and staying out of dark places.

Even without them Singapore is a three-ring circus and a year-long Mardi Gras. It has a million people packed into a short stretch of waterfront suitable for fifty thousand at the most. It is a Chinese city, despite the Union Jack overhead and the fact that it is more than a thousand miles from China proper; there are only twelve thousand Europeans, mostly civil servants and traders; four out of five are Chinese and the fifth is an Asiatic of some other sort.

Properly speaking, the whole city is a slum, so tightly stacked are they one on another. But it is so alive, so cheerful, so bursting with energy that the slumlike quality of it is not depressing. There are admitted slums near the waterfront, hovels built of trash and lived in by people who have neither pot nor window, and there are many, many narrow back alleys that are slums as the term is used in Chicago or New York. But even the "good" streets are so jampacked as to be slums to anyone used to mountain and prairie—or even in comparison with the endless apartment houses of our big cities. The first thing Ticky said, when we turned off the quay boulevards into the city itself, was, "Oh, look! They've got all their flags out. I wonder what they are celebrating?"

A second look showed that they were not flags; the swarming mercantile street we were on was arched over by housewives' laundry, threaded on bamboo poles which stuck out and up from almost every window. Most of the clothes were brightly colored and the effect was very gay, but the effect was accidental and went on every day.

Singapore is the place for shopping. You can buy anything; they will sell you your own hat if you lay it down on the counter. The city is loaded with bargains, most of them real, and waiting to be dickered over—treasures of the Far East, manufactured goods of the West, and careful copies of the latter from Japan and elsewhere. Some few spoilsport innovators have introduced fixed prices but they may be ignored; most buying and selling is still a joyous game, each trying without malice to outwit the other.

It affected Ticky the way fresh catnip affects a cat. Dickering in South America she had never really gotten used to; their shops are too much like ours and South American politeness is so overwhelming that it seemed rude to suggest that the price was too high. But in the bawling, brawling atmosphere of Singapore bazaars and stalls she was able to swing into the spirit of it and enjoy it—so much so that I began to wonder what would happen when we got home. The butcher would say to her, "That will be three dollars and eighty-seven cents, please"—and Ticky would look at him scornfully and say, "Don't be silly! I'll give you a dollar and a quarter. Wrap it up."

I made a mental note to be present when it happened; I wanted to see the butcher's expression.

The prices, even the fixed prices, really were preposterously low. In general a Straits dollar would buy about as much as a U.S. dollar back home—but our dollar would buy three Straits dollars. Ticky bought a little handmade silver bracelet charm, a Chinese junk complete to rigging of silver thread, for five cents American—and this was at a fixed-price store. Later on, one of similar quality purchased at the Royal Hawaiian Hotel in Honolulu set us back eight dollars.

The most colorful place to shop is Change Alley, a narrow passage ten feet wide and a block long but crowded with a hundred permanent shops, uncountable sidewalk merchants, and swarms of money changers. The money changers will swap any currency for any other currency, operating directly out of their pockets while people jostle their elbows on both sides, performing complicated arithmetic in their heads without any noticeable pause, and coming out with an answer that you had better check carefully, then count your money carefully.

Then count your fingers. And the fillings in your teeth.

The little holes in the wall forming each side of Change Alley will sell you anything from really valuable precious stones, or carved jade of high quality, to plastic Buddhas made in Jersey City. Between them, almost covering the already-crowded and too-narrow pavement, traders operating from card tables, push carts, or even old newspaper spread on the street to protect in part their handfuls of merchandise, will sell you anything from a full meal to a Chinese New Year's greeting or a ring with a peepshow built into it. The feeling is Coney Island combined with Woolworth's, all with a lusty flavor of its own. I wish I could go there every day.

A little shopping and a little sightseeing and it was time to go back to the hotel for lunch and a sight of our new room. We had selected the Raffles Hotel from Colorado Springs, because of its fame in history, legend, and fiction. It really is a fabulous old pile, a luxury hotel in every sense, ancient through it is, and a place where one expects an E. Phillips Oppenheim spy to be lurking behind every potted palm.

We picked up our key at the desk and I led Ticky across the "World-Famous Palm Court" (it says so right here on this postcard), up a flight of outdoor stairs, and onto the gallery which led to our room. I let her in and watched her.

She did not say much at first, but wandered around looking at things and touching them. The living room was twenty-five feet long, fifteen feet wide and about twelve feet high, furnished in ebony and trimmed in Chinese red lacquer, with several easy chairs, tables, lamps, a couch, and a buffet. There were two electric punkahs overhead. Beyond the living room was an enclosed porch with two day beds, a large and fancy bar, more easy chairs. Opening off it to the left was an open porch just as roomy which was furnished lavishly with smart garden furniture.

Ticky turned back to me with her eyes wide and her expression solemn. "Yes, darling, but where do we sleep?"

"In here," I answered, and opened double doors wide with a manner suitable to the janitor of a cathedral.

The bedroom was twenty-five feet long, big as the living room, and contained two king-size Hollywood beds, chairs, two chaise longues, two enormous wardrobes, an oversize dressing table, and an executive desk. Two airconditioning units served it, one at each end. Beyond it was a tiled bath fifteen feet square.

There remained one door I had not opened when I had taken the "room." We found beyond it a service porch, not shared with anyone, which had clothes lines, wash tubs, and other useful, homely items.

Ticky came back into the bedroom, sighed deeply and said quietly, "But can we afford it? Heavens, can we even pay for it?"

"Brace yourself. This so-called 'room' costs just three dollars a day more than the 'minimum' room we were in. At that differential I didn't think we could afford *not* to enjoy oriental splendor once in our lives—we never will again."

Ticky gasped, sat down suddenly, and began to giggle.

"Do you remember," I went on, "what we paid for just one room about half the size of any one of these four at Sun Valley last year? That one room without meals cost just what this suite plus six meals a day costs here."

"Are you sure there isn't some mistake?"

"There is no mistake . . . but I never saw a sharper proof that our own economy does not match in with the rest of the world; we are getting this much too cheaply. But I haven't told you the rest of the joke. The manager was reluctant to show me this place. He asked twice when we would sail; I told him I did not know but Wednesday looked like a good bet. He shook his head solemnly and said that he had one more 'room' but it was reserved for Wednesday.

"So I suggested that he could move us a second time, if necessary, and he finally showed me this. But the last thing he said was, 'You understand now, if you take this room and stay past Wednesday, I'll have to move you. Mr. Rockefeller always has this room and he has reserved it and he will expect to have it this time.'"

As it turned out, Mr. Rockefeller stayed as a houseguest of the Queen's Commissioner and canceled his hotel reservation, so, although we did not sail on Wednesday, we did not have to move. We enormously enjoyed the use of "his room" and could well understand why he would ask for it specifically.

With the room came Foo. I think Foo was number-one boy for that floor, but he took care of the end suite himself. Kwai Yau had introduced us to the perfection that the Chinese can bring to domestic service; Foo continued this level of intelligent, anticipatory service but with some charming and individual quirks of his own. He was about four feet ten and could not have weighed a hundred pounds in his uniform. At a wild guess I would place his age at sixty, give or take ten years. His usual expression was one of self-contained rage, which gave way at rare intervals to a shy and surprisingly sweet smile.

Foo stood for no nonsense from his guests. They were going to be served properly whether they liked it or not. The conventional term for this is "keeping face," and so it is, but I prefer to state it more explicitly; Foo had a steel-hard personal integrity which made him require of himself nothing less than perfection in everything that he did no matter what anyone else thought of it.

We shared with him a modicum of language, not quite English, not quite Pidgin, which did well enough for domestic matters. Ticky's first chore was to sort out clothes requiring laundering and drycleaning—practically every stitch we owned since we had had no chance for drycleaning since leaving Buenos Aires and had not been able to send laundry the last few days before arrival in Singapore. She was pleased to see that twenty-four-hour service was available for a 50% extra charge, pointed it out on the ticket to Foo, and explained to him most carefully that we wanted everything back the next day.

"Too much money," Foo answered.

Ticky explained that she knew it cost more but that we needed the clothes.

"When you sail?"

Ticky admitted that our ship did not sail until the middle of the week following but told him again that she wanted the hurry-up service anyway. Foo shut up and staggered out with most of the contents of ten suitcases. I had saved out one suit and a nylon shirt and some shorts; Ticky had the dress she had come ashore in and one dinner dress.

The next day a couple of shirts and some underwear came back, nothing else. To Ticky's inquiry Foo answered, "Tuesday!"

"But I wanted them today!" Foo shrugged and would not answer.

We made do with what we had. My one suit was beginning to smell like a bear rug; it was well to be upwind of me. On Tuesday all the rest came back. Foo brought them in, hung up the suits, stowed the laundry, and presented Ticky with the chit, stabbing his finger at it and saying with fierce triumph, "*See?* I save twelve dollars!" (Straits dollars).

We thanked him sincerely and did not laugh until he had left. Then we gratefully put on clean clothes.

We had been there two days when Foo braced me on the subject of shoes. I have never gotten used to the cosmopolitan custom of putting one's shoes outside at night to be polished. In the *Ruys* Kwai Yau had noted this and had taken care of it his own way by selecting a pair each night and putting them out himself; he never mentioned it. Foo's approach was different. He stepped up to me, looked up, glared, and said angrily, "Tonight—you put shoes outside bedroom door! Never mind corridor, just bedroom door. I come in, get!" He grew almost purple and jabbed his finger at my feet. "Your shoes are *too dirty!*"

I put my shoes outside the bedroom door.

Some days later Ticky and I were entertaining in our "room" before dinner. We had become used to having Foo pop up whenever needed and to his being never more than a buzzer signal away. This time for the first time, when I pushed the service button, a strange Chinese appeared. I asked, "Where's Foo?" but could not understand the answer; this staff member had very little English and I had no Cantonese at all. So I said, "Never mind," and ordered drinks—with no difficulty, as such international words as "gin sling" and "martini" we shared.

The drinks arrived in a few minutes. About ten minutes thereafter Foo showed up, in uniform. We managed to get it straight that I had simply wanted bar service, that it had been provided and I wanted nothing else. Foo left.

The next day I remembered to ask him about it. After a certain amount of semantic difficulty I got it clear: The strange bellman, while weak in English, had nevertheless understood that I had inquired for Foo—so a message had been sent out into town, Foo had dressed again in his uniform, left the bosom of his family, and had come at once to find out what I wanted, even though he was not on duty. I tried to apologize; he shrugged and closed the subject.

We did not tip him at all until we left. The amount had been the matter of much thought and had been arrived at by starting with a formula which one of the international oil companies advised their employees stopping in Singapore hotels to use; to this we had added a percentage to allow for the fact that Americans are expected to tip higher than others, plus a percentage for superlative service, plus the amount he had saved us on drycleaning. It added up to a generous tip by Singapore standards but a stingy one (in comparable circumstances) in the United States.

Foo seemed quite pleased with it. But he left rather hastily and returned with the corridor boy who did the heavy cleaning. Foo pointed at him. "He good boy, too!"

I had no formula to help me in this, so I gravely presented the other man with a tip which I hoped was appropriate in view of their relative ranks. Foo seemed to approve—he did not glare at me.

Pleasant as our suite-cum-Foo was, we spent little time in it. A few peanuts fed to a dog in Montevideo began to pay off in most surprising dividends. Señor Maurice Nayberg had given us cards of introduction to business correspondents of the Nayberg firm in various ports; we looked up one of them here, Mr. Ho Choy Moo.

From the moment we met Mr. Ho until the day we sailed we were taken in charge, driven around town, taken to dinner, helped with our shopping, taken sightseeing, taken on a long drive north into the Sultanate of Johore, taken to amusement parks, even taken to church. And when we left, Mr. Ho supplied us with letters of introduction to smooth our way through Indonesia.

It still is not clear to me just why hospitality was so heavily lavished on us. We had made it clear at the outset that our acquaintance with the Naybergs was of the slightest, covering only a few hours of our short stay in Montevideo. Mr. Ho had himself never met the Naybergs and knew them only by business correspondence. It seems to me that protocol would have been more than satisfied had Mr. Ho taken us to lunch and advised what to see and where to shop—not that we had even that coming to us but to show courtesy to the Naybergs.

Whatever the reasons were (and I can't believe it was just our sweet dispositions even though we usually get along all right with children and dogs)—whatever the reasons, we were given a free ride through Singapore which could not have been purchased from a travel agency at any cost. The Hos even included John Lloyd in much of it, simply because he was with us much of the time—John was enjoying an indefinitely long vacation in Singapore at his employer's expense because his permanent-residence visa for Manila had not yet come through.

We were treated to superlative Cantonese food, food which made us realize that even the best Chinese restaurants in the States do not bother to supply the real thing to unappreciative and ignorant heathen. Bird's-nest soup and shark fin were the only items I could identify but I must state emphatically that chop suey had no part in it. Mr. Ho insisted that Ticky must use chopsticks and instructed her in the art to the point that she learned to pick pieces of cracked ice out of a bowl with smooth plastic sticks. Try it sometime when you are feeling lucky; the coefficient of friction between ice and smooth urea plastic is zero followed by a string of noughts. The trick is to use the sticks as gently as possible, almost no pressure; occidentals tend to use them like a pair of pliers.

Often the whole family escorted us, Mr. and Mrs. Ho and four children—Ho Chee Pen, Ho Chee Fei, the one daughter

Ho Mei Ling (after Madame Chiang), and the baby Ho Chee Cheong. Boys carry a generation name, in this case "Chee," as well as a family name and a given name. Mrs. Ho was an exquisitely beautiful little girl who had kept her figure and her sweet disposition through four children. The children were all well behaved but so shy that we did not get well acquainted with them.

Mr. Ho dressed much as I dressed and the kids were dressed like the kids back home but Mrs. Ho usually wore a chang sam, which is the formal, stylized Chinese dress with the high collar, skirt slit at each side, and quite tight. It must be tight— Mrs. Ho, modest herself as a nun, once went home to change because she decided that the chang sam she was wearing was too loose.

Ticky had to have a chang sam and Mrs. Ho advised her where to go. Singapore is a place where they will take your measurements in the morning and deliver a tailor-made suit to your hotel in time to wear it to dinner the same day. Ticky's measurements were not taken until around noon but the dress was delivered about five o'clock. I concede that tailoring a chang sam is not the job a man's suit is, but try to get that service in New York. The dress was midnight blue heavy silk with a dragon of sequins coiled across the chest—price, $10 U.S.

It appeared to have been sprayed on with a paint gun, rather than tailored and it met with Mrs. Ho's approval. The peekaboo effect of the side slits is rather startling. Shorts show a lot more skin but shorts do not dress up the landscape the way a chang sam does.

The Hos took us to one of the "Worlds"—there are three, the Great World, the Happy World, and the New World, and they are the Singapore versions of Coney Island, so much like our own amusement parks that there is no need to mention anything but the differences, the first being theaters for classic Chinese drama and the second being Joget dancing. The Chinese theater was the sort which can be seen in New York and San Francisco in the States—days-long performances, extremely ornate costumes and hair-dos, stagehands that sit and smoke and have lunch right on the stage, very stylized acting and a singsong delivery not like ordinary Chinese speech. Since we did not understand the dialog and did not know the traditional plots it was interesting only as an oddity to us. But I was impressed by one thing: I had been told that all the female parts were taken by men. This may be so; I found it almost beyond belief. Those cunning little "girls" with their high voices were much more convincing than any female impersonators I have ever seen before.

Joget dancing is the sort of social dancing the Mohammedan Malays do—mostly extremely sexy rumbas and foxtrots. The "Worlds" have several dance halls with taxi dancers available, all just as one finds it in America save for one point: their religion frowns on bodily contact, even with the finger tips, so the taxi dancers follow their partners without the help of any physical lead; they "shadow dance." They are very skilled at it and never fumble in even the fastest and most complicated steps. It appears to be a skill developed by years of practice; we noticed several apprentices, nine or ten years old, who hardly ever gained partners but would join some couple and duplicate every motion of the older girl. The kids seemed only slightly less skilled at it than were the grown women.

While the religious injunction forbade touching, it did not seem to forbid anything else. The couples danced only an inch or two apart and the undulant gyrations they went through would cause them to be thrown off the floor anywhere else. A hula dancer would have blushed.

The long drive the Hos took us on into the Sultanate of Johore was remarkable on one point only—a sight of royalty. Singapore is an island like Manhattan, larger than Manhattan but much smaller than Long Island; it is connected with the mainland, which at this point is Johore, by a causeway, one which the Japanese armies found very convenient when Singapore was caught with its guns facing the wrong way.

We passed through customs for once with just a wave of the hand. Singapore is a free port while Johore is not, but the guards at the border did not seem worried about smuggling.

The countryside, the manners, and the people seemed no different from Singapore save that we were now out in the country and passed through only an occasional village; the buildings were substantial in structure and Western in appearance—no grass shacks, no mud huts.

We glanced at the palace grounds from the outside, then went on to the zoo. It was like any other fairly large zoo except for one thing: it was not, strictly speaking, a public zoo although it was open to the public. It was the private property of the Prince Regent ("Regent" because the old Sultan is ill) and existed only because he likes animals and wanted a zoo. While we were poking around among his caged tigers and apes and so forth, we ran across him. Mr. Ho pointed him out.

It is my contention that the least he could have done, with due respect to the romantic notions of citizens of democracies who gain their notions of royalty from books, would have been to show up riding an elephant and wearing a turban. But he was leaning against a borrowed Jaguar sports car and wearing a beaten-felt hat, a sweat-stained khaki shirt, and wrinkled khaki trousers. We knew the car was borrowed because, as Mr. Ho pointed out, the license plate was that of a private citizen.

If this sort of thing keeps up, I shall have to give away my copy of *The Little Lame Prince*.

But the most amazing place the Hos took us to was the Tiger Balm Garden, also known as Haw Par Villa. There is another one like it, named the same and built by the same man, in Hong Kong; otherwise I am reasonably sure that there is nothing else in the world even remotely resembling it.

Several people aboard ship had said to us, "Be sure not to miss Tiger Balm Garden."

"All right," I had answered. "What is it?"

"Well, uh . . ." Our advisor would pause, look helpless, and add lamely, "Never mind. Just be sure you don't miss it."

I am going to have the same trouble now. I will try to describe it but I probably won't manage to put over its essence. Just be sure that when you go to Singapore *you* do not miss it. It is free, it is not advertised, and nobody cares whether you go or not. It is unlikely that a guide or a taxi driver will suggest it, as there is nothing in it for them. But *don't* miss it.

Tiger Balm Garden is a good many acres of ground thickly covered by statues of rather poor quality.

And the *Venus de Milo* is a badly damaged statue of an overweight female with a busted nose.

You see? A factual description of a work of art is misleading; it does not convey the *Gee-Whiz!* element which is the difference—perhaps the only difference—between success and failure in art.

The statues in Tiger Balm Garden are of plaster and are painted in bright, garish colors. The modeling varies from adequate to poor. The statues do not sit alone on pedestals, but are in groups each of which tells a story; the background scene of each group is sculptured in full detail, furniture, landscape, or whatever is needed. Most of the statues are life size and the effect is to find yourself catapulted right inside a comic book. A sex-horror-crime-sadism comic book it usually is, too, for the emphasis is on the two eternal elements of drama, love and death. Most of the stories depicted are Chinese fairy tales, and pretty rugged fare for tots those stories must be—although classic fairy tales of any culture, including our own, run to themes that could give the comic books cards and spades any day and still excel in blood and violence.

But the themes and moods shift rapidly. Just beyond a long and very bloodthirsty tableau of a war between heaven and hell you find yourself suddenly faced by Donald Duck, seven feet tall and grinning down at you. No excuse is necessary for his presence here; Chinese children know Donald as well as their own fairy tales. A bit farther on is a modern tiled swimming pool, deep end, shallow end, diving board and ladders; it is inhabited by a half dozen mermaids, giant plaster fish and enormous crabs. Why? Well, don't you think a few mermaids would improve any swimming pool?

There is a long underground tunnel which is purgatory in gruesome, explicit detail. Chinese notions about these matters are less poetical than those of Dante, fully as imaginative, and much more drastic. The punishment for a woman guilty of adultery struck me as unnecessarily extreme, and the reward of usury was so horrible that I resolved never to touch the banking & loan business just in case there was something to it.

Ticky refused to look at this stretch. She complained that it made her ill.

But most of the groups and sequences did not show torture, but depicted simple, hearty violence and sex—for example wicked witches who disguised themselves as beauteous, bare-skinned maidens in order to lure wayfaring monks into their caves to rob them. The monks co-operated heartily and everybody had a good time right up to the last scene, where the monks were dispatched quickly and without sadistic furbelows.

What is art? Our own artists have been dinning at us all this century that art need not have draftsmanship, subtle use of color, nor any of the classic disciplines. Certainly these statues would make Praxiteles spin in his grave, but there is a mounting effect of awe, amazement, wonder, and sheer delight. If the scrawls and blobs of our own modernists are art at all, then these lusty creations must be great art.

The Tiger Balm Villas in Singapore and in Hong Kong were built by Aw Boon Haw, multi-millionaire publisher, banker, industrialist, and vendor of patent medicines. His Tiger Balm remedies, the most popular of which is Tiger Balm itself, are used throughout the East. I am told that they are quite useful. In any case they made him fantastically wealthy, much of which wealth he gave away. The Tiger Balm Gardens alone, which deserve to be classed with his charities, would have cost millions of dollars to build here and must have cost in excess of a million even in the Far East, yet there is not even a box in which to drop a voluntary contribution.

I heard two stories as to why he did it: one that he believed that as long as he was creating something he would not die, the other that he could teach basic morals through these frozen morality plays to that part of the population too poor and too ignorant to have had the opportunity to gain moral wisdom from textbook and schoolmaster.

I doubt if either story is true; I suspect that he did it because he wanted to.

United Press reports that he died in Honolulu 4 September 1954. May his unique spirit rest in peace.

As we were leaving Haw Par Villa with the Hos, something came up which made it appropriate and necessary for Ticky and myself to mention what church we belonged to. We had avoided the subject of religion up to then because we did not know whether the Ho family was Buddhist, Confucianist, Christian, or what. The precaution was not uncalled for, as an educated Chinese who also speaks English is not necessarily a product of missionary schools, nor certain to be a convert even though educated by Christian missionaries. On another occasion Mr. Ho had learned that I had studied oriental religions and some mention was made of Confucius—I may have quoted one of his extremely quotable proverbs, or perhaps he did. Two nights later Mr. Ho introduced me to another Chinese gentleman who got me aside and said solemnly, "I understand that you are a student of the Scholar."

I made an intellectual standing broad jump of fifteen thousand miles, recalled that I was somewhere east of Suez and "the Scholar" was not Aristotle, in these parts, but Confucius—so I nodded solemnly and admitted that I had that honor, in a small way.

From then on he treated me not as a tolerated white barbarian, but as an educated gentleman like himself, an equal. My actual knowledge of the great sage is microscopic, but my point is that I would never have been accepted as an equal had I given the impression that I believed that all wisdom and virtue was a monopoly of the Christian faith.

But the situation did come up whereby it was necessary and polite for Ticky and myself to admit that we had been reared in the Methodist Church—whereupon Mr. and Mrs. Ho said with delight, "Why, we're Methodists, too!"

Almost at once we found ourselves attending services in the Straits Chinese Methodist Church.

I found myself projected both in time and space, not merely back to the American middle west but back thirty years as well. This was no boulevard church with a microphone at the pulpit; this was a piece of my childhood. The ladies in the choir wore chang sams, all else was the same, even to the notice board with its movable figures which set forth the attendance last Sunday versus the attendance this Sunday, even to the announcement that the Ladies' Aid was giving a box supper next Thursday evening. I think perhaps it was the nicest thing the Hos did for us.

We visited other churches, among them several Buddhist temples and one Mohammedan mosque. I was not favorably impressed by the Buddhist temples, either by their alleged beauty nor by the attitude of the priests, who seemed to be indifferent to anything but the cash entrance fee. The mosque was much more attractive in its bare, austere beauty than were the temples, which were tastelessly jammed with ornate, overdecorated junk.

We had to remove our shoes to enter the mosque, of course, and Ticky swears that that was when she picked up athlete's foot—which I consider unfair to Islam, as there were daily opportunities to contract it in hotels or aboard ship, especially aboard ship. Ticky just resents that she was told that she must take off her shoes, or stay out.

Earl (the student of yoga) and Marianne, his wife, were also at the Raffles and were tracking down Hindu fakirs among the Tamil colony . . . but this was one religion we did not choose to look up; we had had enough fakirs for a lifetime in one day in Mauritius. There was one adept in town who did a very odd stunt: he would cut off the tongue of one of his followers without letting it bleed—then (so it was seriously claimed) stick it back in place and heal it. I don't know and I did not trot along after Earl and Marianne to find out. But it seems to me you would soon use up a lot of followers that way.

Instead, we went to the botanical gardens the morning that show was supposed to take place, a choice less educational, for me if not for Ticky, since my knowledge of botany is limited to digging dandelions, but a good deal more fun and easier on the stomach.

It was fun because of the monkeys. We purchased a supply of peanuts and bananas from junior merchants near the entrance; as long as the supply lasted we had little time for plants. Wild monkeys swarm in the gardens and they expect tourists to feed them. They gathered around Ticky like a kindergarten class, accepted bananas from here, peeled them carefully, and ate them daintily. Ticky sat on the grass and stowed the peanuts in her lap in order to have both hands free to make fair distribution and maintain discipline, as the monkeys, like children, tried to shove and crowd and each get a lion's share.

While she was thus busy, one more enterprising monk sneaked behind her, made a long arm, and snatched her entire supply of peanuts out of her lap. He headed for a tree top while Ticky shouted, "Hey! come back here."

When she was forced to realize that he was not going to come back, then or later, she turned to me with her eyes round with astonishment. "Did you see that? Why, he's *dishonest.*"

In two more years they will have to let those monks vote.

The day was on us when we would have to leave Singapore, with its crowds and its pungent odors and its trishaws (the coolies no longer pull; they pedal instead) and its pint-sized taxis and its febrile, sleepless activity. We did not want to leave. While it symbolized all the ills of the East and the sins of colonialism, we found the city itself warm and friendly and wonderful, from the little goats that scampered loose on the streets and never quite got hit by the automobiles to the bazaarkeepers who would look you in the eye and try to cheat you, all with the warmest good will.

We wanted to entertain the Ho family at least once before we left; the obvious thing—almost the only thing we were equipped to do—was to invite them to dinner at the Raffles.

But a worry was niggling at the back of my mind. "Ticky, have you considered that we might have trouble? The Hos are not 'European' as the South Africans so squeamishly put it . . . and this place is the last stand of the pukka sahib. We may run into 'Jim Crow' rules. I certainly would not want to subject them to embarrassment."

Ticky nodded. "I've thought of it," she replied crisply, "and I've thought of an answer. We'll serve drinks up here; they can't stop us from doing that. Then we will go down to dinner and if anyone makes the slightest fuss we'll come back here and have dinner served privately up here. Then after dinner you and I will check out of the hotel and as we leave we'll set fire to it."

It seemed a good plan. But it turned out to be unnecessary; no one lifted an eyebrow at "non-Europeans" eating in the main dining room of the Raffles, although we had seen no others. The Far East is changing—Rudyard Kipling might have trouble recognizing the place.

X

The Underside
of the Orient

THIS CHAPTER IS not for the squeamish.

On second thought, I will not be any more graphic than I have to be; if you get the notion that Indonesia is a good place to stay away from, that will be sufficient.

You may remember that we had not only been unable to book transportation from Singapore to Australia but also had not been able to get an Indonesian visa. The visa we did manage to get in Singapore through the intercession of a shipping agent who knew the ropes and was able, by personal favor, to get the consulate to bypass the processing of our papers through six different government departments. We made out endless forms again, naturally. Indonesia not only has the longest and most complicated forms in the silly business but also wants them made out in quadruplicate-original. But we did get the visas.

We found out that our experience was not unique but customary, for we ran into a couple in Singapore from California who had tried to get Indonesian visas from the consulate in San Francisco, only to be forced to sail without them. They tried again in Singapore, as we did, and found their own papers in Singapore, on file with the consul there—whereupon they were required to pay ten dollars apiece to have their old papers canceled before they were allowed to start over and reapply. There is something wildly comical about such super red tape; it excites admiration rather than fury.

I had wanted to go to Bali, but our visa was good only for Djakarta. I did not go to the foot of the line and start over, not merely because I was worn out with red tape at that point but also because I had learned something much more disheartening. For the tourist and photographer Bali has long had two outstanding points of interest, endlessly reduplicated. But the revolutionary government, in its wisdom, has decided that the folk ways of Bali were destructive to the dignity of the new nation; a law was issued requiring sarongs in Bali to start just under the armpits, as they do elsewhere in the islands, instead of considerably lower down as has always been the Balinese practice. Now Bali is just like the other islands of Indonesia.

"Come to Beautiful Bali" indeed! I'll take Minsky's.

And besides that, we couldn't get to Bali anyway. Shipping was awfully tight and we took the only ship we could get, one which stopped only at Djakarta, then went down the east coast of Australia to Brisbane and Sydney. We wanted to land on the west coast of Australia, cross the continent by train, and leave from the east coast. But we had no choice; the only cabin we could get from Singapore to Australia was the one we took, and we got the last cabin in that ship. There was a sister ship going to Fremantle at the same time, but it was chock-a-block, not a berth to be had for love or cumshaw.

The ship we managed to get would have been uncomfortable at best, for she was an old tub which had been designed for Chinese coastal service, overnight trips with two to three thousand Chinese stacked almost like firewood. Now with the Reds running China and that trade gone perhaps forever she had been sketchily refitted as a cargo liner, but the result was far from comfortable. Our stateroom was a third the size of the one we had in the *Ruys* and there were, of course, no private baths. The toilet and bath facilities for men were adequate if not appealing but Ticky found that she shared one facility, bath and toilet combined, with all the other female first-class passengers in the ship; in the course of a three-week voyage this produced more than one acute and embarrassing emergency.

But the worst thing about the ship was that it was filthy dirty. The ship had no purser; the chief steward, an Indonesian, doubled in brass and carried out neither the duties of a purser nor the duties of a chief steward properly. In consequence his Chinese staff, with whom he could communicate only through his Chinese assistant, ran the ship to suit themselves. Now it is an unpleasant fact that lower-class Chinese have no notion at all of Western concepts of sanitation; this is not a racist remark, it is simply a fact. Inasmuch as the stewards in this ship received no instruction in these matters and were subjected to little or no discipline, they did as they pleased—and what they pleased was often disgusting.

For example (and I will keep the examples down to a minimum), discarded towels were laundered only if visibly dirtied; otherwise the room stewards would let them dry, refold them and serve them as "clean" linen. The same practice was followed with napkins. The menus were fancy jobs of four-color printing but the cooking was poor and the food and the dishes were dirty—I once found a cockroach baked into a dinner roll. I won't describe the food-handling methods nor the condition of the galley, but they were nauseating.

The ship's doctor could have and should have made sure that the ship was run in a sanitary fashion, but he himself was a loafer who did not care. Some ship's doctors are excellent but there is a percentage who are the drones of medicine, who sign up for the easy life and are too lazy even to carry out the scanty duties of a ship's doctor. Unluckily ours was this sort. The ship's rules required him to be in his office at nine in the morning and five in the evening; he seemed to feel that he had no other obligations. I recall one morning when a passenger hurt his knee rather badly at deck sports. The ship's doctor was sitting a few feet away, watching and sipping a drink; the passenger went up to him and showed him his damaged and bloody knee. The doctor glanced at it and remarked coolly, "I shall be at your disposal at five o'clock"—and turned away.

While we were not well off in first class, the passengers in second class and in third were in squalor. Second and third class in the *Ruys* were modest indeed, but they were spotless and smelled clean. In this ship they were filthy, reeking holes with a stench better left undescribed. The major shortcoming about ship travel is that, if you do have the bad luck to get a bad ship, you are stuck with it as thoroughly as if you had received a jail sentence. For three endless weeks we could have quit this ship only at Djakarta—which we would have done had Djakarta been an improvement, which it is not.

Of course the Captain should have tightened up his ship by cracking down on the doctor, the chief steward, and his first officer. But, while there is never any real excuse for a Captain since he can never be relieved of responsibility for everything that takes place in his ship, nevertheless I felt a sneaking sympathy for the poor man in this case; he was so busy handling his ship that he hardly had time to worry about the internal administration. The passage from Singapore to Brisbane is no soft snap.

We first became aware of this the first day out, at boat drill. Abandon-Ship drill is never perfunctory in a well-run ship but in this case I was surprised at the extreme and careful thoroughness with which it was conducted. It had a wartime flavor to it; one might have thought that the ship's officers expected the ship to go down at any moment.

We decided later that such was very nearly what they did think; those waters are still infested with mine fields left over from the War and never swept. I once got a look at one of the charts we were using; penciled into it in many of the passages between islands were mine fields.

This voyage would not have been the sinecure which cruising the open ocean is in any case; we were hardly ever out of sight of land, the charts are only moderately reliable (some of the surveys are much more than a century old), and shore lights are not too well tended. The second half of the voyage, through the Great Barrier Reef of Australia, is comparable to driving a narrow and twisting mountain road; reefs and shoals abound, the channel is narrow and must be piloted with great caution—we passed the wrecks of ships whose masters had not been cautious, or lucky, as may be.

The ship had neither radar nor gyro compass to make the shiphandler's task easier, nor did the master have any pilot but himself for the dangerous passages. It meant that he was on duty almost continuously a great deal of the time, night and day—his skill and years of experience against very real dangers. I know that he gave unsparingly of himself to keep his ship safe, so I don't quite have the heart to blame him personally for the faults in the ship's housekeeping. He kept us safe.

But just the same, it was a filthy tub.

Every ship that leaves Djakarta takes its quota of Dutch refugees who are leaving "Holland in the East" for good. The Dutch have been there for three and a half centuries; many of them have known no other home for generations. Those who still remain run the risk of surprise arrest and imprisonment, even of assassination—while we were there, in a town we visited, an entire family of Dutch dairy farmers was murdered by terrorists.

One of the refugees gave me a genteel tongue-lashing aboard ship, the theme being that the United States had forced Holland to surrender the Dutch East Indies to "communists," and that we would someday be sorry for our folly.

But Indonesia is a very complicated place; whatever the truth may be, it is certainly not that simple. It is true that we played a role, through the United Nations, in helping the Indonesians to gain their freedom. We were not alone in it, nor could the United Nations have forced the outcome on the Dutch had the Dutch been physically able to maintain their rule there after the defeat of Japan. Out of the maze of facts and allegations, one thing is sure: the Indonesians were fed up with the Dutch and wanted their freedom—and the Dutch were not able again to subjugate them.

But that, too, is oversimplification. Here are two facts which illuminate but do not tell all. After three hundred and fifty years of Dutch rule 92% of the natives could not read or write—nor did Batavia, the capital city, have anything resembling modern sanitation. These facts prove little but they do cast doubt on the

validity of the long-standing reputation the Dutch have enjoyed
for being the world's ideal colonials. To my simple mind a lack
of schools and sewers after centuries of rule spells exploitation
of the natives—not benign paternalism.

But one may ask how the Dutch could reasonably be expected
to take education and sanitary engineering into remote jungle
villages? That is not the situation at all. Java is an island a
bit smaller than North Carolina and the Dutch built fine roads
into every corner of it, to take out its incredible wealth. As for
"villages," Djakarta, formerly "Batavia" and capital of Holland-
in-the-East, is a city as large as Chicago. Imagine, if you can,
Chicago without running water and sewers—or go to Java and
see what the result is, though I do not recommend this course.

One of the results is an infant mortality estimated at 75%
in the first year.

But I am oversimplifying again and Indonesia is not simple;
a lifetime of study would not be ample in which to dig out the
facts about it and put them in their true relationships. Despite
the notion (and, in some part, the fact) that it is a "small"
country, "unimportant" and certainly one we hear little about,
it has half as many people in it as the United States, some
eighty million. Java, which is effectively three-quarters of the
nation in population and wealth, has a population density of
more than a thousand to the square mile, versus about fifty
for the United States. No country in Europe is so crowded,
not even Holland itself.

This new nation is broken up into five major islands and
countless smaller ones. There are twenty-five major languages
and two hundred and fifty dialects. It has undergone centuries
of colonial rule, four years of Japanese occupation, four years
of revolutionary war thereafter, and civil war was going on
in Sumatra while we were there . . . even in the "quiet" areas
the bushes still held terrorists. They are undergoing drastic
inflation, most of them can't read or write, and they have no
experience in the difficult art of self-government. They are in a
vulnerable position both to communist invasion from the north
and to communist infiltration at home. Wish them luck; they
are going to need it.

The harbor at Djakarta is a good one, well equipped by the Dutch with docks and facilities. As our ship stood in, the marks of war were plain to see; I counted seventeen sunken hulks as we approached our berth. We were told that Surabaja, the former Dutch naval base farther east, displayed even more wreckage of war.

Our time was limited and we were anxious to go ashore, but even after our visas were checked (Indonesia requires a visa to permit even a through passenger from a transient ship to step ashore, which most countries do not)—after our papers were checked, it was necessary to buy Indonesian money from the chief steward and then arrange transportation.

It is against the law to take any foreign money or traveler's cheques into Indonesia. The chief steward sold us rupiahs at 11.4 to the U.S. dollar, and it is much more than possible that he made a good thing out of it, as the black market rate was about 25 to one. I think it may be assumed that the chief steward of a ship calling regularly, himself a citizen of the country, would have means, if he chose, to get dollars ashore and change them back into rupiahs without going through official channels. I have no slightest evidence that he so operated, but the opportunity was there. The Chinese crew members used a simple and straightforward way of beating the currency laws; they were not permitted to go ashore, but they sailed currency ashore to confederates in paper darts. No doubt such transactions were well planned in advance; all sailors throughout history have been part-time smugglers. The stewards in the *Ruys* made most of their income from smuggling between the Far East and South America, with Japanese pearls figuring largely in the undercover trade.

At the customs gate I was subjected to the only body search I encountered in any country. I was not required to strip but my person and my pockets were most carefully frisked. I took it with beaming good nature—we had been warned in Singapore not to argue with a policeman or a soldier in Indonesia no matter what happened, as they would show no hesitation, if angered, in shooting you down on the spot. I don't know if this is true as I never put it to a test; I co-operated and was never treated with anything but smiling courtesy. Indonesians are more than friendly under peaceful circumstances, but news items confirmed the rumors that they could be quite dangerous if crossed. I was happy not to find out.

The customs officials looked like soldiers, which is not the case in the other countries we were in. Soldiers were very much in evidence elsewhere in the country, too, helmeted and always armed. If there were policemen who were not soldiers, I did not see them; the country simply seemed to be under martial law.

Women were not subjected to search at the customs barrier, none of any sort, not even their handbags. They were simply waved on through while the men were detained. The logic of this escapes me. But in consequence of this Ticky was decidedly miffed with me that I had not let her bring dollars ashore. The logic of this escapes me, too, since I had no way of guessing the circumstances in advance. Once through the barrier we stood in the rain for nearly an hour while trying to arrange for any sort of transportation. The docks are far from the city and there was neither bus nor taxi. At last, through phone calls put in for us by a Eurasian clerk who spoke English, two cars showed up and three carloads of tourists piled in; we headed for town.

Singapore is a city, a true metropolis, of slightly less than a million; Djakarta is a village of more than three million— it lacks almost every attribute of a city save people. It has just one modern hotel, Hotel des Indes, and even it is not modern compared with the Raffles, or even by comparison with the little Hotel Paragon in the remote town of Nelspruit. I do not remember seeing any building as tall as three stories and not many that were two stories high. Some of the downtown buildings are Western in type, of masonry, stucco, or sheet metal, but the overwhelming majority of buildings are typical Javanese homes of poles, woven matting, and thatched roofs crowded in together almost wall to wall. We had been told that here, if a family of swallows moved into a house, the family of humans moved out, because then other swallows would follow and the nests would be of much greater value than the house—as an article of commerce to be sold to the Chinese for bird's-nest soup.

This was hard to believe until we saw the houses.

I am not sneering at the houses; they suit the climate; the temperature in Djakarta averages 79 degrees the year round and never varies from that by more than a few degrees. The constant high humidity makes it seem much hotter, however; grass-and-bamboo shacks are not inappropriate.

The most unforgettable feature of Djakarta (and the one I would like most to forget) is the canal which runs for miles through the city and is paralleled by the main highway into the mountains. This canal has no perceptible current and contains opaque yellowish soup; it is used for every conceivable purpose—*every* purpose, it is sewer, bath, laundry, and well. Every fifty yards or so there was a stone staircase leading down into the water and at each there would be people using the canal for all of the above purposes. I don't want to be too graphic about this, but in Java most bodily functions are performed in public.

Our guide pointed out the swarms of people bathing in the canal and said proudly that people here were very clean; they were likely to come down to the canal for a bath three and four times a day. I could understand how it could be an endless process, since bathing in that filth would leave a person dirtier than ever. The so-called bath was rendered still less efficient for females by the fact that they bathed with their sarongs on, whereas the men just stripped naked and went in—though I don't suppose it really mattered either way; filth is filth.

People stooped to drink, housewives dipped up pans from it to take home for cooking, and at one point we saw a woman dipping a toothbrush in the canal to scrub her teeth— an unexpected refinement. Just upstream from her the canal was currently being put to use in its aspect as a sewer; the guide glanced at both activities and said happily, "People never get any disease from the canal. The sunlight, beating down all day, kills the germs."

It was a comforting thought even though without scientific basis. The people here are Moslems and I think I see in the guide's remark a modern version of the very old Mohammedan belief that water in a stream will purify itself in a few feet.

Djakarta is not pretty but it is colorful. Traffic is dense everywhere, some automobiles, many trishaws, many two-wheeled carts drawn by tiny, dispirited little horses much too small for the loads, countless swarms of people on foot. Coolies trot along with poles over their shoulders, carrying loads heavier than they are—sometimes the load is a portable restaurant with charcoal stove smoking and the bearer himself the chef. The sarongs of the women and the jackets usually worn on top of them are in the garish, bright, and somehow beautiful color combinations and patterns made famous by Gauguin. Twelve-year-old mothers not much more than four feet tall stagger along, made lopsided by a child riding one hip. Gums made bright red by betel-nut chewing startle one from time to time and there are depressing sights of leprosy, twisted limbs, and numerous blind beggars—a spate of humanity as overpowering as an avalanche and one which produces the same feeling of helplessness.

Ticky and I located a friend of a friend at Hotel des Indes, an American motion picture producer brought out by the revolutionary government under contract to build up a motion picture industry in Indonesia. I could not help but feel that Java needed a movie industry the way great-grandmother needs a pogo stick, but the new government is determined to make Indonesia self-sufficient in everything—"Export everything, import nothing" is the implied slogan of resurgent nationalism right around the world. In any case the wisdom of it was no responsibility of the American in charge; his firm had sent him out to do a job the Indonesians wanted done and he was doing it. I have no doubt he did it well, as he was Mr. Lothar Wolff who produced the world-famous *Martin Luther*.

Mr. and Mrs. Wolff seemed to be glad to see people from home, drove us around town, and took us out to a very pleasant seaside country club for a drink—a club which had been built for the Dutch masters but which was now used by the uppercrust irrespective of skin or race. Perhaps I should have used the opportunity to have pumped him about the "real" Indonesia; instead we talked about an imminent eruption of the super-volcano Krakatoa, located in the Sunda Strait a hundred miles away. In 1883 Krakatoa produced a disturbance which makes H-bombs look like toys: 3600 people were killed, the noise was heard 3000 miles away, the air wave traveled three times around the globe.

Now the giant was rumbling again and Mr. Wolff was about to leave to take pictures of the explosion. He was as pleased as a child with a new balloon; the possibility of becoming a statistic did not seem to fret him.

We stayed aboard ship that evening not only because Djakarta is not safe after dark but also because there is literally no place to go. But there was amusement aboard ship, for it was Chinese New Year's. We noticed first that the ship suddenly became without service after dinner, no one to answer a ring, no bar boy to sell cigarettes or drinks; they had all gone aft and below, where they were whooping it up with noise and gin and firecrackers and feasting. We moved back to the fantail to watch.

Fireworks are fireworks, and, while the stern of the ship was kept spectacularly illuminated for hours, there is no need to describe it. After all, some of our own best fireworks originated in China; these were the same sort we use on the Fourth. But we met back there a Scot just discharged from the Gordon Highlanders and who had been serving for several years in jungle warfare in the Malay. This is an area which has for some time been officially free of communists, terrorists, liberation forces, and other freewheeling soldier-bandits. But according to our shipmate the "police activities" that continued still added up to daily slash-and-run warfare; the casualties were still high even though news stories no longer appeared.

His report seems strengthened by the fact that mere possession of any firearm on the part of a native in the Malay States carries with it the death penalty—contrast this with our own custom wherein such possession is not only not a crime but a constitutionally guaranteed right.

Some of this we had to get through an interpreter, a young Australian who was present. The Scotsman had spent the first fourteen years of his life in a highland village, the next ten in a highland regiment, and his accent had never been corrupted . . . and Ticky and I had never before heard pure Highland Scottish. At first we were unable to follow it.

He was a handsome, well-mannered young man with the social and political attitudes of a barracuda. To him, all who were not white were "slanties" and deserved killing on sight. The only trade he knew was war; he was on his way to Australia where he expected to join the Australian army— he had been ten years a private but expected to do better in the Australian army. During the voyage he got into a certain amount of trouble, as he was traveling third class but demanded the privileges of first class, because of his white skin. The Indonesian chief steward could, of course, do nothing with him; the young Scotsman ignored his pleas to stay in his own part of the ship. Finally the Captain told him that he would put him in irons if he again showed up in the first-class lounge. After that he was a little more careful, but not much.

We arranged the following day to go to Bogor, a town in the mountains in the middle of Java which is noted for botanical gardens started by the Dutch a couple of centuries ago. We went through customs as before; I was searched but Ticky was not. As soon as we were clear of the barrier she said, "Fine! Now let's locate that black market."

"Huh?"

"I brought my traveler's cheques. Let's cash a few. I want to do some shopping today."

"I thought I told you—"

"I know what you told me, but I don't intend to be cheated out of sixty per cent of the value of my money. Ridiculous! The whole thing is a swindle."

I shut up. My objections were purely pragmatic anyway; my opinions matched hers. I have no moral scruples about dealing in a black money market. (Rationed foods and such in wartime are an entirely different matter.) Wherever there is an attempt to control currency there will be found a black market in money, as the control laws are not merely an attempt by the government to get something for nothing at the expense of its own citizens and their customers, they are also an attempt to defy natural law, to lift by the bootstraps. *Fiat* cannot determine the value of a country's money; only free exchange can do that.

I admit that fiscal theory is much more complicated than my sweeping generalizations, but the last sentence above expresses an easily observed fact to which there are no exceptions in history. But I do not mind going along with the gag and treating the process as a form of concealed taxation if the controls are moderate, as they are in general in the Commonwealth. But where the scheme approaches confiscation, as it did in Indonesia, my reluctance to deal in a free market is based only on a fear of getting caught.

But Ticky is never afraid of getting caught. When the time comes, she will no doubt tell Saint Peter that his bookkeeping is all wet and that she intends to make some drastic changes in the way the joint is run.

On the previous day some of the passengers had managed to sneak contraband money ashore; our driver had, without hesitation, told them where to find a black exchange. Ticky had listened to this and had asked him, "But will they deal with you when they don't know who you are?"

The driver let go the wheel and made an imploring gesture with both hands so oriental in its histrionic emotionalism that I was forced to suppress a laugh. "Madame—they will *beseech* you!"

"Oh." Ticky threw me a dirty look and shut up. On that day we had nothing with us but a few high-priced, official-rate rupiahs and she wanted to buy some sarongs.

So on the next day we drove to the black market. "I didn't tell you," Ticky said happily, "because I knew you would get cold feet."

"You won't like the jails here. Insects . . . cockroaches. Centipedes and tarantulas and scorpions. Things crawling over you and fluttering in your face in the dark—and I won't be there to protect you."

She looked uncertain, for I had flicked her on her one weak spot. Java has an exceptionally intense density of population of the true dominant races of this globe; in that hot and humid climate insects abound in a fashion almost unbelievable to inhabitants of colder, drier places, and Ticky cannot stand creepy-crawlies of any sort. They change her from an Amazon to a frightened little girl. She can't abide anything with six legs—except trios, and not all of those.

I have explained to her that most insects do not bite, sting, nor carry disease, and that even bees, wasps, and hornets are polite to people who are polite to them and do not startle them. But she remains unconvinced; insects panic her. Except butterflies, of course, which she does not class as insects at all, but as self-propelled flowers.

I could see that the remote possibility of spending even a few minutes in a calaboose that was sure to be heavily infested with her mortal enemies was worrying her. "Fleas . . ." I added. "Lice—"

But she shrugged and squared her shoulders. "You're just trying to frighten me. I won't have any trouble."

Nor did she. And they did beseech her. When our car stopped in the little side street where the money changers hang out we were immediately surrounded by a crowd, each member of which swore by Allah that he gave the highest rates.

Ticky opened her purse and got out her book of traveler's cheques. "How many rupiahs for twenty U.S. dollars?" she said briskly.

They all stopped cold. One of them said hesitantly, "No cheques, please, Madame. Cash dollars."

"These are the same as cash dollars. They were purchased for U.S. dollars in the United States of America. Didn't you ever see traveler's cheques before?"

"Certainly, Madame, we know all about traveler's cheques . . . which is why we don't want them. They are very hard to handle. But for your dollars, please, I give you very good rate."

"But I don't have any dollars. Not a single one."

"Madame is sure?"

I thought she would take offense at the implication—which she would have back home. But she took it for the purely professional gambit that it was and answered, "Quite sure. We changed our last cash dollar in Singapore. Now does anyone, anyone at all, want to buy American traveler's cheques, good for their face value in American dollars? Speak up, or I'm leaving."

Nobody answered. On the face of the spokesman was a mixture of doubt, cupidity, and very real apprehension. He withdrew a few yards from us and the rest followed; they went into a huddle. Although the money changers were all in competition he seemed to hold some sort of leadership by prestige. The committee meeting went on for some time, then he came back to us. "Very well, Madame, as a favor to you. Will you come this way, please?" His gestures indicated that he wanted us to come inside a restaurant, out of the public eye.

Ticky held back. "What's your rate?"

"Eighteen rupiahs to the dollar."

"What! That's ridiculous. They are paying at least twenty-five rupiahs for a dollar anywhere."

"For your dollars, Madame, I will pay twenty-six rupiahs. But these are cheques."

"They are the same as dollars."

"To you perhaps, Madame, but not to me. I must pay again to get them changed. Even twenty-seven rupiahs for dollars."

"I really don't have any cash dollars. None. But I'll save these cheques and spend them in Australia before I'll let them go for any silly price like that. What is the best you will pay?"

"Aaaeeh . . . nineteen, Madame. I make no profit."

Ticky looked stubborn and so did he, they managed to look alike. I was getting fretful at the delay and a bit nervous; I interrupted with, "See here, give us twenty and get it over with."

He did not answer but produced a fountain pen and started counting out rupiahs. We left almost at once with my pockets all bulging with rupiahs—dirty, sweat-stained, ragged, and worn, and (I was afraid) possibly counterfeit. Our driver was not outside, nor the car; I looked up and down the street, then saw him waving to us at the intersection. He had moved the car around the corner to another street.

He waited while we walked toward him. Just as we reached the corner an open touring car filled with soldiers, each with a Tommy gun and wearing U.S. helmets, swung around the corner and cruised slowly down the street. They glanced at us, but said nothing. I looked back. The street was empty except for a dog and one child; the swarm of money changers were nowhere in sight. "Get in the car," the driver said. "Let's go."

When we were a few blocks away our driver-guide asked, "What rate did he give you?"

I told him and added, "Was that a fair rate?"

"It's all right. He cheated you only a little—traveler's cheques are no good; they can be followed. How much did you change?"

I hesitated, then decided that if he was asking because he intended to collect a commission later, there was no reason for me to make it difficult, so I told him. He dropped the subject and asked, "You want to go to bazaars now?"

"Yes," said Ticky.

"No," I said firmly. "Let's try to get to Bogor before lunch." It being a Moslem country he did as the male said. Ticky did not debate the matter, as she was almost as eager to see botanical gardens as she was to shop. She seemed quite happy; if the close encounter with the soldier-police had been noticed by her, it had not dampened her. Presently I noticed that she was whistling a tune; I identified it as "Working for the Yahnkee Dollar."

I said morosely, "You know what you are, don't you? A dollar imperialist . . . a jackal of Wall Street. Probably a warmonger as well."

She gave me a sunny smile. "I'm going to buy the *prettiest* things!"

The drive from Djakarta to Bogor is shown as out in the country by the map, but the houses stand almost solidly along the roadside the whole way, with more houses glimpsed behind the others as you speed past. Once in a while there would be a break and the rubber plantations or the rice paddies would come right up to the road. This is a place with climate but almost no seasons; the rice is cultivated through the year, crop after crop. Java is normally a rice-exporting country, and is becoming so again, now that the dislocations of war have been somewhat smoothed out. We could see water buffaloes, the tractor of the East, patiently pulling plows through the water-covered mud, followed by a driver himself knee deep in it. I asked our guide what the wage rates were for farmhands?

I had a little trouble making myself understood, although he spoke excellent, almost-accentless English. I explained again, then added, "Or do they all own the land they work?"

"Oh, no." He considered it, then added, "But they don't get *paid* anything; they get a place to live in and their food. That's all they expect."

I shut up and mulled over the implications of this. Java is one of the richest places in the world, possibly the very richest for its size, both in agriculture and in mineral resources. Yet it is so crowded that the ratio of people to arable land is four to the acre, whereas U.N. estimates of the proper ratio for a decent diet is four to *ten* acres. These figures are clouded by the fact that an acre in Java produces much more than does an acre of good farm land most other places. Indeed, if it were not so, Java could never have reached its present crowded condition; starvation would have prevented.

But things are badly out of whack and I wondered if it were possible for the island to feed its inhabitants no matter how efficiently its riches were managed. We passed the studio and sound stages of the Indonesia national motion picture industry about this time and I wondered again if the country could afford such luxuries? The installation looked comparable to those along Melrose Avenue in Hollywood and must have cost quite a lot of foreign exchange—then I wondered if it were not utterly necessary in the long run to build up the motion picture industry and things like it and thereby swap labor at home (which they had in plenty) for food grown abroad.

All I could really be sure of was that I did not envy President Sukarno his job.

To add to the already innumerable troubles of his possibly insuperable problems the feminists of Indonesia are now after his scalp—and all the poor man did was to take a second wife of the four permitted him by the Koran.

We sped on toward Bogor over excellent paved roads, dodging barrows and buses and foot traffic and dragons. The dragons were in honor of New Year's and each one was animated by six to a dozen Chinese school kids. The dragons could not see very well, decked out as they were, and anyhow they were very busy rearing up and snake dancing and being fierce, as proper dragon manners require. Fortunately our driver had good reflexes. We got to Bogor with only some near misses.

The charge for admission to the botanical gardens was only half a rupiah, or about two cents American. They are very old and very grand. The scientific names of the plants and trees we saw may be found on p. 975 of volume 12 of the 1954 edition of the Encyclopaedia Britannica; I am not going to cheat by copying them down here. But the gardens have representatives in lavish numbers of all the plants to be found in the tropical rain forests ("jungles" to us Tarzan fans) of the Sunda Archipelago, the most impressive of which are the tall, graceful trees, one hundred and fifty feet or more in height, which reach up to the sky and form the roof of the jungle. As for the rest, there was everything from magnolias to mangoes spilling over hill and canyon and all beautifully kept up.

A barefoot laborer with good command of English (which he asserted that he had acquired simply by talking with tourists) spotted us and took us in charge; Ticky had her usual half-Latin, half-English shop talk while I swatted at mosquitoes and appreciated the deep shade—the sun outside the gardens had a Mad-Dogs-and-Englishmen intensity. Finally I insisted that we leave, as Ticky had not taken her anti-malaria pills. The laborer graciously permitted us to make him a small gift and we parted on a high level of international amity.

We were forced to eat lunch in Bogor or go hungry. I say "forced" because the best restaurant available was far from appetizing. Bogor is a pretty little town compared with

Djakarta; it is green and nestles into the mountains. But its standards of sanitation are reminiscent of Djakarta's canal. We ate hot, cooked food and drank no water and hoped for the best. It was a Chinese restaurant and the food tasted good, but the dishes and place itself were dirty. We sat on an open porch at street level; traffic moved past six inches from my elbow, an arrangement which resulted in us being braced by beggars as we ate. Our guide recommended that we ignore them or there would simply be more of them hanging around . . . which was true but I do not have the courage to eat in the presence of a skinny, blind man who is being led around by an equally skinny little girl—and do nothing about it. While I know it is bailing the ocean with a spoon and changes the situation not at all, nevertheless when his filmed eyes stare past your plate and his nostrils quiver the only possible course is to pay and pray Allah to forgive you for being yourself and not the beggar.

So we paid and paid again, usually to blind men, and got out of there as quickly as we could, then crossed the square to the market. Bogor is far enough from the sea coast that the bazaars are intended for the local trade rather than for tourists. I don't suppose that we paid native prices, but even the asking prices were about half the best we could do at the bazaars around the Hotel des Indes back at the port. Over my objections, Ticky bought a coolie hat the size and shape of a large umbrella, the sort worn by the farmers in the rice paddies. It was a beautiful job of basket weaving but about as manageable as a mattress. Then she turned to sarongs and scarfs and blouses.

She looked them over while the Javanese women looked her over and I looked them over. They stared at her silently, quite a crowd of them. Their faces showed nothing, but I wondered what they thought of her, with her white skin and her red hair and her purse full of rupiahs—and her height. Ticky is not big; she has a twenty-two-inch waist and I tower over her, but she was a foot taller than most of these women. Even the Javanese men seem small and smooth and childlike to us; they are not the big-boned hairy apes that we of the colder regions are. Very possibly our appearance alone is enough to make them think how pleasant it would be if we were dead; we offend just by existing.

But they simply stared, while Ticky bought enough batik to start a small tent & awning company. I got her back into the car as quickly as possible, as we were already short on packing space. The coolie hat would not, of course, pack at all and it was already a nuisance in the car. On the trip back we continued to encounter dragons, but they were getting a little tired by now and did not dance quite as much. Perhaps they were beginning to realize that the New Year hardly ever lives up to its promise.

When we got back to the ship we found that we had missed a chance to reach the west coast of Australia and with it the chance to cross the Australian continent. The sister ship of our own, the ship for Fremantle which we had been unable to book in Singapore, had been lying in the berth just forward of us; it had sailed an hour before our return. There had been a cancellation for one double room at the last minute and its purser had come aboard to see if any of us wanted it—so a search had been made for us and the space had been held for us right up to sailing.

I swore feelingly for a bit, as I had wanted very badly to make the trip overland across Australia . . . and, besides, the other ship might even have been clean. But it was impossible to do anything about it; we had literally missed the boat.

Ticky displayed her plunder and our Indonesian chief steward taught her several ways to wrap a sarong. It seems that each island has its own style of wrapping—none of them the way Dorothy Lamour wraps one—and you can tell what island a woman is from by the way she ties her sarong. He also showed her how to judge quality by sniffing the cloth. The rule seemed to be that the worse the odor the better the batik, though I may have been wrong about this.

We had planned for the next day several visits intended to be both educational and instructive. I wanted to take advantage of Mr. Lothar Wolff's invitation to visit the movie studios, this being a subject I knew enough about to form some opinions, and I wanted to see a Chinese school which was run by a relative of Mr. Ho. I had been told in Singapore that the school had more than four hundred pupils, grammar and high, but nevertheless met in the small home of the principal as the school buildings had been a casualty of the War. I had asked how this was possible and had been told that each pupil attended only one hour a day, just long enough to recite and be assigned homework for the next day. The Chinese thirst for knowledge in the face of difficulties I had met before; it seemed to me that such a school was well worth seeing. I planned too, to call on a newspaperman to whom Mr. Ho had given me a letter; working journalists can, if they wish, give the real low-down on a situation better than anyone.

The next morning there was a steady tropical drizzle that seemed likely to keep up all day. The ship's newspaper, posted on the bulletin board, reported the murders of an entire family of Dutch dairy farmers at Bogor; it appeared that we had passed in front of their house about two hours before it happened. Another news item reported the arrest of the Dutch personnel of one of the two major steamship companies; they were charged with sabotage, nature unspecified, and the government had moved in on the firm.

There had been one incident right inside the ship, one which had everyone nervous. One of our shipmates, a nurse from Sydney, was traveling alone, taking the round trip to Singapore as her vacation. She had a single cabin. She was awakened in the middle of the night to find one of the Indonesian soldier-police leaning over her bunk—the cabin doors locked but the locks were the old-fashioned sort which could be opened by almost any skeleton key.

She had been too frightened to scream. He said to her softly, "Oh? So you are alone?" then had gone back and locked the door from the inside. Most fortunately her cabin connected with the next one by a door which could be used to make the two rooms a suite; she jumped up and unbolted it and ran into the next cabin, where an Australian married couple were living—to her great good luck they had not bolted it from their side.

By the time she had made her alarm understood the soldier had disappeared. She had reported the matter to the Captain but there was nothing he could do about it other than to make a useless report of it ashore. A merchant ship tied to a dock is part of the soil of the country it is in, regardless of the flag it flies; the soldier-police-customs-guards were free to come and go in the ship as they pleased, and which they did, night and day. Could she identify the man?

No, she could not; he had simply been a helmeted face in the dark.

I read the depressing news bulletins and thought about the fright the nurse had received, then turned to the rail and stared out at the rain. Ticky came out of the dining saloon and joined me. "Delightful day!"

"Just ducky, for ducks. See here, are you anxious to do more shopping?"

"Not really. But I'd give a nice price for a small snow storm."

"So would I. And I've just remembered that I've seen a movie studio; I don't need to see another one."

"You certainly don't! If you never take another Hollywood job it will be soon enough for me."

"Maybe so, but I wish we were in Hollywood right this minute. To tell the truth, hon, I've had just about all I can stand of being polite to little brown men with Tommy guns. What do you say we stay aboard today?"

She looked relieved. "I was hoping you would say that. This place makes my flesh creep. But I wasn't going to let you go ashore alone; you would get into trouble without mama to look out for you."

I did not argue this amazing perversion of the facts; I simply said, "Swell! I'll skunk you at crib. Or maybe we can get up a game of liar dice."

I suppose that it was a foolish waste not to go ashore in a foreign port, having spent the money necessary to get there, but I did not regret it then or now. Nor do I intend to go back. When our ship stood out of the harbor early the next morning it made us happy.

The next two weeks through the Java Sea, the Flores Sea, the Timor Sea, the Arafura Sea, around the northeast corner of Australia through Torres Strait (transited by the indomitable blackguard Captain Bligh in the longboat of the *Bounty*) and then south through the Great Barrier Reef, were not comfortable but were not entirely unpleasant. The weather was so hot that we slept naked without even a sheet, but no exertion was required of us—we had steadfastly refused to sign up for the deck sports contests organized by the untiringly athletic Australians. The hardest work of the day was to shower just before dinner, then dress and get out on deck before clean clothes were soaked through with sweat. We had Mollie and Bert with us as table mates, the Australian couple who had been with us in the *Ruys,* and they were unfailingly good company at all times. Just to grouse with them about the filthy condition of the ship made the conditions more tolerable.

Most of the other passengers were Australian sheepmen and their families, extremely wealthy but not showing it in any fashion. Several of them owned sheep stations, or "selections," larger than the fabulous King Ranch in Texas; a typical Australian sheep station will have an airfield of its own for the convenience of family and friends—but Mum will nevertheless be doing all the cooking for family and hired hands; the great wealth that has come to them in recent years has not changed their way of daily living. We found them easy as an old shoe and we were offered unlimited station hospitality, which most regrettably we were unable to accept.

The ship did not have the facilities for amusement that the *Ruys* had; most of our time was spent sitting around talking or in non-athletic games like liar dice. Liar dice was a game introduced by Bert; it can be played by any number of people as long as they are dishonest. It requires a set of five poker dice and an ability to lie convincingly, the idea being to pass the poker hand (of dice) from player to player, each player being permitted to roll once to improve the hand but being required to pass the hand along at a higher poker combination each time. The hand is not shown, that is to say the dice are always kept concealed until some player refuses to accept the declared valuation and challenges. If he challenges correctly, the other player puts a chip in the pot; if the hand turns out to be as high or higher than the declared value, the challenger contributes a chip. It is a freeze-out game; the last player surviving takes all.

This game brings out the very worst in people.

The three best at it were Bert, whose honest brown eyes would have served well a confidence man, Ticky, who is ordinarily painfully honest but who turned out to have a deviousness in her that I had never suspected, and Brian Salt, a young Englishman who not only had the natural advantage of a full set of blond whiskers to conceal his expressions but also was possessed of a telekinetic ability to roll five of a kind whenever he really needed them. Or perhaps he had the rare manual skill to roll dice without the usual element of chance— you can never tell with liar dice; it is an immoral game.

I am happy to say that we played only for chips, or I would have arrived in Brisbane in a barrel.

The thousand miles and more inside the Great Barrier Reef passed placidly and monotonously through water with hardly a ripple. As we came out of the reef we edged into a cyclone which had been tearing up roads and bridges all through Queensland, destruction so extensive that many of our sheep-raising shipmates were unable to go home and chose to go on to Sydney to wait out the weather. I concluded that we had had a narrow squeak; the Barrier Reef is no place to encounter a storm and there are plenty of wrecks inside the Reef to prove it. The Reef itself is not spectacular from inside, being usually just a vague line of white on a horizon that seems a little too near, plus numerous rocks and coral islands. The coral formations are said to be marvelously beautiful close up and there are many resorts along the reef to permit people to enjoy the phenomena, but from the shipping channel little can be seen but a line of white on one hand and the coast of Queensland, lush and green, on the other.

XI

Wildlife and Red Tape

WHILE THE POPULATION density of Java is more than a thousand to a square mile, the density in Australia is only three to the square mile. All other comparisons between the two countries are subordinate to this one. In almost every possible aspect Australia, the Australian culture, and the Australian people are as different from that which we had just left as is conceivable, but each of the differences (other than skin color) is strongly related to the fact that the Australians are a handful of people inhabiting a vast and almost empty continent.

Australia's people are almost entirely English in ancestry, but the culture is not English. Americans are more easily at home there than are Englishmen. But it is not our culture, either; it is simply one that we fit into without much friction. It is aggressively democratic in a fashion quite un-English, much more so than our own far west. The Australian working stiff isn't taking no nonsense off cops, or platoon sergeants, or bosses, or nobody, and if you want to make something of it, he is happy to drop what he is doing and oblige, with bare hands, boots, broken beer bottles, or take your choice. On the other hand he is quite willing to be civil to anyone who is civil to him and does not pretend to be better than he is. The attitude and manners are only an extension to the logical extreme of a common American *mores;* any American with enough sense to pound sand should be able to stay out of trouble and get along in Australia. They think as we do, only more so.

We arrived in Brisbane early in the morning and were able to go ashore with a minimum of red tape, since we were not disembarking here. The port doctor looked at our wrists, the immigration authorities looked at our passports, and we went ashore. Brisbane is located up the river of the same name; ships are able to tie up right inside the city, although in this case our berth was a mile or more from the downtown area. When we came out the customs gates we found ourselves in a middle-class residential area of small homes each on its own lot.

The climate and vegetation were strongly reminiscent of Southern California, but there was an even stronger impression of utter and homely familiarity, combined at the same time with strangeness, which I could not at first figure out. Then, as a street car came winding noisily down the street, I suddenly got it: this place had precisely the flavor and appearance of the American middle west of thirty to forty years ago.

I was to have that feeling many times in Australia, a feeling as if I had slipped slightly in time, like the *Connecticut Yankee* but in a lesser time span. I felt it most intensely in that neighborhood of modest homes in Brisbane but it never quite left me. Much of Australia feels the way America used to feel about a generation ago.

I know this sounds patronizing but it is meant simply as careful reporting. Australia is anything but a backward country, but it is rich in food rather than in manufactures, as of today. It is hardly surprising that its trams and much of its physical equipment look as if left over from the Mauve Decade, since such is often literally the case; the imported stuff is expensive and hard to replace.

The immediate effect on me was to make me feel at home for the first time in many months, most especially so after the depressing strangeness of Java. I liked Australia and I wanted it to like me.

We hailed the street car and rode it downtown. Downtown Brisbane looked a bit more modern but not much. It was a pleasantly busy large city, not too dirty and not too bustling.

We walked its streets for a while, tried a few of its shops and bookstores, and enjoyed the sound of English being spoken. But one sign, frequently repeated, began to bother us; it read: "CASKET IS CLOSING!"

About the tenth time we spotted this Ticky turned to me and said quietly, "I think we've blundered into an undertaker's parlor, dear."

"I'm going to find out what it is all about." I turned into a newsstand, attempted to buy a copy of *Walkabout,* an Australian travel magazine, then asked the proprietor, "What is this 'Casket' business?"

"It's closing. If you are interested, you had better hurry."

"Yes, but what *is* it?"

"Why, it's closing, this afternoon. If you want to get in on it, you had better move fast."

"Why is it closing? Who is dead?"

This might have gone on indefinitely if he had not suddenly gathered the idea that I really did not know what "Casket" was. Rather pityingly he explained that it was a lottery. The Australians are gamblers; they will bet you that it does, or that it does not, on anything. Lotteries and horse races are among the favorite legal forms of gambling, but legal or illegal the Australian will gamble. Perhaps the favorite illegal form is "Two Up," a game as simple as matching pennies—in fact, it *is* matching pennies, except that sometimes thousands of pounds will change hands simply because a pair of coins show heads at the same time.

A friend of ours in Sydney told me later that the basic interests of Australian men were "—beer, the races, women, and work, in that order." Nothing that we saw in Australia caused me to doubt the accuracy of his statement.

The subordinate position of women in this hierarchy of interests caused a good deal of friction during the War between Australian men, such few of them as were home, and American troops. The Australian male does not believe in spoiling his women; an attitude of, "Shut up and get hoppin' before I bash you one," is not uncommon. The American G.I. showed up with more money and an attitude that undercut the position of the local swains; the G.I. spent money on taxis—worse yet, he helped the Australian lass in and out of same. He bought flowers for her, candy, dinners, and shows, and in general exposed her to the Cinderella pattern which is common courtship among us, but not in Australia. He behaved like the city-slicker villain in a melodrama and naturally he was hated for it (by the Australian men) just as such villains always are.

The emotional attitudes generated by this unfair competition have not entirely worn off.

We had only a few hours to spend in Brisbane, so we hired a taxi for sightseeing. Instead of asking for the usual sights I asked the driver if there was a place nearby where we could see koalas. There was, at Lone Pine Sanctuary just outside town, so we went there. This trip alone made the journey to Australia worth while; these little animated teddy bears are Australia's finest jewel. I still regret being forced to miss the trip across Australia, but, had our trip to the koala bear park been our only glimpse of Australia, I would have considered the money well spent.

Lone Pine Sanctuary is a small, private zoo located in a grove of eucalyptus trees—I did not spot the "Lone Pine" but it surely must have been lonely. They have there several dozen teddy bears and the place is small enough and informal enough that visitors are permitted to handle them. This does a koala no harm; he loves it. A koala will cuddle with anyone who wants to cuddle; left to themselves, they cuddle with each other. In the wild state—and there are many, many of them still wild in the eucalyptus forests on the east and south coasts—koalas have no natural enemies and have never learned to be afraid. Consequently if you pick one up, he assumes that you are a friend, hugs you and snuggles up. The Marquis de Sade could hardly resist such a response.

Ticky had her picture taken holding Little Mo, who was just two, barely adult. The picture shows Little Mo clinging to Ticky and wearing a bemused, just-woke-up, good-baby expression characteristic of all koalas and shows Ticky with a wide grin of utter delight which is equally characteristic of humans on coming into first contact with these most endearing of beasties.

The picture taken, the keeper took Little Mo from Ticky's arms, set her on the ground and said, "All right, go home." Little Mo started ambling slowly for the open door of the large cage she shared with her brothers and sisters. She came to a concrete curbstone six inches high; instead of climbing it she sat down and started to nibble at it. The keeper said, "Cut that out!" spatted her bottom and boosted her over the curb. She ambled on back to her family.

The keeper said disgustedly to us, "That happens every day. She knows that curb isn't good to eat—but each time she tries, just in case."

Koalas are not long on brains, but they don't need to be; their only food is the foliage of the eucalyptus trees they live in. What they do have is innate genius for being pets. If their diet was not so restricted (they cannot live without certain varieties of eucalyptus leaves), they would be much in demand the world over.

As it is, they may not be shipped out of Australia; each is a ward of the government, whether wild or tame—I mean "caged or loose," as there is no such thing as a "wild" koala; it is a contradiction in terms. Some have been shipped out in the past, to zoos that made special arrangements for their food, but the results were not entirely satisfactory and the Australian government is reluctant to grant such favors.

Even inside Australia the government keeps a close eye on them. They may be owned, yes, if the owner is well equipped to care for them. But let us suppose that the Lone Pine Sanctuary in Queensland were to sell one to the Sydney Zoo in New South Wales. The Zoo would pay the Sanctuary as a private transaction—but the state government of New South Wales would also pay the state government of Queensland an indemnity fixed by law to compensate Queensland for the loss it suffers in having one of its koala citizens emigrate to a neighboring state.

This stringent policy concerning the teddy bears does not indicate that the Australian government is exceptionally sentimental about animals. Bounties are paid for killing kangaroos, as a pair of kangaroos will eat as much grass as three merino sheep, and any means at all is used to kill rabbits, even biological warfare in the form of a virus disease—the offspring of a dozen rabbits introduced in 1788 grew to an estimated half a billion and almost bankrupted the country. But in the case of the koala, an animal utterly useless unless killed for its pelt, the Australian government recognized that the world would be a much poorer place in the warm intangible values if it were allowed to die. I, as a representative non-Australian, wish to thank them.

Although koalas are almost as scarce as unicorns in the rest of the world, it hardly seems necessary to describe them since they are so frequently pictured. Everybody knows that they look like toy teddy bears; indeed, the toy teddy bear is modeled after the koala, not after the carnivorous bear. I will mention only that which does not show up too well in pictures. Man is rightly proud of his opposable thumb; that and his brain set him apart from the other animals. The koala was short-changed on brains, but he has *two* opposable thumbs on each hand. His clown face always has a gentle, muddled look, like a person with one too many glasses of sherry. His bare and oversize nose I had always assumed to be a sort of horny beak (I was misled by the platypus, I think); instead it is soft and rubbery and the little fellow will gladly rub noses with you like an Eskimo or a Maori; it seems to be a gesture of the overflowing affection they feel for everyone.

When unhappy they weep with a cry like that of a human baby, pawing at their eyes as if to wipe tears away. This happened once while we were at Lone Pine; it is unendurable, one must console the little fellow at once—by cuddling it, of course.

There were other Australian creatures at the Lone Pine Sanctuary; we managed to find time to give them a cursory glance despite Little Mo and her relatives. Here we learned for the first time that, with Australian parrots, Polly does not want a cracker, but "Cocky wants a cup of tea." We discovered, too, that besides Old Man Kangaroo and the wallaby there are many, many other varieties of kangaroos, including a tree-climbing one. This struck me as being as inappropriate as overshoes for fish, but you can never tell about Australian fauna; they all seem determined to be as exotic as possible. Consider the bower bird, that builds a hideaway for seduction purposes only, like a roué's flat, and presents his light of love with "jewels." Or the platypus, which can't make up its mind, if any, whether to be bird, beast, or fish. Or . . . never mind; they are *all* on the lunatic fringe of the animal kingdom.

We met an emu there. He stared at us with big blue eyes and said, "Glug!" from way down inside, like a molasses jug on a cold morning. I said, "Glug!" back at him and he said, "Glug! Glug!" Whereupon I gave up, we were getting nowhere.

Looking around the sanctuary that day was a smooth black man with a crop of fuzzy hair. He was barefoot and wearing a skirt, with a white shirt above. I got our taxi driver aside and asked him, "Is he one of the natives?"

The driver looked at him. "Yes, he's an abo [*aborigine*] all right. Must have brought him here on account of the Queen's visit." I accepted the explanation and looked him over with interest, trying not to be seen staring. Later that day, in a local paper, we saw a picture of the man—he was a Protestant missionary from the Fiji Islands, present in Brisbane as an honored guest speaker at a church conference. This illustrates a fact I had not realized; the Australian aborigine is so scarce that many of the people on the thickly populated east coast have never seen one. Most of them are in the Northern Territory, where they are either cowboys or are living in their native state. No one—literally *no one*—who has seen both a Fiji Islander and an Australian aborigine could mistake one for the other. Had I known, the bushy, kinky hair of the reverend gentleman would have told me the difference; the Australian aborigine has wavy hair quite unlike the dense, almost felted structure which tops a Fiji Islander.

We never did see an "abo." We probably would not have seen one even had we been able to cross the continent, as there are less than 50,000 of them left, almost all of whom live far from the centers of white population. There were estimated to be some 300,000 of them when the white settlers arrived; these two figures alone make it clear that the past history of the contact between the two races is not one of which the white race may be proud. On the other hand, we need not lie awake nights over it, since the entire record of the human race of all hues is one of bloody conflict; the end result has been that nine million people now live in peace and civilized comfort in an area formerly occupied by one-thirtieth that number of stone-age savages more primitive than any other people on this planet.

Indeed, so primitive were the aborigines that most Australians in the past (and many of them today) seemed to have believed that they were subhuman. There is no scientific basis for this belief even though their almost animal-like customs give it a superficial plausibility. The brain weight of this race falls within the normal spread in brain weight of the European racial groups and the accomplishments of individuals among them tend to show that their native condition is environmental rather than hereditary.

It is possible that their potential genius is as great as our own, since even Shakespeare or Einstein would find it difficult to leave any permanent mark on the world if born into a culture without writing, one in which the opportunities to display brain power were largely limited to throwing boomerangs at kangaroos. Contrariwise, lack of opportunity does not prove that opportunity is the only lack; there seems to me to be no reason to believe that this race as a whole lacked any racial opportunity possessed (let us say) by stone-age savages of the Mediterranean.

As may be, the present Australians are as race conscious as any people in the world. Their racism is much easier to swallow than that of the South Africans, since they have no wish to exploit other races. (The remaining aborigines are not exploited; their numbers are too few for them to be of any economic importance.) Present-day Australians have no wish to have a servant race; they will do their own hewing of wood and drawing of water and are not ashamed of menial labor even at the highest financial and social levels. But what they do want with apparent complete unanimity is to keep all other races out of Australia. Not just the coolies, but *all* of them, educated or not. So far as we could tell, the "White Australia" policy was the one political issue supported by everyone at all times.

They are almost as anxious to fill up their great empty country, in order to make it strong enough to resist any new colonization by other races. They prefer immigrants from the British Isles but will accept, and subsidize the immigration of, people from any of the white Western nations. They are afraid of the great hordes of humanity north of them, of which the crowds in Java are only a sample. Although never invaded, they remember a time when the government was prepared to surrender everything north of Brisbane and make a last-ditch, last-hope stand in the south. (American troops saved them from that and some of them are grateful, a rare thing in international relations!) They fear the communist menace even more than we do; an overall triumph of communism means to them that they will be swamped in a tidal wave of millions of Asiatics.

Which, of course, they would be.

If the communist powers win this present struggle, the present Australian nation will cease to exist even as a puppet state; it will be replaced by an Asiatic nation occupying the same territory. Knowing this, they are not as vulnerable to the creeping neutralism which daily makes England less and less our ally; they know that, if it comes to all-out atomic war, their only chance of survival lies in the potential ability of the United States to stand the first shock, strike back, and possibly win. Nor will they sit by and wait for us to win it for them. Australians will fight.

We left Lone Pine Sanctuary and rode back downtown, where we dismissed the taxi at the corner of Queen and Edward Streets, an intersection equivalent to Broad and Chestnut in Philadelphia. Brisbane is a standard Western city, very proud of its new city hall. It is about the size of San Jose or Mobile, with somewhat similar subtropical climate. It was started as

a penal colony a hundred and thirty years ago and relics of
the early days are still on display. But no Australian cares to
have the convict system mentioned, unless he brings up the
subject first. They are still sensitive about it. But there is no
real cause for them to be sensitive; the United States and
Australia were colonized by the same sort of riff-raff in the
main. Australia had a higher percentage of convicts in its early
days than we had, but the convict system in Australia was the
direct result of the American Revolution; Britain had to find
some other place to dump her petty criminals and politically
obstreperous after that—the first shipment to Australia was
in 1788. Today one may hear matrons of Atlanta, Georgia,
boast of ancestors who arrived in Georgia in such-and-such
a year in the eighteenth century—when a quick check will
disclose that no one but convicts arrived that year. Perhaps in
time Australians will acquire the same smug, undiscriminating
pride in ancestors, just any old ancestors, which characterizes
our South, Philadelphia, and Boston. But they don't have
it now.

"Nice" people, the prosperous and respected, hardly ever
emigrate; they like it where they are. Colonists are the unsuc-
cessful, the ne'er-do-wells, the outcasts, the indentured, and,
quite often, the criminals, where "criminal" means anything
from a murderer to a hungry petty thief and includes people who are aggressively dissident in their political or religious opinions. The United States has done very well on
such a mixture and so has Australia. It has enriched each
country with a very useful anarchistic strain of impatience
with officiousness and rebellion against injustice, and has left
England and Europe poorer by the loss of those very convicts.

But Australians don't talk about their ancestors.

(I wish we did not. It is a subject always boring to the victim.
Worse yet, it contains a veiled insult not easily answered,
unless the listener cares to indulge in calculated rudeness.)

It was a hot day in Brisbane and poking around its streets
was thirsty work; I started looking for an oasis. I did not find
one easily; the street signs by which one spots a cocktail bar

in the States were absent. Feeling that a longer wait might endanger our health, I stopped a man on the sidewalk and explained our predicament, adding rather unnecessarily that we were strangers in town.

He was all helpfulness, politeness, and gallantry, with gestures, expressions, and manners like those of W. C. Fields at his ripest. He was not typically Australian, if there is such a thing; he was himself, a unique individual. "Ah, sir! Madame! You are expecting to find a cocktail bar. But this is not Paris, this is not New York. You will not find such here."

I inquired rather blankly what one did about it.

"One goes to a hotel. Not into the bar—oh no! Into the lounge. You will find one just around this corner."

I answered that we had just come around that corner, actively searching, and had spotted no indications. He put up a hand. "Never mind. I will show you. Come."

I protested that we did not wish to take him out of his way.

"Not at all. A privilege. This way, dear lady."

"Uh, look . . . do you have time to spare to have one with us?"

He stopped short, hesitated, and seemed at a loss for an answer. Ticky, by instinct I think, guessed correctly the trouble. "I don't believe we introduced ourselves. I'm Mrs. Heinlein and this is my husband. We are visitors from one of the ships in the harbor."

He immediately relaxed, smiled warmly, and told us his name, Mr. Sheppard. There was no further reluctance about joining us for a drink. He consulted his watch, remarked that he should be back at his office, but added that it was a far, far better thing to spend a few sociable moments with kind people. We marched around the corner with an invisible brass band leading us.

In Australia liquor licenses are granted only to hotels. Each hotel has a bar, but it is strictly stag; if a woman were to walk in, it would create some sort of a major crisis. But near the bar is a lounge, where women are permitted to drink seated at tables, out of sight of the bar itself. These rules are empty formalisms but are strictly observed. Mr. Sheppard took us into such a lounge.

Although we had asked him to have a drink with us, he brushed aside my attempt to pay—we were visitors, guests. Ticky ordered her usual Scotch-and-water, Mr. Sheppard ordered beer, and I decided to try beer myself, for I had heard of Australian beer.

Australians cause beer to disappear faster than an elephant drinks water; I had to hurry to catch up and I again lost a check fumble. I was not really anxious for a third round but, for my country's honor, I had to pay for at least one round; this time by getting my money out in advance and insisting, I managed to pay. In the meantime Mr. Sheppard kept us endlessly entertained with anecdotes. He was a man who had been everywhere and seen everything, and he could talk about it endlessly, with charm and droll humor. Before World War II he had traveled for years on business in Europe; he had returned home and was now a glass wholesaler.

I don't remember his stories too well. Australian beer is good stuff; two bottles of it and you think you are Old Man Kangaroo. Three bottles and you are ready to tear up lamp posts by the roots and bash policemen. I had three bottles.

American beer is a nice cool drink on a hot day, but it does not deserve the name "beer." It is sickly aftermath of Prohibition. I had not been able to understand, before I visited Australia, why it was that Australians were reputed to drink almost nothing but beer. There are three reasons: their beer, imported whisky, and their domestic whisky. Imported whisky is much too dear for any but the wealthy to drink; their so-called domestic whisky is a poor grade of radiator anti-freeze put up in bottles. But their beer is the authentic joy juice, the stuff that made the preacher dance. It helps to explain why the Aussie soldier fought as well as he did and why he was insolent to sergeants.

I never tried it again.

At long last we had to leave Mr. Sheppard. We bade each other good-by warmly and blurrily, and Mr. Sheppard assured us that he was going to use his good offices to get us a steamship booking from New Zealand to the States. I don't remember the ride back. I climbed the gangway with my ears roaring, ate heartily, and went at once to bed.

The inhabitants of Sydney are convinced that they have the most beautiful harbor in the world and the longest bridge. They are wrong on both counts; the Rio Harbor is much more beautiful and the Golden Gate bridge is longer both in free span and in total length. There are several other bridges bigger than the Sydney bridge, no matter how you measure—the Firth of Forth bridge in Scotland, for example, or the George Washington Bridge. Nor is it, in my opinion, an outstandingly handsome bridge, though I admit to a prejudice in favor of suspension bridges. If you want to know exactly what it looks like, take a look at the Hell Gate Bridge, a twin about two-thirds the size of the Sydney bridge.

Don't raise either of these points in a Sydney bar; it would not be safe. Deep in their hearts, they *know* they have the biggest bridge and the most beautiful harbor.

It is in fact a most beautiful harbor and an enormous, handsome, and most impressive bridge. The harbor is a drowned river mouth, most irregular in shape, with a multitude of coves, creeks, and bays. In consequence all of Sydney seems to look out over the magnificent harbor; many residential neighborhoods are right on the water. There are many beaches right in the city, with some of the best surf bathing in the world—possibly the best, if you like big, muscular rollers and don't mind risking sharks. The Sydneyites don't mind either one; they take their chances on sharks (people are killed by them each year) and they prefer the biggest waves. All Sydney swarms to the beach each weekend, to swim, hold surfing carnivals, or just spine-bashing in the sun and the sand.

We got off the ship fairly promptly in Sydney, but from there on nothing went quite right. Immigration formalities were not too lengthy, the port doctor looked at our wrists again (I never did find out why), and we got through customs without too much bother. Brian Salt, who had been right behind us in line, had to wait an extra hour because customs closed for lunch, but we just made it. Most of our fellow passengers got caught by the same ploy, but we were lucky.

This practice of closing customs for lunch, tea, and so forth is one that any country would do well to avoid at all major ports of entry. A visitor's first impression of a country is at customs. He is usually tired, nervous, hungry, at least subconsciously afraid, and often legitimately in a hurry. If he is forced to cool his heels for an hour or more, usually in a most dismal shed, often under a "no smoking" rule, frequently without a place to sit down, while a petty civil service employee goes to lunch, he is likely to wind up with an almost pathological dislike for that country that no later impression will quite replace.

There is no more reason why a customs gate should close for lunch than a gasoline filling station, a telephone exchange, or any other public service. I noticed with interest and pride that, when we finally returned to the United States, we went through customs without delay although we arrived there right in the middle of the lunch hour, 12:30 P.M. I strongly hope that all United States ports of entry operate the same way. It is no harder for a civil service organization to arrange relief rotation of lunch hours than it is for a private firm. Most countries spend large amounts of money trying to build up good will abroad; it is moronically stupid to squander the investment through such petty inefficiency. I do hope the United States customs office we encountered is typical of them all.

Getting through customs just under the wire seemed to use up the last of our luck. We had originally planned to stay in Australia almost a month, but our failure to obtain passage to the Australian west coast had disrupted our schedule and left us with only a scanty nine days before our booked departure for New Zealand. I still wanted time to go outback and see the interior of the country . . . possibly even accept one of the numerous invitations we had received to stay on a sheep station. To do this we needed to swap our booking for New Zealand for one a week or so later.

After we checked in at the Hotel Australia we hurried over to the office of the Union Steamship Company of New Zealand to accomplish the rearrangement. I anticipated no trouble, as two large passenger ships maintained almost a ferry schedule between Sydney and New Zealand, with sailings about every six days.

The booking clerk had our reservation but when I proposed exchanging it for one a week or so later he shook his head. "I can't promise you anything the rest of the season. The best I could do would be to put you on a waiting list."

I thought about it and suggested, "Perhaps you have a couple who wanted to sail the day you have us booked but had to accept the sailing a week later?"

"Well, yes, probably, but I don't see what we could do about it."

"You wouldn't have to do anything, really. If you can give us a list, or let us copy one, I can get in touch with such people and see if they want to swap."

He shook his head. "We don't do it that way. If you give up your booking, someone else from the waiting list for that day will go in your place. You'll just lose out."

"You wouldn't permit us to exchange with someone sailing on the seventh, let us say?"

"Sorry."

I thought about it. There were always the airlines, of course, but I did not want to suggest to Ticky a 1400-mile flight over the ocean; she would rather have a tooth pulled. I knew now that over-water flights really frightened her.

Oh, well! If nine days was the best we could manage, nine days it would be. I knew I could talk her into flights over land; between airplanes and trains we could see quite a lot of Australia. It would be hard work, but we had managed to see a great deal of Africa on a similar tight schedule, and it did not really matter if we were exhausted by the time we sailed. I answered, "We'll keep the reservation we have. Do you have the ship's plan?"

He got it out. "This is your stateroom."

It was an inside room without a bath and seemed rather small. Ticky said, "Don't you have one with a bath?"

"Oh, no, there aren't any."

"But what are these?" I asked, pointing.

"Eh? Oh, those are *de-luxe* cabins. I couldn't let you have one of *those*."

"Why not?"

"Why, they are booked. Everything is booked. You got the very last reservation."

His last remark was a gambit I have come to recognize. No doubt it is true one time each for each fully-booked voyage, but it is statistically impossible for it to be true as often as one hears it; what it often means is: "Shut up and consider yourself lucky."

So I pressed the matter. "We made the cash deposit for this reservation by mail from the United States to your main office in New Zealand nearly six months ago. Do I understand that all of those outboard cabins with bath were booked that long ago?"

He shrugged. "I really could not say. All I know is that the home office did not release any of them to me."

So I shut up. "All right, we'll take it." I got out a book of traveler's cheques. "How much is the balance?"

"Oh, I can't issue your ticket today."

"Why not? You have the reservation, I have here the receipt for the deposit, and here is the money for the balance."

"But you haven't made out your income tax. Or have you?"

"Income tax? What do you mean?"

He said patiently, "I can't sell you a ticket out of the country until you have filed your income tax return. Obviously."

"*Income* tax! Why, I'm hardly *in* the country as yet—we got off the ship not two hours ago. How could we possibly have made any money here?"

He shrugged. "That's the law."

I could hear Ticky winding up and getting ready to pitch, so I stepped on her foot. "All right," I agreed. "What do I do and where do I go?"

At least he had the forms. So we went through all the old tired rituals again: age, sex, citizenship, marital status, home address, temporary address, occupation, length of residence, and a dozen other matters even less consequential. It did not

take as long as an income tax report back home for the reason
that all of the significant entrées were either "no" or "none."
At last we handed them in, swore to them, and signed them.
"Where do we turn these in?"

"You can give them to me. You said you were staying at
the Hotel Australia, didn't you? The Company will leave a
message for you there when you have permission to leave the
country."

"You mean you still can't sell us a ticket?"

"Not until these papers have been processed, certainly not."

"How long will that take?"

"It shouldn't take long, not over three or four days I should
imagine."

"Uh . . . well, thank you. You've been very patient."

"Not at all."

I took a deep breath, dismissed the income tax matter from
my mind, and turned to the next matter, an attempt to get
passage from New Zealand to the United States. The Union
Steamship Company had ships which made this run, but they
had refused to book us from the States and had returned our
deposit, saying that they could not book that far ahead—but
the letter contained a weasel-worded phrasing which, while it
accepted our names for a waiting list, implied that it would not
do us much good as New Zealanders would probably want the
space. I had written back and inquired specifically on this point
but the inquiry had been ignored.

So I asked the booking clerk, not very hopefully, about
booking passage from New Zealand to the States. He referred
us to another clerk, where we were told that no bookings were
available. Nor was our name on the waiting list so far as records here showed. I asked them please to let the home office
know that we had arrived and were still interested. Would they
accept a deposit?

No—but the clerk did promise to write a letter to the home
office. Perhaps when we got to New Zealand—

We left with a list of shipping companies which had ships
to our west coast—or to Canada, Hawaii, or Panama City. We
even asked about ships to the west coast of South America, for

we were beginning to realize that the situation was desperate, but there were none. It would appear that there is no trade of any sort between South America and Australia plus New Zealand even though they face each other across the Pacific.

It did not take "three or four days" to get our income tax clearance; it took the whole time we were there. In consequence we were never able to get out of Sydney any distance greater than could be driven in one day; our longest drive was about four hundred miles and did not take us past the Great Dividing Range which parallels the east coast, never got out of the coastal, eucalyptus forest geographical region.

Each day we would first telephone the Union line and ask about income tax clearance and our ticket; each day we would be told to call back the following day. Then we would do local sightseeing—except that the first Monday was spent in tramping from one steamship agent to the next, trying to find anything from a raft to submarine which would accept us for passage to any port on the other side of the Pacific. There were none.

Perhaps I should not say "none" for we had one very promising false alarm and once were actually offered passage the long way round via Manila and Hong Kong, then back across the Pacific, in the Cunard Liner *Coronia,* which was making a circum-Pacific cruise originating from London. The agent had to stop to figure out what our fare would be for that portion we wanted. Presently he looked up and said cheerily, "Better sit down first."

"Pretty expensive?" I asked. I had done a rough calculation in my head, based on the number of days we would be in the ship and what I knew of usual first-class fares; I had estimated it at $2000, or perhaps a few dollars over—almost twice what it would cost to fly home, but worth it in view of the way Ticky felt about flying over the ocean. So I was braced for a sizable figure.

"Just over seven thousand dollars," he said.

I blinked. "I don't want to buy the ship, I just want to ride in it."

"Yes, I know. It is a fantastic cost. I wouldn't pay it."

"Nor I. It's way out of my price bracket. What do they give you for that? Dancing girls? Pheasant for breakfast?"

"Well, it *is* a luxury ship. It has a swimming pool and dancing in the evening, all that sort of thing."

The *Ruys* had had a swimming pool and dancing in the evening, and all that sort of thing, but no megalomania about the worth of such. From curiosity I studied the ship's plan. The *Coronia* had a swimming pool not noticeably bigger than the one in the *Ruys* . . . for ten times as many passengers. Her other "luxuries" were on the same meager scale when compared with the ample arrangements of the *Ruys*. She was a floating sucker trap. Seven thousand dollars indeed! "Hmm—" I said. "Would you do something for me? Tell them to take the *Coronia,* fold it until it is all corners, and—"

"Robert!" Ticky said sharply.

Ticky was right. The agent was a nice chap and seemed as shocked by the larcenous attitude as I was. So I thanked him and we left.

The second false alarm concerned a ship whose owners had no delusions of grandeur. She was going to Panama, an acceptable enough destination by then, from where we could fly home or might even manage to catch the good old *Gulf Shipper*. The home office was in New Zealand, and the booking clerk in the Sydney office, a most pleasant lady, could not tell us positively that space was available, but was glad to attempt the booking through the home office.

"Good!" I agreed. "Suppose we wait while you phone them."

"Excuse me? Did you say 'telephone them'?"

"Certainly. There is telephone service between here and New Zealand, is there not?"

"Well . . . yes," she conceded.

"Then let's telephone them at once. I pay for the call, of course—perhaps I didn't make that clear."

"But I couldn't *telephone* them."

"Why not? There's a telephone right there on your desk. Just call them and we will know at once."

The poor woman seemed quite agitated at my insistence. I finally found myself talking to her boss; where she was agitated, he was bland, but he was quite as firm in his refusal to permit a call to be made to the home office. "Airmail will do nicely, my dear chap. We'll get one off at once and we will hear promptly, probably tomorrow."

I explained that it was decidedly worth the cost of a long-distance phone call to me to tie down the reservation at once. "It is possible that someone might walk into the New Zealand office later today and book the last available stateroom in that ship. I don't want to chance it; it means too much to me."

He frowned and smiled, seemed perplexed by my stupidity, a little surprised that I would propose anything so obviously improper, even though I was an American. "But we can't, you know. That isn't the way we do business. Sorry."

And there the matter stood. The phone call was not made. We Americans are used to telephoning twice the distance from Sydney to New Zealand, as casually as we call the corner grocery, on any matter of business important enough to warrant the minor expense—or simply to inquire about a relative's health, for that matter. A branch office will phone the home office several times a day; that is how business is done.

But apparently not so in Australia. My willingness to pay the cost had no bearing on the matter; one simply does not telephone the home office. It is not done.

We had still hoped to make a flying trip outback, starting Tuesday, but this delay kept us in Sydney two more days . . . to no avail, as the New Zealand office turned our request down. Then we still hoped to make a trip at least to Melbourne the last two days of the week even though our income tax clearance still had not come through. This time we were stopped not by red tape but by a chance in a thousand: Queen Elizabeth was in Melbourne that day, which meant very simply that a hotel bed was not to be had under any circumstances in Melbourne . . . plus crowds dense as a Mardi Gras, plus choked public transportation.

So we never got out of Sydney. I do not know what would

have happened had we entered the country at Fremantle, crossed by train, and arrived in Sydney only a couple of days before our scheduled sailing. Would we have been allowed to catch our ship and leave the country? Or would we have been held there while our null & nothing "income tax" returns were processed? I don't know, but I have no reason to think that Australian red tape will budge for anyone no matter what the predicament. I suspect that it might have been like the telephone call that "couldn't" be made. (And I shall always wonder if we missed being able to reserve passage by that one day's loss of time.)

This income tax nonsense for tourists, indulged in by both Australia and New Zealand, caused me to wonder if our own country indulged in such a useless, time-wasting irritation, so I inquired of Internal Revenue on our return. We do not— neither under the old law nor the new (1954). A non-resident alien, tourist or other visitor, who has earned no money in the United States, is not required to make any income tax report of any sort—nothing! Which is as it should be.

Nevertheless we liked Australia on the whole. In seeing Brisbane, Sydney, and the environs of Sydney we did see that part of Australia occupied by more than half of the population, even though we did miss "the salt pans in the middle of Australia" where Yellow Dog Dingo chased Old Man Kangaroo. We saw two of their three biggest cities and found them no worse than and much like American cities of similar size. The countryside outside those two cities was magnificent; I kept feeling that a landscape architect had been through ahead of us, rearranging it into perfect composition and beauty. In fairness I must admit that the random views around Sydney for a hundred miles or so (as far as we got) are superior to random views in the U.S. countryside save for certain areas overtly touted as tourist beauty spots.

But before we leave the subject of the shortcomings of Australia, let's list the others that came to our attention. The hotel we were in was not very good and Australians readily admit that their hotels are not much. The Hotel Australia is comparable to the Commodore in New York in size and age;

it is the best Sydney has to offer, which is hardly true of the
Commodore in New York. But the Commodore is a much
better hotel in plant and immeasurably better in service and
in cuisine. The prices of the Commodore are about half again
as much as those of the Australia—which makes the Hotel
Australia quite expensive in view of the scale of other prices
in Sydney and *very* expensive compared with a similar hotel
outside New York.

No need to itemize the shortcomings of the Australia, but
here are a few that are typical: we were placed in a room
built like a railroad tunnel with a single window at the far
end. The only shaving mirror was located the room's length
away from the wash basin, which made shaving a source of
healthy exercise. The beds—well, never mind the beds; we
didn't sleep much anyhow. The cooking was adequate but
dull; the menu never changed. Food was available only at
set meal hours and a late Sunday morning breakfast in your
room was a metropolitan luxury not to be had.

That was Australia's "best" hotel, not bad but not good. The
primary cause of the poor hotels in Australia—and the ordinary
run of them are conceded to be much worse than the one we
were in—is the liquor licensing system; a hotel is primarily
a saloon. The profit lies in beer sold over the bar; lodging
and meals are supplied only to meet the requirements of the
law. The secondary cause lies in union rules; organized labor
dominates Australian politics to an extent that American union
men would find amazing and union rules of a type undreamed
of in most parts of the United States are taken as a matter of
course there. In my opinion they have taken advantage of a
good thing in a fashion of no real benefit to the union workers
and detrimental to all.

For example, I tried to get a glass of water in the restaurant
of the Australia and I made the mistake of asking the table
waiter for it. But by union rules he is not permitted to pour
a glass of water, nor is the bus boy; water being a "drink"
must be handled by a liquor waiter or not at all. But a barman
was not available at that time. I could see empty glasses and
carafes of water not ten feet away, but the table waiter was

literally afraid to touch it; the job was not authorized by his union classification.

Groceries may not legally be purchased on a weekend. This makes it tough on working housewives. There are grocery "bootleggers" of course, with their back doors open and with higher prices. I went to one of them with a Sydney housewife; it reminded me of a speakeasy during Prohibition.

Ticky and I, one day when we were sightseeing in Sydney, decided to wait until the business lunch-hour rush was over before eating, for Sydney is a place where more than a million people try to crowd into restaurants sharp at noon. So we waited and so we missed lunch—the restaurants close as soon as the midday rush is over. Union rules again.

This list could go on tediously, so let us consider the examples multiplied by almost any one you can think of and many that, fortunately, have never been thought of in this country. I mean to say, we have proved repeatedly that short hours are not incompatible with high production and good service. The feather-bedders in Australia don't seem to know that. This anti-productive attitude was the very last thing we ran into as we left Australia. Our ship was trying to make the tide and there was just one more sling to be loaded—when it came time for the dockmen to have "smoko," the midafternoon break for a cigarette. Our captain sent down word asking the men to *please* postpone "smoko" for twenty minutes and get that last sling aboard. No go—the rules, rules with the force of law from a government "awards" commission, said to break at that hour. So the ship missed the tide.

Of course, any decent person will prefer the unionism-gone-wild of Australia to the serfdom existing in Russia and South Africa. But there can be a golden mean, fair to everyone—and we are much closer to it than is Australia.

But most Australians seem more than content with their own ways in these matters. I learned from a reporter on one of the Sydney daily papers that a reporter was not permitted to drive his own car nor even a company car while on duty; while out on his news gathering rounds he must be driven by a union chauffeur in a company car. I told him that this struck me as a silly waste of manpower. He informed me quite stiffly that I did not know what I was talking about and that any other rule would be the "—thin entering wedge" which would destroy their rights. The quoted phrase is one that they are fond of and use to justify their most ridiculously non-productive practices. I suppose that the cited practice could be justified in the fierce traffic of Manhattan, but Sydney is not Manhattan; its traffic is not as dense as it is in any American city of comparable size. Carried to its logical extreme, this so-called principle would require every man who moves around in the course of his day's work to be accompanied by a driver who did nothing else—plumber, real estate agent, milk man, police officer, traveling salesman, building inspector, and so forth. Such a rule would reduce the working force of the United States by several millions without any gain of any sort.

But I have no doubt that this is just what they are trying to achieve in Australia. Remember the waiter who could not pour a glass of water.

This is not the way to increase a country's standard of living.

We made our usual effort to see the slums in Sydney. Sydney's slums are much like our own, neither worse nor better—to the shame of both countries. But I noticed two interesting and depressing variations from our pattern. We saw dwellings, or human lairs, that were entirely underground save for air holes—you could not call them windows—on the downhill side only. We saw also the narrowest row houses imaginable, eight feet wide and five stories tall. It was hard to imagine how a staircase was fitted inside such a building, or why such uneconomic structures would be built in the first place, even as tenements with Scrooge himself as proprietor; the ratio of parasitic structure to rentable space in such a building is all out of proportion.

But on the whole there was not too much to criticize in Australia. Ticky reported to me that ladies' rooms were the worst she had ever seen—not merely primitive but uniformly filthy. I found the men's room much the same sort, but I have seen some bad ones in the United States. Housing in general is old-fashioned and dreary, more of that 1910 feeling. Public transportation in Sydney is almost as bad as it is in Los Angeles. But faults of this caliber can be found in any country; our own beloved country has some dillies.

We never did encounter the intentional rudeness which we had been warned to expect, even warnings from Australians. But we did experience rather frequently a naive, almost child-like way of speaking one's whole mind without thought to how it might sound to the listener, a trait which would have been considered rudeness were it not so ingenuous. For example, our closest friends in Australia informed us that they hoped that, in this coming war, the United States would be bombed rather than England—since it was our "turn." I admit that the wish had a certain bleak logic to it, but it never occurred to them that we, as one of the targets, might not relish the role they had chosen for us.

Another time our host at dinner expressed his admiration for the United States and said that he wished Australia would join up as a forty-ninth state. "Only," he added, "I suppose that if we did, we would have a flood of American tourists and there would be no way to keep them out." He knew, of course, that we were American tourists.

But these remarks were utterly without malice; the speakers would have been shocked and mortified had their unintentional rudeness been pointed out. There were many such remarks, but never a one intended to hurt.

Another custom struck me as naive though not at all rude. In introducing a university graduate to a stranger in Australia it seems to be quite the usual thing to mention the fact that this person is a graduate; the possession of a college degree of any sort seems to be sufficiently unusual to warrant mentioning it, just as we tack "doctor" on the name of anyone possessing a doctor's degree. They do have a rather small number of degree-granting institutions for the size of the population, by our standards, but I have not been able to track down comparative statistics as to college graduates. However, it is evident that the privilege of going to college is more highly regarded by them than it is by us.

American books and magazines are forbidden entrance to Australia, which is commonly the case throughout the Commonwealth. The excuse is dollar exchange, although the printed word is no important fraction of foreign trade. The result is not really harmful to us *as trade* (and I make my living by just such trade), but it is, I think, quite harmful to both countries in that it cuts us off from each other; it is an important and ugly barrier to free communication.

Another result is (since their numbers are not large enough to support writing as a profession to any extent) their magazine stands and bookstores are filled with some of the most amazing trash to be found anywhere. It is as if our stands contained only confession magazines and comic books—no *Harper's,* no *Time,* no *Saturday Evening Post,* no *Scientific American.*

But let us speak of the good things about Australia, for we did like it a lot. First, the people themselves are remarkably likable, even when blurting out some opinion better left unstated. Second, the culture as a whole is a good one, filled with a generous amount of social justice, founded on human dignity, and honed with a determination to live and fight for freedom. Even the frustrations engendered by silly union practices (and they *are* confoundedly annoying!) derive from good intentions toward the common man.

And finally, the land itself, what we saw of it, is grand and beautiful, worthy of love—and their birds and animals are simply wonderful!

The Sydney Zoo is one of the best in the world. To reach it you cross the harbor in a busy little ferry boat which takes only passengers, no cars. I commented on this, since their proud bridge is relatively new, and was met with stares; it seems that the notion of automobile-carrying ferries is one which never reached Australia. Until the bridge was built it was taken for granted that a car could be used on one side or the other, but not on both. It is, possibly, a weakness in the Australian temperament that they are too prone to take shortcomings and inconveniences for granted. Their far-from-docile spirit is quick to resent the loss of an expected privilege, but annoyances they are used to they seem to regard as natural phenomena like the weather. Perhaps the government knew what it was doing in forbidding American magazines, as it might cause Australian housewives to be unwilling to put up with what they call "kitchens."

From the ferry boat landing a tram runs up to the top of a high hill to the main gate of the zoo; you may then plan your tour downhill all the way, ending up at the ferry landing. The zoo is beautifully gardened and rich in specimens from all over the world, but our interest was in the Australian fauna not often seen elsewhere. There were lots of koalas but they could not be touched nor even seen from close up, which made us glad indeed that we had visited Lone Pine Sanctuary. We had the good luck to see a platypus. They are not easily seen even at the zoo, as they spend most of the daylight hours in their burrows. But we saw one come out and forage on the bottom of its tank for worms.

A platypus in the flesh is even more unbelievable than one pictured in a book; he looks as if he had been assembled by a taxidermist with a warped sense of humor. Duckbilled, egg laying, fur bearing, and it suckles its young—it seems to have been created for the express purpose of giving nervous breakdowns to taxonomists.

The platypussy does not seem to have good eyesight nor a keen sense of smell. The bottom of the tank was liberally carpeted with worms but the duckbill had a terrible time finding them. He went blundering along, missing nine by millimeters and gobbling greedily the tenth, while Ticky frantically coached him from the sidelines. The coaching had no effect, but she does not speak fluent Platypussian at best.

Australian birds are as freewheeling as Australian animals. The emu, cassowary, and black swan, the bower bird, budgie, and kookaburra or "laughing jackass"—all of these are exotic enough for anyone. The whole continent has been a bird sanctuary, cut off from the rest of the planet and lacking natural enemies, for many eons—during which the feathered kingdom ran wild. Ticky and I loved them all but our favorites were the birds of paradise. Describing a bird of paradise is ordinarily about as useful as parsing a poem; the color plates of them in

any good encyclopedia are much more rewarding. But I want
to mention one fellow.

We had been easing slowly past their cages, admiring their
kaleidoscope patterns and colors, struck almost breathless by
their flamboyant beauty, and reading the names of each—
the Great Bird of Paradise, Crown Prince Rudolph's Bird
of Paradise, the King of Saxony's Bird of Paradise. Then
we came to a cage labeled simply: "The Magnificent Bird
of Paradise."

There was a little fellow in there no bigger than a robin, not
brightly colored and not conspicuously plumed; we felt that
there had been some mistake—no doubt he was just being
kept in there temporarily and they had not bothered to change
the sign, for he certainly was not "Magnificent" and it seemed
unlikely that he was a bird of paradise at all.

Then he caught sight of us, chirped excitedly, and hurried up
to the front of the cage. There was a little perch there, about a
foot in front of our noses; he settled on it, shook himself, and
started to run through his act.

He was magnificent. It had been precisely the right word for
him. He was the most applause-hungry ham I have ever seen
and his routine had everything but "Shuffle Off to Buffalo."
First he threw his neck feathers up into a ruff which framed
his head. He paused for us to admire him, then dropped it and
puffed out all his feathers until he was four times normal size.
He deflated and opened a zipper all the way down his belly.
That is what it looked like—a zipper. The feathers moved aside
in a straight line about a quarter of an inch wide and disclosed
bright iridescent down underneath.

He waited for the laugh with truc Barrymore timing, then
closed the zipper and opened his mouth. All the inside of his
mouth was bright Paris green.

He closed it, braced himself, and gave the climax of his act:
he sang for us.

It was unbelievably, hysterically bad. I can perch on a stick
and sing better than that, and I have been chucked out of some
very inferior quartets. But he was as cockily sure of himself as
Mario Lanza. So we clapped and screamed bravos.

He looked smug, took a bow and an encore, running through the whole routine again without variation. We applauded again and were about to move on reluctantly, when we learned that he had a special encore with which to wow 'em. He hopped into the air, turned a hundred and eighty degrees and landed with his back to us—whereupon he ran through exactly the same routine, including the rusty-iron song, with his back to the audience. This time we discovered that the lining of his ruff was bright yellow. I think he did not want us to miss it.

He ran through his act twice with his back to us, finishing with that awful song, then flew away; the show was over and we could not entice him back. We crept away from there quietly, realizing that we had been in the presence of genius.

The aquarium at the Sydney Zoo is one of the best and may possibly be the best in the world. In addition to all the usual small exhibits and many not usual it has sharks up to eight feet long in a pool large enough to hold them comfortably. In another immense pool they have a giant ray about fifteen feet square. They grow much larger than that, but this specimen is quite large enough to inspire terror and disgust. The aquarium has many octopi and we saw two large ones fighting. No, I really do mean fighting; in this breed lovemaking cannot be mistaken for fighting—the means by which octopi get little octopussies is even more preposterous than what fish do. Look it up sometime; you will be amazed.

That zoo merits at least a week of careful study, but we had to hurry to catch the last ferry.

We prowled downtown Sydney by ourselves, were driven all around Greater Sydney by Vol and Laura Molesworth, and were driven for hundreds of miles through the surrounding countryside by Brian Foley. Vol teaches at the University of Sydney; Brian is a partner in a literary agency. This was typical of the hospitality we enjoyed there. Although we knew no one in Australia when we left home, nevertheless I do not recall that we ever ate dinner alone in Sydney, except on the day of our arrival. Australians are not cold and stand-offish.

The trips around town included ones to Botany Bay, symbol in song and story of the convict system. It is a wide, shallow

unattractive bay which never was the site of a convict settlement; it was the destination of the 1788 First Fleet but the
actual settlement was made six miles to the north in what is
now Sydney. Botany Bay is now a place of yacht basins,
boat yards, light industry, second-hand car lots, and suburban
homes.

The trips out into the country were an endless succession
of prize vistas and musical aborigine place names, names
like Yerranderie, Burragorang, Wollondilly, Woronora, Wol-
longong. North and south from Sydney are endless haughty
cliffs and fine beaches; inland are hills and low mountains
and canyons. We saw the famed tree ferns, living fossils of
the carboniferous era.

Despite the not-inconsiderable inconveniences, when the
time came we were reluctant to leave. But Australia had one
more magnificent piece of red tape to speed the parting guest.
Attached to our ticket, when at last they deigned to issue it,
was a notice that we must apply for an export license from the
Commonwealth Bank of Australia (equivalent to our Federal
Reserve Bank) for any monies we wished to take out, whether
in cash or in traveler's cheques. I had been aware of the limits
placed on cash and had planned our spending accordingly, but
the second category was so worded as to include American
traveler's cheques.

Ticky suggested hiding our American Express cheques and
ignoring the business. The notion suited me but I doubted the
practicality of it; the officers at the docks would know that
we must have funds of some sort; if we failed to show an
export license, we would simply be in trouble. So I set about
getting one.

It did not seem to be too difficult, since there was a branch of
the Commonwealth Bank right in the hotel. I went there. They
examined my papers with interest, talked it over, and decided
that there was nothing they could do for me. They suggested
that I go to the main office of the bank.

The breaks were with me; it was less than half an hour
away. I went there, queued up at the foreign-exchange window,
eventually was referred by the teller to one of the officers of

the bank. He considered my problem and told me that I did not want to be in the bank proper at all, but should go to the eighth floor to the controller of trade & export licenses. To get there I should leave the bank, go around the corner, enter the office-building entrance, and find the lifts. I whistled to my dog team and mushed on; I was beginning to find the search fascinating.

The office I was sent to was not quite the right one, but it was close; the side activity which actually dealt with such matters turned out to be on the same floor. By now the morning had passed (and our three o'clock sailing was coming apace); the man I wanted to see was out to lunch. No one else was permitted to stamp the form, naturally; these things have to be done properly.

But the wait was hardly thirty minutes and the official was quite helpful when he did return. By now we had only some forty-seven checks left and it did not take very long to inventory them, list them by denomination and number, and fill out the rest of the blanks; in another half hour it was all done. The bank official was a bit dubious about the fact that some of the cheques were made out in my name and some of them in Ticky's name, but, since she was not present and our ship was sailing very shortly, he stretched a point and made out a license which mentioned both our names and issued it to me, granting me permission to remove from the sovereign Commonwealth of Australia bits of paper showing that I had paid dollars to the American Express Company back in Colorado, U.S.A.

I hurried back to the Hotel Australia where Ticky was waiting in the lobby. She had been sitting there, watching our baggage and wondering what had happened to me, since we had had to vacate our room earlier in the day—in general, hotels in the Commonwealth do not follow the gracious custom of extending the courtesy, on request, of a later check-out to a guest who is not leaving town until after the regular check-out time, so she had stayed with our baggage in the belief that I would return in ten minutes or so.

All it cost us was our lunch.

XII

The Dreary Utopia

OUR STATEROOM IN the New Zealand steamship *Monowai* turned out to be even smaller than I suspected from the berthing diagram; if one of us inhaled it was a good idea for the other one to exhale. There was a single straight chair which had to be moved in front of the door to permit us to get at the wash basin, then moved back in front of the wash basin to permit us to go out the door.

I went at once to the purser's office, having in mind that a shipping company will often hold a V.I.P. room right up until sailing and sail with it empty, provided no politician, lord of industry, or relative of the chairman of the board needs it. I planned to offer the purser a sackful of Yankee dollars and ask him to shift us to the V.I.P. room, if any.

Either New Zealand lines do not follow this practice or the V.I.P. had claimed the room earlier; the purser assured me that there was no unoccupied stateroom of any sort in the ship. I was inclined to believe him, as the ship was as crowded as a department-store elevator on Dollar Day. Besides that, although the ship was in all respects luxurious in its fittings and furniture, everything about it was a little bit skimpy, like a wartime suit. The passageways were not quite wide enough for two people; when you encountered anyone it was necessary for one of you to stop and flatten against the bulkhead to avoid collision. I felt, the whole time we were in her, as if I were taking a shower in a stall too small to permit me to raise my elbows.

I went back and told Ticky the situation. She had been trying to sort out what we needed and what we could do without from the ten suitcases, and she was hot and tired and dirty. She looked up, wiped dust across her face, and made a suggestion both unladylike and impossible. I reproved her. "Besides, you don't even know the purser."

"I don't want to. Knowing his ship is enough."

"He's really a very nice man. It isn't his fault. Come to think of it, it's your fault. If you weren't old-fashioned and a pantywaist besides, we'd be half way to New Zealand this minute, by air, and we'd be sleeping in a nice, big hotel room tonight, with a big bed and a big bathtub." She did not answer so I added, "Come on now, 'fess up. We're here because you wanted it this way."

Ticky took refuge in the Nineteenth Amendment.

I said, "You don't mean the Nineteenth, you mean the Fifth."

"I know which one I mean! The Fifth is the one the communists are always hiding behind. I'm not going to hang around with *them*—so I use the Nineteenth."

I looked it up later. She really did mean the Nineteenth.

We had signed up for second table but shortly before dinner the chief steward came around to our little smokehouse. Captain's compliments and would we join him at his table?

We looked at each other, astounded. I managed to say, "Tell him 'yes,'" and the steward left. Ticky said slowly, "I don't really want to sit at the Captain's table."

"I know, and neither do I. But what else could I say? You can't refuse such an invitation, you simply can't. Not from a master in his own ship."

"Oh, you did just exactly right. But I don't have to like it."

"No, you don't have to like it. But you do have to be polite, or I'll keel-haul you myself."

"You and eight sturdy seamen, maybe. Want to swap a little judo?" I refused with dignity. Ticky knows some awfully dirty holds.

To our surprise, we enjoyed sitting at the Captain's table. Captain F. W. Young was both a taut shipmaster and a cultured, charming man of the world. The shortcomings of the *Monowai* were either inherent in her design or derived from company policy ashore; he himself ran a clean, disciplined ship. His other guests at his table were most pleasant people, too—Mr. and Mrs. Adman from Sydney, Mr. Field from Victoria. But we never did find out on what basis he had selected us. Ticky and I finally concluded that it was possible that we had been tapped simply because we were the only Americans aboard, which still left open the question of whether we were picked as curiosities or whether our country was being honored through us. We never asked—I suppose we were a little afraid that we might find out.

As we became better acquainted with our table mates it was natural that they should see our stateroom and we should see theirs. Mr. Field had a large cabin outboard of ours, with portholes, a private bath and plenty of deck space; the Admans had an equally nice one forward, with a semi-private bath, shared with one other couple. We showed the dark, cramped Iron Maiden we lived in and told them our story. Had it been necessary for them to make reservations months ahead to get the accommodations they had?

Not at all—in one case the reservation had been made two weeks ago, in the other case a little longer.

I thought of our cash deposit made the previous year and I began to burn. At the earliest opportunity I braced the Captain himself about it, telling my story and then saying bluntly that I thought that the company had a fixed policy under which Americans were not given even treatment with Australians and New Zealanders.

He smiled, did not comment, and changed the subject at once. I am not sure whether he knew of such a policy and did not care to admit it publicly, or whether he simply considered my remarks silly and wished to avoid unpleasantness. It is even possible that he was unaware of the truth either way; after all, captains do not sell tickets.

But I remain convinced that Americans are discriminated against by this line. We had clear proof that they could have given us decent and comfortable accommodations at the time we put up our deposit, and I strongly suspect that they could have booked us out of New Zealand in one of their ships running to the United States if they had honestly followed the policy of first-come-first-served.

New Zealand maintains travel commissioners in major American cities to try to persuade us to come to New Zealand and spend those dollars. Hmm . . .

The four-day passage to New Zealand was without incident; it was merely uncomfortable. The Captain invited us up to the bridge to see the landfall and passage in through the heads into Auckland Harbor, but we could not see much as the weather was dirtying up rapidly; we were scooting in just ahead of a cyclone—a cyclone in these latitudes is the same as a hurricane; it is not the local twister of the Kansas plains. I was surprised to discover that the harbor was on the east coast of North Island, as a small-scale map makes it appear to be on the west coast.

"It's not surprising," Captain Young told me. "All the world's best harbors face east."

"So? How about San Francisco Bay? Or San Diego?"

"You've named two. But take a look at your own east coast. Take a look at the map of the whole world. For every fairly good harbor on a west coast there are half a dozen excellent ones on the east."

I thought it over and decided that he was largely correct, but I certainly had never realized it until he pointed it out.

Entrance into New Zealand required more paperwork than did any other country, plus an unusually tedious process at customs. I had another minor crisis with Ticky, for New Zealand had thought up a brand-new piece of nonsense: every visitor must sign a statement and swear a formal oath before an immigration officer not to do anything harmful to the Queen.

They handed these forms out the morning we arrived; Ticky read hers and blew her top. "I am not going to swear allegiance to their blankety-blank queen!"

"Now quiet down, honey. It doesn't say anything of the sort."

"It does so. And I won't sign it!"

"No, it does not. All you are promising to do is to obey the laws of New Zealand while you are in their country. I know you won't, but I'm hoping that you will be discreet enough not to get caught. So why not sign it?"

"It doesn't say anything about their laws; it's an oath that I will uphold their queen. I won't."

I tried again to explain it in a way she would accept— very wearily, for I considered it as nonsensical as she did. A criminal or a foreign spy would take such an oath and not turn a hair, while an honest man surely did not need to take it. "See here, baby, it's just a peculiarity in semantics. When they frank an envelope they put on it: 'In Her Majesty's Service,' while we put on it: 'Penalty for Private Use to Avoid Payment of Postage $300'—and they both mean precisely the same thing: 'Official Business, Free.' All this means is that you promise not to break the Queen's laws, which right here means the laws of New Zealand. You obeyed Perón's laws while you were there, but that didn't mean that you approved of Perón."

"All right, I'll sign a statement that I won't break any of their silly laws—but I won't sign that thing!"

I gave up, which is often the only way to win with Ticky; lack of opposition makes her unsure, I think. "Have it your own way. If you won't sign, they won't let us off the ship. We will have to stay right where we are for three days in port and then four more days at sea, then we are back in Australia. I suppose the police there will want to know why we were deported from New Zealand, but at least our visa is still valid. We can start tramping the streets of Sydney again, trying to book some sort of passage back home."

With that I dropped the matter. When the time came she signed the form, put up her right hand when she was told to, and muttered something. I did not hear what she said and I am sure the immigration officer could not hear it either. Perhaps it is just as well.

But will somebody tell me, please, why it is that countries will advertise for tourists, then do their very damndest to make the tourist feel like a child being kept in after school?

Once we were through customs we piled our bags into a taxi and asked the driver to take us to the Waverly Hotel, where a room had been reserved for us by the Union Steamship Company. The ride turned out to be only a few hundred yards, as the docks in Auckland rub elbows with the main downtown business districts, instead of being weary miles away as is so often the case. But during that short ride I looked around more eagerly than ever before, for New Zealand, of all countries in the world other than my own, interested me the most.

From time to time for more than twenty years I had made a hobby of New Zealand, studied its history, its laws, its geography, pored over statistics of its economy and its foreign trade. I knew how it was explored, how it was settled, the organization of its government; I had studied its Polynesian people from tattooed lips and cannibalism to their present status as political and social equals of the white English. So far as study will take one I felt that I knew New Zealand. Here was a country that had everything, physical wealth, an ample food supply, a people with high educational standards, civilized culture, democratic traditions, and homogeneity save for a colored minority with whom they had worked out the most decent *modus operandi* in the black history of the white race's relations with other races. Spurning communism, without resorting to socialism save on a purely pragmatic, non-doctrinal basis where needed, they had produced an economy with comfort and security for all, more entitled to the name "The Middle Way" than was that of Sweden. Their laws were ideal objectives for liberals all over the world, conceded to be at least fifty years ahead of any other nation.

Why, they had even solved the baby-sitter problem with graduate mother's-helpers!

I wanted to see this utopia, get to understand it. We had talked seriously of the possibility of renting a housekeeping flat in Auckland or Wellington and remaining for two or three months. I could pay for the stay by gathering material and doing a novel with a New Zealand background while I was on the spot and could check my background facts. Ticky could keep house and resume her scientific study of sub-tropical plants, interrupted when we had moved from California to the high Rockies. The plan seemed particularly attractive to her since it seemed possible that we would have to wait about that long to be sure of steamship passage back to the States, she being frantically opposed to flying the Pacific.

So we looked around eagerly, thinking this might be our temporary home.

The first impression was not too rosy, I had to admit. Where Brisbane reminded me of 1910, this looked more like a movie set for 1890. Still, I conceded, no city looks well when the weather is bad—the cyclone was still playing hop-scotch around us—and very few cities are attractive near the wharfs.

But I was a little surprised when the taxi stopped almost at once without leaving the unattractive neighborhood. Nor did the Waverly Hotel seem very cheerful; it looked like the sort of beat-up job a drummer stays in when he finds it necessary to be very, very careful about his expense account. But a decent bed and a hot bath was all I asked; we got the bags in and I registered. There were many other passengers from the *Monowai* checking in at the same time; it was likely that this was a comfortable inn despite the unattractive exterior.

I learned, without much surprise, that private baths were not available. "That will be seventy-one shillings per day, including breakfast and dinner."

"I think we would prefer just bed and breakfast, please. We will probably be eating out most of the time."

"We don't do it that way. You are charged for dinner whether you eat it or not. Do I understand you are staying more than one night?"

"Probably." Up to the time I walked into the lobby I would have said, "Certainly," but I was beginning to have doubts. I had not yet seen our room but the lobby itself was grim.

"In that case it will be six shillings less after the first day."

"Eh?"

"Linen charge, you know."

I did not know, but I let it ride. Ticky had been sitting on our luggage, as there were few chairs in the lobby, all occupied. An elderly porter helped us up to our room and I helped him with the bags, as he hardly seemed fit for it. Our room was long and narrow, with two narrow iron bedsteads placed end to end on the left wall, an old wooden bureau and a wash stand (real marble!) on the righthand wall. There was a single window at the far end, a clothes closet near the door— no coat hangers, however. There was a single dropcord in the middle of the room and a light over the wash basin. There were no bedside tables nor bedlamps, but there was a wicker chair and a kitchen chair. The floor was covered with wall-to-wall carpeting which seemed to have been laid when the building was built; its pattern had vanished under successive geological layers of dirt.

I paid off the porter, dismissed him, and turned back. Ticky was standing and touching, with a gloved finger, the dirty, faded bedspread over one of the cots. She looked up and said meditatively, "I don't think Mr. Duncan Hines would stay here."

"It reminds me of that trailer camp we got stuck in once. You remember? Mud and no plumbing?"

"I've been trying to forget it for years—but I wish we were back there right now. At least our trailer was clean. Honey, I don't think I can take this."

"I don't intend that you should. Come on."

"Huh?"

"This is a fairly big city; there must be a hotel room in it somewhere better than this pig sty. Do you have that little guide they gave us aboard ship?"

She dug it out of her purse and we consulted it. Hotels in New Zealand are graded by the government from "five stars," the highest, on down. To my shocked surprise the Waverly had a rating of four stars, just under the best, but there were two five-star hotels, the Grand and the Trans-Tasman. I telephoned the Grand at once and asked for a double room and bath, and was told that they had no rooms of any sort. How about tomorrow, then? Anyone checking out? Sorry, everything booked.

I had some trouble getting through to the Trans-Tasman Hotel but the guide showed it to be nearby. "Let's go there. Sometimes you can accomplish things on the spot which you can't by phone. You know—reservations not picked up, or a probable check-out that we might wait for."

We could not find a taxi, so we walked; it was not far. As we approached the number I said, "I don't see anything around here that looks like a hotel. Let me see that street guide again."

We were on the right street and the numbers indicated that the hotel should be almost on top of us. And so it was—there was a sign, THE TRANS-TASMAN BAR. It was a jerry-built frame structure which I would never have suspected of being a hotel, much less a "five star" hotel, but beyond the doors to the saloon was an inconspicuous second entrance which possibly might lead into a lobby.

We walked slowly past it, glancing inside, then walked back. Both of us were reluctant to go inside. "What do you think?" I asked doubtfully.

"It looks even worse than the Waverly. A joint like that would not have private baths. It is a terrible firetrap, too. Look at it—it ought to be condemned."

"Well . . . we're here; I suppose I should inquire."

Ticky put a hand on my arm. "Don't. I don't want to move into there. Bad as the Waverly is, this looks worse to me."

"Well, what should we do?"

"What can we do, you mean. Let's put up with the Waverly, just for this one night. And right now let's go to Thomas Cook and see if they can route us out of here tomorrow."

We had planned on a sightseeing swing around North and South Islands, but with a few days in Auckland first to get our bearings and check on steamship possibilities and launder clothes. I reminded Ticky of that.

"Never mind those things," she said earnestly. "I just want to get out of that home for unfortunate fleas. Maybe Wellington will be better."

So we walked to Thomas Cook & Son. On the way I recalled something. "You remember that chap we had a letter to? Sir Ernest Something-or-other?"

"Yes. What about him?"

"Wasn't he supposed to own a string of hotels?"

"I believe so. Or was it breweries?"

"Both, I think." I studied the matter, frowning. Up to this time we had never used a personal connection to get us favors which would not otherwise have been coming to us. We had had many a fine favor done for us, but we had asked for nothing, certainly not on the basis of being a friend of a friend. We intended to look Sir Ernest up, surely . . . but we had not intended to put the bite on him for special favors.

But this was an emergency; I had to get Ticky out of that squalid, dirty room. "When we get back to the Waverly I want to look up his address and give him a ring. If he is a hotel owner, he is sure to have at least one decent room in reserve to take care of legacies like us. I'm going to cry on his shoulder and get that room."

"Mmm . . . maybe. You know how we feel when people look us up at home during the tourist season. Let's try Thomas Cook's first."

The office of the Thomas Cook agency was on Queen Street, the main street of Auckland, just down the way from the Waverly. There we unloaded our troubles on Mr. D. M. Gunning, who was competent, cheerful, and as helpful as circumstances permitted. "It will be difficult, probably impossible, to set up a tour for you starting tomorrow morning. Have you tried any other hotels? We do have a couple of good ones."

I told him that the Grand had turned us down and recounted our impression of the Trans-Tasman. "I can see why you would think so," he answered. "But it actually is quite a bit better hotel than the Waverly. While it does not look like much outside, they have spent a lot of money fixing it up inside. Let me try them for you."

"Okay, if you say so."

But the Trans-Tasman was filled up, too. We dropped the

matter, since it could not be helped, and worked out with Mr. Gunning a tour which was to start with a flight to the far end of South Island, then bring us back by easy stages to Auckland via bus, train, and ferry across the channel, and would cause us to see every city and every major tourist attraction throughout New Zealand. It looked like a most attractive trip and we cheered up at the prospect of getting out of the Waverly and on the road.

"I'm going to work very hard on this," he assured us, "to get you started tomorrow, if possible. But I can't promise anything; there are too many hotel reservations and too many travel bookings involved in it to be sure. I'll set up the flight to Dunedin and your lodging there first, then we will see."

Ticky told him earnestly that if he could move us to Dunedin the next day, we would take a chance on the rest of it. He nodded. "Give me a ring at six o'clock, will you? I'm going to stay late and work on it."

We thanked him and left with a list of steamship agencies; the first two had nothing for us, but by the time we were through with them the others were closed. We spent an hour simply walking up and down Queen Street, then reluctantly returned to the Waverly.

I remembered to look up the address of the man who was supposed to own hotels. Or was it breweries? It turned out to be both: the Hancock Hotels and the Hancock Breweries. I was just looking up his telephone number when the phone rang.

It was Mr. Gunning of Thomas Cook & Son. "I'm terribly sorry but I can't get you away tomorrow. This cyclone is kicking things up south of here and all flights are canceled."

"Oh. Well, how about Sunday?"

"The airline does not operate on Sunday. I'll try to get you away early Monday."

"Well . . . thanks for trying."

We were downstairs and waiting outside the dining room before I recalled that I had intended to phone the boss of the Hancock Hotels. Oh, well, it was too late to do anything about it today and it would probably be best to call at his office anyway.

We quickly found out why guests were required to take, or at least to pay for, their dinners; no one having freedom of choice would have eaten there. We were soon to learn, too, that the compulsory boarding system used by all New Zealand hotels also resulted in independent restaurants being extremely scarce; a guest who was disgusted with hotel fodder found it extremely difficult to eat anywhere else even though willing to pay twice.

We started to walk into the dining room but were stopped by the manager-hostess—if "hostess" is the word. "You will have to wait a few minutes," she said bleakly. Since I could see empty tables I could not understand why, but wait we did. There were no chairs. Presently, although no one had come out, she signaled for us to come in and we were seated at a table for four. We had arrived at the beginning of the meal hour; the table had not been used by others.

The other two seats were not occupied. Another couple had arrived at the door right behind us, but had not been permitted to enter when we did. But after we had been at the table about ten minutes, they were let in and were seated at the same table with us.

I began to see the system by which the hostess worked and later observation confirmed it in detail. The dining room was open exactly one hour for each meal; this means that you must finish your meal before the sixty minutes has passed; it does *not* mean that you will be fed if you arrive at the door before the doors are closed. At the end of sixty minutes they stop serving and clear off the tables—and woe betide any guest who is still trying to finish his dinner. There were as many places at the tables in that dining room as there were sleeping accommodations in the hotel, but the "hostess" would not permit them to enter and sit down as they arrived. Instead she waited until she had a waitress free, which was why we and the other couple had had to stand in the corridor until she saw fit to let us come in and sit down.

We now experienced for the first time the delights of New Zealand cookery. The country is bulging with good food and it exports great quantities of the best. It should have been, like Argentina, a gourmet's paradise.

Australian cooking is not very good; hotel food in New Zealand is just barely short of inedible. Entrees are such things as boiled mutton, boiled bacon, and, if you are lucky, boiled beef. Clear soups are merely rain water; cream soups are sour paperhanger's paste. They have some means of vulcanizing potatoes. If by chance there is steak on the menu, you will find that they have cut it along the grain, cooked it grey, and the cut is one we would grind into hamburger. The difference between "lamb" and "mutton" appears to be that lamb is slaughtered whereas mutton apparently dies of old age. But they do not cook mutton with the wool left on. This is a canard, they sell the wool separately. But I have had many a piece of bacon served to me with the rind still on it and pig bristles, black and stiff, still sticking out of the rind. Under these circumstances it hardly matters that the bacon is only half cooked, cold, greasy, and undrained; you would not wish to eat it anyway.

Instead of a hot dinner roll there is a little square of stale, dry bread resting on the tines of your forks. No butter, of course. Toast is served cold in a toast rack and is much like building tile. For a sweet, or dessert, you will be offered stewed fruit, acidly sour, to which no sugar has been added.

This first night, following my custom of trying things which I did not recognize, I passed up the fruit and ordered "steamed sponge." So far as I could tell the thing they brought me was just that: steamed cellulose sponge. I tried a bite of it; it had no flavor and a coarse, resistant texture. I was toying with it with my spoon, wondering what to do with it, when the waitress leaned over my shoulder. "It helps a bit to soak it in milk," she advised.

But the milk was gone and she returned shortly from the kitchen to report that there was no more. I tipped her for her good will.

I might as well get this unsavory subject over with and not return to it. The food at the Waverly was typical of the food all through the country, consistently and amazingly bad—sloppily cooked, usually dirty, and often cold. Fly screens seemed to be unheard of and no attempt was made to check flies; cold buffet dishes such as salads and cold cuts were allowed to sit out on the sideboard for as much as an hour before meals, getting warm and stale, while flies wandered over them unmolested. Service varied from indifferent to rude. Once at the Waverly I asked the waitress to hand me a menu from a table at her elbow which was unoccupied, inasmuch as the menu at our table was in use (one menu in that case for ten people), but she refused to give it to me. I asked why not?—and she became quite angry about it.

As we left the dining room on that occasion, I told the hostess-manager about it. She looked at me as if I had lost my mind and told me the waitress was perfectly right—one menu to a table; that was the rule.

I answered, "Is that rule of your making? Or is it one laid down by the manager of the Waverly?"

"Why do you ask that?" she said sharply.

"Because I see no sense to it and intend to bring it to the manager's attention if the matter is beyond your control. So is it your rule? Or his?"

She looked disgusted. "Well, it isn't exactly a *rule* in that sense. But everybody knows it. One table, one menu—that's the way things are done."

I gave up and did not bother to speak to the manager. The notion that certain things "are done" and other things "aren't done" is the unanswerable argument of the provincial, to whom the customs of his tribe are laws of nature, as Shaw pointed out long ago. The odd rule about menus was not important anyway; I had spoken to the manageress simply because I disliked being bawled out in public by a person who was being paid to make me comfortable. But I did check as we went along to see if this oddly inefficient practice really was the uniform custom of the country.

It was, without any exception. Shortly before we left I tried to break it once more, simply as an experiment. We were eating alone in the dining room of another hotel, having been granted permission to eat lunch at twelve-thirty instead of one o'clock by special dispensation of the manager because we had a travel connection to make. There was one menu at our table, but about fifty menus in sight elsewhere in the room, so while Ticky was studying the one I turned to the waitress at my elbow and pointed at a menu less than four feet away. "Will you hand me that menu, please?"

She shook her head.

I had tried it on her because she looked good-natured. I now answered pleasantly. "Why not?"

"Huh? It's for *that* table."

"So it is. But it is not in use now and won't be until one o'clock. What harm is there in letting me see it for a moment? I won't damage it and I'll give it back in a moment or two."

She seemed to be undergoing some inner struggle. Finally she visibly braced herself, reached out and handed me the other menu. "Just this once!" she warned.

"Thank you."

She looked at us curiously. "You're Americans, aren't you?"

"Yes. Why? Our accent?"

"No, you talk all right. But Americans *always* want extra menus."

We tried to avoid the slops served at the Waverly by dining at public restaurants, but we found the cooking just as bad and the food even less attractively served. One large restaurant which looked all right from the outside served nothing but meat and potatoes, fish and chips—two sorts of potatoes on the same plate, both sorts rendered indigestible. We ate because we were very hungry, drank some tea (no coffee) and never went back. Coffee was served at the Waverly, since it "catered" to travelers, but not in the dining room, only in the lounge; coffee with your dinner cannot be obtained in New Zealand. Every hotel has a lounge, which always has some claim to posh swankness no matter how dreary and dirty the rest of the place may be, and here coffee is served in demi-tasse—which means that you have to wait up to forty-minutes or even longer to get it, that you can almost never get a second cup, and that cream is rarely available. All of which is of little importance as the stuff is usually not fit to drink. I don't know what they do to it. I've encountered bad coffee before, but it must take real talent to make New Zealand coffee. It tastes like a mixture of sorghum and used crankcase oil, but it surely cannot be that.

At last we spotted an ad for the Hi Diddle Griddle, which promised "that Heavenly American Food." We were suspicious as we had encountered "American" restaurants in other countries before, but we had nothing to lose, so we hurried there. It turned out to be a real, honest-to-God American hamburger joint, owned by a New Zealander who had lived many years in the States and only recently returned (through family necessity) and managed by a young Hollander freshly arrived in the country. It was *clean* and the coffee was wonderful, made fresh in Silex pots. They served rare, tender T-bone steaks, six versions of hamburgers, ham and eggs, chicken-in-a-basket, waffles, tender hot cakes, three-decker sandwiches, and home-made American pies. It was the sort of hole-in-the-wall restaurant which can be found two to the block in almost any side street in America but it was the only one of its sort in all New Zealand. We ate there every day we were in Auckland after that. It did not open until evening, so we made do in the daytime with fruit and biscuits that Ticky bought and fetched to our room.

But we did not find it until we had endured several Waverly meals. During the course of our first dinner there I happened to notice the inscription on the silverware, then asked for the menu again to confirm what I had found. There it was, across the top of the menu: *The Waverly, a Hancock Hotel.*

Silently I showed it to Ticky. When she had read it I whispered, "There goes our last chance." When we were back in our room, we sounded each other out, found we had the same point of view: not even to get out of this smelly squalor would we demean ourselves to ask favors of the man who was responsible for this squalor. "The only possible thing I could have to say to Sir Ernest," she said, her tones making the noble title a swear word, "is to tell him what I think of this room of his. But to do that properly I could not first meet him socially through a mutual friend. So we won't look him up."

Nor did we. We had another introduction to a former prime minister who was a warm friend of the United States. We intended to call on him, but, by the time it came to do so, we had had such a taste of New Zealand that we decided that it was more polite not to do so, as we would either have had to drink his tea and lie to him, or drink his tea and tell him the harsh truth of our opinion of his country. Neither alternative was acceptable, so we stayed away from him. In all, we accepted no personal hospitality of any sort in the country, for which I am glad.

We went to bed soon after dinner, as the weather was still stormy and the room was cold. It was only early fall in New Zealand, nevertheless that weekend was cold. The hotel had no provision of any sort for heating the rooms, nor did any but one of the hotels we were in there—Auckland is of the latitude of Norfolk or San Francisco, with a similar ocean-moderated climate. But imagine a San Francisco hotel without heated rooms!

The plumbing was far down another hall, a pot for women, a pot for men, one each, and nearby were shower rooms—or I should say "room" for it was one room with two doors, divided into two shower stalls by a partition which missed going all the way to the ceiling by about four feet. I did not mind this and Ticky told me later that she had not realized that the men's bath connected so intimately—but I wonder how a single and timid woman would feel to realize that men could watch her bathing by the simple expedient of dragging a chair up to the partition and looking over? That he could even climb over and assault her? Unlikely, I suppose, and no skin off our noses, since we made a habit of showering at the same time.

No tubs, of course. No amenities of any sort—and the toilet tissue appeared to be ancient parchment. After the first day we supplied our own.

Ticky killed a couple of cockroaches and we went to bed. The beds were beds in name only and we could not read, the only light being high in the ceiling. Nevertheless we got to sleep at last.

I woke up covered with mosquito bites and some other bites I was not sure about. Or, rather, I was awakened, for at seven-fifteen there came a sharp knock on the door, it was opened before I could answer, and a Maori chambermaid shoved a mug of tea in my face. Ticky tried to tell her to go away, but the girl was not listening, so Ticky accepted it. She sat up, sipping it and looking at me. "You're wearing a fright wig, did you know?"

"You wouldn't take any beauty prizes yourself this morning, my sweet. But I love you even if you are old and ugly."

"And I love you even when you're horrid, which is pretty often. But I don't doubt I look awful. Honey, could we have breakfast sent up? I've had a terrible night and I'm just not up to facing people and being polite. So please?"

"Did you read the house rules over there on the bureau? No room service. No parking of automobiles. Rooms must be vacated by 10:30 A.M.—or they sock you for another day. And a big, bold-face boast at the bottom 'The Comfort of Each Guest is the Objective of the Management.' "

"Only they failed to capture their objective. I had forgotten that quip about room service. Oh, dear!"

"They haven't, so pull yourself out of that sack. That dining room opens in exactly thirty-four minutes now and they slam it shut sixty minutes later. Get up and make yourself beautiful. Want me to draw you a nice hot tub with lots of bath salts?"

"Don't be nasty." She got up and started brushing her teeth. Presently she said, "They never did bring any face towels and this skimpy little bath towel is still wet—and I'm afraid I got it sort of dirty in the shower last night. There wasn't any place to hang it. May I use yours?"

"Go ahead. Where's my grey suit?"

"Still in one of your bags. There weren't any coat hangers and the maid would only bring me two, when I asked her. Your towel is wet, too."

"Don't fret about towels, the maid will bring some fresh ones when she makes up the room. And we'll buy some coat hangers this morning, if we have to."

But we did not buy coat hangers, as we discovered later that in New Zealand everything buttons up at five P.M. on Friday and remains closed until nine on Monday. The exceptions are negligible. Australian closing hours are inconvenient, but

New Zealand closing hours are more in the nature of paralysis. We did not know it yet, but our weekend was to be a complete blank.

Nor did we get dry towels. The comment about the linen charge was an indirect way of telling us that, in a New Zealand hotel, you use the same towel (one, for all purposes), the same napkin, the same sheets and pillow case for the duration of your stay. There was no use to complain; these things are regulated by the government.

I wonder if a government that decides when to change the sheets really has time to take care of more usual government business?

After breakfast (let's not mention it!) I urged Ticky to stay in and work on her clothes and mine. The cyclone seemed to have moved in on Auckland; it was rainy, very windy, and cold out. She agreed. "But be sure to try to find some American cigarettes."

"I'll try." I went first to Thomas Cook & Son. Every place I passed was closed and I was beginning to wonder, but I found it open and Mr. Gunning inside. He looked up, smiled ruefully, and shook his head. "Trouble?" I asked.

"Trouble. From the weather reports now I doubt if there will be any flights even on Monday. Besides that, I can't even get you out of here on Monday even if they do fly. Half the telephone lines are down and I can't begin to complete your reservations."

He showed me what he had planned and how little he had accomplished. Finally I said, "Mr. Gunning, what does South Island have that is unique? That can't be seen on North Island?"

"Mmmm—the Southern Alps. Fjords."

"Is that all?"

"Just about. The best hunting and fishing is there."

"Well, I don't hunt or fish, we live in the Rocky Mountains and much as I love mountains, I can get along without seeing another range of them. And I've seen plenty of fjords, too. If we limited this tour to North Island would it be easier?"

He looked happy. "Much easier."

"Then do it that way. Cut out all plane flights and keep us on this island—my wife will be pleased about that, anyway. She hates to fly, it frightens her. Can you get us out on Monday then?"

He shook his head. "I wish I could, but there is no use in giving you false hopes. This is a weekend. Half the places I'll have to reach will be closed—even if I can get a call through."

"Hotels? Transportation companies?"

"Hotels will be open, of course. Some of the transportation companies may be. Suppose I phone you later in the day? I'll do my best."

I agreed. Then I decided to turn over to him the matter of getting a ship back to the States. I was going to have very little time to haunt the steamship agencies and he probably stood more chance than I did, anyhow, since he knew the ropes. He was obviously able, and willing to try very hard— and the nicest person we had met yet. So I did so, then went out to look for American cigarettes. There were none, of course, but I was very lucky in that the sale of tobacco was permitted up until noon on Saturdays. I bought two or three brands that were recommended as "mild, much like American cigarettes," and went back to the room. I found Ticky swatting cockroaches again.

I do not remember too many details of the rest of that long weekend. I recall it just as the unvarying monotony of that filthy room, long treks down the corridors to try to find other toilets somewhere else in the hotel whenever the single facility reasonably near our room was in use, which seemed to be two times out of three, showers ended by smearing off with a towel that never did dry, a few sober drinks in the funeral-parlor splendor of the lounge, and watching the storm out the window.

I am not blaming New Zealand for that cyclone. Most of the weather while we were there was delightful; New Zealand has an almost ideal climate. We had encountered bad weather in every country we were in; given clean and cheerful indoor surroundings, bad weather is a very minor inconvenience or none at all. It is another matter when you are forced to hole up in filth.

We had tried to go out Saturday evening, but ran into one of New Zealand's most characteristic institutions, the six-o'clock drunk. Their saloons close at six P.M.; the customers spend the last fifteen minutes trying to get really plastered and most of them succeed. At 6:01 the drunks come pouring out on the sidewalks outside every hotel in New Zealand—in fact, marriage of the hotel business to the liquor trade appears to be the cause of New Zealand's scandalous hotels.

Ticky and I were standing at the taxi rank at the Waverly, which is just outside the Waverly Bar. We were waiting for a taxi and minding our own business, when simultaneously an empty cab drove up and the drunks started pouring out of the bar. Before I knew what was going on I found myself faced with a fist fight simply because Ticky and I had started to get into the cab.

I avoided the fight simply by accepting insults, obscenity, and by surrendering the cab. I am no hero and I do not relish facing a judge on a street-fighting charge in a strange country, and I relish even less the broken nose, broken glasses, and so forth, that may be picked up in such a brawl—and still less the prospect of Ticky's getting involved in such a useless, silly, and dangerous business . . . which she would surely do if she saw me getting the worst of it. So I crawled.

Much later, after all the drunks were served, we got a taxi. I was still shaking with rage and so was Ticky. But it turned out that she had not realized what had almost happened—because the notion of grown men fighting on a sidewalk was foreign to her experience. In thinking it over I realized that the last time I had seen anyone really drunk—fighting, mean drunk and not just happy—was over twenty years earlier and in a Central American banana port at that. For all the liquor consumed in the United States, drunk and disorderly on the streets is something one reads about in the newspapers but hardly ever sees in the flesh.

In New Zealand they do not warrant a police-court news item. So far as I know they are never arrested, for they are common as lamp posts. Nor are they limited to six o'clock in the evening; that is simply the time when the sidewalks are literally crowded with them. But you can see them at any time of day on the streets of Auckland, staggering, too drunk to navigate. Nobody pays any attention, not even the bobbies.

On Monday the weather was much better, although still overcast with some rain. After breakfast I told Ticky I intended to go at once to see Mr. Gunning. "Better get out of this hole and come with me. And say—where is that Auckland guide? Not the little one, but the big one the Chamber of Commerce puts out."

"Over there under the wash stand. What do you want if for?"

"What's it doing on the floor? And—good grief, what have you been doing with it? It's all messy."

"Swatting cockroaches."

"But why use the Auckland City Guide?"

"I had to use something . . . and it seemed appropriate."

"Mmmm, maybe you have a point." I opened it gingerly. "I want to look up the American consul. It is just barely possible that he might be able to help us get a ship back home."

Ticky had been standing at the window, looking down at the grim and antiquated buildings of Auckland. She did not say anything for a long moment, then she turned rather suddenly.

"Bob—"

"Huh?"

"Don't bother."

"Eh? What do you mean?"

"Don't try any further to get us a ship back to the States. Let's go down right now and buy an airline ticket home."

"*What?*"

"Let's fly home."

I said slowly, "Honey, I thought you were the girl who would put up with anything rather than fly over the ocean? I thought the very idea frightened you?"

"I was. It does. It just scares me speechless. I'm almost sure we'll be killed. But—" She began to cry. "B-b-but I'm just so homesick and miserable that I'll do *anything* to get home. I just can't stand this filth and the dirty food and, and everything. So let's fly."

I put an arm around her. "Take it easy, honey. All right, if that's what you want. Let's go over and tell Mr. Gunning and have him cancel the tour. Then we'll make a reservation."

"Oh, let's!"

It turned out that we could not possibly fly for four more days at the earliest; Ticky decided that such being the case we might as well make the tour around North Island and leave immediately on returning, a week hence. The notion of the tour did not upset her nearly as much as the idea of four more idle days in Auckland. So we spent the rest of the day happily, in a holiday spirit, making preparations for the tour and buying our ticket to San Francisco. We had a party at the Hi Diddle Griddle that night and let the Waverly do what it liked with the dinners we had already paid for. What Ticky suggested that they do with them was more appropriate than eating them.

When we checked out the next morning we found that they had charged us for one extra day and two extra meals. I called it to their attention with a minimum of comment, waited while they corrected it, and returned my key—ten shillings deposit. But they had the last laugh anyhow, for they gave us less than the established exchange rate for our dollars and I was too much in a hurry to go out to a bank for the correct rate. As we climbed into a taxi I shook the dust of the place from my shoes and did not look back.

The trip around North Island was very pleasant, in spite of hotels almost as bad as the Waverly and food that was just as bad in most cases. We used the hotels just to sleep in and were on the move, out in the open country, all day long. New Zealand is truly a beautiful place; once away from the eyesores they use for towns and cities one could easily fall in love with it.

The first jump was to Waitomo, by bus. The bus had been described as a "luxury bus" to distinguish it from their ordinary cross-country buses, which are known as service cars. It was not bad, but the seats are so narrow and close together that they are really suited only to married couples still in love—so Ticky and I happily held hands the entire trip. Brazil could tell them something about luxury buses, however.

The first stop was at the Waitomo Hotel, by itself in beautiful country. There we had the only decent hotel accommodations in all our stay in New Zealand. It was just a simple room and bath, but good, clean, new, and comfortable—say an $8 room in a decent commercial hotel in America. But it looked like heaven to us.

The Waitomo was the only good hotel we found in New Zealand, and even it had oddities which would not be tolerated in America—the habit, for example, of paging a guest by loudspeaker: "Mr. Tompkins, room twenty-five, report to the desk!" We had run into this army-barracks procedure first in the steamship *Monowai;* if the purser wanted to see a passenger, he ordered him, by loudspeaker, to report to his office, instead of sending a messenger with the message couched as a request. This rude practice is common throughout New Zealand. The peremptory knock in the early morning, even on Sundays, the lack of room service, and the boarding-meal hours and style of serving are common to all hotels that we saw; New Zealanders apparently do not mind being strictly disciplined on their holidays. But, allowing for these customs of the country, the Waitomo was a good hotel. Even its cooking was markedly better than that of the Waverly—not good, but edible and usually clean. By contrast it seemed wonderful.

After dinner, during an unusually long wait for coffee in the lounge, we met the manager, Mr. W. F. Swift. I had remarked that the two pages serving coffee were doing it in such a back-handed, steps-retracing fashion that they seemed unlikely ever to finish, whereupon the gentleman next to me introduced himself as the manager. It became evident that he knew his job and wanted to run the best hotel possible—and his efforts showed.

He asked us what room we were in; Ticky answered, "Number three." He nodded and said, "Ah yes, the Royal Suite."

Ticky said, "Why do you call it that?"

"Eh? Because it is. The room you have was the Duke's room; the one connecting with it, number four, was the one occupied by the Queen—let me see, uh, just four weeks ago today."

I looked at Ticky and she looked at me. We managed not to laugh until we were safe in the "Duke's room"—then we got slightly hysterical. Not that there was anything wrong with the room; it was in all respects comfortable, proper, and decently furnished. I am sure the Duke of Edinburgh was comfortable in it, even though you could have lost it and never missed the space in the incredible "room" we had enjoyed in the Raffles. But the notion that we had had to acquire the Royal Suite to enjoy accommodations adequate but less luxurious than those of any of thousands of motels in America hit us, in our weakened state, as riotously funny.

The bathtub in the Royal Suite was exceptionally long and I suspect it was specially installed in consideration for the Duke's height—certainly all the fixtures were new. I know I found it a luxury even though I am two inches shorter than the Duke. But it had one oddity which I learned presently was characteristic of New Zealand plumbing: they do not revent drain lines and consequently, when a drain is thirty-five feet or more above its discharge, the drain hole will show a full fifteen pounds per square inch of vacuum, enough to be startling and moderately dangerous. I found this out by stepping on the drain hole in the tub, to my great surprise and moderate pain. I wrote a story once about a man who sealed off a vacuum leak by sitting on it; I really should rewrite that story since I did not know at the time just how absorbing a trick it is.

I managed to pull my foot loose with nothing but a large strawberry mark to show for the mishap. I hope the Duke did not step on the drain.

Waitomo is a limestone-cave resort. There are three caves, all quite good, but I am not going to describe stalactites, stalagmites, and such. If you have seen limestone caves anywhere in the world you have seen much the same thing; if you have seen the Mammoth Cave or Carlsbad Caverns you have seen much more. I am not running down the Waitomo Caves; I love limestone caves anywhere, never miss a chance to go through them, and these are excellent examples. But if you have seen one, description is unnecessary; if you have not, description is almost worthless—it is time you treated yourself to the experience.

But there is one aspect of one cave there which is unique, to be seen nowhere else in the world: the Glow-Worm Grotto. It is a surpassing emotional experience which may well be worth making a trip of thousands of miles to see and worth even the indignities of New Zealand hotels. The glow worm referred to in the name is the larva of a small fly, *Arachnocampa luminosa,* whereas our glow worm is the larva of a beetle— but the difference is important only to another glow worm or an entomologist; it is a worm that glows by the same biochemical process which makes our fireflies light up. The larvae, an inch to two inches long, live on the ceilings of Cave Waitomo, where they spin threads like spider webs to catch other insects.

We went through Cave Waitomo the evening of our arrival. The first part of the tour is the usual limestone-cave trip, beautiful and impressive but not unique. Then the guide explains that he is about to turn off the lights, as the glow worms shut off their light if disturbed by light or sound. We are enjoined to keep absolute quiet. In the darkness we are led down to a big boat in an underground river; each visitor is handed into the boat in darkness, seated, and given whispered orders to sit still, keep quiet, and show no light.

With no sound but breathings and the water lapping gently against the side of the boat we are pulled along in pitch darkness, the guide moving the boat by means of steel rope let into the rock walls. The boat makes a turn to the left, following the course of the underground stream.

There is a chorused gasp, muffled at once. The ceiling of the cavern we have just entered is covered with many, many thousands of tiny blue lights, so many and so bright that we can now see the awed faces of our companions in the boat, enough light to read newspaper headlines. The sight is most like that of the Galaxy spilling across a clear desert sky on a moonless night, the gasp from the boat like that one always hears when the "stars" first come out in a planetarium show. It does not feel like a cave; it feels like open sky and glimmering stars.

The above is correct, as far as it goes. I am afraid I cannot convey the eerie emotional experience of the silent walk through darkness down to an underground river, the spooky, River-Styx feeling of that black and muffled voyage. It is good that the glow worms are shy, for a single gaggling word would blemish the awesome spell of that unearthly place.

We went from Waitomo to Wairakei by train and bus, stopping overnight at the Chateau, their best-known resort hotel in the middle of National Park. Their trains are good, but smaller than ours; their goods wagons look toylike compared with our freight cars. The Chateau would be comparable to the hotels in our own national parks if it were well run. It is not. Poor food, a sickening stench in the dining room, and more of the army-barracks spirit in handling the guests. We were bawled out for daring to sit down at an empty table in the dining room—cold, dirt, and tongue-lashings are routine for the visitor to New Zealand; you must harden yourself to it while there.

The bus ride from the Chateau to Wairakei was one of the most interesting parts of the tour, even though it was scheduled simply as a means of getting us from one tourist attraction to another, for the reason that it took us intimately into New Zealand farming country and let us see a little of how the New Zealand countryman lives. The bus traveled much more than twice the road distance, wandering around through small villages and up side streets, delivering newspapers, picking up mail, stopping at a hail to pick up a note from a farmer's wife and deliver it to some farm farther up the way. We could see clearly for the first time that the whites and the Maori actually did live intimately together in the country, with no apparent color line. The countryside is fertile and has a feminine beauty, the paddocks and fields being separated by hedge rows rather than fences, English style. The back roads are poor, the houses small and rather grim, the cross-roads stores very poorly stocked; the much-vaunted high standard of living is not evident. In several places there were kennel-like housing developments, with whole families living in cramped boxes that made the worst of company towns in America look like well-planned suburbs. Housing is New Zealand's most acute shortage, but it is hard to see what obstacles prevent solving it, other than those they have deliberately placed on themselves through legislation. But even the best houses are uniformly dreary, made more so by an all-prevalent use of drab yellow paint, and even new houses are built in the same nineteenth-century style which accounts in part for the 1890 overall impression the country gives one.

New Zealand seems to be a place where no one goes hungry, but where life is dreary and comfortless beyond belief, save for the pleasures of good climate and magnificent country-side.

The bus delivered us at last to Hotel Wairakei, having taken four hours to cover seventy miles. Wairakei is a thermal-activity neighborhood rather than a town; it has geysers, hot springs, boiling mud springs, and colored formations in abundance, and is also the center of the government's experiments in harnessing volcanic steam for heat and power, a project pictured last year in *Life* magazine. The geothermal bores are located near the hotel and the hotel is alleged to be heated by them; perhaps in time heat for hotels will become a common thing there. As yet, the experiments have not realized commercial results but there is every reason to expect that they will. The amount of dry steam underground here is illustrated by one thermal activity which is not duplicated or excelled in Yellowstone (grand as they are, all other thermal activities in New Zealand are no match for Yellowstone, a demonstrable fact no New Zealander will believe). This exception is the Karapiti Blow Hole, which incessantly blows dry steam at 180 lbs./sq. in. pressure and has been doing so without let-up at least since the Maori arrived there in the fourteenth century. The guide there referred to it as "New Zealand's Relief Valve" and suggested that the island might blow up if the blow hole were stopped up—Ticky was all for sneaking back at night and dumping rocks and cement into it, but she is a vandal at heart as well as an anarchist.

Speaking of vandals, our several visits to the geysers and so forth of Wairakei area were made less than pleasant by the New Zealander's own disregard for his country's natural wonders. Even the guides joined in the casual sport of tearing up the vegetation, roiling the lily pools, chucking refuse into hot springs and the like. After the firm discipline of our own National Park Rangers plus the unending and quite successful warnings to us all not to disfigure our parks it was shocking to see these people witlessly damaging their national treasures. Yet we never once heard a government guide protest or warn.

In fact, in the Waitomo Caves we saw one of the guides break off a stalactite (which took endless years to grow) just to show a party of twenty people its inner structure. In these caves the formations were covered with disfiguring chicken wire where they could be reached, just to stop such rape— but the formations in our Carlsbad Caverns have no such protection and need none, for each party that goes down is so indoctrinated before starting that, should a tourist be so reckless as to harm a formation, the Rangers would almost certainly have to intervene to save him from violence at the hands of the outraged majority. We have our vandals, certainly—out we regard them as vermin. Not so there.

This same guide at Waitomo mentioned something else that surprised us almost as much as the destruction of the stalactite. It turned out that Ticky had the only flashlight in the party, whereupon the guide mentioned that the week before the lights had failed and a guide had been forced to lead a party out in the pitch blackness, relying on his memory of the twists and turns underground. Despite this incident, our guide had no torch of any sort. One of the New Zealand tourists remarked that the government certainly should buy him a flashlight, whereupon all the rest of the party and the guide himself agreed solemnly that the government certainly should, as the present situation was dangerous. Ticky and I kept quiet. No one at all suggested that a professional cave guide, not supplied with a free flashlight, might consider investing ten shillings in a flashlight of his own rather than wait for a bureaucrat to think of it.

The Wairakei Hotel had the usual swank lounge and dining room, poor food and lack of service; it was exceptional only in having the smallest room we encountered around the world. It contained a double bed and there was barely room for one person to walk down one side and the end, with the bed jammed against two walls.

We went on from there to Rotorua, fifty miles away. Rotorua is a town built right on top of a thermal area; there are geysers, hot springs, and plumes of steam popping out at odd places in back yards, in parks, or by the roadside. The Wairakei area and Rotorua and its environs comprise most of the thermal area in New Zealand. One gets the impression that thermal activity in New Zealand covers a vast area, much larger than Yellowstone, but this is not true; a map of Yellowstone, to the same scale, placed over a map of New Zealand, will show that the area of thermal activity in Yellowstone is more widespread than the corresponding area in New Zealand. After trying this comparison I wondered why the New Zealand area seemed larger and concluded that it arose from one difference: the New Zealand thermal area is not a reserve, except for certain very small areas of intense activity; farms and houses and villages fill up the space between these very limited enclaves; on the other hand, in Yellowstone we have chosen to block off the entire space, all 3500 square miles of it, more than 2,000,000 acres.

This comparison is not a criticism of the New Zealand policy, as New Zealand simply could not possibly afford to block off an area the size of Yellowstone in the middle of North Island. Besides, while I would not change Yellowstone by one pine needle, nevertheless there is a quaint charm about a country town in which the houses and fruit trees and privies intermingle with geysers and hot springs.

The Hotel Geyser in Rotorua did nothing to sully New Zealand's unchallenged record for the worst in hotels. Our room was larger than the one at Wairakei, but, since it had twin beds, it was not roomier. Since we were going to be there longer than overnight I started to ask for a chair, there being none of any nature in the room, then refrained from doing so after I had considered every possibility and discovered that no jigsaw puzzle maneuvering could possibly make room for a chair in that lovely boudoir.

The mattress on my bed was such that I took it off the bed each night and placed it under the bed. In my opinion this improved things somewhat, as there was a hard boxlike structure under the mattress which seemed to me to make better sleeping than the alleged mattress. Ticky chose to sleep among the hills and valleys of her mattress; I don't know which one of us came out ahead, but we both resorted to sleeping pills every night that we were there. There was no danger of us sleeping through breakfast as a Maori maid came in at seven each morning to wake us with tannic acid solution and another Maori girl toured the corridors, banging on a Maori war gong—allee-samee lid of garbage can, with decorations—at seven-thirty to make sure no one failed to sit down on time. This clamor went on even on Sunday mornings.

We were unable to keep the maid out of the room at seven A.M. because we could not get a key to our room, nor could it be bolted from inside. Immediately after checking in I went back to the desk and made a fight talk for a key, somewhat exaggerating the value of my camera equipment and of Ticky's jewelry to justify the unusual (in New Zealand) request . . . in fact, between camera, binoculars, typewriter, engagement ring, and a few gewgaws, we did have items with us which it would have grieved us to lose.

The manageress told me somewhat frostily that we did not need a key since everyone around there was honest. Right at this point a bellman came up to her, stuck out his hand, and asked for the key to the linen locker; she reached under the desk and got it for him while still talking to me. I looked at him, looked back at her, and said, "I thought you just told me that keys were quite unnecessary around here because everyone was honest?"

This made her angry and she informed me quite huffily that the linen locker was another matter entirely. I did not get the key.

While we were there Ticky took her baths wearing all her jewelry, such as it was. Insurance compensation does not interest her.

Perhaps everyone around there was indeed honest; we did not miss anything. But New Zealand is the only country we visited where we were cheated in making change and it happened there so frequently as to justify fairing a curve and declaring a trend.

The hotel was standard in all other respects. The room had no coat hangers, of course; the food was bad and dirty; the coffee was one point worse than any other, for it was not drinkable at all—and I will happily drink very bad coffee rather than do without; I am a coffee addict. But the meals were rendered somewhat cheerful by Maori waitresses in old Maori costumes, very fancy indeed. The Maori are a handsome people and Maori girls are very pretty indeed, if you like them a little on the plump side. The girls were not only smiling and attractive but actually seemed to want to please the guests. They dressed in a skirt much like a hulu skirt made of New Zealand flax, scraped, rolled and dried in such a fashion that the strands look like strings of beads. When they walk the strands make a cheerful clacking sound. Above the waist they wear fancy embroidered bodices, strapless, with arms and shoulders bare.

The Geyser Hotel is almost next door to the Maori village of Whakarewarewa, which sits right in a geyser basin with houses built on the crusts deposited by thermal action. We paid a guide fee and joined a party of four Englishmen who were being shown around by an old Maori woman. The houses in this village are of the same style as almost every other house in New Zealand; they are not Maori architecture. So far as I could find out no Maori lives as his ancestors lived; there seems to be nothing in New Zealand parallel to the pueblo cities and the Navajo hogans of our southwest. But nearby the occupied houses, the Maori have built a replica ancient Maori village for the benefit of tourists; the tour includes the modern village, the thermal activities, and a lecture on Maori culture illustrated by the replica empty village.

The modern village sits where it does because the Maori use the natural steam and hot water for cooking, for washing, and for all domestic purposes. Iron pipes run here and there above ground, carrying water and steam from natural source to houses, and there are boxes and Dutch-oven contrivances placed over steam holes and used as stoves. The heat is great enough for boiling or simmering, not great enough for broiling or frying. Laundering is done outside in natural basins and the children, at least, bathe outdoors. I had the impression that this method of living was continued primarily as a tourist exhibit even though the houses really are inhabited, but it is no more the normal way for Maori to live than it is for the whites. The overwhelming majority of Maori have no more opportunity to use natural steam than have the residents of Auckland. Nevertheless it was very interesting.

We left the village and were conducted around the rest of the geyser basin and over to the replica village. We had had the bad luck to draw a guide who was intensely racist; she was bent on proving that Maori were equal to white men in most ways and better in all others. While we could sympathize with her chip-on-the-shoulder attitude intellectually, it was nevertheless tediously annoying. I am not going to give this woman's name as she has had much too much publicity already, being conceded to be the leading guide there and the one always chosen to conduct V.I.P.s—you have probably seen her picture in American magazines several times.

When we joined her party she was busy baiting the four Englishmen, making invidious comparisons between Maori and English, criticizing the government of England, and so forth. The Englishmen endured it in dignified silence. When she found out that we were Americans she shifted her attention to us, but limited herself at first to boasting about how much the village had done for American service men during the War (which may well have been true) and how thoroughly impressed "Eleanor" was with what she had seen there.

A few minutes later I accidentally brought her wrath down on us. She had asked us if we had seen Yellowstone Park; we admitted that we had. She answered, "I'll show you things you don't have at Yellowstone." Shortly thereafter, during the geyser basin tour, she stopped and pointed around us. "Note," she said, "how the greenery, the trees and bushes, come right down to the edge of the geyser basin. There's nothing like that in Yellowstone."

This was a wonderful place for me to have kept my mouth shut in the interests of international amity. But I answered, "Excuse me, but somebody has misled you. The trees and greenery in Yellowstone come to the edge of the thermal basins just as they do here."

"*What?*" She stopped and glared at me. "But I know they don't! I've seen pictures."

I realized almost at once how she could have gotten honestly mixed up from pictures. There are several geyser basins in Yellowstone so many acres in extent that one may take any number of pictures without having trees and shrubs in the background; nevertheless similar conditions produce similar results and where the burned-out thermal area stops the trees and shrubs begin at once.

The basin she was showing us was not on that vast scale; it could have been lost in one corner of the Norris Geyser Basin, for example. Consequently trees and shrubs were never far away. In the enormously bigger basins of Yellowstone the nearest greenery might be several hundred yards away, but the basic arrangement was precisely the same—in the smaller thermal areas of Yellowstone the spatial relationships were just like those around us.

There was no reason for us to quarrel. I did not design Yellowstone and she did not design the Whakarewarewa thermal area. So I tried to straighten the matter out. She was still boiling, shouting that every other American who had ever been there had told her that she was right and anyhow the pictures proved I was wrong. I said, "I think it is just a mix-up, a misunderstanding. You see—"

"You can't argue with photographs! I'll *show* them to you!"

The Englishmen were beginning to look at us oddly and I was growing embarrassed. "Let me explain how it is at Yellowstone. You see—"

"I've no time to listen to explanations now. Come on, we're late!" She turned and stomped up the path.

I shut up, realizing that she did not want explanations. The superiority of "her" thermal area was a matter of dogma; it was emotionally, though illogically, related to the superiority of the Maori race. Several times during the next hour she turned to me and said, in several different ways, that it was very funny that I was the only American who had not agreed and so forth; she did not quite call me a liar but she made it clear that I must know that I was not telling the truth. But every effort to explain she brushed off; she had no time to listen to heresy.

Her attitude was not typically Maori but it was typically New Zealand. The New Zealanders know, beyond any argument, that they have the best thermal displays in the world. I certainly agree that the New Zealand displays are wonderful and beautiful. But let me quote the Encylopaedia Britannica, which states that the geysers of Yellowstone render those "—of New Zealand almost insignificant in comparison" (X, 319, 1954). This truth is self evident to anyone who has seen both—but few New Zealanders have; indeed, their government forbids them to travel to our country save under very special circumstances.

But neither Ticky nor I ever told any New Zealander that Yellowstone was better, and I gather from what I heard that other Americans had been equally forbearing. (Even when I incensed our guide I had not been claiming that Yellowstone was "better"; I had simply attempted to correct an explicit error—nor was I successful even in that.)

The party went on to the replica village where our guide lectured us and several other parties on the virtues and wisdom of the ancient Maori, directing most of her remarks at us. The Maori emigrated here from Tahiti about six centuries ago; every Maori of today traces his descent back to a particular canoe of that heroic migration. Maori social organization was based on blood relationships and each village was a super-family, communal inside the family village. Exogamy was not required but consanguinity closer than second cousins was "tapu" or taboo.

The lecture was very long, the day was hot, and we were packed into the stuffy, windowless "city hall" of the replica village. Besides, the talk was compounded of boasting and of many statements which were, at least, imaginative and idealized rearrangements of history and anthropology. Ticky became faint and I happily excused ourselves and led her away.

A lot of nonsense has been peddled both about the modern Maori and their ancestors. Most modern Maori are fine people indeed, handsome, good-natured, civilized, and acceptably well-educated; they are a real pleasure to know.

But the notion that their ancestors were nature's noblemen is preposterous; the Maori, before the English fought them and tamed them, were the mad dog of Polynesian peoples. They were not simply barbarous, they were bloodthirsty savages, perhaps the worst this wicked planet has seen. Physical courage and family loyalty were their only virtues. They exterminated the unwarlike aboriginal inhabitants of New Zealand, then turned their attention to eating each other, a practice to which they were addicted as the present-day New Zealander is addicted to his beer. Compared with them the lowly Australian aborigine was a civilized gentleman.

All of which has nothing to do with the Maori today; all of us have savage ancestors. It is New Zealand's boast that the present Maori are political and social equals. This boast has a large and admirable measure of truth; the status of the Maori in New Zealand is, in most respects, better than the status of colored people of all sorts in the United States. But it is not literally true. Maori will usually be found in menial jobs and there is much unspoken, "Gentlemen's Agreement"-type discrimination. Politically the Maori may not be a second-class citizen but he is certainly a special-class citizen, for he does not cast a white man's ballot. Instead he votes only for legislative representatives of his own race. He is allowed four out of eighty, or five per cent. But his birth rate is nearly twice as high as that of the whites and his present proportion in the population is nearer ten per cent than five. Exponential growth curves being what they are, one may wonder what the white man will do when these proportions are more nearly equal; will he ever permit the Maori to outvote him, or will he hold him to five per cent and a separate ballot?

In the matter of schools, most of them are mixed; others are "Jim Crow" schools for Maori children.

We attended a concert given at the City Hall of Rotorua under the direction of our guide at the Maori village. She had apparently forgotten her anger at me, or perhaps our meekness under her abuse had mollified her, for she greeted us as old friends and insisted on seating us down front. (Ticky had almost refused to attend; she wanted to claw the woman— with a cannibal feast for the victor, I gathered.) The concert consisted of Maori war dances, story dances, and songs, among them the famous "Now Is the Hour"—which is Maori. The war dances were characterized mainly by sticking tongues out as far as possible, said to be a gesture of defiance. Possibly through years of practice, a Maori can stick his tongue out much farther than a white man, sufficient to cover his chin. The arts and crafts displayed were of the usual barbaric level found all over the globe in all early cultures and almost monotonously alike wherever found—garish colors, overelaboration of detail, and highly traditional, unindividual design. It is considered the proper thing these days to gush over peasant and native art, admire the "marvellous" designs and the patient workmanship. I cannot go along with this fad; most primitive art is obviously poor art, of kindergarten quality, if judged on its own merits without sentimentality about its origin. As for the patient workmanship, to spend pains on such fiddlin' stuff indicates a person with lots of time on his hands and lacking knowledge of anything better. These are simply stages that all of our ancestors went through; we should respect them for what they are but not gush over them for what they are not.

Maori story dances are much like other Polynesian dancing such as hula, but made more interesting to me by the addition of the poi. Poi are light-weight balls on strings, which are swung like Indian clubs with remarkable dexterity. It is a form of precision juggling worked into the choreography and is most pleasing and quite difficult. There are "short poi" with six-inch strings and "long poi" with the strings about as long as the girls' arms, and they produce varied rhythms and incidental slapping sounds. It is an art most graceful, unique with the Maori, as traditional and stylized as classic ballet and (I suspect) almost as difficult.

During our stay at Rotorua we had signed up for one of the government tourist trips scheduled to leave at 2 P.M. from the bus station in town on Saturday afternoon. We showed up there, only to be told that the trip was canceled because nobody wanted to go that day. Nobody but us, that is. I am rather glad, now that it is over, that we were disappointed as it gave us a chance to enjoy a real New Zealand Saturday afternoon.

We asked the clerk at the bus station what else there might be to do in town that day? Nothing, so far as he knew. Now Rotorua is the center of their principal holiday area and it was the height of their tourist season, so I persisted: How about a cricket match? Where could we expect to find one? Ticky had never seen cricket and I thought it was time that she learned why cricket had never displaced baseball in spite of the obvious inanities of our own national sport.

No cricket match scheduled, sorry . . . nor any place he could suggest to look for a "sand lot" game. Well, how about a movie?

Ah yes, there was a cinema performance, starting in about fifteen minutes just down the street—but have you booked tickets?

It had not occurred to us. He shook his head dismally; nevertheless we tried the cinema. It was not a continuous showing, but one performance only, reserved seats only . . . and every seat sold. The one-performance-only rule was, like the sixty-minute meal hours, one of their multitudinous restrictions on working hours; we observe a forty-hour week just as closely as they do, but their approach to it is entirely different.

So we wandered the streets, trying to find something, anything, open. Rotorua is not a large place, but it is more than a wide place in the road; it has more citizens than has Annapolis, Maryland, a few dozen less than Princeton, New Jersey, and in addition has droves of vacationers staying in it. It is also the shopping center of a large farming community, and this was Saturday afternoon when any such farm community in America would be bursting at the seams.

You could have sprayed a machine gun down its main street and never hurt a soul. We were the only people in sight.

We strolled the silent business district, stopping occasionally to peer into locked shops. A drug store had a notice in the window stating that it was the authorized emergency chemist shop for that weekend, prescriptions filled on certified emergency from nine to ten in the morning and from six to seven in the evening. I wondered what would happen if a heart patient had to have digitalis in the middle of the day; would they let him die? A closed filling station had a similar notice, giving the address of another station at which petrol might be purchased in a certified emergency.

At last we found a small restaurant and soda fountain open, one which we had patronized the day we arrived, so we went in, even though we were not really hungry, and ordered milk shakes and sandwiches.

"Ah no," said the waitress.

"No? Well, what can you serve us?"

"Tea."

"Tea? What else?"

"Just tea."

We had tea. There was no lack of food in the place; it was in sight all around us, entertaining the flies. But tea was all that might be legally sold then.

East of the business district we found a large and beautiful park; here there were people, reveling in sports—croquet and bowls. We watched a doubles match at croquet, played for blood, the sort where you take vicious delight in knocking your opponent's ball into the next county. We were beginning to take real interest, when someone rang a dinner bell and all the players on all the courts stopped at once, racked their balls and mallets, and stopped for tea. They did not even leave the balls in position to resume play. It seemed to me a perfect example of the New Zealander's willingness to accept regimentation even in his pleasures. I began to understand why girls' marching teams were a major sport in New Zealand; close order drill suits their temperament and, besides, there isn't much else to do.

After the break for tea, disgusted with the croquet players, we watched bowls. Bowls is not bowling; it is a game played with lopsided spheroids about the size and shape of a loaf of pumpernickel and the principles are those of pitching pennies for a line. But it is a game requiring high skill to play well, as the unbalanced bowl will not go in a straight line. However, as a spectator sport, it cannot compare with chess. It is played mainly by elderly men and I think I could learn to enjoy it in my declining years.

Having exhausted the resources of this holiday resort and ourselves as well we went back and waited for the bus. There was just one, as the movie let out, and it would not hold all the crowd. I don't know whether it went back and picked up the few left behind or not. But our own experience earlier with an unannounced cancellation of a scheduled bus trip made it seem doubtful.

New Zealand is a good place to hunt and fish.

The trip from Rotorua back to Auckland was longish, five hours and a half. Ticky relieved the tedium by singing endless verses of, "In eleven more months and ten more days I'll be out of the calaboose," while I pretended not to know her. The bus stopped for tea at Hamilton; not wishing a mug of tea and ersatz, fly-tromped sandwiches, I inspected a magazine stand instead and bought one somewhat resembling our *Harper's* magazine to read on the bus.

The lead article was "The Great American Hoax," which undertook to prove that the American standard of living was much lower than that of New Zealand. The author had figures to "prove" that most of us live in abject poverty, unable to buy necessities, much less enjoy any comforts, such as autos, radios, decent clothes, etc.

But he did not mention that, per capita, we have more than twice as many automobiles as do New Zealanders, twice as many telephones, four times as many radios. But at the end of the article he advised us to use the legislative measures that had brought such great prosperity to New Zealand.

New Zealanders believe this sort of drivel. They know they have the world's highest standard of living; they have been told so repeatedly. Since they are not allowed to travel to the United States without very special permission (they can get a passport but they are not allowed to buy dollars to make the trip) and since our magazines and books are forbidden entrance to their country, they are not likely to change their opinions.

The embargos against American printed matter seem to me to be one of the most serious breaches between the United States and the Commonwealth nations. It is not a barrier to understanding as tight as the Iron Curtain but it is certainly no small fence. The excuse given, of conserving dollar exchange, is preposterous; the result has been to contribute, at least, to the potentially disastrous drawing apart between former allies which has been increasing since 1945. It is true that a trickle does get through. Some technical books printed in America are allowed under special import licenses—and I did find a dealer in Auckland who bootlegged American pocketbooks under the counter and another dealer who sold old, second-hand American magazines. But these driblets merely point up the tragic lack of communication.

The magazine of opinion and the opinions it inspired took me on into Auckland. It was raining when we arrived and we needed a taxi to take us to the Trans-Tasman Hotel. But the Union Bus Depot of New Zealand's largest city has no taxi stand, nor can one be called. So we carried our bags two blocks in the rain, stood in the rain for forty-five minutes, and arrived soaked. Why the taxi rank should be two squares from the station on a dark, unsheltered corner instead of at the curb in front of the rain shelter immediately outside the station I do not know; it seems simply to be part of the New Zealand genius for doing things the hard way. It will never matter to us again, but it surely inconveniences thousands of local people each year . . . to *no* purpose. Why do they put up with it? Yet I heard no lone complaint from those who got soaking wet with us.

The Trans-Tasman did turn out to be a better hotel than the Waverly, in that it was cleaner and our room was more cheerful. But it had the same boarding-house & reform-school rules, the same paucity of plumbing, the same lack of central heating; on the scale under which it had won New Zealand's highest official rating of "five stars plus" the Muehlbach in Kansas City would get about seventy-eight stars and a sunburst.

The next day was a very busy one. I had wanted very much to see a kiwi bird but chores incident to our departure the following day left no time for a visit to the zoo. First we had to pick up a suit left to be drycleaned and intended by Ticky for my use on the trip home—we found that they had broken three buttons on it and ripped one off. We neither argued nor complained, having learned that to do so was to invite a tongue-lashing. Since we were flying we wanted to ship back the excess over our air baggage allowance, but when we tried to do so, we found the red tape so appallingly complicated and the service so poor, that we gave up and I limited myself to mailing back as parcel post a suitcase full of books and papers. This required a trip to the customs house for export license before I could mail it. Once I had permission to send it out of the country I returned to the hotel, got the suitcase and went to Auckland's General Post Office, only to find that I could not mail it there. One could do many other things there—deposit money, place a long-distance phone call, send a cablegram overseas, pay insurance premiums, straighten out social security accounts, or even buy stamps—but the mailing of packages was not one of the functions of the General Post Office; that was done at an office several blocks away.

The trip was not entirely wasted, as I wanted to check on an expected cablegram from America and had found myself unable to do so by telephone. I found out why—the cable office in Auckland maintains no file of undelivered messages; they have no way to answer the question: "My name is J. H.

Glutz—is there a message for me?" But a good-natured clerk took the trouble to check through every cablegram that had arrived in the country during the past two weeks (that being the only possible way to do it) in order to locate the one intended for me.

The suitcase being heavy I had taken a cab to the G.P.O., but had dismissed it on arrival. Now I had to lug the suitcase to the other office in order to mail it as I could get neither taxi nor tram. One of the first things Ticky and I had learned about Auckland was that the traffic cops simply were not interested in pedestrians, nor were the drivers; no quarter was given or expected, you were quick on your feet or you got hit. But in this case the heavy burden slowed me down. By the time I got that suitcase to the parcel-post office I was shaking with rage and adrenaline shock . . . most particularly because a bobby had looked right at me, then signaled a solid mass of cars to come on anyhow, stranding me in the middle of traffic, unable to run or jump. Latin Americans drive with courage, but the hazard thereby to pedestrians is as nothing to the cold ruthlessness of Auckland drivers. They give the impression that they seriously intend to hit you if possible, while their police seem to encourage the sport.

The suitcase mailed, it was necessary to obtain a different export license at still another office to take out of the country our remaining traveler's cheques. This required the usual questionnaires and declarations but did not take as long as it had taken in Australia; however, New Zealand charges a revenue fee for this gracious privilege.

We still had to arrange customs clearance for about half our suitcases and check them into the airline. Mr. Lees, of New Zealand National Airways Corporation, had pointed out that we could save quite a bit by classing our excess baggage as air cargo rather than as baggage—Mr. Lees was extremely helpful throughout—but this did entail one more chore the day before. But at the end of a long, hard day we were completely ready to go, stripped down to toothbrushes and a change of underwear. We celebrated by going to Hi Diddle Griddle for dinner.

But I still wanted to see a kiwi bird. The kiwi is not only the national symbol of New Zealand, the nickname of its soldiers, and the brand name of the world's best shoe polish, it is highly interesting in its own right. Most of the other flightless land birds are giants like the ostrich and the emu, able to compete through size, muscle, and speed; the kiwi is no bigger than a chicken. New Zealand had practically no animals before man introduced them; a flightless bird, even though small, was able to get along. Indeed, he made out better than his colossal cousin the fabulous moa, a bird that towered twelve feet in the air and which was relished by the Maori even more than they relished their neighbors—by the time the white man came it was extinct.

The kiwi hung on and still hangs on, wild in the bush. But the Auckland Zoo has a few. There was time enough the last morning, before we had to be ready to take the airport bus, to make a fast trip to the zoo provided we took a taxi and hung onto it, which we did—having the driver park and paying his way into the zoo with us.

While the Auckland Zoo cannot compare with the Sydney Zoo it is a remarkably good one for the size of the city. But I had just one thing on my mind—kiwis. So I stopped the first attendant I could find and asked where they were. He scratched his head, admitted that there were some, but he did not think we could see them. Why not? Well, they were night birds and they hid out in the brush in the daytime and were very hard to find. Ah no, he did not think we would see any, but we might try the director's office.

We tried the director's office but there seemed to be nobody at home. We walked away from there rather disconsolately, wondering whether we should sample a few caged tigers and such, or go at once back to town.

We heard someone running behind us, turned and found a slender, very pretty girl waving to us. "Hello! You wanted something at the office?"

We introduced ourselves and said what we wanted. She was Miss Margaret Wilson—"Pat" to her friends, who must be numerous—secretary to the director. She said, "You are visitors, aren't you? Not New Zealanders?"

"That's right. We're from the States."

"Then I think you ought to see a kiwi if that is what you want to see. Come along, I'll try to arrange it."

But we did several things else first. Miss Wilson was not a zoologist nor veterinarian herself, but she loved her zoo and was proud of it; we had to meet her friends, including a lioness who let Pat put her hand in her mouth, a Canadian timber wolf who fawned all over her and whined when she left, and a baby lion which Pat went into a cage to fetch, then brought out and let Ticky hold.

She showed us Komodo dragons, left over from an era even rougher than this one. I remembered our ship passing their home island after we left Java and regretting that I had never seen one. She showed us blue penguins, native to the islands between New Zealand and the south pole and a variety rarely seen in captivity. These had just arrived and the birds were not used to pens; they had hidden. Pat got inside with them and started groping back in under rocks, almost standing on her head. "Come on out, please! Come, darlings"—she called them all "darling" and "dear" from lions to budgies. "Come on out, dear, please! I won't hurt you. Darn! You *bit* me. You shouldn't have done that. Now come on out and be nice."

She talked him into it and reappeared with a penguin that was unquestionably blue. He looked at us and did not seem impressed. Then he bit her again.

The kiwis are kept in a large, wild although enclosed, stretch of native bush. This suits the kiwi but it makes him a wash-out as a zoo exhibit as he simply hides and sleeps through the day. Miss Wilson had one of the keepers poke around until he found one, which he then fetched to her. She held him, petted him to sooth his nerves, and talked about him. "He eats worms and lizards and things like that. He can eat one hundred and sixty-eight worms before he gets sick," she told us solemnly— I quote verbatim.

The kiwi's feathers look and feel like coarse hair. Its bill is the size and shape of a lead pencil but curved. Its wings are useless, featherless little stubs, hidden under the body feathers and looking like a chicken wing just before frying. The kiwi takes a dim view of humans and presently we let him go, whereupon he hurried into nearby thicket and was soon lost to view.

I think Miss Wilson would pet a brontosaurus if she could find a rock to stand on. She would probably call him darling, too. All in all, she was just about the nicest thing that happened to us in New Zealand.

Our taxi driver had seemed to enjoy visiting the zoo on a paid basis and we had grown rather chummy. But when he got us back to the hotel he looked me in the cye and charged us just double what I knew the legal tariff to be for the mileage and the waiting time. I paid it without a quiver, not minding since we would be on our way in an hour or so. Our ship was a DC-6 sleeper of the British Commonwealth Pacific Airlines (since then merged with Qantas). The day was clear, the take-off uneventful; we settled down for a long flight to the Fiji Islands. As we headed north we could see North Island stretched out under us and behind, its odd shape recognizable, just as on a map.

And I was determined to leave it on maps from then on. Australia had had its drawbacks but Australia was a place we wanted to return to and see what we had missed. But New Zealand— To get us back to New Zealand they would have to drag us, kicking and screaming all the way.

I had time to try to get my thoughts straight about New Zealand. Certainly poor hotels were not reason enough to detest a country. I myself had been born in a house without plumbing and had lived much of my life without much of the physical comforts. I was sure in my heart that I could have loved New Zealand, beautiful place that it is, had there been not a single flush toilet in the whole land.

I admitted that part of my reaction was disappointment. I had been sold on their propaganda about what a paradise the place was—no doubt it had seemed more dreadful in contrast to my expectations. But that alone was not it, either; every new place turns out to be quite different from anticipations. The reality quickly erases the preconception and causes one to forget it;

it took a careful effort of memory to recall what my former concepts had been.

Perhaps I had placed too much emphasis on poor hotel food. But food is basic to life. It need not be fancy but it should be clean and reasonably well prepared. The plain fare of an American freighter had suited us well enough—but in New Zealand Ticky had lost eleven pounds in eleven days.

But it was not even bad cooking that had appalled us and taken our appetites. One can live a lifetime on tasteless food. It was hair in the coffee, flies in the sugar, dirt on the dishes, and an atmosphere of incivility that tightened up the stomach and made it impossible to eat. The last especially—Australian manners are rough but warm; New Zealand manners are often colder than the proverbially chilly English, with an icy and intentional rudeness not characteristic of the English.

"A guest should never complain." Ah, but we were not treated as guests; we were merely sources of revenue to be exploited, "suckers." It is their country and they are entitled to run it as they see fit, but they are not entitled to advertise for tourists, as they do, and then treat them as they do. They are obtaining money under false pretenses.

But, I reminded myself, not all New Zealanders are rude, or drunken, or dirty, or dishonest. Not at all! I remember at least three taxi drivers who were fine gentlemen, one who apologized on behalf of his country for the manner and speech of a drunk, another who returned half of a tip which he considered too large, another who did us a gracious service and refused pay. There was the manager of the Waitomo Hotel, a conscientious host, Mr. Gunning of Thomas Cook & Son, Mr. Lees of the government airlines, and the lovely and sweet little woman we had met at Rotorua who was so upset at the nastily anti-American talk we had been subjected to one night at dinner at the Hotel Geyser. There was Miss Pat Wilson, bless her warm heart, that very day.

I loved them all, every one of them, and was grateful for what each had done to make us feel happy in their land. But it does not take a very high percentage of boors to make a country dreadful for strangers. No doubt, even in New Zealand, the boors are in the minority . . . but nevertheless New Zealand has several times the minimum tolerable percentage; a visitor gets slapped around so frequently that he is in a constant state of shock.

But New Zealand unquestionably does have some of the finest hunting and fishing in the world. At Lake Taupo near Rotorua the trout, they say, average over five pounds. As for game, you may even shoot doe and be paid a bounty for shooting them. The game do not have to be stalked; just bang away until your shoulder is sore. If that is what you are after and you can stand the hotels and the numerous and-so-forth, then New Zealand is for you.

But is that "sport"? Shooting cows in a pasture is actually more sporting; you have the farmer to worry about. As for fishing, it is a long way to go to catch a fish.

Plan your trip to avoid the place. This is not hard to do; only Tristan da Cunha is harder to reach, harder to leave. New Zealand claims to have the finest variety of natural wonders in the smallest area of any place in the world, but let me tell you how to plan a trip which will cover no more territory than all of New Zealand, involve no more mileage in the area described, and involve thousands of miles less to reach your starting point—and will provide everything New Zealand has to offer, including hunting and fishing, and excepting only the glorious Glow-Worm Grotto:

Lay a map of New Zealand down on a map of the United States of the same scale so that the south end of South Island is at North Rim, Arizona, with the north end at Yellowstone. Place the toe of the shoe of North Island at Puget Sound and the heel at Glacier National Park; this will leave a space between the two islands roughly equivalent to Cook Strait at a point just above Arco, Idaho.

In the area of the United States covered by the outlines of the two New Zealand islands superposed on your map as described above you will find:

Several Indian reservations, in place of Maori villages
The thermal areas of Yellowstone Park

Many caverns including Lehman Caves National Monument

Mountains, glaciers, fjords (Puget Sound is not called "fjords" but the name is not important)

Yellowstone Lake instead of Taupo Lake

Freshwater and saltwater fishing of many sorts

Hunting—elk, deer, antelope, bear, game birds, even mountain lion—but you will have to hunt in most areas; it will not be shooting cows in a pasture.

In place of Auckland, you have a choice of several cities but let us name Salt Lake City which is the same size as Auckland, but much prettier and immeasurably cleaner, and possesses some of the finest hotels in the world, run by Mormons, a people who make almost a fetish of being polite and hospitable to "gentiles." They are wonderful cooks, too.

And (I almost forgot!) several hundred miles of beaches, ocean, freshwater, and salt lake

The above list equals or tops everything that New Zealand has to boast about in the way of scenery, natural wonders, and holiday advantages—except the Glow-Worm Grotto. But as a bonus you will also get the following:

The Grand Canyon of the Colorado, unparalleled in the world

The Grand Canyon of the Yellowstone, smaller but incredible in its combination of canyon, thermal activity, waterfalls, and amazing colors

The Great Salt Lake and the Great Salt Desert

Sun Valley

The Craters of the Moon National Monument

Bryce Canyon

Zion Park

Kodachrome Flats

The Grand Coulee Dam

A choice of several petrified forests

The Arco Atomic Energy Plant

Several cities, a list too long to enter of lesser natural wonders, a few hundred miles of the great divide, mountains
such as the Tetons and the Olympics having the spectacular beauty which distinguishes lordly mountains from
"just another high one."

But there are two additional bonuses: first, you need not
spend the time nor the money to make a fifteen-thousand-mile
round trip to see this super-New-Zealand wonderland; and second, you can stop anywhere on the way and be sure of clean
quarters, private bath, decent food, and no regimentation. If
you care to tuck the Duncan Hines guides in your car, you
can be sure of luxury and gourmet food. I can guarantee that
you will *never* be offered boiled mutton! So bypass the smug,
provincial, and conceited place called New Zealand. Leave
them to their lotus eating. If you ever follow the route we took,
turn north when you leave Australia and see the Philippines
and Japan instead; thus you will not be wasting your money
on things more readily available at home.

The flight was uneventful and as monotonous as over-water
flying in good weather is bound to be. Just after dark we landed
at Nandi on Viti Levu in the Fiji Islands, walked fifty yards to
an excellent, modern hotel and had a simply wonderful dinner.
But it could hardly be called a trip to the Fiji Islands, since
all we saw of the Islands was that one hotel, all we saw of
the Fiji Islanders were a dozen tall, grave, barefoot black
men who were the waiters at dinner. We could tell we were
back in the tropics by the heavy, smothering heat, and the
glimpses of luxuriant gardens outside in the dark. But it was
all hello-and-goodby.

They bedded us down when we took off from there, beds
much like Pullman berths, but with safety belts. Ticky did not
fasten hers, since the flight was smooth as a superhighway.
But early in the morning we passed through some turbulence
and she was awakened by finding herself two feet over her
bunk, from which position she descended rather suddenly to
her mattress. It solidified her opinion that we had placed our

lives in forfeit to escape from dirt and rudeness, but she did not complain. However, it did upset her very much and when we landed on Canton Island I took her ashore for a stretch and a cup of coffee. Canton is an atoll just north of the equator, and a British-American condominium, which means that nobody quite knows who should do what. We could barely see the lagoon and could not make out the shape of the atoll ring— another hello-and-goodby.

We had the luxury of breakfast in bed, served by a pretty airline hostess. About noon we sighted lordly Diamond Head and at twelve-thirty, having crossed the date line in the night, we landed at Honolulu on the same date we had taken off from Auckland but three hours earlier than when we started. There was the Stars and Stripes flying over the port, we were *home*, back in the United States! My eyes filled up and my mouth began to tremble and I had to grope to get down the stairway without falling.

Only the fact that the runway was smeared with spilled oil at the spot where we deplaned kept me from falling on my knees and kissing my native land. I *wanted* to do it. I wanted to hug it and never let it go.

XIII

Paradise

WE ZIPPED THROUGH immigration in nothing flat and through customs in about five minutes, at least four of which were occupied by the customs officer chatting with us about where we had been and our own bubbling over about how happy we were to be *home*. He shook hands and welcomed us back.

Waiting at the door of the inspection room were Bob and Vi Markham, our chums in the *Gulf Shipper*—how many miles and months ago? They were loaded down with flower leis and grinning like pups. The leis were placed around our necks with kisses and warm aloha and again we could not see for tears. Home!

It had been years since I had last seen Honolulu. It seemed a bit bigger, a bit brighter, more automobiles and more curving, beautiful boulevards, but essentially unchanged. Aloha Tower still offered welcome, the royal palms still swayed in the warm and steady trade winds and the breakers still rolled in on Waikiki. But I had forgotten how splendidly beautiful it is.

There are those who complain that Honolulu is too artificial, not a South Seas sort of place at all. I am not one of them—I have seen Auckland! Honolulu is as shiny and up to date as a new car and it is that way because most people want it that way. It is impossible to take proper care of more than fifty thousand visitors a year with just a few grass shacks on a beach; fine big hotels are indispensable. For those who want

333

untouched nature and solitude there is plenty of it on the Big Island, miles and miles of empty beach without a soul in sight. But one should not ask for silence and solitude at Waikiki any more than one would expect it at Rockefeller Center.

Bob and Vi drove us out to their home at Aina Haina, beyond Diamond Head. I stared and stared the whole trip, still in a state of shock at the sudden transition from grim and dreary Auckland to this chrome-plated Land of Oz—like being dumped from an icy tub of water into a warm bed. But I am not going to give a blow-by-blow account of our stay in Hawaii. Hawaii is home, just as New Jersey is home; neither one belongs in an account of a trip around the world told from an American viewpoint. So I will simply dust off the high spots just to get us back to Colorado, where the argument with Ticky had started a year earlier.

We did all the usual things—shopped, ate in restaurants where we could see hula dancing, drove around Oahu, saw the place of murdered ships and murdered men at Pearl Harbor, inspected the pineapple fields and went through the Dole pineapple cannery, of which Bob was an executive, attended a luau and ate poi and laulaus, having learned first how to prepare and tie a laulau, stood in the wind on the high Pali where King Kamehameha the Great sealed in blood the unification of the islands as one nation, and took a packaged commercial tour by air and automobile of Hawaii much as we had taken such a tour in New Zealand, a tour which had as its high spot a stay in Volcano House on the rim of the great, live crater Kilauea where the firegoddess Pele lives.

But you have probably been to all these places, too. If not, mark it down in your book. This is one of the fairest parts of the United States. You need no passport, you undergo no red tape, you don't have to worry about the drinking water; all you require is the price of a round trip ticket from the Mainland, $250 by aircoach, plus what you care to spend while there. Prices in Honolulu are higher than they are in San Francisco as almost everything has to be imported, but they are not much higher. What you spend depends mostly on how much liquor you drink, where you eat, and what you buy. An all-expense luxury tour (and I do mean "luxury") of the outer islands costs about $30 a day, but you need not spend that much if you do not wish to be spoon-fed. On the other hand it is no trouble to spend a hundred dollars a day in shops and night clubs if you wish.

Whether you pinch pennies or spend it like water, you will be treated with courtesy. Much more than half of the population is of Chinese, Japanese, or Hawaiian descent, three cultures outstanding for politeness, and the Caucasians or haoles have absorbed and taken for their own the leisurely, informal, almost excessively courteous spirit of the islands. Besides that, the Chamber of Commerce and the territorial government have been pushing a Be-Kind-to-Mainlanders movement which is carried to such extremes that it is considered bad form to call us trippers "tourists"—we must be called "visitors" or "guests" and every resident has been reminded repeatedly that it is up to each one of them to make us feel welcome.

Of course this last point is not just altruism; tourists bring money into the islands and the purpose of the drive is to remind the islanders not to mistreat the goose that lays the golden eggs. But one real and important result is that here is a place where a tourist who thinks he has been cheated or mistreated need not swallow the matter and try to forget it; the Visitors' Bureau will take a warm personal interest in his complaints. Besides that, politeness feels good whatever the reason.

The visitor will want to be equally polite. Just as three words of Spanish are enough to go all around South America three simple rules are sufficient for visitors to get along smoothly in this variant of the basic American culture:

1. Honolulu is pronounced with the "o's" long and fully sounded, as in "Oh, no!"—not the way it is generally heard elsewhere; and Hawaii is pronounced "Hav-wah-ee," not "Ha-wah-yuh." The "vw" sound is a slurred labial not found in English and should be sounded as a single consonant; if you have trouble with it, make it a simple "w"—but *don't* let a "yuh" get into the ending. There is no "y" sound and it is either a prolonged "ee" or two distinct long-E sounds said very

rapidly one after the other—Hawaiian Polynesian is filled with
vowels unseparated by consonants.
    2. Never, never, *never* speak of "going back to the United
States." This *is* the United States. That bigger piece over there
to the east is referred to as "The Mainland." People from it are
"Mainlanders" or "malihini" and the term "Americans" is used
only inclusively and must never mean mainlanders as distinguished from islanders, no matter what their race or color.
    3. And never forget that here there is no color line of any
sort. The Mayor of Honolulu is of Japanese descent. One of
the most distinguished of jurists here looks like Kamehameha
the First. A mistake on this score will convince you that even
an islander can be impolite if you push him hard enough.
    But if you follow these easy rules you find that when you
leave you will join in the ancient toast *"Me ke aloha pau
ole"* (May our friendship be everlasting)—and mean it with
all your heart.
    A word about the word "aloha"—its usual literal translation
is "love" but it also means "friendship" or good feeling of any
sort; therefore it is used as a toast, as a greeting, as a farewell—
which tells more about the Hawaiian culture than anything else
could; Hawaii is a place where "love" is the commonest word
in daily use.
    What this weary planet needs is a lot more aloha.
    The islands affected Ticky the way catnip affects a cat; she
decided that she wanted to stay there forever, raising orchids
outdoors, a prospect that dazzled her after the short growing
season of our Rocky Mountain home. Soon I was subjected to
a well-organized campaign, led by Ticky and ably brain-trusted
by Vi, to get me to agree before we left Hawaii that we would
come back and build a home there.
    I tried to combat it with logic; I should have known better.
"Look," I said, "use that knot on the end of your spinal column.
We've *got* a house; you've *got* a garden—back in Colorado
Springs. Remember?"
    "The deer eat all my tulips."
    This was true. I don't know why mule deer prefer Dutch
tulips to all other forms of salad, but they do. "I thought it

pleased you to have deer wandering around our house?"

"It does. But they ruin my garden. And just look at the garden Vi has! I could never have flowers like those in Colorado no matter what I did."

This also was true. In Hawaii one does not need to encourage flowers; one needs a flamethrower to subdue them. "Ticky, you know perfectly well that, lovely as this place is, in six weeks you would be homesick for your mountains."

"Sure! But that's just the beauty of it—we'll commute. When the weather gets cold and nasty in Colorado, we'll come here. When we get tired of perfect weather and begin to long for mountains and flash floods, we'll go back to Colorado. About three months each way, maybe. Perfect!"

I winced, then took a deep breath and started the fatherly, facts-of-life approach. "Look, baby, my name is not Ford, nor Morgan, nor Rockefeller. You probably should have married that Philadelphia banker chap, assuming that you could have hooked him. As it is, I can't afford two households, neither the initial cost nor the overhead. I have to write like mad, an overworked hack, just to keep up with your whims and—"

"I didn't want to travel," she broke in. "I merely wanted to build a greenhouse. Traveling was *your* idea."

One simply cannot hold a woman to the point in a discussion. "Never mind that," I answered with dignity. "The point is that, after all, you can't have everything."

"Why not?" she wanted to know.

I have never been able to think of an answer to that one, not one which is emotionally convincing. "The cat won't like it," I said feebly and shut up, which I should have done much sooner. But the economic facts of life did soon slow Ticky down a bit; she started pricing building lots in suburban Honolulu and found out that too many people just like herself were very anxious to obtain the choice sites which were all too few. Choice home sites near the city were not for sale at any price; the best that was offered was long-term leasehold at a ground rent which seemed very high to people from the wide open spaces. Ticky did not stop trying but the difficulties subdued her and she quit lobbying at me about it.

But she had planted the germ in my mind. The idea really did have attractions . . . to be able to throw away my snow shovel, to be an upholstered beachcomber, yet able to return to our mountains whenever we began to yearn for the dry-wine air off the snow fields. We didn't have to compete for that expensive beach property near Honolulu; we could go clear to the other side of the island if we wanted to. Just a little grass shack of whitewashed cinder blocks and only one bathroom, nothing fancy or expensive—oh, a lanai, of course, and a barbecue. One I could build myself, naturally.

Maybe just a little one—

But the cat certainly would not like it and we hardly ever do anything without the advice and consent of the cat. I put it out of my mind . . . mostly. Ticky surprised me by not taking up one minor feature of Hawaii; she is probably the only white wahine ever to go there who did not attempt hula. All of the white female residents have studied hula at some time, as a graceful accomplishment and a delightful exercise, whereas the women visitors from the Mainland sign up in droves for about three lessons each, then go home and demonstrate to their friends that they have "learned" the hula—an accomplishment requiring ten years or more and for which study should start at about the age of five.

But, knowing that Ticky delighted in every form of dancing from rumba to waltzing on ice and including ballet and square dancing, I found out the name of the best teacher available to beginners and signed her up for a quickie course. But she never got there, not when she discovered that bare feet were obligatory. "I'll wear heelless sandals," she had said comfortably.

I looked shocked. "Would you take a swimming lesson in riding boots?" For once, Vi formed an alliance with me, instead of against me, and convinced Ticky that anything but bare feet for hula would be as ridiculous as a tail coat at a picnic.

Whereupon Ticky canceled the lessons and never did study hula. I had known that she disliked to go barefoot but I had not realized that she carried it to such extremes—I had had not too much difficulty in persuading her not to wear shoes to bed and she always takes them off while bathing. But it seems that some no-nonsense adults had forced her to go barefoot in the country during summer while a small child, which had offended her baby dignity. So no hula.

Now I am the one who demonstrates hula to defenseless guests. I don't do it any worse than most females who visit Hawaii.

I have promised not to take you step by step around the islands but I cannot refrain from listing some things which you must not miss when you go there. The first of these is Volcano House on the Island of Hawaii, a fine hotel which sits on the edge of a great live volcano in the middle of one of our National Parks. You will probably not have the luck (good or bad, depending on how you look at it) to see Kilauea in eruption but you will see steam rising and will be awed by looking down into the crater, and you will see the scientific demonstrations and documentary motion pictures prepared by the vulcanists who maintain a research station there. The last are in color and are at least as frightening as having a tomahawk thrown at you out of a 3-D screen.

Despite the continuous watch by scientists Kilauea last went into major eruption without any warning. It might do so while you are there, making of you either a victim or an extraordinarily favored observer; the possibility is one of the fascinations of the place. After all, you don't want to live forever. Or do you?

Orchids you cannot avoid seeing; they grow here as easily as dandelions on the Mainland, and the residents grow them in their back yards and in their living rooms. But while you are on the Big Island go see the commercial orchid nurseries in Hilo—if you are on a guided tour you are certain to be taken. The sight of tens of thousands of blooms in hundreds of species makes one a little drunk.

There are at least three thousand cultivated species of orchids, an estimated fifteen thousand species wild and tame, and nobody has ever tried to count the enormous number of varieties. I was amazed to learn that there were some forty native species in my own mountain area—I had not known there were any. The flavoring in vanilla ice cream comes from the seeds of the vanilla orchids. The common cattleya, the "orchid"-colored orchid used in the United States by wolves to break down the resistance of females and which costs from three to eight dollars a bloom on the Mainland, is so common in Hawaii that you are likely to be given one as a free sample.

Most temperate zone orchids grow on the ground but tropical orchids, as almost all cultivated orchids are, grow on trees, clinging to them and never touching the ground. They are air plants; the term is "epiphytic"—since "epidemic" means a disease raging among humans and "epizootic" means the same thing for animals, "epiphytic" sounds as if it should mean a pretty sad state of affairs for fish, but what it does mean is a plant that rests on another plant without deriving nourishment from it. Orchids sometimes are called parasites but this is an unfair slur; they use trees only for mechanical support. Just how they do make a living has me buffaloed—apparently by taking in each other's washing.

If you want to raise them yourself, go right ahead. Don't let Nero Wolfe fool you, it is not hard. A few years ago Philip Wylie had an article in *The Saturday Evening Post* telling how to do it and the periodical index in any public library will locate it for you.

You will want to attend a luau while in the islands. These feasts are a great treat socially, but the authentic Hawaiian foods do not especially appeal to me. Here "poi" are not little dancing spheres but is a sticky grey paste made from taro root, sort of an underprivileged tapioca eaten with the fingers. It was the staple of the natives until they encountered corn flakes and hamburgers and such, and a great deal of it is still eaten. You will be served it at luau; if you really like it, let me know. Laulau is a chunk of pork, a piece of fish, and a handful of taro leaf, all wrapped in ti leaf (the long leaves from which grass skirts are made) and baked. Laulau makes quite acceptable food but nothing to get excited about. The rest of the feast is likely to be fish, possibly raw, pig barbecued whole, fruit, and much aloha, some of it liquid. Pig is the authentic main dish as the Hawaiians never did have the vice of "long pig"—they were never cannibals. They fought among themselves until Kamehameha the Great put a stop to tribal war with one last big one, but they never ate the slain.

Sophisticated modern variations of primitive island cookery are delightful indeed. Honolulu is bulging with gourmet restaurants, some of them surprisingly reasonable. The Sky Chef at the airport terminal building is as good a restaurant as may be found in New York and New Orleans taken together, but I would hesitate to say that it is the best restaurant in Honolulu because there are so many fine ones. If you do not like poi, you need not lose weight. Ticky gained back the eleven pounds she lost in New Zealand and I gained weight I did not need. Oh well, the Hawaiians say it takes a big opu (belly) to hula properly.

I found myself wondering constantly why it was that Hawaii was such a paradise while New Zealand was such a grim washout. The two island groups are basically much more alike than they are unlike, except that New Zealand is much, much richer in resources, having far more usable land, much gold, much coal, oil and many other minerals, and unlimited water power. Hawaii has nothing but farm land, no commercial minerals of any sort. If there is any advantage in climate, it lies with New Zealand, not with Hawaii. Hawaii is much overpopulated for its resources, while New Zealand is underpopulated—an economic advantage unless the population is very small, but New Zealand nevertheless has four times the population of Hawaii.

Hawaii does have an advantage in tourist trade in being more centrally located, but in all other ways New Zealand is more favored, being bigger and very much better endowed. Even in the tourist trade New Zealand is not too badly at a disadvantage, as she is much nearer the heavily populated east coast of Australia than Hawaii is to our west coast and also she draws on the entire pound-sterling area for tourists, a trade not available to Hawaii because of the money embargos placed against us.

Then *why*?

I was forced to conclude that the difference must lie in the people themselves. The New Zealanders have saddled themselves with endless laws and government regulations restricting competition, reducing production, discouraging incentive, and almost prohibiting initiative. The wage fixing, price fixing, licensing, and forbidding outright of many economic activities considered routine with us is almost beyond belief. New Zealanders themselves complain that their own people will not put in an honest day's work. Between fixed wages with no incentive to work harder on one hand and a social security system so pervasive that not working is almost as good as working on the other hand, the New Zealand employee has precious little reason to do a good job—and his employer has even less incentive to risk new capital in a game that is intentionally rigged against him. To a stranger, the result looks and feels like stagnation.

The economic environment in Hawaii is essentially like that in all the rest of the United States. We do have government regulations, certainly, enough of them to make some of our citizens apoplectic, but compared with New Zealand we live in economic anarchy. Whether we think we have too much or too little, or perhaps the wrong ones, nevertheless our rules are not such as to make ambition fruitless. Hard work and imagination still pay off, despite what the crepe-hangers say, and Hawaii is a showcase proof of the fact. The residents of Hawaii work like beavers in spite of the lazy climate and they get rewards for their efforts. Even unskilled labor receives the highest wages in the entire world. As for those higher up the ladder the material evidence of their rewards are everywhere around you in Hawaii.

But of course no one in Hawaii is satisfied with his share, any more than people are on the Mainland. Perhaps that is the real difference between the two sets of islanders: those in Hawaii are hustling to get more while those in New Zealand sit back content with the government-controlled minimums assigned to them. Why hustle when the prizes are predetermined?

We were having a wonderful time in Hawaii but I had to get Ticky out of there before she picked out a building site— and before I weakened and leased it. Leaving by air is not very ceremonious, thank goodness, for neither one of us was in emotional shape to stand at the rail of the *Lurline* and listen to "Aloha Oe" as the ship warped slowly away from the dock. A plane departure is mercifully swift. As it was, we were both weeping as the Markhams piled leis around our shoulders. I wonder if anyone ever leaves those glorious islands without promising himself through tears that he will return? It was a short sleeper flight back to San Francisco. By the time we finished breakfast the Golden Gate bridge was in sight. Before eight o'clock we were standing on the soil of the Mainland and were home for a second time. I had caught cold on the flight, so I rested up in a hotel bed for a couple of days while Ticky shopped. Despite Singapore and Buenos Aires she considers San Francisco tops for shopping and complains that I never allow her enough time for it there; my indisposition was convenient. As soon as I was able to totter around we had a drink at the Top o' the Mark, then caught an evening flight to Denver—and we were home for a third time.

To us, softened up by summer in both hemispheres and months in the tropics, Denver was unbelievably cold. It was too late to catch a shuttle flight to Colorado Springs, so we hurried to the Brown Palace with our fingers numb and our teeth chattering while Ticky pointed out that we would be warm through had we stayed in Hawaii. I concealed the point but was interested then only in getting into a hot tub of water as quickly as possible. Our room turned out to have a nice big tub and all the hot water I could want; we got warm. The room was luxurious in every way and reminded me of New Zealand because it was so different. But I must admit that it cost twice as much as our room in the Waverly.

But it was worth at least six times as much. The next foreigner to make a disparaging remark about bathtub & plumbing as the vulgar criterion of culture in America in my presence is going to get a swift poke in the eye. Decent bathrooms do not constitute civilized living, but they are as necessary to high civilization as water is to a fish. Music festivals and such are necessary, too—but we have *both*.

The shuttle flight from Denver to our little town is only twenty-five minutes; one does not even unfasten seat belts.

For the last time I made sure that all the suitcases went with us, then breathed a sigh of relief, feeling that all worries were over.

Ten minutes after we took off that confounded daisy clipper caught fire. The pilot made a sharp U-turn and headed us back for an emergency landing while the hostess hurried up and down the aisle, assuring the passengers that there was no danger. Ticky leaned over to me and whispered bleakly, "If we walk away from this, I'm going the rest of the way by bus." I did not have an answer.

The plane filled up with smoke to the point where we could not see each other's faces and I began to wonder if we would smother even if we did not burn. But the hostess—gallant as airline hostesses have proved themselves to be in many an emergency—turned out to be right; the fire was not dangerous, being merely some excess oil in a cabin heating system and involving neither structure nor engine. We landed easily and walked away untouched.

I did not attempt to argue with Ticky's determination to go the rest of the way on the ground; I kept quiet while cursing silently the perversity of chance that took us forty thousand miles around and up and down a planet without a single mishap, not a missed connection, not a missing piece of luggage, not even a flat tire—then saddled me with a fire in the air when we were actually within sight of the mountain we lived on. I felt sure that I would never live it down, that I would never again persuade Ticky to risk her slender neck in one of those pesky flying machines.

So I did not argue; I simply guided her steps toward the cocktail bar and administered several doses of nerve tonic to her as rapidly as possible. I had one, too, to keep her company—and just a bit because I had been a touch nervy myself when the cabin filled up with smoke and the plane lost altitude rapidly. Nothing important, mind you, since I am a fatalist. But the first dose of medicine tasted so good I had a second one.

It took them an hour and a half to get that bucket of bolts ready to fly again, but by the time they did Ticky was no longer talking about catching a bus. With only a little effort she could have flapped her wings and flown down unassisted. The second try at getting to Colorado Springs was uneventful, though we were amazed to find that we had been away so long that they had had time to build a new airport terminal while we were gone. But we did not stop to admire it; friends were waiting there to meet us, with hugs and handshakes and more tearful kisses. Ticky, with great care, had managed to keep one orchid lei fresh; she wore it, and carried that ubiquitous and utterly unpackable big coolie hat she had bought in Java. Between the two she looked quite out of place in that bleak and cold mountain day. We were home.

Thirty minutes later we were home for a fifth time and truly home at last, in our own living room, with our friends around us and our cat bumping our legs and demanding to know where in the *hell* we had been?

XIV

Unpacking

THIS TRIP WAS taken for itself; I had not planned to do a book about it. I am a fiction writer by trade and it seemed to me that John Gunther and Robert Ruark and James Michener and their peers had the globe-trotting business pretty well sewed up. But I found it necessary to write one anyhow, just to get the jumble of impressions in my mind sorted out. A confirmed writing addict can't think clearly without a typer in front of him. (Writing is not a profession, it is a disease.) Since I was compelled to write about it anyhow, why not whip it into some sort of commercial form? It might possibly bring in a few royalties.

But now I reach the point where I must state what I learned from it, which is the hardest part. "Is this trip necessary?"— as those accusing placards used to read during the War. Was a trip around the world worth what it cost in money, in working time, in very considerable physical effort?

There is an old story about a gangling youth, back country, who saw a merry-go-round for the first time and just had to ride on it, to the disgust of his mammy. When he got off, his mammy looked at him sternly. "Sammy, you has spent your money, you has had your ride—*but where has you been?*"

Did he get anything out of it that made it worth the cost? A fair question—

For me, it has always been worth it. I have never sailed from a port in my life, any port anywhere, but what I was glad to do so. When I was a kid, on a Sunday we would climb on a street car and ride all the way out to the end of the line, then ride back again. It was almost as good as a John Bunny nickel show. Now I have been on the biggest merry-go-round of all, the street car with the longest run; I've paid my money and ridden all the way to the end of the line and back again. It was worth it, I don't regret the expense.

Even today in wealthy America the people who can manage a trip around the world are a very small handful of the population, which is another reason for writing about it. Those who can spare the time usually cannot afford such a trip; those who have the money to spare usually find it difficult to spare so much time from their business responsibilities—one does not become wealthy by trotting off on long junkets with no one to keep an eye on the business.

Now, Ticky and I are far from being wealthy—wealthy writers are as scarce as albino crows; I know of only one. Most free-lance writers are just two jumps ahead of the installment collector and borrow money from their agents and importune their publishers for advances. But a free-lance writer does have the advantage that he is not tied to the shop; he can usually arrange his time to do what he wants to do. Therefore, if he can scrape up the money, he can travel. To me, this is probably the greatest single advantage of an otherwise not-too-satisfactory trade. My colleagues seem to think so, too; free-lance writers are, I am almost certain, the most tireless vagabonds in the whole population, not counting those people who are paid to travel.

We were able to make this trip because I found myself, for the first and only time in my life, with enough money not already committed elsewhere to permit us to make it. A prudent man would have taken such money and invested it in something solid; to spend your only nickel on the merry-go-round is not sensible economics . . . unless you believe in your heart (as I do) that a ride on the merry-go-round is worth more than cash in the bank. You must be able to laugh in Poor Richard's

face. Now that the money is gone I'm saving my nickels again
for a trip around the world northern hemisphere, and after that
for a trip all the way across Asia come the day we get the communist apes civilized or liquidated. After that— Well, after that
I will really have to save my nickels because I figure the first
scheduled tourist trip to the moon will be pretty expensive.
But I rather think that, by the time I am ready to pay for
tickets, Mrs. Feyock will be ready to sell them to me.

In the mean time, what did we learn on this trip? Not what
we saw—we saw funny birds and people who ate bananas
with knives and forks and lions in the bush. What did we
learn? What was worth the effort?

In the first place, travel to see scenery is not worth the trouble. Scenery is everywhere. Hollywood has long since listed all
the outdoor backgrounds in the world, right in California. The
hypothetical trip I described whereby one could see everything
New Zealand has in a few states of our west could be duplicated for any part of the globe, if not inside the forty-eight
states, then certainly within North America. If your principal
interest is in natural wonders, then the usual two-week vacation
is long enough; we've got them all, right here at home.

Nevertheless I am certain that I got my money's worth and
a big fat profit in the people we saw and encountered and the
things we learned. I am going to split the list up into two parts:
practical matters, and heavy punditing of the Walter Lippmann
sort. The practical minutiae will give you something, at least,
for this book; the wise conclusions you can read or ignore—
I'm new at the pundit business.

Practical matters: Packing and preparing for a long trip of
many weeks or months with many stops is different from
packing for a fortnight's vacation. There are two approaches,
to pack only for health and reasonable comfort, or to pack so
that you are prepared to dress smartly for every occasion you
are likely to encounter and to have with you every convenience
you are likely to need.

I strongly favor the first approach and believe that luggage
should be limited to two bags apiece, one for each hand, no

matter how long the trip. But many wives (and some men) prefer Ticky's approach, which is more like that of the White Knight in *Alice Through the Looking-Glass.* You remember? The White Knight had never yet been troubled with mice on his horse but, if one ever should show up, there was a mouse trap waiting for it. Ticky would be happiest with a camel train.

But she did manage to have us smartly turned out under all possible circumstances for months on end, and we had with us typewriter, books, extensive camera equipment, binoculars, an electric iron, and a dozen other things, all within the limitations of ten suitcases and no trunks.

But first let's list items indispensable even when traveling light. I am not going to list clothing in detail, as that is personal choice and the requirements of destination. British Overseas Airways Corporation, 342 Madison Avenue, New York 17, has an advisory service on how to make the most of your international flight allowance of 66 pounds—which is just about two large suitcases. *Esquire* had an article on this same subject this past year and *Holiday* runs such advice from time to time. But I will not presume to pick out for you your clothes or toilet articles.

But I do want to make certain remarks. Make all possible use of the new synthetics such as Orlon, Dacron, and Nylon, the ones which do not wrinkle and which may be washed out in soap and water. Reliable drycleaning is not only hard to come by, but frequently there is not time for it, whereas you can always wash out a garment in a tub or hand basin, *if* it can stand soap and water. I had with me two pairs of slacks which looked like tropical-weight wool which I wore almost constantly. They have never been drycleaned, have repeatedly been sopped in hand basins, and have never been pressed. But the creases in them are as knife sharp as the day they were purchased; they simply do not wrinkle. I had a formal dark blue suit as well, which looks like blue serge—but it was washed in a bathtub with soap and water one time when we were long away from drycleaning. Without drycleaning and with the circumstances of travel, hot train compartments, planes, and buses, and such, wool clothes will soon begin to stink, even when they still look smart. Avoid them as much as possible.

I do not like the feel of most of the synthetics against my skin, so I used cotton shirts and underwear. But this is a personal idiosyncrasy.

We each carried just one all-purpose coat. Mine was a dark blue topcoat-raincoat; Ticky's was a long coat in an oatmeal shade which could be worn day or evening. This shade will show dirt but it was made of Orlon, which is the same plastic as Plexiglas and washes just as easily. It could be, and was, washed out in a bathtub, then allowed to drain dry, whereupon it was ready to wear without pressing. Besides this she carried a plastic raincoat and plastic boots of the sort that fold into an envelope and fit into a purse. Since my topcoat was a raincoat and since men's shoes are not the frivolities that women wear, I did not have this equipment—but it is worth considering.

The drugs we found indispensable are these: aspirin, laxative, the opposite of a laxative (even more important), vitamin pills (we started out without any; Ticky got both scurvy and pellagra), Dramamine (there is a new seasick remedy which your doctor can recommend which does not have some of Dramamine's side effects), iodine, Band-Aids, and a fungicide (I prefer Upjohn's Benzo-Salicylic Compound, plus Desenex foot powder, but be sure to take something; the fungus skin diseases and diarrhea are the two greatest physical hazards of travel abroad).

In addition to the above, which I regard as an irreducible minimum, if you are dependent on thyroid extract, insulin, nitroglycerine, or any other special drug, take along a bit more than necessary for the entire trip. Although chemist's shops are everywhere your prescription may not be honored, the local chemist may not have it, or you may not be able to get to one in time. If you are chained to spectacles, as I am, two pairs are an utter minimum—remember what happened to me in Africa, when I broke two pairs in twenty-four hours.

If you use an electric razor, take along the sort of blade razor you hate least; you will not be able to use your electric razor about half the time.

Some sort of a robe is indispensable whenever you have to share a bath. Pajamas are not utterly indispensable. Slippers are not indispensable but a pair of very light-weight ones are a desirable comfort. Extra shoe strings can be carried no matter what your weight allowance and not only are they needed in a hurry when you break one but they double as clothes lines most opportunely. A small flashlight is always a convenience and you can count on it saving your neck at least once. But I said "small." The ordinary household or automobile torch is too heavy and too big; get one of those which looks like a fountain pen and fits in a lady's purse or a man's vest pocket.

You can save weight and space by transferring medicines and toiletries to polyethylene bottles obtainable from any drug store. This also eliminates breakage—have you ever had a bottle of hand lotion spread itself through an entire suitcase of clean clothes?—and it also lets the bottles "breathe" at high altitude. In the latter connection, fountain pens and lighter fluid are not things to take in airplanes; use a ballpoint pen and refill your lighter in tobacco shops. Matches are hard to obtain the world round; you will probably want a lighter with you. If you are a steady smoker, you can resign yourself to smoking some odd mixtures, for, if you attempt to carry with you enough of your favorite brand of cigarettes, you will not only weigh yourself down to an impossible degree, but you will also find yourself paying around a hundred per cent duty over and over and over again. So relax to the inevitable, or ask a waiter to buy you American cigarettes on the black market—he will almost certainly be able to do so.

We have already been over the horrors of getting the numerous papers needed for foreign travel. Remember that the State Department puts out a pamphlet on passports, the Public Health Service puts out one on medical requirements, and the Treasury Department puts out one about customs requirements. Then when you are traveling be sure to *carry on your person* your passport and all other travel papers including spare photographs and traveler's cheques whenever you cross an international boundary. They are bulky but it is usually only for an hour or so, and the one they want to see is always the one you packed away.

Make up a small notebook, as small as possible, and list in it the number of your passport, the cable address of your bank, all the addresses you will need while out of the country and any that you might by any wild chance need, including the addresses of all those relatives, neighbors, and acquaintances you promised to send postcards to. Then write in this notebook all memoranda you need before you leave (such as prescriptions for spectacles, promises to buy things abroad for people, etc.). Then never use anything else for memoranda. If you don't follow this rule, you will never be able to find a piece of necessary information when you need it; you will be smothered in little pieces of paper. Most especially use this notebook to record foreign purchases since an exact record of such things will speed you through customs on your return and may save you quite a lot of money. We got through customs swiftly in Hawaii because we could present the inspector with an itemized list showing when, where, and how much, all prepared from our little notebook. The inspector glanced at it, congratulated us on having taken the trouble to comply with the law, asked us to open just one bag, and sent us on our way.

But make it hard for him and and he may make it hard for you.

A medicine which you may need but which I did not list is a malaria preventive. This depends on where you are going. But there is no way today to vaccinate against malaria.

A deck of cards and a few items to read are not necessary to minimum-luggage travel, but I consider them worth their weight. I feel the same way about a small camera.

Barbiturates and Dexedrine are dangerous drugs, but used with care they can smooth over the inevitable disturbances of travel most wonderfully. I carry them—but use your own judgment.

Everything mentioned above is compatible with two suitcases per traveler. Now let's see what Ticky did to run it up to five each—with my help, I must admit. Typewriter—Corona puts out a seven-pound model these days called a Skywriter, but the cost is rather high unless a typewriter is a necessity. I carried one that weighed more than twice that much; it was a mistake. Ticky carried an "international" electric iron, which worked on any current and had plugs for any sort of socket. It was a mistake, too, as electric irons may be borrowed or rented for a few pennies almost anywhere there are facilities to use them. She hardly ever unpacked her own iron. But pressing cloths are hard to lay hands on; it is worthwhile to carry one. I carried lots more camera equipment than is necessary to "Kodak as you go" and camera equipment is always heavy. We carried binoculars, but they were featherweight; both the Germans and the Japanese make powerful binoculars which have been miniaturized remarkably. Unfortunately they are rather expensive. Between us we carried about fifty books. This is quite unnecessary unless carried for business reasons (which some of ours were)—buy pocketbooks and magazines, read them and throw them away, or mail them back if you want some of them.

Ticky carried capsules of detergent, much advertised these days for travel. She found them not worth the space. She carried some little dabs of spot remover called "Spotwix" and these, she feels, are worth having along, since cleaner fluid cannot be carried if one is to fly. She packed everything in polyethylene film freezer bags, which simplifies packing, keeps clothes in good condition, and adds little or nothing to weight—and most importantly makes it possible for a customs officer to examine baggage without actually handling or mussing a lady's fancy frillies. She carried shoeshine cloths but we never used them, not once.

Ticky strongly recommends carrying enough hangers for all your clothes, because hangers are scarce everywhere outside the States and non-existent some places. I have strong doubts about this recommendation. Hangers are remarkably clumsy to pack. I favor putting up with one inconvenience rather than adding another.

We carried extensive maps, an atlas, and books about each country we visited—a luxury well worth while if you aren't trying to stay under the 66-pound limit. I wanted to carry a globe but could see no way to do so other than in my hot little hand.

But most of the additional space was taken up just by clothes. Ticky simply prepared us for any occasion, sports, informal, and formal. I had both a tuxedo and a white dinner coat, with shirts, pumps, ties, and accessories to match. She had plenty of evening dresses and dinner dresses. We had swimming suits and shorts and a wide variety of sports wear. She had handbags to match all outfits. We both had plenty of shoes. Men's shoes are very heavy and both men's and women's shoes use up a lot of space. None of the above is necessary; all of it makes life pleasanter—except for the maddening business of handling it when you are on the move and of keeping track of it.

The problem of keeping track of it she simplified by making a careful inventory of each bag and by having me paint large numerals on each bag. The latter enabled me to "call the roll" in a hurry and at least twice kept bags from being left behind; the former enabled her to go right to the proper bag to find something, without pawing through them all. The inventories were set down in the little notebook mentioned above. If you do travel abroad with lots of luggage I strongly recommend both expedients; they will save you many headaches.

I asked Ticky to list the variety items other than ordinary clothes which she had found useful. Here they are; some of them are quite light in weight and might be classed as indispensable: whisk broom, sun glasses, sun hats, run-proof nylon hose, sun tan oil, adhesive tape, fever thermometer, Aureomycin, sulfa pills, Scotch cellophane tape, Kleenex, a box of pins, paper clips, rubber bands, string, and needles and thread.

You will want phrase books, of course, but don't let foreign languages scare you; if you are patient, there is always a way to communicate. Our geographical isolation has made us Americans very poor linguists, of which I am an outstanding horrible example. But I had no trouble once I overcame shyness. In the first place a most amazingly large percentage of people have

English as a second tongue. But in the second place, if you will write things out, using a phrase book, and have the other party do the same, you can get around the baffling hazards of pronunciation. In particular, numbers, addresses, dates, hours, and prices—anything numerical—can be written out in the figures common to all languages and often these items are the single barrier to understanding.

Don't be afraid to wave your hands around. We've been taught that talking with your hands is vulgar—and so it is, in the finest sense of the word. Gestures are the oldest, the noblest, and the most truly international form of communication. You can say almost anything in pantomime; just let yourself go and enjoy it.

Don't be embarrassed by the amusement created by your wild mistakes in grammar, syntax, and pronunciation. Your listener will feel tolerantly superior because of your ignorance; this will make him feel kindly toward you and he will go out of his way to help you.

Travel by ship is an invitation to stargazing. Simon & Schuster puts out a pocketbook called *Stars,* part of their Golden Nature Guide series, which will pay for its slight weight (four ounces) in pleasure. If you start stargazing, you may want to find out something about how the ship is navigated. Mr. S. Y. Tupper, our jovial companion in the *Gulf Shipper,* taught himself to navigate after a long, full life ashore, bought himself a sextant, and navigates right along with the mates wherever he goes. It is most unlikely that you will wish to emulate his gentle hobby (sextants are expensive and heavy) but there is usually a sociable and good-natured ship's officer who will teach you how to read a sextant and let you take a sight or two—it is no harder than aiming a rifle and much like it.

It has suited celestial navigators throughout history to pretend to laymen that the art is difficult and mysterious. This is a lot of guff. I have practiced and taught navigation and I will swear on a stack of Bowditches that the basic principle can be taught to any normally-intelligent grammar-school graduate in twenty minutes and that he can be given sufficient skill to enable him unassisted to establish the position of a ship accurately through star and sun sights after only four hours instruction. Never mind those screams of rage from the old salts in the rear of the hall—it is *true*. Oh, he won't be a navigator; as with any art it requires study and practice to attain speed, accuracy, and self-confidence. But he will be able to get a decent "fix" by himself.

Let me give one illustration of the single, simple principle of *every* sextant sight. The mate uses the sextant to measure how high above the horizon the sun (or a star) is, in degrees and minutes; the sun is ninety degrees high if it is directly overhead, zero degrees if it is at the horizon, something in between for a typical sight. The process is no more mysterious than measuring an angle on a piece of paper with a protractor, but with a sextant an angle can be measured with great accuracy . . . with great ease, too, as the process is almost exactly like that of focusing a camera which has a split-image focusing arrangement. You simply look through a peephole and turn a little knob until the sun appears to touch the horizon line. It is easier than firing a gun or using a camera, because your accuracy does not depend on holding the sextant perfectly steady; you can sway around all you please as long as you can still see the sun through the peephole.

The rest of the job is the simplest sort of arithmetic not to be compared with balancing a check book. You compare the altitude of the sun as you just measured it with the altitude you thought it should be based on where you thought the ship was. Not very clear? Well, we're doing this without diagrams or pictures, so look at it this way: if you were down at the equator you would expect the sun to be overhead, wouldn't you? Contrariwise, if you were at the North Pole you would expect the sun to be near the horizon— above it, below it, or on it, depending on the time of year, but near it. All right, let's leave the North Pole and travel due south; for every degree of latitude the sun will get one degree higher in the sky. By the time you have traveled south ninety degrees of latitude the sun will have climbed ninety degrees high in the sky, be right overhead, i.e., the sun's altitude tells you at once and directly just what your latitude is.

That illustrates the one and only principle of celestial navigation: as you travel toward a star or the sun it climbs higher in the sky, as you travel away from it it sinks lower. If you compare the body's measured altitude with the altitude you thought it should have for where you thought you were, you get a correction, a difference between the two altitudes, which you can draw with a ruler on a map to correct your estimated ship's position and make it what the stars show it to be—simple addition or subtraction, nothing more.

It is true that there are hard parts, very difficult, but they are all done by astronomers and mathematicians ashore; a navigator does not have to bother with them. It used to be that a navigator, after he finished taking a sextant sight, had to solve a very tedious and fussy problem in spherical trigonometry— but not today. All that work is done for him now, by young females employed by the Naval Observatory; the answers are all arranged in tables for every possible combination of date, latitude, longitude, heavenly body, and time. All he has to do to impress the passengers is to look up the answer in a book.

To make it still easier, the nautical mile (6080 feet) has been made just the proper length to match in with these measurements of angular altitude of heavenly bodies. If you were to travel south a distance that made the sun one degree higher in the sky at noon, the distance traveled would be *by definition* sixty nautical miles. This is the only reason why miles at sea are longer than miles ashore; it makes the arithmetic easier in navigating.

Although celestial navigation is simple, piloting and ship-handling are very difficult; there is no easy gimmick, but there is endless pleasure to be derived from watching a master handle his ship in tight waters, such as going up channel, or docking. The beauties of it cannot be seen too easily from the parts of the ship where passengers are usually permitted, but there is a way to get around this. Do not ask the captain for permission to come onto the bridge at such times. Instead, ask him for permission to watch him handle his ship from the *flying* bridge, where you will not be in the way. Put this way, he is almost sure to grant permission—and there is at least one chance in three that he will invite you onto the conning bridge itself. He does not want you there, but captains are human and respond to sweettalk just like anybody else.

If he does invite you to the conning bridge, stay out of everybody's way and don't ask questions of him when he is busy. Then you will be invited back.

Almost immediately after our return to Colorado I had to go to New York, thus completing our journey around the world with a trip coast to coast in our own country. In the last thirty years I have made this crossing about twenty times but this time I looked at my own beloved native land with new eyes, trying to see it as I had seen the countries we had just visited. How did it stack up? What was good about it? And what was bad?

Jacques Barzun has just done a beautiful and sagacious book on this subject *God's Country and Mine,* so I won't try to say what he has already said so well—but read his book. The first thing that anyone is bound to notice is that prices in the United States seem terribly high compared with most prices elsewhere. But prices are relative. I for one will always feel emotionally that the "right" prices are the prices of my childhood, with grade-"A" milk five cents a quart and large eggs ten cents a dozen. This conviction is nonsense and I know it intellectually as well as you do. True prices depend on wages and salaries—how many minutes a journeyman carpenter has to work to earn a kilo loaf of standard bread. I tried to get answers to that question around the world, and the answers I was able to get, plus the statistics I have been able to dig up since, show clearly that a workman works a shorter time to earn the staff of life in the United States than is the case anywhere else in the world. Australia looked pretty good by this scale but even there it took him half again as long; New Zealand was far outclassed. All the other countries we visited were not even in the same league.

Of course everybody screams about high prices, but no matter how you work the above problem the answer always clearly shows that we, as a nation, are eating high on the hog, higher than ever before in our history, higher than any other nation on the globe, higher than any nation ever before in history. The consumption of luxury items makes the difference even more marked, whether it be telephones, automobiles, or soft drinks. (Not alcohol however, as we drink much less alcohol than we could afford; we are far from the drunkest nation.)

This is the only country in the world where a man will drive his own car down to pick up his unemployment compensation check.

How do our manners stack up with those of other countries? I had about decided that ours looked pretty good, on the whole, when I hit Pennsylvania Station, took a cab, and at once found myself an unwilling spectator to a screaming argument between my driver and one in another cab, followed by a wild ride which bruised my kidneys and gave me a headache . . . a type of ride, I am sorry to say, that I experienced almost every time I stepped into a cab while I was there.

On the other hand, manners in general in New York were about on a par with manners all through our country, except that everyone is always in a hurry. Our manners cannot match the courtly politeness of Latin America, but they are not bad; we have no reason to be ashamed on that score. Even New Yorkers, always hurrying nowhere, are almost all willing to listen, to help, to take friendly interest. The extreme rush that characterizes New York is a burden of its size; distances are so great and the channels are so choked that everyone must hurry or perforce waste most of the day simply getting from point to point.

New York is a very special case, both the most gigantic and wonderful mechanical toy the human race has ever built, fascinating in its incredible complexity, beautiful in its intricate, functional design—and a colossal slum by sheer weight of bodies too closely packed together. More conscientious cleaning goes on there than anywhere else; the city remains dirty, even the air is dirty. More genius has gone into its services and its transport than into any other city; it remains the most uncomfortable place to live in the United States.

I am proud of New York and awed by it. I am glad we built it—and I hope we never build another one. Like the stegosaurus it has grown too huge for its functions; like the stegosaurus it is bound to become extinct. It is the biggest and juiciest H-bomb target on the globe . . . too big to decentralize, too big to evacuate, too big to escape being hit.

When we arrived in New York everybody seemed glued to television receivers, listening to hours of silly wrangling as to whether a certain Senator had or had not been rude to a certain general, and whether a certain private had or had not received more weekend passes than privates usually get. The interest in these rather trivial events was amazing. I don't think it has been equaled in any presidential campaign, even the 1940 election. The tragic events in Indo-China were then coming rapidly to their disastrous close—but nobody in New York seemed to be paying any attention; they were more interested in learning why a V.I.P. had let his picture be taken with a private.

We were out of the country when the McCarthy madness swept over the land; consequently we arrived home as detached observers, not as partisans of either side. I tried to maintain that Man-from-Mars attitude but found it difficult; people were almost violently on one side or the other. What color rose do you wear, man?—red or white?—for you are either for us or against us.

I still cannot manage to work up a fever; I seem to have been away during the infectious stage of the epidemic. Was it anything like the time the gunmen shot up the U.S. Congress? Oh no, nothing like that; this affair was conducted entirely with words. Had anyone been deprived of life, liberty, or property contrary to the Bill of Rights? No, but— Had anyone been *hurt*? Well, not physically. Financially perhaps? Well, yes and no, some persons had lost jobs after refusing to answer politically embarrassing questions.

But, my informants insisted, I simply did not understand the real danger, the real importance, how every single one of us was vitally endangered by the things that had happened in these committee rooms.

Well, I still don't see the overpowering importance. The McCarthy fit strikes me as the most astounding example of senseless hysteria since the Mississippi Bubble. Let me make it clear that I am neither supporter nor constituent of the Senator from Wisconsin; I just don't think anything that he has done is important, one way or the other. As a "fighter against communism" his efforts seem to have been rather futile; as a modern Torquemada the effect on his victims seems to have been public embarrassment only. In many of the cases, though not all, the embarrassment seems to derive from unwillingness to answer questions that vitally concern loyalty to the United States.

If anyone cares to assert that the central character in all this is a big, hairy, horse's rear end, I will not argue the point. But I will point out that we have had some choice examples of the genus oaf in the United States Senate at other times; somehow, the Republic weathered the strain.

But two things struck me very forcibly about the matter, coming as I did direct from months abroad. First, it has been asserted repeatedly by several prominent journals that the "real" danger of the McCarthy fit lay in the friends it lost us abroad and the prestige it cost us.

This is nonsense almost complete. No one abroad was hurt— among our friends. It is true that the dust-up received much attention abroad and was used to make propaganda against us. But it was simply seized on as a chance to kick the Fat Boy by our enemies, who will do so on any excuse or without any excuse (as in germ warfare). Slandering Uncle Sam has gone on for years; the McCarthy row did not start it. For another reason which I will go into presently we should ordinarily pay no attention to what the press of any other nation says about us, but make our own decisions quite irrespective of what the world will think.

We may have good reasons of our own to curb this Senator's activities, but to do so because our enemies or our putative friends dislike what is being done *inside the United States* would be to decide our national policies on an emasculating "Nervous Nelly" basis. To our dreadful cost in blood and treasure we have for years been making crucial decisions on just this unsound basis, worrying about what other people might think of us instead of worrying about what is right and what is wrong. If we find it proper for reasons of justice to clip the wings of the ubiquitous gentleman from Wisconsin, then by all means let us do so—but let us not act from fear of what the neighbors may think!

For, I assure you, they don't give a tinker's dam what *we* think about *their* actions. American criticism of events in other countries—most particularly of anything as intimately domestic as the McCarthy row—is *always* rejected with indignation. *Always* . . . if you can think of a single exception, please write and tell me.

Yet those selfsame citizens of second-rate powers, nations that have nothing standing between them and inundation by the communist flood but the strength of the United States, are almost unanimously ready to criticize Uncle Sugar on any score, ready to tell him what to do and how to do it, expecting him to foot the bill and most ready to vilify him if he fails to do just exactly what they advise. The most distressing truth that we learned in traveling around the world was how painfully few friends America has. We traveled entirely in territory and in ships of our allies in World War II, but only in Uruguay did we find a general feeling of friendliness toward the United States. Nowhere else!—not even in Australia.

Once or twice we heard kindly remarks about the United States when people learned that we were from the States, but dozens and endless times it was simply an opportunity to read us a lecture on the "sins" of our country. To be sure, the McCarthy uproar was often used as a weapon to lambast Uncle Sam, but any excuse was sufficient and it was usually something else. Baiting Uncle Sam is a favorite sport among our supposed friends.

For this reason I assert that it does not matter what others think of the McCarthy mess. It should not be a factor in our thinking about the matter.

The second thing that struck me forcibly about the McCarthy issue (on viewing it immediately after some months abroad) was how remarkably little McCarthy had been able to do even to those "victims" he had attacked most savagely and with least attention to fair play. No one seems to have noticed that our complicated system of safeguards to protect the innocent has stood up under this test and worked amazingly well. No one has been jailed other than after trial and due process— McCarthy himself has jailed no one; he has not the power. In fact no damage to an individual has been alleged other than damage to reputation and even that usually followed refusal to answer questions. I am not trying to "try" the McCarthy case, but I want to point out that it is not an example of breakdown of civil liberties but, on the contrary, a most outstanding triumph of civil liberties, *one that probably could not happen anywhere else in the world*!

In the communist half of the world a man in McCarthy's shoes would *really* have power. He would be a "people's judge" and his victims would never live to complain. Their friends would not dare speak. In most of Latin America those politically out of favor hide out, or seek refuge in embassies, to avoid rotting incommunicado in jail. Even the British countries have no record of gentleness toward dissidents as gentle as that termed "McCarthyism"—oh, I admit that England has a very soft attitude toward communist treason at present but look at the whole record: Gandhi in jail repeatedly for passive resistance, the Black-and-Tans in Ireland, the present law in the Malay States making mere ownership of a gun a capital offense, the speed and harshness with which British courts act. I am not excusing any wrongful act that McCarthy may have committed; I do assert that we have failed to notice publicly the proudest aspect of the whole sorry business—that our safeguards for the individual stood up under pressure.

The third thing that I noticed about the matter, confronting it cold on my return, was the amazing amount of stew for such a skimpy little oyster. The true importance of the whole thing has been vastly overrated.

During our trip we were in the British Commonwealth about half way around the world. We had time to think about some facts well known but which we had not considered until we had our noses rubbed in them, i.e., the potentiality of the British Commonwealth for balanced economic self-containment. We, like most Americans, had sent food parcels to Britain during the years of drastic rationing following the War. Now I am beginning to wonder why it was necessary? South Africa, Australia, and New Zealand all have large surpluses of food; all of them need manufactured goods. England needed food badly and was only too anxious to barter manufactured goods in exchange. I do not regret a one of those food packages; they were badly needed by hungry people—but what went wrong? What happened? It looks like a set-up designed by a wise Providence for a balanced economy with plenty to eat and plenty of goods for all. But it did not work out that way and even now it creaks badly. Why, with over 120,000,000 sheep in Australia, should it be so hard for a man in London to enjoy a mutton chop? England manufactures Kleenex and sells it to New Zealand; why should a box that costs seventeen cents in America cost five shillings in Auckland? (Seventy cents by direct conversion, more nearly a dollar and a half in view of the over-all price scale.) It can't be just a transportation differential, as eleven thousand miles by water is not as expensive as hauling goods across the North American continent by railroad.

The old, tired excuse of "We can't get the dollars" does not apply here; this is all pound area. Nor was it that we were dunning England for the repayment of war loans, quite the contrary; we were handing over billions of dollars as a free gift.

I have no degree in economics, nor do I have access to the statistics used by ministers of finance of the various Commonwealth countries to determine their policies. No doubt there are excellent reasons—but I suspect that the "excellent reasons" are of the same quality as those that have kept the little continent of Europe balkanized and pulling against itself. The longer I worried about this matter and tried to find out *why* the Commonwealth was in such sorry shape compared with what it seemed to be capable of achieving the more I kept finding the same facts—balkanization. The Commonwealth is not an integrated economic unit all operating under the same basic laws, as the United States is. On the contrary, every part of it is dragging its feet and trying to be one up on all the rest—precisely in the same fashion that our individual states have often attempted to do, only to be slapped down by our Supreme Court. But the Commonwealth has no supreme court, no overriding body of law; the once-great Free Trade area of the British Empire is now bogged down in local tariffs, taxes, import and export licenses, restrictions, and embargos, each intended to rig some advantage against the others and each player engaged in the same knife-in-the-back game.

Perhaps I don't see the Big Picture, but to me it looks like a hell of a way to run a railroad.

(I am aware that our own trade policies are criticized on somewhat similar grounds. But there is a big difference; we are very nearly economically self-sufficient and our tariffs and other laws have not been such as to ruin us in the respects in which we are not entirely self-sufficient. But none of the Commonwealth is self-sufficient; they need each other.)

Another question that fretted my mind was the contrast between Uruguay and New Zealand. The two countries are comparable in size, in population density, in stable democratic government, in basic industries, each being a rich primary producer not yet heavily industrialized. Each country has a sheaf of most remarkable social-welfare laws which superficially add up to about the same thing. Yet New Zealand is a phony utopia; its social measures are strangling it—while Uruguay appears to be a true utopia, as near perfect as our race has achieved.

I confess I do not know the answer to this one. I cannot see a basic difference in their laws and I have no evidence on which to attribute basic differences in the temperament of the two peoples. All I can see that it proves, if it proves anything, is that social security laws need not be destructive to high production and a high standard of living, if properly designed and wisely administered. My reservation weasels out of it, of course; I have not said anything. But I want to know why, for there is something to be learned here that could be of crucial importance to the United States. I intend to go back to Uruguay in the next year or two and stay until I think I have found the answer. But my temporary license as an apprentice pundit does not seem to warrant my answering now.

However I do have a hunch. New Zealanders are addicted to price-fixing as a permanent (not just wartime) policy. King Canute could give them a few tips on this subject.

The most important thing that I believe I have learned from a trip around our planet is that no progress whatsoever is being made on the prime problem facing the human race, that the problem is bigger than I had dreamed, and that, most tragically, it probably has no solution.

I don't mean communism and I don't mean the chilling probability of atomic war; I mean something much worse: too many people.

The basic problem was stated a century and a half ago by Dr. Malthus, then his depressing theory was "exploded" by new lands being opened, new farming methods, new advances in science—only it turned out not to have been exploded after all; his equations for starvation are working out to the last dismal decimal place. A modern discussion of it was published last year by Charles Darwin the Younger. There is no longer any way to get around it; this planet has too many mouths, too few acres.

We beat the game for a long time by opening up new frontiers, but now there are no new frontiers to open up. *The only place left for the billion people in China and the Indian subcontinent to spill over is into areas already occupied by the white Western nations.*

This fact is more explosive, more dangerous than H-bombs.

I had known this—as who did not?—before this trip. We had certainly been told often enough, by flippant little paragraphs in *Time* magazine, by dry and rarely read hand-outs from UNESCO, through diagrams in atlases and geographies. But, for me, it took a personal look at the dreadful condition of Java to make the statistics about China and India and the other overpopulated areas come alive in my mind.

The worst of it is that the problem won't hold still; it gets worse every day. We have already passed the crisis point; we need two and a half acres of farm land for each human, but we now have about one and a half. But there were eighteen million more people on earth when my wife and I came back from this trip than there were when we left; since we got home fifteen million more have been added—a total four times the population of Australia.

Too little food, too many mouths. How will they be fed? Where will they sleep?

It is barely possible that you and I will be able to duck the issue; our children must solve it or be overwhelmed by it. Not our grandchildren, but our children, for the problem grows too rapidly. The crisis is with us, the catastrophic outcome cannot be more than one generation away. More probably we ourselves will face it, in the form of World War III.

Quite aside from the life-or-death practical matter of who will win the next war, when or if it comes, is the unavoidable moral problem: do we, with our acres to waste on golf courses and parks and tobacco fields, have the right to hang onto what we hold? Or are we, as our brothers' keepers, morally obligated to accept two or three million Asians as fast as they can be shipped to us?

Are the ten million Australians and New Zealanders required by good morals to let the eighty million Indonesians swarm over them? I can give one sort of answer to that one. Both of the Anzac nations are strongly humanitarian at home—but they will fight and die to the last digger, the last Kiwi, before they will let that happen.

But that does not solve the moral issue. My own ancestors came to this continent, pushed the Indians aside—or killed them—and made far better use of the land for far more people. I feel no special qualms about it now. But suppose the teeming crowds of Asia now give us the same treatment, seeing that we are making something less than maximum use of the land for maximum population. Have I any right to feel indignant?

I will not duck the issue. I have always believed that a man who accepts capital punishment should not be too squeamish to serve his term as hangman. The tail goes with the hide. I have not been able to find a moral answer which pleases me; nevertheless I know my answer—precisely that of the Australians. I'll fight before I'll let the spawning millions of Asia roll over Colorado and turn it into the sort of horizontal slum that Java is. Maybe this decision damns my soul; if so, so must it be. I don't see any solution to the problem of Asia at all, for they won't stop breeding . . . in fact, the psychological truth is almost certainly that they *can't*. But I am not willing to move over and give them room here to breed another hundred million—or half billion. We have here a pretty good nation, at least for the time being; I will not willingly see it turned into a slum.

Are we our brothers' keepers? Just what does our Western culture owe to the rest of mankind? Let us not be too humble about it. It may well be true that the potentialities of all parts of the human race are about the same. Nevertheless that minority of the human race called loosely the Western democratic peoples and consisting mostly of Caucasians even though not identical with the Caucasian race has added twenty, eighty, a hundred times as much to human wealth, human knowledge, human dignity and freedom, as all the rest of the human race put together. Sanitation, scientific farming, mass production, civil liberties—these are *our* inventions, not theirs. We have shared them, what they would accept, and that is good—but we *do not* owe the teeming rest of the world a living!

Lastly, this trip around the world cured me of One-Worldism; I have fully recovered and am as immune to it as I am to measles. The idea of one sovereign world nation, free forever of the peril of war, working together in peace and harmony, is an appealing one. I do wish we could afford it. But, the earth and the human race being what they are, we cannot . . .

not unless we are willing to accept the logical and inevitable consequences. "One World" means a situation in which the United States is not sovereign, any more than one of our states is truly sovereign. That means that the United States would be outvoted . . . which just as certainly means that they would swarm over us immediately after counting the votes.

That which I am willing to fight for I am not willing to surrender as a result of counting noses in China and India. Therefore, no World State for me. It's a trap.

I could wish for a better world, but, as the stranger in the poker game told the sourdough who warned him, "Sure, sure, I *know* the game is crooked—but it is the *only* game in town."

I came back to the United States convinced that it was an even better country than I had thought it was. This our land is not perfect, but it looks just about perfect from even a short distance away. It is immeasurably a better place to live than anywhere else I have seen.

But I came back, too, convinced that our peril was very great and our friends very few. The extent and the viciousness of the propaganda campaign against us must be heard to be believed. Its prime source, of course, is Russia, but there are many ears willing to listen and many mouths willing to repeat. Envy and hate are the inevitable concomitants of wealth and power; we have been uneasily aware of this and have tried to curry favor wherever we could. But it is not possible; we are hated not for our behavior but for what we are—and they are not.

England, in the days of her strength, paid no attention to what other peoples thought of her; she acted in her own best interests as she conceived them to be and ignored world opinion. We should learn from our predecessor at least part of this lesson: never let a decision be swayed by what the neighbors will think, for they will gossip about us whatever we do. Let us be honest and brave—but not politic. We have tried to be politic for ten years now—and look at the mess we are in! We have bumbled around, an awkward giant, apologizing for our big feet and our bulging muscles, scared witless that the fortnightly French cabinet might fall or that the British foreign office might say "boo!" at us. We have had many, many chances to act forthrightly and call a halt to the world's rush toward disaster; instead, each time we have again been persuaded to pay Danegeld.

We know, as surely as we have ever known anything, that we may have but a short time more to live. The Soviet Union is determined either to nibble us to death or to smash us, whichever seems easier. On what can we depend?

Primarily on ourselves. Turkey has the resolute courage to fight, that seems certain. There are one or two others perhaps. But what of major allies? England? Suppose Bevan were prime minister, as may well be the case when the time comes. For that matter, can we reasonably expect England to risk a saturation attack of H-bombs to support us? But, in any case, will she? With Churchill, probably, with Atlee, maybe—with Bevan? The man hates us.

Will France support us? Let's not joke, this is serious.

So far as we can count on it . . . for all practical purposes . . . we already stand alone. Let us therefore get on with that "agonizing reappraisal"—but let us quit agonizing about it. We are not liked, we have few friends; therefore we should quit being afraid, stand up and assert ourselves. The only friends we will lose thereby are those we never had.

We might even gain a few. Courage is respected and admired where timidity is scorned.

If we are to die as a nation, let us die proudly, with neither head in sand nor led around by the nose, but calmly aware of our peril and fighting it with our utmost. There can be no safe course for us, but, if we deserve to win, we are more likely to win.

But let us not be afraid, not even of our friends.

SESTINA OF THE TRAMP-ROYAL

by Rudyard Kipling

Speakin' in general, I 'ave tried 'em all—
The 'appy roads that take you o'er the world.
Speakin' in general, I 'ave found them good
For such as cannot use one bed too long,
But must get 'ence, the same as I 'ave done,
An' go observin' matters till they die.

What do it matter where or 'ow we die,
So long as we've our 'ealth to watch it all—
The different ways that different things are done,
An' men an' women lovin' in this world;
Takin' our chances as they come along,
An' when they ain't, pretendin' they are good?

In cash or credit—no, it aren't no good;
You 'ave to 'ave the 'abit or you'd die,
Unless you lived your life but one day long,
Nor didn't prophesy nor fret at all,
But drew your tucker some'ow from the world,
An' never bothered what you might ha' done.

But, Gawd, what things are they I 'aven't done?
I've turned my 'and to most, an' turned it good,
In various situations round the world—
For 'im that doth not work must surely die;
But that's no reason man should labour all
'Is life on one same shift—life's none so long.

Therefore, from job to job I've moved along.
Pay couldn't 'old me when my time was done,
For something in my 'ead upset it all,
Till I 'ad dropped whatever 'twas for good,
An', out at sea, be'eld the dock-lights die,
An' met my mate—the wind that tramps the world!

It's like a book, I think, this bloomin' world,
Which you can read and care for just so long,
But presently you feel that you will die
Unless you get the page you're readin' done,
An' turn another—likely not so good;
But what you're after is to turn 'em all.

Gawd, bless this world! Whatever she 'ath done—
Excep' when awful long—I've found it good.
So write, before I die, "'E liked it all!"

(1896)